COURAGEOUS
OUTCAST

To Lenny;

From my heart —

To my Pen —

To you!

Susan I. Leppert

January 12, 2005

COURAGEOUS

OUTCAST

SUSAN ILEEN LEPPERT

To order additional copies of this book, contact:
Xlibris Corporation
1-888-795-4274
www.Xlibris.com
Orders@Xlibris.com
21180

With special thanks to:

Rose Csercse for always believing in me and my writing, from day one, Chris Cornell for struggling through my rough copy and never complaining, Earl L. Colmus, Jr. for help I didn't expect, badly needed, and deeply appreciate, Bryan Locey for proofreading that saved the day, Joyce Mathews for all the encouragement given, and tears and laughter we shared as I wrote, Sharron Smith for helping me to get the "ball rolling," Autumn, Laura, and Debbie, my friends at Beaverton Branch-Gladwin County Library, Dr. Marcelino Barreto for giving of his time to answer my many questions, Bruce Drew for inspiration: One writer to another! One cousin to another!

And to those who listened patiently to every word, every page, every chapter, as it was written: Earl L. Colmus, III and Kim Sult.

And for those who cheered me on with prayers, positive support, and loving smiles: Cathie Yager, Arygle Winona Fassett, Eric L. Colmus, Jr., Johnny Colmus, John R. Colmus, Kelsey Colmus, Diane, Evelyn, Lauralee, Lesa M., Lisa H., Evelyn Litkowski, Carla Dick, Homer Bixler, Sister Mary Pelagia Litkowski, Pat Alberda, and many others!

A special thanks to Ramona Woodbury for answering my many questions about horses, and to Deb Diamond, owner of the beautiful "Glory" horse, on cover.

May God bless each and every one of you always,

Susan Ileen Leppert

Dedicated to:

Blake Andrew Colmus
"Peanut"
(I love you a bushel and a peck!)

and

William Andrew Burke, Jr.
"My Beautiful Billy"
(Your love and encouragement continues to warm me!)

and

Samuel I. Leppert III
"A Wonderful Brother"
(I Miss You So!)

AUTHOR'S NOTE

My great-great Uncle, John Bruce, passed away long before I was born. My Grandfather, James Bruce, entertained me, as a young child, with many wonderful and hilarious stories about John; all "supposedly" true! Although John Bruce never, to my knowledge, traveled any farther west than Carrollton, Michigan—and certainly not to Hastings, Minnesota—I have carried my grandfather's stories—and John—in my heart for over 50 years.

CHAPTER ONE

Clouds, white as snow, hung suspended like thick mounds of soapsuds in the azure-colored sky as a pair of eagles soared in effortless spirals, screeching a warning to all below that man was coming: "Beware! Beware!" Wildflowers in a profusion of colors swayed gently from the slight breeze. A myriad of shapes, rippling like a patchwork quilt, hung on a line to dry, undulating with each whispered breath of wind.

Sarah Elizabeth Justus ran through the flowers and tall prairie grasses, her skirt held up above her ankles, as her eyes took in the splendor of her surroundings. She was certain no one had ever come this way before. No one from town, that is. Only a few deer, grazing on the far side of the meadow, their eyes and ears ever alert for the slightest sign of danger. A quick flash of white, and they were gone, plunging into the woods beyond in urgent bounds. Then stopping and turning back, they watched cautiously, safely hidden among the bushes and trees—ears straining—heedful of the slightest sounds of pursuit. She slowed her pace, walking now. Her steps were long like a man's, a habit she had acquired from childhood walks with her father. Pausing to pick a handful of flowers, her thoughts soared like the eagles that flew above. She smiled at the happiness she felt inside and spread her arms far out to each side, turning around and around in carefree abandon, dipping and rising, her thoughts peaceful and serene.

Then she stopped turning, giving herself a hug of joy, and began again to walk toward the woods to the west. She lifted her skirts to cross the shallow creek that coursed its way in swift abandon to the valley below. The icy water felt good on her bare feet, and she splashed and laughed at herself, feeling immense delight. Today was her birthday. Already her twenty-eighth, and what a glorious day it was!

How she loved this beautiful land: the flower-filled meadow, the peaceful valley, and the quiet sun-streaked forest. She had never been as happy anywhere before. She still remembered the day she and her father arrived in Hastings, dusty and trail-weary, but anxious to begin again in this new territory. It seemed a million miles from the fort where he had been in charge of "taming the West." "A most grievous and dangerous job," he had said, "thanks to the murderin', stinkin' Indians."

There were no Indians near Hastings, or so people said. No fears of being scalped, or murdered, or worse, from what the old-timers said who sat on the porch of the general store, soaking up the sun and chatting every afternoon. She hadn't been afraid of the Indians back at the fort, regardless of what she overheard her father tell her mother after he had been out with the troops, hunting and tracking the worst of them. Truth was, Sarah had never seen an Indian. Not a live one. But she had seen the dead one, hauled into the fort on a rope, dragged by his wrists past the commander's office and over to the stables. Her mother had screamed at the sight and pushed Sarah's face into the folds of her skirt. Then, gaining her composure somewhat, she rushed off in the direction of their home, dragging Sarah along in her haste.

Later, Sarah had heard that the Indian had killed a woman in one of the settler's cabins outside the fort and had been shot by her husband, who had run in from the field when he heard the woman's screams. The Indian had died from the dragging, not from being shot, and someone said he was old and sick and had only wanted some food, but the woman started screaming and . . . well . . . no one knew what the real story was.

Sarah's father said it was a good lesson for all the stinkin' Indians, and he paced the floor a long time before his anger was spent. Sarah knew her mother hated such talk, and also the brutality that was so much a part of life at the fort. Her mother—a pale, timid woman with nervous mannerisms—was the gentlest woman Sarah knew, and she couldn't help noticing the sadness in her eyes that seemed to grow with each passing day.

Jenny Marie Tallson, of the Virginia Tallsons, if it hadn't been for her marriage to a handsome cavalry officer with a promising future in the West, would have spent all her days among the genteel folks of Virginia. She hated the West, the fort, the uncouth and uncivilized ways of the folks of the fort, and had become more and more quiet and withdrawn as each year passed. Her world became the rooms they called home, the everyday burdens and responsibilities of caring for her family, and her intense love and devotion to her daughter, Sarah.

Sarah gave her mother's life purpose and fulfillment, and above all, satisfaction. She lavished attention and time on her daughter, teaching her to read, write, sew, and later, to cook, bake, and do other womanly tasks. From Sarah's first breath, till the fateful day ten years later when Jenny closed her eyes and smiled no more, Sarah received through her mother's love, a wonderful legacy. "A victim of consumption," the doctor had said, shaking his head and lowering his eyes, "a woman grown old, though only twenty-eight at the time of her death."

"Twenty-eight," Sarah said aloud, no longer lost in thought. "Twenty-eight when you died, Mother, and today I am also twenty-eight." She paused and then added, "And an old maid. Oh, Mother, I miss you so much," she said, looking up toward the sky.

A melancholy smile momentarily traced its way across her lips. She sighed and began once more to walk. How she would have liked to have shown her mother the meadow and wildflowers. She knew Jenny would have been happy here. She halted where the meadow ended and the woods began, glancing around for any signs of movement or intrusion. The air was still and the sounds of birds assured her she was alone. Quietly she entered the hardwood forest, stepping gingerly among the ferns and bramble, careful not to trip on fallen branches or other undergrowth. Here and there a lonely pine tree stood like a shivering child surrounded by giants, its feathery branches seeking any ray of sunlight that filtered through to grace it with a halo of golden light.

There was an enchantingly ethereal beauty here that Sarah always felt when she entered the forest, as if it contained some magical essence that spoke softly and directly to her heart. The music of the forest seemed written especially for her to hear: the whisper of the pines, the chirping of the birds, the harsh, sharp call of the jays, and the occasional tiny squeaks of the chipmunks she startled. After the rain, the woodland symphony included sundry other sounds: the click of the cricket's song and the deep melodious chorus of the bullfrogs where the swamp edged the pine-stand to the west.

Sarah felt no fear now on her many visits to the forest, though once she had encountered a bear on this very trail! She had stood still, unable to move if she had wanted to, hoping it would not notice the slight rustling of her skirt, she was trembling so. She also hoped it would not catch the scent of the biscuit she carried in the small cloth bag tied at her waist. The bear stood up, reaching with its massive paws, its nails raking the air, nostrils flared. Loud growls and snorts rumbled from within it, and Sarah stared straight into its fierce brown eyes, willing herself to remain frozen in place.

After its great show of fierceness, the bear lowered its

massive bulk to the ground and ambled off the way it had come. Sarah let out a sigh that seemed to come from her very toes, and gathering her courage, turned toward the north and continued her journey. After that day, foolhardy as it may have been, she never feared her sojourns through the woods again.

"I'm the most courageous girl in Hastings, Mother," she spoke aloud. "The others won't even walk to the meadow, let alone the woods." She noticed the stronger rays of sunlight ahead, and the large patches of light-blue sky, and knew she was nearing the far edge of the forest where her journey's end always took her. Ahead lay a clearing surrounding a large lake of crystal blue, flanked on two sides by steep cliffs of red and brown limestone and smooth gray boulders. Here was her uncommonly beautiful, hidden retreat. Sarah had been coming here ever since the first summer that they moved to Hastings. It afforded her the privacy she needed to sort out her many thoughts and the serenity life at Hastings seemed to lack.

Perhaps it was because she had lost her mother at such a tender age. Or perhaps, as her father said, because she was a dreamer. But Sarah always felt on the outside somehow, as much now as when she was growing up. Not that she didn't have a lot of friends. She did. But it seemed that she just couldn't get interested in the things that interested the others. She could dance, but she couldn't waste time in silly discussions about which fellow was the best catch, or about the sparse shipments of fabrics to arrive in town. To Sarah, those things were frivolous and foolish pastimes, and they afforded her no amusement. She would rather run a race, or practice shooting, or spend the day alone at this special place, thinking thoughts or dreaming dreams.

Well, maybe my father is right, she thought, and I'm an incurable dreamer! She knew most of the women her age were married now, and most even had children. She wanted children. Why, she even had their names picked out: Jenny Marie, like her mother, if a girl, and Samuel Abraham, after her father, if a boy. She could picture her son in her mind's eye: young Samuel: a tall, gawky child with dark eyes and a shock of golden hair the color of wheat kissed by the sun. She would teach him to read and ride and see to it he had a sense of adventure, balanced by a strong faith in himself and in God. As for her daughter, she would teach her all the things her mother had taught her—and more! She would show her the meadow, the flowers, and the woods, telling her the names of the trees and birds. And someday she would bring her to this special place and share her innermost thoughts, hopes, and dreams.

Sarah raised her eyes to the sky, checking as she did, the path that wound its way up the side of the cliff to a ledge high above. There a pile of brush covered the entrance that she knew led to a cool, secluded cave. She began her ascent, placing her feet carefully amongst the rocks and brush, ever alert for snakes and other dangers that might bring misfortune her way. She climbed upward, breathing easily, feeling the welcoming warmth of the sun upon her. She reached the cave and bent to enter. Then stopped, turning to look down from where she had come, surveying the countryside and enjoying a sense of communion with her surroundings. The scent of flowers wafted lightly in the air from a bush beside the cave's entrance.

It was here she wrote, as her mother had taught her, page after page of thoughts. Someday she would collect her writings and put them together as a book to read to her children. It was also here that she stitched for her father a patchwork quilt from a kaleidoscope of fabric scraps that she had accumulated over the years. Some came from her mother's scrap collection, and some from occasionally trading with her friends. It would be a grand quilt, warm and protective against the coming winter cold. She took up her sewing basket, quickly threading the needle, and began a series of small stitches, intricate and precise, as her mother had taught her. She was proud of her ability, and her needle flew quickly across the pieces of fabric, joining them securely. This would be a fine gift for her father, one she knew he would appreciate, as those her mother had made long ago were wearing thin. Before long, she would have to make one for herself, also.

As she stitched, her thoughts assailed her. She thought of "Old John," her closest friend in Hastings. Old John, with his gnarled hands and scratchy beard that had reddened her cheeks as he hugged her close when she was young. Old John, who mothered the motherless child from age ten to her late teens when she began to blossom into womanhood and was no longer as comfortable carrying on in boyish ways. She began acting more ladylike then, like the other young women, though she never blushed when a coarse word was overheard, or shrieked and fainted at the sight of a snake. She prided herself in knowing the things he taught her about nature, and animals, and even about people. It was like she was the son he never had, and he, the father she never had. Oh, not that her father meant to ignore her. He just hadn't known what to do with a little girl after her mother died and left her more or less on her own. Except, of course, for Rosie O'Day Mitchell, the preacher's wife, who taught Sarah the proper things a young girl should know. She enjoyed the time spent with Mrs. Mitchell. She especially liked to hear her sing in her husky Irish brogue, songs from her homeland as she bustled around the kitchen, baking and cleaning. Rosie Mitchell had fluffy carrot-colored hair that she wound round her head in a large thick braid that reminded Sarah of the coat of the wily red fox she had seen in the meadow one day. The color of Rosie's hair made her plump, reddish cheeks seem always afire. She was a stocky woman who wore somber-colored dresses lacking the adornment of lace or frills. A large white apron covered her clothing when she busied herself with chores. But, unlike her clothes, her dazzling green eyes—the color of emerald waters—sparkled with happiness and gaiety as she went about her tasks, and Sarah could not remember a time when she wasn't smiling. She sat many evenings, telling Sarah about her homeland, Ireland, and how she came to America on a huge, creaking ship. The mishaps and adventures that had befallen her as she lost first one family member or friend to illness at sea, and then another, and how, at last, they had arrived in America, and how homesick and frightened she had felt.

As luck would have it, she found a position as an upstairs maid for a wealthy Boston family and remained with them nearly two years, enjoying their employment and kindness, and "working very hard," she had added. Then, one fine Sunday morning while returning from church, she happened to meet young Reverend Emory Mitchell, who was heading west the following month. Being a good Irish girl—raised Catholic—she battled with her conscience day after day, and when he left a month later, she went with him as his new bride, carrying her Catholic faith within her heart.

In the ten years of marriage they shared, she had grown to love him and had no regrets, she said, concerning her decision to marry him. They had worked side by side, shoulder to shoulder, sharing the work, hopes, and joys that filled their daily lives. They also shared the sorrow, which included the death, soon after birth, of their twin infant sons. But, as Rosie said, the joys far outweighed the sorrows, and she had no regrets.

Four years before Sarah's mother passed away, Reverend Mitchell had died of smallpox he caught while ministering to some settlers in a distant settlement, and Rosie had carried on strong in spirit and still smiling. Sarah could not help noticing how different Rosie was from her own mother, who had always seemed so sad.

However, it was Old John whom Sarah felt closest to.

She loved him nearly as much as she did her father—and maybe in some ways, more. She learned the best things from him and dogged his steps as a child, always underfoot wherever he went in and around Hastings. It wasn't long before she knew how to set a trap, how to track, and how to stay upwind of an animal so her scent would not alert it to her presence. She learned to recognize the different animal tracks, and droppings, and even how to get her bearings from the sun and stars. It took him awhile longer to teach her to light a fire with a stone and stick, how to throw a knife with deadly accuracy, and how to handle a gun. At first she would pull up as she squeezed the trigger, or close her eyes, missing the target she was aiming at by a country mile! She was a quick learner, however, and before long she was able to keep her eyes on the target and her hand steady. She soon knew before she even fired that her aim was true and would usually hit precisely where she intended. Old John would hop around and whoop like a wild Indian when she hit her target, making her laugh until her sides hurt. Later he would tell her he was proud of her and get a glint in his eyes that made her feel ten feet tall.

He was muscular and long-legged, slightly worn and weathered. His skin was mottled and tough like an old piece of leather, and his hair fanned out around his head like a soft fur pelt. It was as white as a new-fallen snow and reminded her of the rabbits he often caught in his traps. But it was his eyes that first attracted her attention: the brightest of blues, like the feathers of the jays that graced the meadow and woods. They sparkled like diamonds when he was happy, and flashed like moonlight glancing off ice when he wasn't. Men trusted and respected him, while women stole shy glances when he passed by. Sometimes, he would bow masterfully and sweep his old tattered hat from his head in the most gallant manner. Yet even though it flattered the old maids and made them blush and giggle, he never courted any of them, Sarah noticed. It was she who occupied most of his time and attention, and she was glad.

Sarah knew his full name was John Bruce, and he had come to America from Scotland many years earlier to seek his fortune. Rumor had it, there had been a young woman in Scotland who had his heart, but by the time he could afford to send for her, she had married another. They said he was a brilliant fellow. A professorship at a college in the East awaited him upon arrival in America, but he walked out the day he learned she had married, and never went back. Bought himself a horse, a gun, and supplies and headed west. She also heard he was a direct descendant of the king of Scotland, but she could not imagine this rugged old man as royalty! She knew he was very smart, feisty, and funny, not to mention, as loyal to a friendship as a faithful hound—but royalty? She doubted that. There was never a king or prince in the books her mother had left her who wore a buckskin shirt and pants, or trimmed his beard with a Bowie knife! She had to laugh at that!

Sarah put down her sewing and rose, stretching her arms above her head, then rolled her head from side to side, stretching her neck muscles to alleviate the stiffness she felt from sitting so long in one position. Far below, a doe drank at the edge of the lake, her light-brown tones blending with the tones of earth and rock. She glanced timidly around, ears flickering with alertness, eyes ever watchful and quick. She seemed to glance more often behind her to a thicket of dense brush. Sarah wondered if another deer was bedded there. She scanned the brush, trying to spot the hiding place, to no avail. All was still, except for ever-widening circles in the center of the lake where a fish had just jumped.

Sitting down at the cave's entrance once more, she took from the small cloth bag at her waist the sourdough biscuit she had made earlier that morning. As she broke off a piece of it and put it into her mouth, she thought again of her friend, Old John. Unlike her father he had never spoken badly of the Indians. In fact, she knew he had friends among them, though she was taken aback by this, having been brought up to think so badly of them. She knew they had taught him to hunt and track after he came west, but curious as she was, she could not bring herself to question him. Somehow, it just did not seem right.

She'd overheard some talk at the blacksmiths, while waiting for her father's mare to be shod a couple years earlier, of how John had come west along the Ohio River, taking up with a wagon train of homesteaders. Where the Ohio coursed its way into the Mississippi River, they had turned north, following the Mississippi to Fort Snelling. From there John had gone on alone, westward, following the Minnesota River toward the Dakotas. At Montevideo, they told of how he had gone on north along the Chippewa River. They laughed amongst themselves then, commenting on the foolishness of this, since he lacked even the rudimentary skills needed to survive in wilds such as those. But survive he did, in spite of the fierce winter storm that blanketed the region with arctic cold and billowing drifts twice as high as a horse and rider that year! They paused, seeing in their minds' eyes the illimitable dangers of that situation, and then resumed their conversation.

Sarah listened with rapt attention. They seemed unsure of how it happened, but when Old John emerged from the wilderness two years later, he was no longer a greenhorn or ignorant of the ways of the wild. He could track and hunt as well as the best of them, and he knew many things even they did not. Some said he seemed more Indian than white. His hair had turned snow-white from the ordeal, they added, and no longer was he clean-shaven. Also, there was a look in his eyes that bespoke an almost spiritual depth of understanding, and he seemed reverent of the land and animals in a way most white men could not understand. Often they would seek his advice and counsel when a problem came up, but none of them could call himself a close friend of John's. He was a loner, quick to smile or shake a hand, but private, given to plain talk but not to gossip. Except for his friendship with Sarah, he kept to himself, a man secure within himself and master of himself.

Sarah felt privileged to be his friend and relished the time they spent together. She did not understand how he could be friends with any Indians, but she knew that many of the things he had taught her were "Indian ways," and she figured they must not be all bad or "stinkin'," as her father claimed. She thought again of the Indian she had glimpsed, dragged by his wrists into the fort that fateful day years before. From what she had seen, he was a man like any other man, though his hair and skin were darker. She wondered if Indians prayed on Sundays to God—as white folks did—or if they knew of heaven or hell. Of course not, she decided, coming out of her reverie, how silly.

She brushed crumbs off her skirt and stood, gazing at the stillness below. She knew it was getting late by the sun's position in the sky, so she moved her sewing basket farther into the cave and turned to leave. She placed the pile of branches in front of the entrance once more and then began her descent to the ground below. The lake beckoned to her in its stillness and serenity, and she longed to take a swim, but she turned reluctantly from its spell and began her trek down the path. She would have to hurry if she was to have supper ready when her father got home. She paused, glancing once more to the lake, and then up towards the cave. She smiled and couldn't help thinking of how special it was to her. She thought once more of her mother and how she wished she could share it with her. "I'll be back," she whispered, looking beyond the cave to the cliff above.

Suddenly, her heart stood still! Her breath caught in her throat, her mouth dropped open and her eyes widened in surprise and disbelief! There, on the cliff's edge, a short distance from the cave, stood a lone figure. A man bronzed by the sun, naked except for a loincloth and moccasins. An Indian, she thought. "My God, an Indian!" she exclaimed aloud, feeling her heart begin to pound wildly, willing herself to stand still, only her eyes moving as she looked along the ridge crest for others. She saw none. He was alone, or so it seemed, and he was watching her!

Slowly, forcing herself not to hurry, she turned and began walking toward the woods, straining every nerve to listen for the sound of silently approaching moccasins. Her pulse pounded hard at her temples till she could hear nothing else. "Easy," she commanded herself, "go easy." She walked quickly, making no sound, trying to listen for danger or sounds of pursuit. Above all, she did not run or let herself panic. She did not want to look afraid. She knew many trails back to town that she could use if only she could get to them. Quietly, quickly, she walked through the woods, careful not to stumble or trip in her haste. When she got to the creek that edged the meadow, she leaped across, glancing quickly around, and began to run! She ran rhythmically, her feet barely touching the ground, her strong legs carrying her easily, skirts flying!

She was five feet, six inches tall and weighed one hundred twenty pounds, with small, firm breasts and a tiny waist. Her hips were rounded and solid, her legs shorter than she wished, but strong and able. She ran easily, still frightened, but not winded, as many of the other girls in Hastings would have been. She prided herself on her stamina and endurance. She had outrun all of them at church socials. She ran steadily till she reached the clearing near her cabin and then, pausing long enough to catch her breath, walked quickly to her house.

She did not tell her father about her encounter with the Indian, because she knew he would forbid her return to the cave and the lake. How could she tell him? He would also sound an alarm and rush blindly in pursuit, unleashing his hatred of all Indians on the one lone Indian she had seen. She could see no reason for such action, and above all, she could not bear the thought of her father and others invading the sanctity of her special place.

She fixed supper and later washed up the dishes, her thoughts restricting every attempt at normal conversation.

"Somethin' wrong, Sarah?" her father asked as she washed the dishes. "You've been awful quiet tonight, gal," he added, sensing her nervousness. "You and Tommy have a fight or something?" She blushed, and he added, "About time he got 'round to proposin', I figure."

She thought of Tommy Dawson and blushed again. "No, Pa, nothing's wrong. You know I don't want Tommy proposin'. We're just friends."

"If you say so," her father replied, looking up from some papers he was reading, smiling a quick smile. "You know you're not getting any younger, gal." He paused and, setting the papers aside, took a small box from his pocket. "Here's a little remembrance for you, Sarah," he said. "Happy birthday."

She went to him and bent, kissing his cheek, then opened the small package he handed her. In it was a tiny golden cross on a delicate gold chain. It was engraved with both her mother and father's initials on the back. "This was your mother's," her father stated, his voice sounding subdued. "I gave it to her the day we were married." He cleared his throat and continued, "I should have given it to you sooner, but I just couldn't bring myself to part with it." He cleared his throat a second time and added, "Happy birthday, Sarah. She'd want you to have it." Sarah felt her eyes fill with tears at the enormity of love that accompanied his gift. She kissed him again on his cheek, thanked him and felt even more anxiety over the secret she kept from him.

Later that evening, as she sat before the fire, mending, she asked him hesitantly the question that lay heavily on her mind. "Pa, are all Indians murdering savages?" She saw his jaw tighten as he quickly glanced over at her.

"Sure are," he answered. "Every last one." He looked at her questioningly. "Why'd you ask?"

"Oh, no reason. I had a . . . a dream, that's all," she replied, hoping he could not tell she was lying.

"Dreams don't mean nuthin', girl. Best you just forget 'em," he added, already taking up his paper again.

"Good night," she said. She heard him acknowledge with a grunt and closed her door. Quickly she undressed and unbraided her long auburn hair till it hung loose, covering her shoulders and caressing her back. She brushed it carefully with long, gentle strokes, her thoughts racing back to the Indian on the cliff. His hair had hung as long as hers, she remembered, though it was black and seemed to glisten in the sunlight. She thought again of his muscular shoulders and bronze skin, of the scarcity of clothing he wore and of the gray-and-white feather hanging from his hair. She wondered how long he had been watching her, and if he too was, at this very moment, thinking of her. Growing restful, she curled up in the old but comfortable quilt upon her bed, her mind drifting. Her father thought it time she married; how many times he had hinted at it, always linking her with Tommy Dawson. She snorted and shook her head. Tommy Dawson was one of the few single fellows in Hastings, her childhood friend and most eager pursuer. Only pursuer, if the truth was known. Tommy was one year older than she, tall and thin with pale skin and hollow cheeks that burned fire red when he was embarrassed, which was often! He lived with his widowed mother at the east end of Hastings and worked in the general store from dawn till dusk. It had been his father's store and now was his, and though he managed it with pride and unquestionable loyalty, Sarah knew, in his heart, he dreamed of becoming a wagon master and traveling west, leading a large wagon train to the fields of gold being spoken of beyond the great mountains. "Someday," he would say, wistfully, his eyes glistening with hope. "You'll see," he'd say. Year after year Sarah had listened to his ideas and dreams, as enthused as he at first. Then one year became two, two became three, now ten. No longer could she feign interest or cheer him. Though the dream still beckoned, his hope was gone.

Over the past ten years, Tommy had grown sullen and morose, reminding her of an old horse yoked to a cart too heavy for it to pull. Faithfully, patiently, he carried his load, burdened by the weight of it. He mentioned marriage to Sarah once, but it was spoken of in a joyless tone, and it wounded her instead of pleasing her. She had kissed him quickly on the cheek and hastily changed the subject. She would stay an old maid, she vowed, rather than marry into such dismal circumstances. She could never bear such a hopeless and forlorn alliance.

She had always thought of Tommy as a friend and, perhaps when younger, had even imagined marrying him. But his life had narrowed to a bland, mechanical, limited existence, while her dreams were quite the opposite! She dreamed of so many things that Tommy Dawson could never even imagine! Like the books her mother used to read to her, she wanted adventure and love, wanted to seek her fortune, to ride full tilt into her destiny, and stand face to face with her fate as the knights of old had done, fearlessly and courageously! Tommy talked of "someday," but lacked the courage of his convictions, while she, on the other hand, grew stronger in her determination to step beyond the mediocre and mundane.

How often she had lain in her bed, as she was now, imagining the day her own true love would ride into town. She would know him at once, as he would her. He would be tall and ruggedly handsome, with dark flashing eyes and sinewy muscles that belied his strength. His greatest feature: a smile that bespoke the tenderness within his heart. She would take one look at him, as damsels of old long before had done of their true loves, and *know* in that instant that he was the one. She would marry him and travel to far distant lands as helpmate, and mother to his children. She would share his dreams, dreams that most folks never dared to dream.

She pulled the quilt up over her shoulders, imagining what he would look like, as young women often do. As sleep enveloped her, she saw, in her mind's eye, a silent figure with bronze skin and long ebony hair, standing straight and tall. And in her heart, she knew that, for her, nothing would *ever* be the same again!

CHAPTER TWO

The next two weeks went slowly, though Sarah was busier than usual, when a young family of California-bound settlers stopped at the cabin while mending their hitch and restocking some of their supplies. The homesteaders, Josiah Winthrop, his wife, Cassandra, with their infant son, Jebadiah, had heard the stories of gold in California that had recently begun to filter east, and had plans to stake their claim as soon as they reached the gold fields. Sarah questioned the sensibility of their intentions, doubting their belief that gold lay so thick upon the ground that a man had only to scratch the earth with the toe of his boot to become rich. She questioned, also, the wisdom of their traveling alone along the Minnesota River to Browns Valley, South Dakota, and, once there, to spend a whole month visiting old friends before resuming their journey. But, she said nothing.

She remembered the stories of the hardships Old John had suffered, when winter blizzards had overtaken him, and knew in her heart that the same hardships could lie ahead for them if they lingered too long into the fall. She decided to speak of this to Cassandra and Josiah before they left. They had come west with great hopes and even greater expectations, but the more they talked, the more Sarah doubted the viability of their plans.

Josiah Winthrop was a tall man, nearly a head taller than

Sarah's father. He had shoulder-length brown hair and gray-green eyes that held a gentleness whenever he looked at his wife or son. He was a quiet, peaceable man who spoke softly in a reassuring manner. He was in his early thirties and had a very confident demeanor about him that made him easy to like. His legs were long, and he had broad hands that gave evidence of the hard work he was used to doing. Both Samuel and Sarah liked him at once.

Cassandra Winthrop was nearly as tall as her husband, with hair the color of honey, and soft features that enhanced her looks. Sarah liked her immediately and enjoyed the camaraderie that came so easily for both of them. They talked happily as they prepared the meals, sharing the chores equally. Sarah welcomed the chance for "woman's talk," a rarity she hadn't realized she missed, as they shared cherished family recipes passed down from generation to generation and spoke of Eastern fashion and events.

The men checked wheels and greased the wagon axles, inspected harnesses and hooves, and shared stories they had heard of the long trip ahead, of other homesteaders who had passed this way, and of the possible dangers that might arise. Sometimes, they sat side by side on the large fallen log, out near the barn, in silence, watching the stars, contentedly listening to the night's sounds, and thinking whatever thoughts came to mind as night, soft as velvet, settled in around them.

Inside, Cassandra taught Sarah the steps to the latest back-east dances. They laughed joyously as Sarah mimicked Cassandra's steps, whirling gaily, skirts billowing and feet flying as both women stomped and whirled, arm-in-arm, in the confines of the cabin. Cassandra sang, in tones as sweet as a meadowlark, the words to the tune as they do-see-doed, bowed and curtsied, cheeks flushed and hearts racing! Acting much younger than their age, for both were twenty-eight they had discovered, they fell upon the bed, side by side, giggling happily and panting as they tried to catch their breath. Their cheeks flushed with excitement, their eyes bright with merriment.

"Oh! Cassandra, I've never had such fun," Sarah stated breathlessly, sitting up and grasping her new friend's hand in her own.

"Nor I," Cassandra replied. "I wish we were staying here," she lamented, her eyes suddenly welling up with tears. She spoke then of her widowed mother and the four sisters she had left behind in the East. As she talked, she rose and walked over to the willow basket where her tiny baby son slept near the fireplace. She bent, her face serene in its motherly tenderness, and straightened the dark-brown woven blanket that covered him. Her eyes were damp with unshed tears when she returned to Sarah's side.

Sarah felt her own sad longing then, too, knowing she had never felt as close a friendship with any of the young women she had grown up with. Memories of her own mother's love for her, long since gone but not forgotten, overwhelmed her suddenly. She reached out, taking Cassandra's hand in her own once more, and they sat in silence, each aware of how quickly one's life could change and unexpectedly take a new direction. After a few moments, Sarah spoke, telling Cassandra of her life in Hastings, of her friends, Tommy, Rosie Mitchell, and Old John. Soon they were laughing aloud and happily conversing.

In the mornings that followed, Sarah washed quickly in the basin in her room. She dressed in whichever dress caught her fancy of the three she had, and ran a comb through her hair. Donning the long, faded apron that had been her mother's, she went quickly about the task of cooking breakfast. She prepared large saleratus biscuits, which her father liked to sop in homemade syrup, and broke eggs into the large skillet on the stove and ground coffee, when they had some. Coffee, sugar, and flour, were often scarce and costly. Butter was stored in stone crocks, but wouldn't last long in the summer heat, unless stored in the icehouse by the creek. They had a hardy supply of eggs from the half dozen chickens they kept, and plenty of milk, butter, and cream from their golden brown Jersey cow that Sarah called simply Pet.

Pet had a gentle disposition, and Sarah liked to press her face into Pet's side as she milked, enjoying the warmth and softness of her. She especially loved the sweet smell that emanated from her because of the molasses she often added to Pet's feed. Pet never kicked, or stamped her feet, upsetting the milk bucket as other cows were often wont to do. And she never tossed her head sideways, catching Sarah with her horns.

She was a fine animal, and Sarah loved the Jersey. She smiled, thinking of Pet's first calf, born in early spring, when crocus heads pushed up through the disappearing snow. A knobby-kneed bull calf that grew quickly to a nice size on his mother's colostrum, then milk, and later, grass, corn and oats. He was soon traded for two fine half-grown pigs to be fattened, to provide lard, bacon and ham.

Setting the plates and cups in place at the worn wooden table, Sarah called her father and the Winthrops in to breakfast and poured coffee for all. The biscuits were light and fluffy, and Sarah was proud of her skill in making them. Both Cassandra and Josiah ate theirs slathered in fresh butter, while Sarah spread wild berry jam on hers. Her father preferred his sopped, as usual, in homemade syrup. The eggs were a treat for the Winthrops, and they ate heartily, amid talk of the weather and their pending journey.

Later, as the women washed dishes, they talked and laughed. Sarah was delighted to hear that Cassandra could read as well as she, and hastened to a corner shelf where several books lay. She thought of her mother and how she had sat many evenings by lamplight reading and rereading the many treasured books, her brown woolen, homespun shawl wrapped loosely around her shoulders, her face peacefully serene.

"Here it is," Sarah exclaimed, carefully lifting a brown leather-bound book from the shelf, touching it with great tenderness as she handed it to Cassandra. "This is my favorite book. It's called *Twice Told Tales*. It's by Nathaniel Hawthorne, the rather new writer so highly praised by Longfellow. I want you to have it, Cassandra, to remember me by when you're settled in California."

Cassandra took the book, her eyes misting with gratitude. "Thank you, Sarah. I'll treasure it always," she replied, hugging it to her, then hugging Sarah. Books were rare and precious treasures to those who could read, and a comfort during lonely times.

The women talked quietly as Cassandra held Jebadiah to suckle at her breast. Sarah was moved by her friend's adeptness at mothering, and wondered if she would be as capable and loving when she had a baby. Quite unbidden, across her mind flashed the memory of the tall bronzed figure with long ebony hair standing ever so still, dressed in loincloth and moccasins, on the ledge above her cave. She felt her cheeks flush and glanced quickly at Cassandra.

"Sarah?" Cassandra asked questioningly. "What is it?"

"It's nothing," she replied, longing to share her thoughts about the Indian. "Nothing," she repeated with stronger conviction. She felt a momentary wave of sadness overshadow the bond of friendship that, in so short a time, seemed to have blossomed within her heart to more of a "sisterly bond" than mere friendship.

Quickly, she moved to the table, peeling the potatoes and carrots she had gathered from the root cellar behind the cabin after milking Pet. She added them to the Dutch oven, along with a handful of flour to thicken the juices from the rabbit which her father had shot and cleaned earlier that day. She hung it in the fireplace to cook and then made salt—rising bread to go with it. Every piece of potato skin with eyes was saved for the next year's crop, as her mother had taught her, and could prove a matter of life and death through a harsh winter. She took pride in her cooking skills and knew the Winthrops would not leave hungry. She hated to think of them leaving at all, but knew they planned to start west in the morning. A sense of loss filled her heart at the thought.

Deciding to pick some peas, she took up a wooden bowl and walked quickly down the path behind the cabin. Cassandra had finished feeding Jebadiah and, after a resounding burp, he slept peacefully in the willow basket, his tiny lips sucking as though his mother still fed him.

"Can I help?" Cassandra asked, hurrying to catch up with Sarah.

"Yes. Come," she replied, happy for her companionship on this, their last day together.

"I hope to have two children someday," Sarah said. "A boy and a girl." She paused and then added, "Someday."

"Are you soon to wed?" asked Cassandra.

"Oh, no!" Sarah exclaimed.

"Is there someone special in your life, that Tommy you spoke of earlier, perhaps?"

"No!" Sarah stated emphatically and felt her cheeks grow hot. She knew she was blushing. "Not Tommy . . . no one really," she stammered, bending quickly to pick the peas that were growing abundantly. "No one really," she repeated, as Cassandra wondered at her friend's obvious hesitation.

Soon, they sat on the fallen log out by the barn, shelling the peas and enjoying the soft breeze that stirred the leaves on the trees around them.

"I want someone special," Sarah said suddenly, as if their earlier conversation had never stopped. "I won't be satisfied with," she hesitated, "just anybody." Her voice trailed off, and Cassandra did not venture to interrupt her, knowing Sarah was sharing her innermost thoughts. "I'll know when he comes. I believe that." Sarah stated.

Cassandra smiled at the look of pure conviction upon her

friend's face. "Then you haven't met him yet?" she asked, seeing Sarah's cheeks begin to redden slightly as she pondered her reply.

So softly that Cassandra had to lean forward to hear her, Sarah shyly answered, "Maybe . . . I have." The bronze figure flashed once more across Sarah's mind. "Yes," she continued, "I . . . think I might have." She said no more, quickly changing the subject.

That evening, after they had eaten and once again cleaned the dishes, the women walked arm in arm down to the pond beyond the raspberry patch. In the still shelter of partial darkness, they undressed quickly and hurriedly entered the water. The cold water was refreshing, and they splashed like children, laughing and squealing playfully. Then they settled down to the job of bathing themselves, washing and rinsing their hair amid soft laughter and murmured conversation. They both felt the bond that had grown in such short time between them, and it filled their hearts and gave them great joy.

While the women were at the pond, the men also shared an enjoyable camaraderie as they watched the baby and spoke of the past and future. Samuel Justus walked to the willow basket and watched the small baby sleep, his thoughts drifting back to his wife, Jenny, and Sarah's birth. He remembered how they had enjoyed the tiny girl-child that filled their lives, their home, and their hearts with love. He became saddened, too, as he thought of Jenny's death, and turned away from the willow basket and the baby, and the disturbing thoughts. Tomorrow the Winthrops would leave, and life would go on as it had before. Before the good Lord had seen fit to send such fine folks into their lives. It had been a long time since Samuel had enjoyed the company of another man as much. He felt relaxed and at peace, wondering, as he had more than once of late, if it would have been different, somehow, if Jenny had given him a son. He poured them each a cup of coffee and sat down at the table as Josiah cupped his hands to his lips and began to play a melody on his harmonica, the notes clean and pure in the stillness of the night.

Long ago, when he courted Jenny, Samuel reminisced, he too had played the harmonica. He smiled as he remembered. It was a memory that brought both joy and sadness. How he wished Jenny were here to share the music and fine fellowship with the Winthrops. He closed his eyes, feeling a dampness upon his lashes, as Josiah continued to softly play.

Later that evening, knowing that tomorrow they would part, the women served the last of the pie they had made the day before, and encouraged Josiah to entertain them with still more music. Sometimes they sang along, but mostly they sat quietly listening, knowing in their hearts that none of them wanted the evening to end.

In the morning, the sky was clear. Having eaten a quick breakfast of biscuits and gravy, and having shared a pot of coffee, the men hitched the horses while Cassandra fed and changed the baby. Samuel warned Josiah of the dangers of traveling too late in the year through the pass in the mountains, because of the great blizzards that occurred there. Heeding Samuel's advice, Josiah agreed that they had best change their plans to visit old friends in Browns Valley, South Dakota, staying a month, and would instead visit only a day or two before going on. Already it was late June and, barring any trouble, they would have to press onward steadily, cautious of Indians and all the other perils that could befall them. Josiah said he hoped to meet up with a wagon train in South Dakota, as his friends there said many passed that way. He knew there was more safety in numbers, and wanted to take no chances where his family's safety was concerned.

With the baby fed and bathed and now asleep once more in his basket, Sarah read to Cassandra from a small book of writings she had written during her sojourn from the fort to

Hastings after her mother had died when she was ten. It was filled with the innermost feelings of the young motherless child: her fears, her hopes, her limited understanding of why her mother had had to die, and how God, Who was supposed to be all goodness, could allow such a thing to happen. Her deepest thoughts and emotions filled page after page as she sought to make some sense of her loss. Sarah felt a similar loss now, knowing she would most likely never see Cassandra again. Reading this journal to Cassandra was the only way she knew to give her friend an in-depth part of herself, a sharing of her deepest thoughts.

Cassandra began to cry, hugging this new—but most dear—friend to her, as the ache in her heart at having to part took precedence over all other feelings. Sarah cried, too, and clung to Cassandra, wishing, but knowing, they would not stay. She pressed a small container into Cassandra's hand. "Seeds," she said, "from my garden to the one you'll plant in California." Then, she pulled away, wiping her eyes. They stood there in silence, knowing that they must do what their lives demanded of them. They looked at each other as though to memorize each tiny feature, thinking of the wonderful moments they had shared the past two weeks. Then, sighing and sniffling simultaneously, they smiled and, arm in arm, walked over to the baby in his willow basket.

The men looked up as the women came outside, noting the sadness that shown in their eyes, their cheeks wet even though they smiled. They felt helpless to ease the pain they knew their womenfolk were feeling. Samuel lifted the basket and baby up into Josiah's waiting hands as Cassandra took a small woven basket from under the seat of the wagon where she would ride. Opening the basket, she took out two things, folded them into a small square, and placed the basket into its place once again under the seat. She walked to where Sarah stood.

"I want you to have these things, my dear friend," she

said, a tear rolling down her cheek, "so you'll always remember me, too." And handing them quickly to Sarah, she turned and got a hand up from Josiah to her place on the wagon seat. Josiah shook Samuel's hand in the firm grip of mutual caring and respect and, with emotions riding high, he snapped the reins. The horses strained forward, pulling the wagon as their journey began.

Samuel put his arm around Sarah's shoulder to comfort her as best he knew how. He remembered that long ago he had also comforted her in the same way. It had not been enough for the ten-year-old girl and he was, even yet, at a loss to know what else to do. A cavalry he could command. Soldiers were strong and resilient. They were men and he understood men. All his life he had dealt with his men with firmness and discipline, demanding strength and orderliness, applauding courage and honor. He had not known how to comfort Jenny in her loneliness, though he had tried. God knows he had tried, though demands at the fort often kept him away and duties kept him too busy.

"Father?" Sarah said, her voice bringing him back from memories that haunted him more and more the older he got. "Are you okay?" she asked watching him closely, having noticed the faraway look that filled his eyes.

"Yes. I'm fine," he answered, smiling a smile that did not last. "I'm fine," he said again, as though to assure himself as much as her, and turned toward the cabin. Yes. A boy would have been easier, he thought. I would have understood the needs of a son.

Sarah stood and looked at the empty, fading wagon tracks. Her hand clenched tightly, she suddenly realized, around whatever it was Cassandra had given her. She opened her hand to reveal a beautiful hair ribbon the color of the sun, a shimmering yellow gold. She tied it quickly around her head, holding her hair off her face, feeling the slight breeze waft gently across her cheeks. She smiled in gratitude and then unfolded the fine piece of tightly woven gray wool, seeing at once the small even stitches upon it. She turned it to face her and read the words:

FOLLOW YOUR HEART

"Oh! Cassandra," she said aloud, a smile as bright as their friendship upon her face. "I shall," she stated decisively. "I shall follow my heart!" and she spun on her heel and went into the cabin.

CHAPTER THREE

For three days, Sarah busied herself around the house: cooking, baking, cleaning, and washing clothes in the nearby creek. She worked furiously, as though driven, trying to rid herself of the increasing desire to return to the cave. At last, she could stand it no more. Strapping to her waist a deer-hide bag containing a knife and two sourdough biscuits that she had placed in an amber-hued scarf that used to be her mother's, she set out on her journey. She knew the knife would be little protection against an Indian, but felt better carrying it. She felt tense with excitement at her intended foray back to the cave. She knew she was being foolish, but somehow she could not help herself. It was as if the destiny her soul longed for was at last within her reach and—come what may—she could not turn back.

Ever alert for any signs of danger or movement, she hurried on, not noticing the beauty of the wildflowers at her feet. Soon, she came to the stream at the edge of the forest and listened intently for even one sound that might warn of danger. She lifted her pant-legs above her ankles and jumped quickly and quietly across the rushing water. Above, a few birds scolded her intrusion into their domain. A fat brown squirrel chattered and hastily retreated, scurrying along on the long lower branch of a tall stately oak, quickly disappearing from sight.

She hurried on, knowing if she turned back now she would never again gain the courage to confront what lay ahead. The cave, the woods, and possibly even the meadow, would be lost to her if she let fear overtake her. She could do this! She would do this! She must! She did not understand the immense need she felt to return to the cave. Was it mere curiosity or just out-and-out foolishness? It felt as though she was being propelled along with no will of her own, as though a powerful force was guiding her, goading her, pushing her to hurry, hurry! She felt as much excitement, as fear, as she arrived at the edge of the clearing, and peered out from behind a large clump of bushes, surveying the familiar scenery. Stillness prevailed, the pounding of her heart all that disturbed the silence. She felt her muscles, taut with tension, relax a bit, and looked to the ledge where he had stood watching her. No one was there. She felt an odd sense of disappointment until she looked toward the entrance to the cave. The brush that she had piled in front of the entrance seemed askew. Or was she imagining it? She peered anxiously up toward the cave, feeling apprehensive. Was he inside awaiting her return, ready to savagely murder her? Had she been foolish to return?

I had to be stubborn and foolhardy, didn't I? she thought. The only woman my age in Hastings who practiced shooting and trapping and all such other manly skills. I should have been born a boy, she thought, studying the path to the cave and devising a plan of action.

No sign of an intruder, she thought, edging cautiously from behind the brush beside the lake. She steadied her shaking hands, carefully removed the knife from her deerskin sheath, and then began the ascent to the cave. The muscles in her neck felt tense from the strain, but she had no time to consider that now. Slowly, with great care, she eased ever upward. The moccasins Old John had given her last spring silenced each footfall as though she were an Indian.

She was dressed in an old pair of brown pants and the

muted green shirt of her father's she usually wore dogging Old John's footsteps in the woods. She was glad she didn't have to worry about holding up a skirt as she climbed the narrow path to the cave. She never did understand why women favored skirts. They might look more "ladylike," as Rosie Mitchell proclaimed, but they were a darn nuisance when it came to hunting, trapping, and other such activities. Let the other girls dress up in dresses and frills. She preferred pants.

She had braided her hair in one thick braid that hung down her back. Her auburn—colored hair would be easy to spot in the woods, and she had thought about tucking it up under the old gray floppy hat she usually wore when hunting or tracking, but had decided against it because the hat was cumbersome and devoid of any charm. It mattered to her that she looked fetching, though it was a subconscious thought she was not truly aware of.

As she neared the cave's entrance, she held the knife in her outstretched hand, and paused to listen for any sounds of imminent danger. There were none. She edged in beside the pile of branches, holding her breath, eyes darting warily around the inside of her special domain. The midmorning rays of sun lit the inside of the cave, making it nearly as bright as outside. Her sewing basket sat near the center of the cave, not where she had left it. Otherwise, nothing looked disturbed.

Sarah eased in and sat on her haunches, hidden by the brush still in front of the entrance. She let out a sigh, watching the area surrounding the lake and path up to the cave. Relaxing a bit, her thoughts turned to the reality that he had been inside the cave. He had touched her sewing in its small woven basket, but had not disturbed her needle and thread, or destroyed her delicate stitches. He had also not stolen the quilt she was making for her father. She traced the rim of the basket with one finger, realizing, in all probability, she was touching where the Indian had touched. She put her finger to her nose and sniffed. No scent was present. The cave floor showed no hint of footprints, she noted, as she stood and surveyed the lake's edge below. Birds flitted happily amongst the trees. Some settled in bushes, pecking and calling back and forth amongst themselves. No warnings. She relaxed her hold on the knife, laying it at her feet within easy reach. She wondered what she should do next.

What if the Indian is on his way to the cave at this very moment? What if others follow, she thought, ready to unleash their savage fury upon me and the other good folks of Hastings? She shivered at the thought and picked up the knife once again, her fingers closing tightly around its handle. She had considered bringing her father's gun, the one she took to practice with Old John. But she decided against it because she felt more "fleet of foot" not carrying it. A gun would slow her down, a knife would not. She also wondered if Indians could run fast. She wondered so many things about them.

She stayed at the cave awhile, taking one of the sourdough biscuits from the scarf that they were wrapped in, carefully setting it beside her quilt pieces in the small woven basket.

Perhaps he would return again, she thought, and eat the biscuit, taking it as a sign of friendship. Then, her courage waning, she decided not to press her luck and started down the path, cautiously alert to any possible danger. She eased down the path, carefully stepping among the small stones, until she was on level ground. Then, she turned, shading her eyes with her hand, and scanned her surroundings. On the cliff's edge above her, she saw him.

He stood as still as the stone statues she had seen in one of her mother's books. Sarah forced herself to stand still, also, wondering what he would do next. She also wondered if others watched or crept closer. That thought gave rise to a host of fears, and she gazed quickly around, clasping the knife tightly. Birds flew above, giving no sign of danger. She had an impulsive thought and, after laying the knife on a rock beside her, quickly removed her mother's scarf from the deerskin bag at her side. She placed the remaining biscuit in the scarf and held it aloft for him to see. Then she placed the scarf upon the rock, picked up the knife, and turning on her heel, walked off into the woods.

She wondered what he would do. She wondered if he would have enough sense to understand her attempt at friendship. She doubted it. But, what if not all Indians were stinking savages? she thought. She wondered if they could be taught to be civilized and decent. Hadn't Old John befriended some of them? She was certain he would not have taken up with a bunch of wild, filthy, murdering savages. Absolutely not! Maybe this one was a good one and even smart enough, she thought, to learn some Christian ways. Well, he had invaded her special place, and foolish as it might seem, she was not about to give it up. Maybe there was a way to tell which were good Indians and which were bad, she thought. She'd have to ask John the next time she saw him.

When, at last, she came to the creek, she jumped across and began running across the flower-filled meadow. She felt a wealth of good feelings as she neared her home and was pleased with the day's adventure. She planned to return to the cave as soon as possible.

Early the next morning, she woke to a heavy rain and the repeated roll of thunder, rumbling in quick succession across the black sky. She was startled by the intensity and pulled her quilt up over her head as great claps of thunder shook the earth just outside the cabin with unrelenting fervor. She had heard all the childhood tales about thunder: that God was angry and throwing great spears at the earth, and as they hit, the resulting crash was heard for miles, ear-splitting and frightening. She rolled on her side, pulling her knees up, only the end of her nose sticking out from under the quilt so she could breathe. She thought of the storm last spring that had flashed and boomed in thunderous reverberations. When it was done, they had found four of "Old Man Pearly's" cattle lying dead beside a large tree that had been struck by lightning. Their eyes were bulged and glazed over, their legs stuck straight out and stiff, their tongues lolled out of their mouths. Fearsome, that storm had been. Plain fearsome! Sarah thought. She lay still counting the seconds after each flash of lightning until the thunder crashed. She relaxed as there were more and more seconds between them, knowing the storm was moving farther away.

At last she could no longer lay still as the day's chores beckoned to her. Today she planned to bake a pie and some cornbread from the recipe given her by Rosie Mitchell. She washed in the basin by her bed, dressed quickly in her favorite blue dress, and brushed and braided her hair into one long, thick braid. She pinched her cheeks, a quick pinch, as she looked into the small mirror that had been her mother's and was now her prized possession. After putting on the well-worn apron that hung by the door, she entered the main room of the cabin. Sarah smiled as she saw the sun just peeking through the window on the far side of her father's bed. She saw that, as usual, his day had begun much earlier than hers, though it was still barely morning. His bed was neatly made— the pillow plumped, the quilt straightened—a habit he had acquired after her mother's death. She picked up a basket and headed outside to pick some strawberries. Strawberries being so small, she knew it would take her some time to pick enough for a pie.

When she returned to the cabin, basket brimming with the juicy red berries, she set at once to hulling them and proceeded to prepare the pie for baking. Then, she took the old oaken bucket her mother had purchased years earlier and headed for the stream that ran beside the cabin and on through the hills leading into town. Stopping only long enough to scoop up a handful of the cool, refreshing water to drink, she dipped the bucket into the stream, filling it. Then, she returned to the cabin. She was barefoot and walked with a spring in her step, happy with herself. She hummed—a little off key—a tune she had learned at church when she was a child, unable to remember the words. She felt at peace, happy with her plans for the day, with the memories of days just passed, and in her hopes for the future.

As coffee boiled on the stove, and the smell of cornbread filled the cabin, her father returned for a bowl of cornbread and syrup, and his usual mug of strong black coffee. Sarah joined him, though she added cream to her coffee to make it more palatable to suit her taste. Everyday, about the same time, Sarah and her father shared their morning meal together and they talked of his earlier trip into town after he had finished milking Pet. Sarah was always interested in whatever news he had heard in town. Today he told her of an Indian attack over at Black Dog Lake, west of Hastings. She had an uneasy feeling about it, wondering if the Indian she saw had any part in it. Samuel also told her that Nancy Pearly was going to wed Silas Haverty the following Saturday. He said there would be a barn dance after the wedding and he thought they should go. She smiled and shook her head, picturing quiet, dreadfully plain Nancy Pearly, who had long ago probably given up any hopes of marrying, due to her domineering and drunken father.

Silas was a short, ruggedly built, bearded trapper, who came to town twice a year for supplies. He spoke such broken English, she was told, that most folks couldn't understand a word he said. But, apparently, Nancy had understood him. Sarah poured her father a second cup of coffee as he ate the last of his cornbread.

Silas Haverty, she thought, of all people! She didn't know where Silas was from. She did know he smelled strong of liquor when he came to town the one day she had seen him, and equally strong of the hides he dressed in and carried on his pack mule. Someone had said he lived in the mountains with a squaw whom he had stolen or traded furs for, but she wasn't sure of the truth of it. Poor Nancy, she thought, to settle for so little just to leave her father's home. Never once did Sarah consider it possible Nancy had met and grown to love Silas Haverty.

Later that afternoon, before her father would return again from town, Sarah prepared a kettle of stew and sourdough biscuits. Then she slipped out of the cabin and headed for the stream. She carried the bucket and filled it once more with the icy water that rushed along on its way toward town. She dipped a cloth in the water, wrung it out, and then washed her face, arms, hands, and feet. It was a hot day, muggy after the thunderstorm, and the water refreshed her.

She gathered up the bucket and turned toward the field where her father's horse grazed when not being ridden. She whistled for it, seeing it raise its head in answer to her call, and start moving in her direction. As she watched it, she glanced beyond it to a thicket of trees where something light in color seemed to be moving. She stared, shading her eyes with her hand, straining to make out the shape. There! There it was! Something the color of . . . was it a deer? She stared, turning her head to the side, stretching her neck and raising up on her toes. A man stood in the partial shadow of the trees. Yes! It was a man!

But who? she thought. Why doesn't he come out in the open? She could just make out his buckskin pants, his shadowed form. Perhaps Old John was returning from a hunt, she thought, but why doesn't he move out into the field? Why is he staying in the shadow of the trees?

Suddenly, she knew! The Indian had followed her and was watching her. Her heart leapt as panic assailed her. She dropped the bucket of water and raced back to the cabin, her heart pounding in her ears. Inside the cabin she found she was shaking so hard she could hardly think. Bolting the door, she grabbed her father's gun from its place on the mantle, making certain it was loaded. Her hands continued to shake as she hurried to the window and peered out, trying to see if she could see him.

She remembered the story her father had told earlier that morning of the attack at Black Dog Lake. Clutching the gun, she searched for him among the shadows, but saw nothing. Her father would not be back from town for hours, she knew, and she chided herself for not telling him of the encounter at the cave. Now I'll be killed by the same Indians my father always warned me about, she thought, and it's all my fault. She heard her father's mare nicker and then whinny, a small trusting sound, and peered out. It whinnied again, shaking its head, but remained where she had left it, looking back across the field toward the stand of trees where she had seen the Indian. She looked out just in time to see the tall buck-skinned figure enter the woods and disappear.

She watched a long time, straining her eyes for any sign of him: a movement or a sound. Her muscles grew taut. After a while, she replaced the gun above the mantle and cautiously unbolted the door. The sun shone brightly in the blue cloud-free sky. She listened, hearing only the twittering of birds and another nicker of greeting from the mare. She walked to the horse and reached to pet the great silver-grey colored animal. The horse nuzzled her hand and shook its head, stomping one foot, a ripple moving across its skin from neck to back. Sarah ran her hand through the thick, tousled black mane, and then she saw—to her surprise and delight—a long gray-and-white feather hanging from the mane. She touched it gingerly and then took it into her hands, realizing what it symbolized. This was his gift to her! He had understood! He had given her a token of friendship in return. A smile broke upon her face as bright as the noonday sun. He had understood her gesture of friendship and returned it. Her heart soared as she twirled in delight, causing the mare to shy away from her.

That evening, to her great relief, her father ate quickly and then returned to town for a meeting. She was afraid he'd notice her unabashed joy, joy she would not be able to explain. She felt ready to burst and wished she could tell Cassandra of her great adventure, and the result of her offer of friendship with the Indian. He had understood! He knew she wanted to be his friend. She smiled at remembering, though immediately she thought of the Indian attack at Black Dog Lake and the lives that had been taken. Didn't anyone believe in the Bible's teachings anymore? she thought. What about loving thy neighbor? Of course Indians weren't God-fearing folks. They were heathens and savages. Everybody knew that. These thoughts gave rise to more somber ones. How could white folks, being Christian, have wreaked so much death and destruction over the years, not just on Indians, but on the "darkies," as her father called them? She heard talk of them being brought over in the holds of large ships. Slave ships, they were called. Of the hundreds on board, half or more died on the journey, usually, due to horrid conditions or ill treatment. As if that weren't bad enough, she'd heard the ones who survived were chained like dogs and sold on auction blocks as slaves, to the highest bidder. Why sometimes whole families were split up and sold to distant bidders, never to see their loved ones again, someone had said. She shivered at these thoughts. She'd heard plenty more, about whippings and such, and felt sick at heart about these things. She heard it was common practice—in the South—to own many slaves, and the thought of it made her feel a sense of embarrassment and shame.

"They just weren't Christians," she said aloud. "I guess maybe there's good and bad in all people: whites, Indians, and all the rest." She had never met a Negro, but had seen one at the livery stable the summer before. He was a powerful-looking man, over six feet tall, she guessed. He was black as the night with large, pale palms and a throaty laugh that seemed to vibrate from deep inside him and burst forth like an explosion. She wondered what he had to laugh at. She had seen the long reddish-purple welts across his wide, muscular back as he loaded great bags of grain into a wagon, his skin glistening with sweat in the blazing noonday sun. His lips were cracked and parched from the heat of the sun, and she wondered if anyone had given him a drink of water to cool him. It had never crossed her mind that she might have done so.

She walked over to where the mare grazed, reaching up, rubbing her hand along its side, feeling the silken skin ripple at her touch. "Good girl, Glory," Sarah whispered softly. "Oh, Glory! What did you think of our new friend?" The horse nickered softly in response, swishing flies with its long black tail.

Sarah fairly danced to the barn to get Glory a handful of grain, her joy was so abundant. She must think now—with caution and Christian considerations—what the next step would be in this new friendship. She had to come up with a plan!

CHAPTER FOUR

On the day of the barn dance to honor Nancy Pearly and Silas Haverty, the sky was filled with a golden radiance, sunny and bright. The sun's golden rays shone across the fields, basking them in beauty. Birds flew here and there, soaring in effortless flight across the cloudless sky. Flowers abounded— tiny pinks, grand reds, whites, and purples—a veritable rainbow of colors, including the cattails by the creek, their stick like stalks topped by thicker tufts of light golden brown.

Sarah's thoughts turned from Nancy and Silas to her own circumstances with the Indian. She pondered the similarities in both instances. Silas was rugged and wild, a man who lived away from society, surviving by his own hands. He lived on his own terms as she imagined her Indian to do, also. She had to admit she admired that in a man, though, at the same time, she felt a great concern for Nancy. Nancy was quite the opposite. She had lived near town all twenty-nine years of her life. She could cook, clean, and sew, more than acceptable stitches. But how would she fair in the woods? Sarah shuddered at the mere thought.

Sarah knew *she* could survive such a life, even welcome it . . . but . . . Nancy? Of course, she knew Nancy had many times walked long distances to sit with a sick neighbor, or to comfort a grieving neighbor. She worked hard and never complained, a trait most folks—especially men—could appreciate. She was plain, it was true, but Sarah had to admit she had a pleasant smile, and a quiet, feminine demeanor that made everyone like her and enjoy her company.

She laughed aloud as she began wondering how she would be described. She could cook, clean, and sew, too, thanks to her mother's patient lessons, but a quiet, feminine demeanor? Looking down at the dirt on her boots and the rip in her pants, she felt sweat on her brow and knew a few errant pieces of straw were most likely tangled in her hair at the moment. She had been mucking out Glory's stall in the barn the past hour and would hate to have anyone, much less her betrothed, if indeed she had one, see her in such a state. She giggled and rested a moment as her thoughts ran rampant.

"Her Indian"—for she did think of him now as her Indian—was probably as wild and smelly, and as self-sufficient a loner, as Silas Haverty. She imagined him riding over the hills, hair streaming out behind him, in pursuit of a deer, or elk, or buffalo. She wondered, suddenly, if either man knew any social graces. A picture formed in her mind of both men arriving at the festivities: one in his loincloth and one in his smelly hide britches. Sarah got to giggling, and then laughing aloud so hard that she had tears in her eyes before she could stop.

Well, yes sir, this wedding ought to be quite the eye opener, she thought. Tossing a small amount of grain in the bucket for Glory, she put up the pitchfork, stomped her feet to get rid of any residue, and went across the yard to the cabin.

Later that afternoon, after a refreshing bath in the lake, Sarah got ready for the celebration. She dried her auburn hair and then brushed it till it shone. With the help of her mother's small looking-glass, she began to braid it and twist it around her head. A few wispy tendrils escaped the braid and graced her cheeks, giving her a softer, more feminine look. She examined herself in the small mirror as best she could and knew she looked womanly now and no longer girlish. She sighed and turned away. Nancy Pearly had long been thought of as an old maid, and she was only twenty-nine. One year older than me, Sarah silently lamented.

She put on the only really good dress she had: a white cotton with tiny pink roses across the bodice, sewn long ago with care, and a young woman's hopeful anticipation of happy times, by her mother. Each stitch was the labor of love of a new bride going west with her handsome cavalry-officer husband to a new life together. Sarah wondered if Nancy Pearly had any hopes and anticipation about the new life she would soon be embarking on. Maybe hopes, Sarah thought, don't we all have hopes? But anticipation? With Silas? Sarah finished her toilette and threw the soft brown woolen shawl from her mother's old pine trunk around her shoulders. It would be cooler during the ride home in her father's wagon, and she didn't want to catch a chill.

Her thoughts again turned to Nancy Pearly. Old Man Pearly must be pretty angry at losing his cook and scrub woman, Sarah guessed. Everybody in town knew how hard Nancy had to work to keep in her father's good graces. Folks would tell of hearing him yelling at her, and once Mrs. Carson—the boarding house proprietor—had turned to wave as she passed by the Pearlys' place and had seen Old Man Pearly hit Nancy a whack with a red-twig broom, nearly knocking her off her feet. Some folks said that things had been different before Nancy's mother died, but Sarah doubted that. She imagined him to have been the same with Mrs. Pearly as he was with Nancy: ill-tempered and, if truth be known, a regular patron of the one saloon in Hastings, the Lucky Lady Saloon.

Sarah shook her head and brushed another unruly wisp of hair off her cheek. Old Man Pearly—for that's what everybody called him—was a stocky man with black hair streaked with gray and thick eyebrows still nearly all black. Sarah guessed him to be about her father's age, or older, but you couldn't always tell. Drink and a mean temperament often aged a person, she had noticed, whereas a pleasant countenance and happy demeanor gave a more youthful appearance. Old Man Pearly was as unpleasant a person as Sarah had ever known. He never conversed with the other men in town, except to argue, it seemed. She reckoned she had never seen him smile. He seemed angry with everyone he met, and about as antisocial as a fellow could be. Sarah wondered if he'd be any different at the wedding and barn dance, or as disagreeable as usual. Poor Nancy, if he was. No wonder she'd marry a trapper who lived in the wilds. Who wouldn't to get away from such a father?

Sarah heard her father draw up to the door in their wagon. She picked up the pie she was taking, and went out, closing the door behind her. Handing Samuel the pie, she took the hand he offered to help her up onto the wagon seat. Thank goodness I have such a good father, she thought, giving him a quick kiss on the cheek. She noticed he had gotten a haircut and shave and smelled nice.

"You look pretty," he said. "Tommy Dawson will be the luckiest fellow at the dance." Sarah blushed, smiling at her father's attempt as matchmaker. She knew it would do no good to tell him, again, that she and Tommy were just friends. Or that she wouldn't marry Tommy if he were the last man on earth. She shook her head and, seeing her father smile, settled the pie she had baked for the occasion on her lap. Once more, she thought of her Indian and he filled her thoughts on the long ride to the Pearlys' farm.

The Pearlys' farm looked no different than the one other time Sarah had been there. Shabbiness was the first impression one got. The cleanliness inside, the second, an impression that somehow seemed to blot out the first impression. Sarah knew, as everyone else did, that Nancy was responsible for the overall cleanliness. A white cotton cloth with tiny embroidered daisies covered the stained wooden table. The dirt floors had been swept clean, boots lined up in neat order beside the door, homespun curtains at the windows, giving the cabin a cheerful, homey feeling. On the table, a jar of fresh-picked wildflowers in a rainbow of colors graced the surroundings, a touch of beauty that brought thoughts of her mother to Sarah's mind, and she smiled at these memories.

Nancy gave Sarah a warm smile as Sarah and her father entered the home. They were the first to arrive, and Nancy invited them to make themselves comfortable, offering them coffee or tea. Sarah was amazed at the changes she noticed in Nancy since she had last seen her in town the summer before. Where was the plain-faced woman Sarah expected to see? Nancy was positively glowing: her cheeks pink, her blue eyes bright, and her light blonde hair curling softly around her face. She looked radiant! Sarah noted the lovely pink cotton dress Nancy wore, its smooth lines accenting her small waist, its bodice hugging curves that Sarah had never noticed before. Why Nancy was positively beautiful!

"And where's your intended?" Sarah blurted out, totally taken aback by the changes in her friend.

"Out by the barn, talking to my paw," Nancy answered, as she seated herself across from Sarah and offered more coffee to Samuel.

"Believe I'll go out and say hello," Sarah's father said, standing. "I'll take you up on another cup when I come back in. It sure is tasty," he added.

"That's 'cause I add egg shells when the hens are laying," Nancy answered, blushing. You could tell she wasn't used to compliments. Samuel excused himself and went outside. Sarah removed her shawl and sipped her tea, noticing the lovely brown quilt on the bed in the corner.

"Do you like it?" Nancy asked, looking also in the direction of the quilt.

"Oh, yes!" Sarah answered. "Did you make it?"

"Yes," replied her host, her cheeks reddening slightly. "I dyed it with walnuts from a tree in the valley to the west. It's a difficult undertaking, one my mother taught me years ago." They smiled in womanly understanding and drank their tea.

Just then the door opened and a man came in that Sarah didn't recognize. He wore an old-style brown suit, and his white shirt buttoned so tightly at the neck that it seemed to make his neck bulge. He was a slight bit taller than Nancy, clean-shaven, with laughing brown eyes that bespoke a happy nature. His long gray-streaked black hair looked tousled, though she could tell he had attempted to smooth it down with a little water. He grinned at Sarah, as if reading her thoughts, his eyes twinkling, then walked over to Nancy. Nancy smiled shyly, first at the man, then at Sarah.

"Sarah, I'd like you to meet my betrothed, Silas Haverty," Nancy said. Sarah almost fell out of her chair in amazement. *This* was Silas Haverty? *This* was Nancy's beau? The bearded, smelly trapper who lived in the wilds? It was all Sarah could do to stammer a "hello."

Silas spoke then, his voice a deep melodious sound that further surprised Sarah, "Hello, Sarah. I'm glad ta meet ya'. Nancy told me of your skills with a gun and all." He paused and then added, "You were taught by the best. I hope your friend, John Bruce, will be comin' today. We met years ago . . . a wiser man I've not known."

Sarah beamed with pride at both his words and his compliments, surprised at how easy it was to understand him, noticing only the slightest accent. "I hope he'll come," Sarah replied, though she knew Old John usually avoided gatherings like barn dances, weddings, and such, as a matter of principle. He just wasn't the social type. Of course, if he knew his old acquaintance, Silas Haverty, was Nancy's betrothed, he just might make it a point to come. She hoped so. It had been quite awhile since she had seen him.

Soon wagons could be heard arriving, so Nancy, Sarah,

and Silas left the cabin and went outside to greet everyone. In one wagon, Sarah recognized four of the old-timers who spent most of their time sitting in front of the general store smoking and gossiping, two were widowers and two were old bachelors who had "never been caught," as they liked to boast for anyone near enough to hear. She didn't figure any of the older and wiser women she knew would give them a moment's notice. Most were set in their ways from being alone or used to the more presentable husbands they had been married to, but who'd now passed on. But life was funny, and who was she to think she had it all figured out?

She waved at an old friend of hers from school days, Melinda Rose Matson, as she was helped from the buckboard she had come in. Sarah could see she was heavy with child and wondered if it was her first baby. Melinda Rose straightened the folds of her dress across her stomach and walked slowly over to Sarah. She was a dreadfully thin girl when younger, but now she seemed enveloped in mounds of fat. Her cheeks were round as apples, her arms and hands looked puffy and swollen, and her body more than ample. She walked as though her feet hurt and Sarah wondered how she could have let herself get in such sorry shape. Surely it wasn't all because of the pregnancy.

"'Lo, Sarah," Melinda Rose wheezed as she reached Sarah's side. "How ya' been?" She panted for breaths in between sentences as beads of sweat poured out across her forehead. "I guess I shouldn't 'a come," she wheezed. She wiped her brow with the sleeve of her dress, which looked worn and pulled extremely tight at the seams.

"How've you been?" Sarah asked, smiling. "I see you're going to have a little one." She nodded toward the obvious pregnancy. "Is it your first?"

"No . . . I been all right, I guess," Melinda Rose replied, swatting at a fly and settling herself heavily onto a bench. "No, not my first. Been in the 'family way' since forever,"

Melinda Rose added, laughing. "Seems all I wanna do with this young'n is eat and sleep." She spoke again, giving a short sad laugh, "No, this ain't my first. Got me three young'ns, all buried up at Falcon Hill. Lost the first two two days after birthing. Twins, they was, little boys. That was three years ago. Then almost a year ago today lost my third, a girl, to the fever. My husband says he don't want no more if'n this one don't make it, but what ya' gonna do? Seems every time I turn around, I'm with child." She sat quiet, at last, again wiping her brow and shifting to get more comfortable on the bench. Sarah saw how swollen even her feet were, and worried if the bench would hold her.

"Want something cold to drink?" Sarah asked.

"Sure. Why, that'd be nice," she replied, and with that Sarah went to get tea for the two of them.

As she walked across the yard, she noticed Nancy and Silas standing close together out by the barn and, once again, marveled at how different Silas was from what she had expected. "I gotta quit listening to folks," Sarah said to herself. "He sure doesn't look like the drunken, smelly, old trapper I heard about." She smiled at them and waved, shaking her head.

As she neared the cabin, she saw old Doc Pearson and his missus arrive and heard the sound of fiddles and a squeeze box warming up in the barn. Doc Pearson was a short, rotund man with tired-looking eyes and thinning white hair that lay back from his forehead in smooth, silvery strands. He was about five-foot-six, but still taller than Mrs. Pearson, who was a petite four-and-a-half-feet in height and had fluffy white hair and a sweet smile. They were both in their sixties, Sarah had heard, and had come to the area some years earlier as newlyweds. Everyone liked them. Mrs. Pearson often held ice cream socials or quilting bees at her home in town. They had never had children, but their home was filled with happiness that emanated from the love they shared.

Doc Pearson yelled a greeting to a family Sarah knew only by sight, but wasn't acquainted with. She watched the children chase each other around the apple trees by their folks and thought again of Melinda Rose and the babies she had lost. Sarah could not imagine losing a child. She felt she would never quit grieving such a loss.

"Lord, I hope my children are all healthy," she said quietly, not really realizing she had spoken aloud.

"And what children would that be?" a voice asked from behind her.

"Oh!" she exclaimed, giving a start. "Are you spying on me, Tommy Dawson?" she retorted.

"No, ma'am," he answered, smiling a little sheepishly. "I just happened to be coming around the corner of the cabin as you were talking, Sarah. I couldn't help but hear you. You didn't tell me . . . you had any children," he stammered, his face getting redder by the minute.

Sarah felt her face go as red as his, even though she knew he was only teasing. "Lots of things I don't tell you, Tommy Dawson, lots of things," she replied, sashaying into the cabin to get the glasses of tea for herself and Melinda Rose.

Tommy stood beside her, still red in the face, a self-conscious grin spreading from ear to ear. "Maybe I better be proposin' again if you got . . ."

"Tommy!" Sarah exclaimed, stopping him from saying more, and hoping no one had heard. She turned and walked outside, stopping only long enough to glance back, giving him a quick smile, and a shake of her head. Then, balancing the two cups, she walked over to Melinda Rose.

Melinda Rose sat on the bench where Sarah had left her, fanning herself with her hand and tapping her foot to the sound of the music that began to fill the air. "Nice, ain't it?" Melinda Rose said. "You and Tommy getting ready to wed soon," she continued, "now that he's all settled in his pa's store and all?"

"No!" Sarah replied, a little more sharply than she intended. Melinda Rose glanced at her questioningly. "We're just good friends, Tommy and me," Sarah stated. "We've been friends ever since school, you know. Just *friends*," she emphasized.

"Oh," Melinda Rose replied, again shifting her ponderous body on the bench as it groaned under her weight. "Always thought you and Tommy were sweethearts," Melinda Rose continued, "even back when Daniel and I were courtin'. We'd see Tommy go by in his pa's buggy heading out your way. Everybody said he was sweet on you. They still do," she added.

Sarah wished she could put an end to the conversation and escape to the barn without being rude, but it seemed impossible.

"Melinda Rose, how's Daniel doing? I see he didn't come with you today," she asked, trying to change the subject.

"Oh! He's doing okay. Don't see him much now that he's working over in the valley at the Crowley Ranch. He only gets home 'bout twice a month. Just enough to check how things are going and," she giggled, "get me this way again." She pointed to her stomach, continuing to laugh.

Sarah felt her face redden once again and wished more than ever to get away. Melinda Rose meant well, she thought. Probably she was terribly lonely from being by herself all the time, but there were some things you just didn't talk about. Sarah felt awfully uncomfortable. Talking about Tommy and her as if they were a couple was one thing, but being so outspoken about private things was another. And to a single woman, no less, Sarah thought, as if I was wed, too. She saw her father come out of the barn and look her way. "Excuse me, Melinda Rose. I see my father looking for me," she hurried on. "Best of luck with the baby," and before Melinda Rose could reply, she sat her empty cup on the bench and started across the yard.

She knew, once again, why she never went to sewing bees and church socials and such. Why she never spent much time with other women her age. A bunch of ninnies, she thought to herself. A bunch of gossiping old ninnies! With that, she took her father's arm, and they walked over to a bench by the barn. Sarah knew that it wasn't really the continuous chatter that had irritated her so. It wasn't even the personal stuff that upset her. It was the fact that Melinda Rose, like Tommy and her father, thought that Tommy Dawson was her beau. Tommy Dawson! As if she'd settle for that old store and sorry old life as Tommy's wife. She fairly bristled with anger. Why couldn't folks understand that there was *more* to life than birthing one babe after another and watching them die, more to life than . . . no dreams. Or hopes. She snorted in disgust.

"You okay, Sarah?" her father asked, glancing at her questioningly. "Something troubling you, gal?"

She smiled to assure him, answering, "Oh! I'm okay, Pa, just tired of listening to Melinda Rose go on and on."

"I feel sorry for her," Samuel replied. "Isn't she your age, Sarah? And her having no friends out her way to keep her company." He went on, "Daniel works away you know."

"I know," Sarah answered, feeling a little guilty now at her hasty abandonment of Melinda Rose.

"I often wonder how she manages," Samuel stated, "alone so much and being in the 'family way' so often. Lost the other babies, I hear," he added, "and doesn't look too healthy with this one."

"I know," Sarah said, feeling ashamed for the anger she had felt.

A group of folks arrived just then, some in wagons, some on horseback. The three on horseback drew attention by their loud shouts back and forth and the dust they stirred as they raced into the yard. Sarah recognized the three of them. There was Kevin Landford, a tall, lanky, sandy haired fellow, about twenty-seven, originally from back East, who had been on his own since quite young, it was said, and gained a reputation as being both trustworthy and responsible. He was now foreman at one of the cattle ranches over in the valley, she had heard. She watched him dismount and brush the dust off his red-checkered shirt and black pants with his hat, and then brush back his hair with one hand, and once more put on his hat. She noticed he seemed to take his cue from the other men as to what to do next, which was to tie his horse to the fence, and then go out by the barn where the men seemed to be gathering to talk. Two of her ninny girlfriends had spoken to her of their interest in the young man, but he seemed to shun their attention whenever he saw them in town. She didn't know if he was too busy or just awfully shy, but she thought he had a pleasant smile and liked his mannerly ways.

The fellows with him were laughing loudly. There was Jay Bullard, a handsome fellow with curly black hair and gray eyes, who seemed to do a double take whenever he happened to spot Nancy walking across the yard. He smiled and bowed gallantly, and even from where she stood Sarah saw Nancy's face redden. Sarah smiled and for just a moment hoped he'd look her way. She had met him the summer before when they literally ran into each other as she came hurrying out of Tommy's store, and her packages had been knocked from her arms before she knew it. She caught herself from falling and remembered again how he had quickly but gently grabbed her arm to help her maintain her balance, at the same time apologizing and asking if she was all right. Her heart had skipped a beat when he looked at her with those light-grey eyes that seemed so intense. She realized he was much younger than she. Before she had command of her thoughts, Tommy had rushed from inside the store, scolding him rudely for his carelessness, and had scurried about her feet picking up her packages. She watched him now as he walked away toward the barn, noticing once more his ebony black curls.

He was much thinner than she remembered, and she hoped he would eat heartily today.

It was then, she noticed that the third rider had also dismounted and was leaning back against the fence, one foot resting on the bottom rung, looking directly at her. Sarah felt her face flush, and she tried to look away, but found she could not! Moses Gentry, Hastings' sheriff, his dark hair hanging to his shoulders, stood watching her and smiling. Oh, Lord, that man had a way about him; that, she had to admit! She watched him run his hand through his hair and found herself unable to look away, it seemed, as if she were spellbound.

Suddenly, she realized her father had spoken. "What?" she asked, feeling her face grow hot.

"I'm going over to speak to Ros . . . ah, Mrs. Mitchell, Sarah. Will you excuse me?"

"Yes, of course," she replied, relieved that he hadn't seemed to notice her discomfort. She looked back toward Moses Gentry and saw him smile that slow, tauntingly devilish smile of his, then give a slow bow of his head at her. "Oh, the nerve of the man!" Sarah bristled. How dare he embarrass her like this! How dare he treat her like she was one of the many saloon girls that fell all over themselves to get his attention, or so she had heard. She whirled around, intent on breaking the foolish "schoolgirl" trance she seemed to find herself in, and was exasperated to find Tommy heading her way across the yard. She turned back, feeling more flustered than ever, and glanced frantically around for a route of escape. At that moment, the sheriff began to walk toward her, his eyes seeming to hypnotize her as he came closer and closer. His smile both angered her and—though she would never admit it—tantalized her senses, stirring odd feelings within her.

"Miss Justus," he drawled as she focused on his worn brown boots, her face burning as if on fire.

"S-sheriff Gentry," she managed to stammer, feeling the pulse in her temples pounding.

"Would you care to walk a bit?" he asked, offering his arm.

"No," she replied, daring to look up at his dark eyes that seemed to envelop her. She turned away, saw Tommy still approaching, and turned back, feeling hopelessly entrapped. "Yes!" she exclaimed, surprising herself and feeling even more unsettled. She didn't want to walk with this man, this rogue with the devilish smile and dancing eyes. He made her feel all fluttery and weak-kneed. But she took his arm and tried desperately to gain control of her reeling senses. "A fate worse than death." Those words came to mind as she started walking, her hand lightly resting in the bend of his arm. She could feel his body heat right through his shirt. Or did she imagine it? "A fate worse than death." The words again raced through her mind. She cleared her throat, trying to regain her control, her mind still racing. A fate worse than death wasn't walking with Moses Gentry. A fate worse than death was being *stuck* with Tommy Dawson! *That's* why she accepted the sheriff's offer to walk! That made sense! She would be bored to death in Tommy's company. She felt calmer now that she understood herself better.

"Would you care to get something to drink?" Moses asked, smiling, his eyes twinkling as he looked at her.

"No," she answered tersely, noticing the texture of the buckskin vest he wore and the design of the fringe that hung from it across his chest. Dark, curly chest hair escaped where his shirt opened at the base of his neck. She cleared her throat, dropping her eyes to his boots, the scuffed brown toes sticking out beyond his tight buckskin pants. She looked up quickly, feeling her face grow hot. What an effect this man had on her! No wonder she heard the saloon girls flocked around when he was near. She knew, without looking, that he was smiling at her discomfort, and enjoying himself immensely at her expense. She glanced quickly around for her father. Not finding him, she looked for Tommy, who had apparently given up his pursuit of her and drifted off to bore someone else.

"I must get back," she said, not daring to look up at Moses.

"Back to what, darlin'?" he questioned. She blushed hotly at his term of endearment and dropped her arm to her side. "There now," Moses drawled, picking up her hand in his and placing it, once more, in the crook of his arm. "We haven't got a chance to visit yet, pretty lady. You don't really want to run off already. Do you, Miss Sarah?" His voice was deep and seemed to stroke her very being.

She stood there, feeling—if he said any more—her bones would indeed melt and she would fall. She took a deep breath, and another, trying to still her racing heart and gather her thoughts.

"I must get back to my father," she stated and, once more, removed her hand from his arm.

"It was my pleasure," he said, in that voice that again began to stir her senses.

"Your pleasure?" she questioned, not understanding.

"My pleasure, darlin', to rescue you from dull old Tommy," he drawled, and she looked up into those eyes that once more smiled in pure devilment and delight.

"Why you . . . ! You're wrong!" she stammered, embarrassed that he had read her thoughts so clearly and reveled in delight at her discomfort. She turned and hurried away, hearing him laugh a deep, soft laugh, as feelings unlike any she had ever known before flooded her very being. Well! she thought, as she walked briskly toward the house. How dare he make fun of her! How dare he hypnotize her with those devilish, dark eyes and that rogue's smile! How dare he! She was beside herself with frustration.

"How dare he!" she said aloud. Though she couldn't help looking back, just once, to see if . . . yes . . . he was still watching her and was still smiling. She turned, continuing her hasty retreat.

She was so intent on getting away from him and all the unbidden feelings he had stirred in her, feelings she was certain no decent girl would feel, that she promptly collided with Amanda Culpepper. Miz Culpepper was the tiny elderly woman who worked for Tommy at the general store. She was a widow who had come to Hastings, a few years back, in an old black buggy with few possessions. She had bought a small one-story house next door to Rosie Mitchell's house and had become not only a dear friend of Rosie's, but an indispensable assistant at the general store. She was a gentle, soft-spoken woman, barely five feet tall, but could be formidable when riled. Everyone in town had heard tell of the day some rowdy cowboys had come into the store and began "cutting up." Miz Culpepper had quickly silenced them, spoken her mind in no uncertain terms, and ushered them out of the store. Tommy had stood there, dumbfounded, his mouth wide open in disbelief, doing nothing. Miz Culpepper returned to what she was doing, stacking yard goods, and except for very pink cheeks, looked none the worse for wear.

Sarah knew from talks with Rosie Mitchell that Miz Culpepper's family was originally from Germany. Her most treasured possessions were two large pictures: one of a handsome young man, the other of a beautiful, dark-haired young woman—probably her parents—and a large Bible, written in German. She was a kind woman who lived modestly. Her main activities: going to church, which she never missed unless ill, and working at Dawson's General Store. She was polite and quiet spoken, a very private person. She never spoke of her life before coming to Hastings, and had no other pictures in her house, not even one of her deceased husband.

Sarah wondered if there had ever been a Mr. Culpepper and, if so, what he had been like. But of course she would never be so rude as to ask.

"Oh! Miz Culpepper, I'm sorry. Are you all right?" Sarah exclaimed, as she nearly knocked the small woman off her feet.

Amanda Culpepper caught her breath and balance, placing a hand upon her breast. "My goodness, child. Where are you off to? Are *you* all right?"

"Yes," Sarah answered, blushing. "I'm . . . I'm just going to find my father," she stated, unable to think quickly of any other excuse.

"Well, you look flushed, Sarah. You're face is red as fire," Miz Culpepper stated, looking over Sarah's shoulder, and beyond, to the man standing watching them, a sly smile on his handsome face. "I'd say you were running away from trouble, Sarah, by the looks of it." Sarah saw where she was looking and knew it was obvious her hasty retreat was from Sheriff Gentry. She felt her face grow hot with embarrassment. "The sheriff giving you trouble, child?" Miz Culpepper asked, smiling a warm smile and taking Sarah's arm. "Let's go over to that bench in the shade, Sarah, and talk."

"Miz Culpepper, I really do have to find my father," Sarah stated, more composed now, since they had put more distance between themselves and Moses Gentry. "No, the sheriff's not bothering me," Sarah added. "I mean . . . he's not giving me any trouble," she stammered, looking down at the ground as she felt her face flush again, and knew her cheeks were blazing.

Miz Culpepper patted Sarah's hand, smiling, glancing in the direction of Moses Gentry. "That man don't have to give trouble. He *is* trouble," Miz Culpepper stated. Sarah looked at the older woman's kind face and smiled. Then, she gave Miz Culpepper a quick hug.

"Yes, he certainly is," Sarah agreed, then she bade her

farewell, excused herself, and left the elderly woman to her own thoughts.

Miz Culpepper took a small white cotton handkerchief, lavished with lace, from her purse. Fanning herself, she watched the tall, handsome sheriff turn and walk toward some other men who were standing out by the barn.

"Oh! You surely are trouble," she whispered aloud. "I used to know one just like you," she continued, "trouble, just plain trouble." She felt momentarily lost in her reveries. How I loved every moment, she thought, as a tear traced its way out from under her lashes, trickling down her cheek. "And where are you now, my love?" she questioned, sadly.

Sarah entered the house that was rapidly filling with guests and the dishes of food they had brought. The aromas rose: of pies and cakes, of stews and biscuits, of roasts with potatoes and carrots, and pans of cornbread, hot from the oven. Coffee brewed on the stove and voices filled the room with laughter and excited talk. Sarah wondered if Melinda Rose was all right and, after pouring two glasses of tea, went outside to find her. She headed for the bench she had left her at earlier, only to stop when she realized Melinda Rose was sitting there, talking and laughing happily, with Tommy. Sarah heard him laugh heartily at something Melinda Rose had said and felt a bit surprised at how easily they conversed. At the same time, she felt enormous relief that Tommy had a woman's companionship and was no longer following her around like a lost pup. She turned quickly, leaving them to their privacy. A smile began to form the more she thought of them.

Too bad Melinda Rose is married, she thought, and has a baby due. She giggled at her thoughts and went over to another bench near the far side of the cabin. It was in the shade and as she drank one glass of the tea, she began to once more watch the latest arrivals. It looked like most of the folk's roundabouts had come to the wedding and barn dance. She knew they came for Nancy's sake, not her pa's.

Of course, some came just to get away from chores and problems, or loneliness, enjoying the chance to visit and catch up on the latest news. Seemed it took a wedding or funeral to get most folks together, otherwise they tended to keep to themselves. Most didn't see much of each other, except when they went to town to get supplies and such.

Sarah stretched her feet out in front of her and stepped out of her shoes. They were her mother's shoes and didn't fit her like they should. But, she couldn't see buying a new pair when they were still in good shape. They were black slippers with tiny bows on the toes, and very attractive. Jenny hadn't worn them much, even though they had come all the way from Virginia with her when she married Samuel. Sarah stretched her toes, wiggling them and enjoying the freedom of being barefoot. She had gone barefoot so much this summer that she was surprised she could get any shoes on, let alone these pretty ones of her mother's. She hoped she would be able to dance in them without tripping or falling.

A carriage pulled through the gate with a large lathered horse, snorting and jerking in its harness. A small man in a top hat and waistcoat yanked the reins, causing the bit to tear at the poor animal's mouth, as he succeeded in stopping. Sarah slipped the shoes back on and watched closely—curiosity getting the best of her—as two women in brightly colored frocks of shiny material, and much adornment, stepped down from the carriage. Sarah watched as the shortest woman opened a parasol to shade herself from the sun. She laughed at something the other said, and then proceeded to walk toward the house. Sarah knew the short one was Ruby Deegs, a saloon girl. She had seen her more than once in Hastings: once at Dawson's General Store, and once at Doc Pearson's when she had to pick up some medicine for her father. She was fascinated at the dress Ruby wore. It was a soft blue with ruffles cascading down the back, from waist to ankle, and the parasol matched perfectly. The front had a swath of lace that started at her shoulders and fell in a deep "v," exposing more bosom than Sarah had ever seen exposed before. She touched the high neck of her own dress, realizing for the first time, how plain it looked and how—well, the only word she could think of was "decent." Decent! Imagine! Ruby could wear *that* and walk like *that*, and practically every man was watching her. And here *she* sat . . . looking . . . *decent*!

Sarah sniffled and watched the other woman with Ruby. She was a beautiful woman, the most beautiful woman Sarah had ever seen! She was tall and slim, and her skin was pale as ivory, her hair a rich ebony that surrounded her face in a mass of ringlets and curled down the back in a large, elegant mass. Sarah couldn't help but stare at this beautiful creature. She looked like one of the heroines in days of old from the books Sarah had read. She watched the tall woman with increasing interest. She noticed that the woman held herself very straight and spoke in a hushed tone, causing even those closest to her to lean forward to hear each word. She had on elegant-looking, lacey white gloves that seemed almost childlike in their daintiness. Her dress was a lovely shade of pink that complemented both her skin tone and her hair. It was form fitting from top to bottom, and Sarah wondered how she would ever sit down in it. Unlike Ruby's dress, the pink dress had a high collar of lace that fit closely at the neck. More lace covered her chest in a risqué fashion down to where the other fabric—Sarah thought it was satin—met, barely concealing her breasts.

Sarah watched the woman slowly head toward the cabin. She noticed how the other women watched, too, though they kept their distance and seemed more than a little upset by the presence of these two women. Probably jealous, Sarah thought, as she saw the homespun clothes the town's womenfolk wore, and the satin and lace that the two saloon ladies wore. How small! Sarah thought. These women are being positively mean! Sticking their noses in the air and giving Ruby and the other woman nasty looks. I'll be nice. I'll say hello and introduce myself, make them feel welcome. Sarah stood up, straightening her dress, smiling at her own wisdom.

As Ruby and her friend got to the cabin, Sarah stepped up and reached out her hand. Her mother had told her there were good and bad in all people, and God was pleased when you showed Christian kindness to one less fortunate than yourself. Sarah smiled and began to speak. "Hello, Ruby. I'm Sarah Justus. How nice to see you."

Ruby stopped, looked questioningly at Sarah, and then extended her hand, taking Sarah's. "I remember you from the general store," Ruby said, smiling, and then turned slightly toward the other woman, who was even more beautiful now that Sarah could see her liquid brown eyes and long feathery lashes. "I'd like you to meet my friend, Jasmine LaRue from New Orleans, Louisiana. Jasmine, this is Miss . . ."

Before Ruby could even finish her introductions, a deep, male voice exclaimed, "Jasmine! Well, I'll be. If you aren't a sight for sore eyes, honey!" Sarah knew the voice even before she saw the gun on his hip and the badge on his vest. She watched helplessly as Moses Gentry grinned his way right into the arms of Miss Jasmine and took in every inch of her with those dark, flashing eyes of his. Sarah suddenly felt weak in the knees and was afraid she was going to faint. She coughed a couple of times and excused herself to get a drink of water. She wasn't sure if anyone had heard her, or even cared. She simply vanished back the way she had come, feeling her face burn with embarrassment.

Why did he have such an effect on her? Why did she make a fool of herself every time he came near? How many times had she caught him looking at her when she was in town shopping, and she acted just as foolish? Why, she had even forgotten her packages the last time. He had walked into the store, said hello to Tommy, looked at her with those devil's eyes of his, and she had left without her packages like a foolish schoolgirl! She couldn't explain her actions. They made no sense at all. Why, her hands were even trembling, she noticed, as she walked back toward the cabin, all the while willing herself to calm down, grow up, and act her age.

She thought of the curly black hair sticking out of the open neck of his shirt, in spite of herself, and felt a warmth invade her inner recesses. "Oh, Lord!" Sarah whispered, her voice hoarse and raspy. "Oh, Lord!"

She went out the back door of the Pearlys' cabin and walked across the yard to where two friends of hers were standing, talking.

"Hi, Sarah," they both said upon seeing her. "Come join us."

Lilly and Lydia Benedict had been her friends ever since she had moved to Hastings at ten years of age. Lilly was the oldest of the two, a slim, reserved, young woman of twenty-six with soft brown curls and large brown eyes that reminded Sarah of fawn's eyes. Lilly was slightly shorter than Sarah, with pale skin and quiet ways. She was still single, though many fellows had taken an interest in her over the years. Her attention always focused on her family, however. That's where her heart lay. Her mother was sickly ever since the birth of Lydia, and Lilly had grown up happily accepting the ever-increasing responsibility of her home, farm, and care of her younger sibling. She had no time for flirtations and courting, and never seemed to miss such things. Or, if she did, she never spoke of it. She took over many of the household chores at the age of seven, when her mother took to her bed. Sarah respected her for her devotion, though she often questioned in her mind how Lilly could tolerate no hope of a life of her own.

Lydia, on the other hand, was shorter still, a mere twenty, as pretty as a picture and as plump as Lilly was slim. Her hair was a mass of dark-brown ringlets that bounced when she walked, and she laughed and giggled and seemed unable to sit still. Though Lilly and Lydia were sisters, they certainly didn't act alike. They seemed like exact opposites, in fact, Sarah often thought. Lilly was so meek and quiet, and Lydia so talkative and always bubbling over with enthusiasm.

"Sarah, how have you been?" Lydia asked, hugging Sarah quickly, her eyes bright and full of merriment.

"I'm fine," Sarah answered, hugging her back, happy to see that both of them had been able to come to the wedding. "How's your mother?" Sarah asked more out of politeness than caring.

"Oh, just fine," Lydia answered, glancing around the yard in childlike abandon. "Did Reverend Cole get here yet?" she asked.

"Cole?" Sarah asked, looking from Lilly to Lydia questioningly.

"The new preacher from over in the valley at the little church on Old Mill Road," Lydia hurried on, bursting with information. "He's sooo nice," she continued, causing all three of them to laugh in unison. Lydia spoke again, her voice more quiet but teasing. "Lilly thinks he's cute, too, but she won't admit it."

"Lydia! I do not!" Lilly gasped. "You must not speak of such embarrassing things," she admonished, her voice raised slightly. "He is a preacher, after all," she added, looking helplessly at Sarah and shaking her head in embarrassment.

"Well, he's *not* Sheriff Gentry," Lydia chortled, "that's for certain! But he is cute."

Sarah felt her face redden. My goodness, she thought. Had that Gentry devil even drawn the attention of this mere child? What was wrong with the women of Hastings? Were they all addlebrained when it came to Moses Gentry?

CHAPTER FIVE

A buckboard full of adults and children entered the Pearlys' yard, stirring up dust as it arrived. Sarah, Lilly, and Lydia looked on in curiosity as women were helped down from it and some young boys jumped from it.

"Oh! It's Preacher Cole," Lydia exclaimed excitedly, heading over to greet them. Sarah squinted into the sun for a better look. She couldn't make out the face under the wide brimmed black hat, but noticed he handed baskets to the women and then helped a small boy from the buckboard.

She recognized the family as the O'Learys. She couldn't remember the parents' names, but knew there were five O'Leary boys, all redheaded, and one older girl, Mary. Sarah watched a sweet, soft-spoken girl of about thirteen or fourteen enjoying the laughter and merriment of the group. She remembered four of the boys' names—Michael, James, William, and Patrick—but couldn't remember the other boy's name. They were Irish, like Rosie Mitchell, and Rosie had spoken fondly of them. Sarah knew they were barely eking a living from their small piece of land. The children wore threadbare clothing and were barefoot even after the weather became brisk in the late fall. They were a happy bunch—all of them good humored—and their home was filled with their youthful exuberance and a deep, familial closeness. The love they felt for each other was highly evident.

Sarah remembered tasting some pies that Mrs. O'Leary had baked for the last gathering of neighbors a while back, and she still relished their moist, rich flavor and light, flaky crust. My, she thought, that woman could certainly bake. Her pies put mine to shame any day.

The preacher had removed his hat and was shaking hands all around while being introduced by Rosie Mitchell. It had been many years since Hastings had been blessed with a preacher who actually lived in the area. Before that there was Rosie's husband, but after he died, there had been only circuit-riding preachers, and folks missed the sense of belonging that a permanent preacher provided. Of course, it was quite a distance from Sarah's house to the church in the valley and, since she didn't attend church regularly anyways, she doubted if she would see much of Preacher Cole.

Sarah had developed a different spiritual awareness from hanging around Old John when she was younger. She felt content with her beliefs and the Christian teaching she credited to her mother. Between her mother's teachings of the Bible and Christian ways, and Old John's reverence of nature, Sarah felt secure in her relationship with God and tried always to live by the faith instilled deep within her heart. She didn't believe you had to attend a church to be a Christian. *She* was proof of that!

She watched Ophelia Denton walk across the yard toward the cabin. Miss Denton was the teacher at the school east of town. Sarah had often visited with her at different gatherings and liked her very much. She was two years older than Sarah, well-mannered, and friendly, though exceedingly prim and proper, and especially well-read. Sarah was delighted to know another woman who treasured books as she did. Often, they found themselves in lengthy discussions of the newest books that Ophelia had access to, or in books of old which Sarah's mother had left her. Occasionally, as winter set in, they would loan each other these treasured volumes and not return them until the weather cleared in early spring.

Sarah knew Ophelia Denton had never married. It had long ago been gossiped that she had once been engaged, only to discover—to her horror—that he was already married. She had left in shame and came west to Hastings, feeling betrayed and devastated, and looked for work as a seamstress. There was none to be found, but it so happened the school lacked a teacher, and being highly intelligent and liking children, she applied and easily acquired the position.

Sarah had heard rumors that old Mr. Wills—the barber— had asked for her hand in marriage, but she had firmly and politely refused his offer, going on as she was, alone. At thirty, she was now considered a spinster and the severity of dress and hairstyle she always wore furthered that opinion. Her sandy-colored hair was drawn back in a tight bun at the nape of her neck. She wore only a tiny locket for adornment, no bracelets or earrings to brighten her severely plain black dresses. Sarah wondered what she would look like if, just once, she let her hair hang loose and donned a dress in soft pastel colors. She felt a pang of sadness for all that this woman was missing.

"Hello, Sarah. How are you?" Ophelia asked, walking over to her. She stopped near the cabin. "I hope you are well," she added, smiling and shifting the basket she was carrying from one arm to the other.

"I'm very well. Thank you," Sarah replied and, not able to help herself, added, "I hope that's one of your delicious pies in that basket?"

"Yes," Ophelia replied, smiling warmly at the compliment. "A strawberry pie," she stated happily. "I barely found enough strawberries to fill the crust, though. Had to pick all morning."

Sarah smiled and asked the question that had been on her mind so often of late, "Have you gotten any new books?"

"Yes," replied Ophelia. "You must come to my home and see them, Sarah. A whole crate was shipped to me from a friend back east recently, and I'm sure you'll be interested in many of them."

"Wonderful!" Sarah exclaimed. "Thank you. I will come." Ophelia excused herself and entered the cabin.

Sarah looked around for Lilly who had apparently gone off to keep an eye on Lydia and happened to notice an exceedingly large man leaning against a tree near the empty buckboard. He was shabbily dressed and stood all by himself, hat in hand, looking miserably uncomfortable. She knew it had to be Jonas Hart, a farmer who lived over in the valley on Old Mill Road near the church. He was a large man—a "giant"—some folks claimed, who lived with his tiny mother in a house surrounded by flowers and fruit trees. Sarah remembered the story of how he had single-handedly lifted an overturned buggy one winter, freeing the occupants trapped beneath it and saving their lives. Many of them spoke of him as a gentle giant after that and expounded on how kind and sweet natured he was. Sadly, though, he became the brunt of many lesser men's jokes because he was horribly embarrassed in the company of ladies, and became tongue-tied if they even smiled at him. Sarah watched him shift his great bulk from one foot to the other. She felt sorry for him and wished she could make him feel less of an outsider. Perhaps he would like a cup of coffee, she thought, trying to decide how to approach him without making him more uncomfortable. She started across the yard, but stopped short when she saw a small girl trip on a root and go sprawling in the grass at his feet. She was amazed to see him move quickly to the girl's side. He moved the girl's ankle first one way, then the other, to see if it was broken, and then lifted her up in his huge arms, snuggling her safely to him and talking to her softly. The child stopped crying almost immediately and began to smile, then to giggle out loud as Jonas pulled out his hanky from his back pocket, spit on it, and carefully wiped the dirt off her shoes. Then he gently set her down on the ground and knelt down beside her. Sarah realized he was talking to the child to comfort her and get her mind off the fall. Her heart was filled with warmth for the kindness he was bestowing.

Sarah realized, too, that she was not the only one who was watching them. Lilly had stopped in the yard near them and witnessed the whole scene. She was looking at Jonas with an expression of deep admiration. Sarah watched, fascinated. The little girl stood up, kissed Jonas on the cheek, and ran off to play. Jonas stood up, dusting himself off and stuffing his hanky back in his pocket. At that moment, Lilly walked up to him and spoke. Sarah could not hear what she said, but Jonas hung his head and nodded, his face becoming a "fire red" beacon. Sarah wondered what she had said, and why, and was beside herself, trying to figure it out. She imagined one scenario after another. Hard as she tried, she couldn't imagine what Lilly would have said to Jonas. She gave up and went in the cabin to see what was going on.

Inside the cabin there was a flurry of activity. Amanda Culpepper and Ophelia Denton were twisting Nancy Pearly's hair into a bun on top of her head and sticking daisies into it. Amid much laughter and excitement, Nancy had changed from the pink dress she had on earlier, to a white one of softly draped fabric with yards of lace that encircled her throat and tiny waist, and then cascaded down the skirt with a large bow at the waist in back. Nancy was protesting that she couldn't borrow Rosie Mitchell's gown. She just couldn't. Rosie waved away her protests, telling her that every bride deserved a special dress, and if it brought Nancy and Silas as much happiness as she and Reverend Mitchell had shared, it was well worth it. Nancy positively glowed with happiness as she pirouetted around so all the women could see how perfectly it fit her.

"Thank you!" she exclaimed, her eyes dancing with delight. She hugged Rosie as tears of gratitude filled her eyes. She knew if her own mother were alive, she would have had as fine a dress to wed in, but she had died many years earlier. Rosie had understood the dreams of a young woman's heart and had insisted she wear her very own beautiful gown.

Ophelia walked up to Nancy and handed her a small box wrapped in silk ribbons. Nancy looked at her in surprise. "A little something to take with you to your new home," Ophelia said, adding, "I hope you'll always cherish it. It was mine when I was young."

Nancy, who was not used to getting gifts, tore the ribbons away and opened the box. Inside lay a small Bible and dainty light-blue hanky, edged in lace.

Nancy hugged Ophelia. "How lovely!" she exclaimed. "I'll *always* cherish your gifts."

Ophelia smiled tenderly at Nancy and said, "And now I'll put on another pot of coffee for everyone." And she walked back into the kitchen.

Sarah had never seen Nancy so happy. She was positively radiant! She wanted to do something nice too, for her, and looked around trying to decide what it could be. Suddenly, she knew! She left the cabin by way of the back door, hurriedly crossing the yard to the meadow beyond. There she gathered a fine bouquet of wildflowers: white and red cosmos, tiny blue bells, delicate Queen Anne's lace, poppies with lovely red petals and black centers, and white daisies with purple-edged greens that she no longer remembered the name of. She also picked a bunch of lavender, the lovely fragrance a delight, and feverfew, a white daisy-like flower with flat yellow centers. If nothing else, it might repel the bees the other flowers would attract. She arranged the flowers so the colors flowed together in a complementary fashion, and then returned to the cabin.

The preacher was standing in the main room by the

fireplace when she came in, and Sarah realized her timing was perfect. The wedding was soon to begin. Rosie Mitchell introduced Sarah quickly to Reverend Cole. She was surprised to see that he was a mere boy, no more than eighteen, she guessed, nineteen at the most. He had a pleasant smile, slim build, straight black hair, and gentle brown eyes that seemed wise beyond their years.

"I'm happy to meet you, Miss Justus," he said, his voice sounding even younger than he looked. "I do hope you'll come to our church Sunday."

"I'm happy to make your acquaintance," Sarah replied. Before she could say more, a guitar began to play outside and he spoke again.

"On with the wedding, ladies. Miss Nancy, are you ready?"

"Yes," came the joyful reply, and as Nancy entered the room, she saw Sarah's beautiful bouquet and was pleased. "How beautiful! Thank you, Sarah," she said, taking the bouquet, and walked outside to become the bride of the mountain man she had grown to love.

Silas Haverty smiled a wide grin when he saw his beautiful bride-to-be and thought himself the luckiest man alive. Nancy stood happily at his side, a vision of loveliness who would soon be his very own wife.

Sarah stood back by the tree near the cabin and looked at all the people who had come to celebrate on this happy occasion. The O'Leary parents stood close to each other, the father's one hand on the shoulder of his oldest son, Michael. The other children gathered around them, each face beaming with happiness. Mrs. O'Leary held her husband's other hand, Sarah noticed, and looked up at him lovingly as Nancy spoke her vows.

Rosie Mitchell stood beside Sarah's father, and Sarah noticed they seemed closer somehow than mere friends. She saw her father wink at Rosie when the ring was placed on

Nancy's finger, and Rosie took his arm, smiling as though they shared a secret all their own.

Farther away stood Ruby Deegs, Kevin Landford, and Jay Bullard. They listened politely to the ceremony, but Sarah noticed both Jay and Kevin kept glancing at Ruby's low-cut gown. She could only imagine what they were thinking!

On the same bench where she had sat earlier sat Melinda Rose, wiping sweat off her brow and face, and, beside her, Miz Culpepper. Melinda Rose wore an expression of sadness, Sarah thought, and she vowed she would try to be kinder to her before she left for home. Miz Culpepper, on the other hand, had a strange look on her face, a look of longing it seemed, and Sarah was surprised to see her wipe a tear from her cheek. She must be thinking of her husband, Sarah mused and turned away lest she be caught gawking.

Tommy Dawson stood behind Melinda Rose and Sarah thought, perhaps, he was trying to make her jealous by avoiding her. She smiled, secretly enjoying his absence, and looked around to see where Lilly and Lydia were. She was surprised to see Lilly by herself over near the tree where Jonas Hart had been standing earlier.

She was even more surprised to see Jonas standing about an arm's length from Reverend Cole. Well, whatever is he standing there for? Sarah wondered, noticing that his hands were folded so tightly in front of him that his knuckles looked white, and he kept his eyes focused on the ground. He looked tense enough to pass out. She felt sorry for him, but wondered why he didn't just return to the tree and not stand right up there in front, where no one could miss seeing his discomfort. He stood at least six feet, seven inches tall and his shirt barely stretched across his massive chest. Sarah noticed the frayed collar of his shirt, and how worn his pants and boots looked as he stood there, and she felt tremendous pity for him and shook her head solemnly.

Then she turned her thoughts back to the ceremony at

hand. Reverend Cole was speaking, "Before I pronounce Silas and Nancy husband and wife, I've taken the liberty of asking my friend here, Jonas Hart, to sing a song to commemorate their special day." There was total silence. Everyone looked surprised. Mouths hung open and everyone stared at the large man as he fidgeted and cleared his throat, his face becoming redder and redder. "It's okay," Reverend Cole whispered, reaching up to place a hand on the big man's shoulder. "You'll do fine," he added.

One of the young men, Sarah wasn't sure if it was Jay Bullard or Kevin Landford, yelled out, "Go ahead, Jonas. The ladies are all listenin'." Sarah turned, giving them a nasty look as her heart went out to Jonas. Folks were still staring at him, some were smiling, and a couple poked the person next to them and grinned, covering their mouths with a hand as others began laughing out loud. Sarah felt so deeply sorry for Jonas. She felt like smacking Reverend Cole for the humiliation he had caused the poor man.

Some friend, she thought, as she fumed with anger while trying to catch the eye of Reverend Cole to show him how horrible and cruel he had been. A sound suddenly stopped her. Jonas Hart began to sing in the most beautiful voice Sarah had ever heard. All the people stared in amazement as notes, as pure as ever could be imagined, filled the air. No one spoke, or laughed, or even breathed, it seemed, as across the Pearlys' yard and meadow beyond a voice as lovely as Heaven itself filled the air.

When he finished, everyone went wild! They yelled and clapped and some went hurrying over and shook the big man's hand. A couple pounded him on the back and then pumped his arm up and down. The God-given talent of this big, ungainly giant touched everyone. Thanks to Reverend Cole, Jonas Hart would never again be the brunt of anyone's jokes. From this day on, he would be applauded and looked up to—and rightly so!

Reverend Cole clapped his hands and spoke loudly to get everyone's attention. "Folks! Folks! Excuse me! Excuse me! You can talk to Jonas later," he laughed, "but let's not forget we're having a wedding here!" Then, as everyone settled down, he continued, "I pronounce you man and wife, and Silas, you can *finally* kiss your bride!" And as he did, everyone cheered.

Sarah felt elated with the turn of events. She hurried over to congratulate Jonas, just in time to see Moses Gentry and Miss Jasmine LaRue shaking his hand and talking to him. She stopped in her tracks, not wanting to become the target of that unscrupulous devil again, but it was too late. Moses had seen her coming.

"Well, Jonas, have you met Miss Sarah?" he drawled, looking at her mischievously.

"N-no," stammered Jonas, looking down at his feet.

"Miss Sarah, did you enjoy his song?" Moses questioned, winking at her and causing her to feel her cheeks grow warm.

"Yes!" she snapped, stepping around Moses to speak directly to Jonas. "You have a beautiful voice, Jonas . . . ah . . . Mr. Hart. I'm *so amazed*. Oh!" she corrected herself, afraid he had misunderstood. "I mean, I'm *not* amazed you have a beautiful voice, I . . . Oh, dear!" she exclaimed, thoroughly upset and exasperated. "I mean, I'm . . . I . . ." she stammered and felt her cheeks burning. She looked down at the ground, afraid she would burst into tears if she said more. Regaining her composure as best she could, she looked up at Jonas and tried once more. "I enjoyed your . . . your singing, Mr. Hart. You have an *amazingly* beautiful voice." To add to her discomfort, Jonas Hart did not reply, but only stood there smiling slightly in her direction. Sarah quickly turned away, but not before glaring at Moses. Then, she lifted her chin and fairly stomped over to the cabin.

"The nerve of that devil, the *very nerve!*" she fumed. She flounced over to the bench at the side of the cabin and plopped down on it, thoroughly beside herself. "Why does he always get to me? Why can't he just leave me alone? Wasn't it enough to have ole Miss LaDue, or LaRue, or whatever her name is, falling all over him? Oh! Such an intolerable man! A beast! That's what he is, a *beast*!" And with that, she straightened her dress and smoothed some unruly wisps of hair in place.

When she felt sufficiently calm, she went into the cabin, where plates were being filled with the delicious foods all the ladies had prepared. Only once, as she stabbed a slice of juicy, succulent bear meat that Silas had provided for the occasion, did she think again, "The beast!"

CHAPTER SIX

After they had eaten their fill, folks headed out to the barn to listen to the music. Sarah helped Ophelia and Amanda clear the dishes and wash the table. She dallied along, dreading the possibility of running into the sheriff again. Seems she couldn't rid herself of thoughts of him. Should have just put up with Tommy, she thought. At least he wouldn't have embarrassed me.

"Sarah, did you hear me? I asked if you want to walk over to the barn with me now. I'm ready to join the festivities. How about you?" Ophelia asked. Sarah smiled, "All right, let's go. Are you coming, Miz Culpepper?"

"No, dear. I think I shall sit here awhile. You young folks go ahead. I'll come along directly."

The two women were only inside the barn a few minutes when Samuel Justus, Sarah's father, entered with Rosie Mitchell on his arm. They smiled at Sarah and Ophelia and walked across the floor to where there were still some empty chairs off to one side.

Jay Bullard had joined some fellows Sarah didn't recognize and was mouthing a harmonica as they tuned-up various instruments and began to play. Almost immediately, Tommy Dawson approached Sarah and asked her to dance, a wide grin upon his face. She shook her head as she took his arm, and they joined the dancing couples. Two dances later, Sarah happened to glance toward the door and was delighted to see Old John standing there in his "Sunday go to meeting" clothes: his less-worn buckskins. His eyes seemed to sparkle with merriment as he spotted her, and she waved and smiled happily in return.

"Sometimes I think you like Old John better than you like me," Tommy said, as he whirled her around. "I think I better keep an eye on him or he'll steal you away," he added, laughing. "You always did favor his type," he continued, "a rugged woodsman and all."

Sarah laughed at Tommy's words. He would be shocked if he knew just how true his words were, she thought, and in her mind she imagined a tall, dark-skinned man with long black hair standing at the door in conversation with Old John, but looking at her. Sarah couldn't help smiling at her thoughts. When the music stopped, she headed across the floor to say hello to John.

"'Lo, Sarie," John greeted her. "You look pretty as a rose among daisies."

"Why, thank you, kind sir," she replied, playfully curtsying in his direction. "You look pretty dapper yourself," she added. He fidgeted a bit, and she couldn't help noticing how white his hair had grown in the years since she had first met him. She stepped close and went up on her tiptoes to kiss his leathery old cheek. He smiled and looked at the floor, clearing his throat a couple of times. Sarah cared so much for John and knew how uncomfortable her kiss on the cheek made him.

She giggled and he looked at her, his eyes full of mischief, as he teased, "You best get back to your beau, girlie. Tommy'll be beatin' my hide if you don't."

She snorted and teased right back. "You just want to go check out all the old widow women," she whispered quietly so no one listening would be offended.

"'Deed, I do!" replied Old John, and at that he winked at her and ambled outside. She watched him go and was filled with pleasant feelings that always came when she thought of him and the easy camaraderie they shared. They were the best of friends, always had been, and she treasured his friendship more than any other.

As she turned back to the dance floor, Kevin Landford approached and asked her to dance. She accepted, and they joined the others. Kevin seemed slightly off balance, and she realized from his breath that he had had quite a bit to drink. He was not much of a talker, but he really could dance! He whirled her around like she was a rag doll, and she hoped they wouldn't collide with the other folks who were dancing. As she spun around, she saw that Jay Bullard was dancing with Ruby Deegs, and Mr. and Mrs. O'Leary were also dancing, as were three or four other couples she didn't recognize. Everyone seemed to be having a swell time.

When the music slowed, Kevin excused himself, thanked her, and headed over to where Ruby and Jay now sat. Sarah shook her head, thinking it was just like a man to fall all over himself in the company of an immodestly dressed, pretty woman. Sarah moved to the edge of the dance floor and stood there watching the dancers. Ophelia Denton waltzed by in the arms of the widowed banker, Johnathon Clark. He was an impressive dancer, Sarah noted, and she wondered where he had learned. She thought Ophelia and Mr. Clark made a very handsome couple. He was on the stocky side, not really heavy, but not tall and thin as most men she knew. His hair was black, every strand combed neatly back in place, and his eyes were a warm, deep brown. He smiled often, a pleasant smile, Sarah thought, that gave him a cheerful appearance. He wore a dark blue, narrow-striped suit, with a vest that matched, and a tie that corresponded in color. Ophelia smiled often at whatever he was saying, and Sarah—always a dreamer—wondered if romance was abloom.

The song finished and most of the dancers returned to the sidelines, as a fast-tempoed tune began. Tommy appeared and asked Sarah to dance. She nodded and away they went. Rosie Mitchell whirled by in her father's arms, feet flying, leaving happy laughter in their wake. Sarah was delighted to see her father so obviously enjoying himself. She couldn't remember when she had last seen him dance—or laugh. It made her feel good just to see them. Rosie waved her fingers at Sarah, her plump cheeks bright red from exertion, and her lovely red hair bouncing as she whirled past.

She then noticed, to her surprise, Reverend Cole dancing with Lydia Benedict. They made a cute couple, both young and full of energy, the reverend much more reserved, however, than his partner. Sarah smiled at them and they smiled back, looking for all the world like brother and sister. Sarah wondered what chance the overly exuberant Lydia had with the soft-spoken preacher, and could not imagine such an odd alliance.

Oh, well, she thought. Better a preacher than a rogue like Moses Gentry. To her dismay, she had no sooner thought this than Moses cut in for a slow waltz that had just begun. Sarah flushed with embarrassment as he took her hand in one of his and his other encircled her back. She nearly stumbled in response.

"Howdy, pretty lady," he whispered near her ear, smoothly maneuvering her around the floor without bumping into the many other dancers. She looked straight ahead, not daring to look up into his face. She knew without looking that he was grinning. Looking straight ahead, however, was almost impossible when she realized her face was just inches from the opened top button on his shirt, where those curly black chest hairs showed so blatantly. She felt her face grow hot and stepped on his foot by mistake.

"Oh," she said, even more embarrassed.

"Don't fret, darlin', I've been stepped on before," he drawled in that honeyed tone she found so irritating. She couldn't answer. She was so beside herself, she was afraid she would swoon if she tried.

Moses saw her face redden and knew the effect he was having on her. He had always thought her a beauty since he first laid eyes on her. An innocent child, his first impression, but that was long ago. Now she was still beautiful, even more so, and—if he was any judge of things—still innocent, but most definitely not a child. He smiled now, remembering how upset she had gotten trying to congratulate Jonas on his singing.

Yep, he thought, I bother her, and he smiled at the thought. Most of the women he knew were not innocent, and he liked the feeling of power it gave him to have such an effect on one who was. He liked the way her green eyes blazed when she was upset, the way she raised her chin defiantly when she had enough of his teasing. Why hell, he mused, I just plain like her, innocent or not innocent, and he laughed aloud at this discovery. He felt her stiffen and pulled her slightly closer, though no closer than propriety permitted.

"What?" she bristled. "*Now* what have I done to make you laugh?" He noticed she had turned her chin up again, just the way he liked it, but avoided looking directly into his eyes.

"Oh, darlin', I was laughing at myself, *this time*, not you," he said, emphasizing "this time" to see how she'd react. She snorted an unladylike sound he wasn't used to hearing, and managed to distance herself a tiny bit further from him. He wasn't too pleased with this and realized to his surprise that he was strangely affected by it. In fact, he felt an overpowering urge to pull her body tightly against him and kiss her like no innocent had ever been kissed.

Later that evening, her feet sore and feeling tired from so much dancing, Sarah caught her father's glance and met him at the door, saying goodbye to all the folks nearby. She noticed Melinda Rose just coming out of the house, carrying a glass in one hand and rubbing her back with the other.

Lingering behind, Sarah asked, "Are you okay? Can I get you anything before I go?"

"Oh, are you going?" Melinda Rose asked, looking back at the barn just as Tommy emerged from it. She smiled at Sarah "knowingly."

Seeing this, Sarah retorted, "You're *wrong*, Melinda Rose. We're just friends. *That's all!*" Feeling angry once more, Sarah said a hasty goodbye and turned quickly, walking to where her father stood beside the wagon. Some people just didn't listen, she thought angrily, no matter what a person said. Her father climbed up into the wagon, looking over Sarah's shoulder as she reached for his hand.

"Goodnight, sir. Goodnight, Sarah," Tommy said, as she took her seat beside her father.

"Goodnight," they both answered in unison, and her father turned the horse toward the road home.

"I don't know why you're so hard on that young man, Sarah," her father began. "He's a good, solid fellow. Doing good with the store," he added. "You could do a whole lot worse, girl." Sarah sighed and turned away. They rode on in silence, both enveloped in their own thoughts. Sarah knew her father would never understand her hesitancy to hitch up with Tommy. How could she explain to him, a retired cavalry officer, that her heart seemed destined for someone he would never accept? She leaned her head against her father's arm as the wagon jostled along.

"Tired?" he asked, glancing over at her.

"Sure am," she replied. She closed her eyes and, as usual, daydreamed like the heroines in the books her mother used to read to her. She saw, in her mind's eye, the tall dark-haired Indian as she had last seen him, and then, to her complete surprise, she saw, too, the grinning face of that irritating devil, Moses Gentry.

CHAPTER SEVEN

Days went by in their usual fashion after the wedding. Sarah cooked, cleaned, and tended to her usual chores with calm deliberation and purpose, while inside her head her thoughts ran wild, causing her much unrest. At last, she could fight it no more. She had to go to the cave. She had to! She had to know if he was still there. She had argued with herself. Should she? Shouldn't she? What if he was one of those bad Indians who were responsible for the settlers' deaths at Black Dog Lake? What if he was setting a trap to capture her and carry her off? What if . . . ? The list went on and on. The worst one being: what if he was gone? She couldn't stand the thought of that.

Finally, knowing her father would be gone until evening, with hopeful heart and unbridled excitement coursing through her, she left her home once more for the cave. Before long, she stood beside the lake, but on the far side hidden by thick bushes. From there she could easily see the entrance to her cave and the cliff above. She stood still, holding her breath, not daring to even breathe. She had heard a sound off to her left and felt the muscles in her shoulders and neck tighten. There! There it was again, coming closer. She froze, her eyes straining, her hand gripping her knife, knuckles white from the pressure. A bush moved, suddenly, and a raccoon—the largest she had ever seen—came toward her until it caught her scent and made a hasty retreat back into the woods. Sarah breathed a sigh of relief, dizziness nearly overwhelming her from holding her breath so long. Her vision blurred and the ground began to spin beneath her feet. She quickly sank to a squatting position, letting her head droop forward until the faintness eased. She took her time getting to her feet, getting control, and then visually began to search the cliff's edge above for sight of the Indian. She looked all around as far as she could see, trying to remember just where she had last seen him. She saw nothing. She looked around the edge of the lake, still clutching the knife tightly, intent on using it if need be. She was alone.

She very quietly walked through the brush to the side of the lake where she usually went into the water. The large, smooth rock beckoned, as she remembered how she used to rest on it in the warmth of the sun after swimming—when younger—and she blushed as she remembered her nakedness, then. She paused beside the rock, running her hand across its smooth gray surface, remembering.

She saw a fish jump far out near the center of the lake, ever-widening ripples spreading in its wake, and wished she could join it. The sun beat down on her, and she turned her face up toward it, enjoying its warm caress.

Suddenly, a feeling of being watched filled her, a feeling she couldn't shake. She turned slowly, looking intently along the cliff's edge. She had just decided that her imagination was playing tricks on her, when she saw him. He stood still, as before, and she remained where she was, while inside her heart leapt with joy. She looked once more at the bronze tone of his skin as he stood there in the sun, his black hair hanging loose and caressing his wide, muscular shoulders. She saw he wore buckskin pants and moccasins, and she wondered how tall he was, not being able to tell from where both stood.

Her breath caught sharply as a stick broke nearby and a

buck ran cautiously toward the lake to drink, unaware of her presence. She quickly glanced back to the Indian, seeing him smile, and could not help but smile, too. At that moment she noticed below where he stood a stream of dirt and sand had begun to pour down among the rocks. Before she could shout a warning, two large rocks just below where he stood began to slide, plunging faster and faster to the ground below. In that instant, the Indian yelled out as the ground crumbled beneath his feet, and as Sarah watched in horror, he fell forward, rolling and plummeting like a rag doll to the ground far below.

Sarah's heart pounded wildly in her chest! Dropping her knife, she began running through the brush and crossed the clearing to where the rockslide settled. Dust rose in the air, covering the rocks that crashed to the earth below. She prayed aloud, "Dear God, let them miss him! Please, let them miss him!" She never thought for her own safety, or that she could be heading into danger, too. She just ran on, terrified of the fate that had befallen the Indian. As she came to the pile of rock, dust still spread, filling the air. She climbed carefully, searching frantically, trying in desperation to find him.

Then she saw him! He lay face down among the rocks, his hair gray with dust and dirt, one arm bent beneath him at an odd angle. She approached slowly, realizing she no longer had the knife and could not fight him without it and win, unless . . . she stood still and listened, watching his body intently. There was no sound, no movement. She bent closer. My God! Was he dead? Her heart tore inside her at the thought of it. He couldn't be. He just couldn't be. She gently touched his back and noticed one shoulder was reddened with bruising. He lay still.

Stepping carefully around him in the debris, Sarah pulled very gently on his shoulder, trying to turn him onto his back. At last, she succeeded. Blood ran from a large cut across his forehead and another even worse cut across his chest. She felt his neck for a pulse. There was none. Her own heart was beating wildly. She felt his neck again, bending closer to him. As she did, she leaned on his chest slightly. Suddenly, the pulse in his neck began to beat, faint at first, then harder.

She looked about her, for the first time aware of the impossible situation they were in. How could she help him, here among the rocks, with no medicine? She felt a helplessness that made her want to cry out. Even more hopeless than the day, years back, when her mother had died. She had stood then—as now—helpless and confused, as the dust of circumstance settled stealthily around her, changing her world irrevocably.

"Oh, Mother. What'll I do?" she asked, looking up beyond her cave. "What ever can I do?" she said aloud and tears started to fill her eyes, smarting as they traced two paths through the dust on her cheeks. She wiped back a tear with the side of her hand, bending closer to the Indian, quieting somewhat as a calm settled upon her.

"You won't die," she stated firmly. "I won't let you!" She spoke aloud, determined to evoke or persuade, perhaps to cajole, some force, if indeed she believed in such a thing, to make her words be truth. Doing so seemed to ease the feeling of helplessness and dispel her sense of hopelessness. Suddenly, she knew what she must do!

She lifted her skirt and tore two wide strips of cloth from her petticoat. She moved easily, quickly, knowing whatever was to be done was up to her. She folded the two pieces of fabric and laid the first on his chest, hoping to stifle the wound. The second piece she lay across his forehead, her fingers gentle and quick. She blotted at the forehead wound, seeing that it already bled less, though it was long and jagged. Looking hastily around to search for any sign of movement or danger, and seeing none, she raised her skirt and raced back to the lake. Once more, she ripped more strips of cloth from her petticoat and dipped them in the cold, clear water.

She hurriedly piled them, like soggy wet balls, upon the flat rock, and then quickly ran to where she had last had her knife. She fell on her knees, running her hands through the grass. She would need the knife, she knew, and she silently cursed herself for dropping it.

"Just like one of those town ninnies," she said aloud, her disgust evident. "Should have kept your senses about you." She swept her arms back and forth in ever-widening circles. Just as she was about to give up, her hand touched the cold, hard blade. She grabbed the knife up to her breast and ran back to the large, flat rock. She held tightly to the knife as she put the wet bunches of material into her scarf, holding its corners to make carrying easier. She hoped to keep the cloth cleaner, also.

Quickly, she ran back to her fallen companion, who lay as still as death, his breathing so slight that she dropped to her knees once again and felt his chest for any sign of consciousness. Unwrapping the wet cloths, she began ever so gently to wipe off and stem the thickened flow of blood that still ran from the tear across his chest. She worked quickly, intent on her purpose. Soon, the blood flow slowed. She stood up, lifting her skirt and tucking it in at her waist, then tore another long piece of cloth from her petticoat and ripped it in half. She wrapped one-half around the Indian's head, noticing, as she lifted his head, the weight of it.

If only you could help, she thought. If only you were conscious, she added, never once considering the danger she might be in if he were. She tucked in the ends of the fabric and tried to wrap the other piece under his arms and across his chest. It took all her strength to roll him, first this way, then that, to place the material beneath him, and it was covered with sand before she was finished. She held it out away from his wound, knowing all too well the dangers of infection. Then remembering the scarf, she reached back for it, quickly folding it so only clean parts were showing, and placed it over the gaping cut. She tied the long ends of the material around him, over it. It held in place, and she sighed deeply, sitting back on her heels to look at her work.

With womanly tenderness, she brushed a long strand of hair back from his face, noting the silky feel of it as she did so. Then, she leaned close in childlike curiosity, until her face was only a mere breath from his, and very quietly inhaled deeply, once, and again. "He doesn't stink," she said softly, surprised at her discovery. She moved her face close to his chest and again sniffed, sitting back to peer intently at him, a look of amazement on her face. She continued to study him, noticing each hair of brow and lash, tracing, in her mind, the shape of his lips, the hollows and contours of his cheeks, memorizing each feature of his face. With a slight hesitation, she ever so gently put her fingertips against his skin, touching his cheek, then his forehead and chin. She let her palm rest momentarily against his cheek, feeling its smoothness, its taut resilience. "You're beautiful," she whispered, feeling a feeling within her heart that had never been there before.

The serenity was short lived. At that moment, the Indian's eyes opened, and in but an instant, the clouded look in them changed to that of alarm as his arm nearest Sarah thrust forward, grabbing her by the wrist. She screamed, sprang up and back, lost her balance, and sat down with a thud. As she fell, his hand on her wrist loosened and fell heavily to the ground. He moaned in pain and then was silent.

Sarah clutched her hand to her breast and scurried away, stopping a short distance from the unconscious figure. Her heart beat so hard she could barely get her breath. She looked around warily, realizing she had cried out, realizing others like him could be near. Her eyes, wide with fear, scouted the surrounding landscape. She saw nothing, but stayed crouched where she was until she could quiet her shaking body. It was a while before she moved. Then, going forward stealthily to where he lay, she paused—guardedly—wanting only to retrieve her knife. He lay still as death as she crept nearer and nearer. Mustering every last ounce of courage, she crept within arm's reach of him, tense, wary, and alert, watchful as a mountain cat near a trap. Then, ever so quickly, she reached out—retrieving her knife—and with it a slight bit of courage. The Indian lay still, his features relaxed as though in sleep, and she wondered, once more, if he was dead. She turned and moved a few feet away.

In time, she again ventured close to check on him and keep watch. She looked at his bare chest and the buckskin pants covering his muscled thighs. She had touched him, touched his face. It was smooth and firm. As she thought of this, she looked at her hand and unconsciously ran her fingers across her own cheek. Her thoughts were shattered as the Indian groaned, slowly moved one leg, and then turned his head in her direction. His eyes were open, watching her. Fingers tightening on the handle of her knife, she tensed, but his head fell limply to the side, and once again his eyes closed. Sarah's muscles in her arms and legs ached from the unaccustomed crouched position. Still, she stayed where she was.

The screech of a bird overhead made her realize that a lot of time had passed. She couldn't be gone much longer or she'd have some explaining to do to her father. She gazed off in the direction where the stream ran through the woods to the meadow beyond the big rocks. She could not leave him like this, helpless and alone. What if a bear came along in the night, or a mountain cat? She looked back to the Indian, realizing once more that whatever was to be done was up to her. Her resolve to help goaded her on. Quietly, she rose, stretching each leg a few times to get the blood flowing through them. She walked closer, quietly, carefully, holding her breath, trying to still her pounding heart. She clutched the knife in her hand, feeling its uselessness. Could she use it if she had to? She knew she could not.

She stepped to within inches of his inert body. The blood pounded so hard in her temples she was afraid she would faint. The bandage on his chest once again ran red with blood, she noticed. She took a step back, realizing her skirt was still caught in at her waist, but the realization seemed to spur her into action. Putting down the knife, she gathered the ripped petticoat to her and tore two more pieces from it, then let it fall freely back in place. She folded one piece of cloth into a thick pad and folded the other in half lengthwise to use as an outer bandage. Trusting her feelings and instincts, she knelt beside the inert figure. Biting her lip to fight the fear within her, she reached forward, untying the old, bloody bandage.

Mustering every last drop of courage, she ever so gently unwound the cloth from his head, lifting his head as carefully as she could. She tossed the bloody cloth off to the side, and the saturated pad with it, then she placed the new pad in place. She thought she noticed a twinge of movement of one of the Indian's eyelids, but forced herself to continue. Kneeling in still closer to lift his head and once more wrap the clean bandage in place, she tucked the ends in on each side to hold everything secure and carefully laid his head back on the ground. As she did so, his eyes opened, and slowly he turned to face her. She knelt beside him, weaponless, a strange sense of calm within her. His eyes sought hers and watched her warily, it seemed, though she remained still, scarcely breathing, feeling a sudden trickle of sweat run down her brow.

Looking at each other, neither moved nor spoke. Then, Sarah forced herself to smile ever so slightly. The Indian's eyes watched her—like two dark coals—and then slowly looked down to her neck, and then to her breasts, and back up, studying her. Sarah felt her cheeks flush red with a mixture of excitement and embarrassment. The smile left her lips, and yet she made no move to look away. The hand that had grabbed her wrist before lifted, and Sarah watched it as though it was something unseen before. It rose slowly until it was even with her breast and Sarah tensed, her eyes widening in fear. The Indian's eyes bore into hers, seemingly paralyzing her every normal reflex. She stared at him, holding her breath. Then, his hand rose up to her face and, with a tenderness that surprised her, brushed her cheek.

Time seemed to stand still for Sarah. She no longer heard the birds, or was conscious of her surroundings. Instead, she felt a calmness and serenity beyond anything she had ever felt before. Without thinking, she closed her eyes, trusting again her instincts, and in a moment's eternity, she felt his hand encircle one of her breasts. His touch was tender. Sarah opened her eyes the second he touched her, but found his were now closed. He posed no threat. He too, seemed calm and perhaps as curious about her. A mere second passed before he opened his eyes and lowered his hand to his side, and Sarah knew she would never feel threatened by him again.

Rising slowly, she looked up at the sky, knowing it was much later in the day than she had planned to stay. When she looked, his eyes followed hers. With an unspoken acknowledgment of understanding, he turned his head, looking as best he could at his chest, moving his legs, and feeling the bandage on his forehead. Sarah watched him take stock of his injuries, and then carefully roll onto his good side. She had no doubt his other arm was broken. It hung limp, bruises beginning to blacken areas of it from shoulder to wrist. Using sticks and more material from her petticoat, Sarah carefully set his broken arm. It was difficult to do, though she was no longer afraid to be near him.

He moaned only once as he pushed up with his good arm, getting his feet beneath him, swaying unsteadily from the effort. Sarah was aware of the tremendous pain he had to be feeling. He straightened up, steadying himself on the edge of a large boulder, grimacing from the pain. Sarah moved toward him, admiring his strength and hoping it would be enough for what was to come.

Looking at him steadily, she raised her eyes toward the entrance to the cave. His eyes followed and he nodded quickly, acknowledging it. He took a step, faltering, lost his balance, and sank to his knees. She hurried to help him, reaching out her hands to him. With great effort, he again rose to his feet. Sarah moved in close to him until she felt him lean his weight against her. Slowly, painfully, step by hesitant step, they made their way up the path to her cave.

CHAPTER EIGHT

It was nearly dark when Sarah reached her cabin. Her breath was short from the long run she had had across the meadow. She peered anxiously through the window to see if her father was anywhere to be seen. She prayed silently that he would not notice her coming in this way: skirt torn, blouse blood-smeared, hair tangled and wild, from running. Though the light on the table burned brightly, there was no sign of her father. She took a few breaths to ease her trembling body and quietly opened the door, entering the cabin. Silence greeted her. Obviously, he was out in the barn.

She hurried to her room barely daring to breathe until she had the door shut behind her. Once shut, she ran to her dresser and hastily gathered fresh garments. She hurried to the bed, tossing all the clothes down on it. Quickly, she unbuttoned the blouse she had on and let it, and the skirt and torn pettocoat, drop to the floor. She cleansed her face and washed her arms from the bowl in the wooden stand near her bed and, drying quickly, began to brush her hair with the wiry brush that had once been her mother's.

Oh, Mother, she thought, as she began to dress, whatever will I do now? How can I help him? She finished putting on her clean clothes just as her father entered the cabin, his voice brisk as he asked, "Sarah, girl, where are you?"

Sarah felt her heart begin to pound, took a deep breath to

steady her voice, and then replied, "Here, Father. I stayed too long in the meadow today. Have you eaten?" She opened her bedroom door and went out into the homey interior of the cabin, a smile covering her anxiety.

"Yes, I did. I've just been to see the widow Mitchell. She sent a cake," he said, smiling a bit, she noticed, as he answered.

Sarah took the cake from him and tried to relax. Setting plates on the table and taking the cake, she cut them each a piece. "Coffee, Father?" she asked.

"Later, Sarah. That'd be nice, but I've been meaning to talk to you."

Sarah quickly sat down, hoping to quell the rising uneasiness within her. She could not remember the last time her father had had a talk with her, and was sure it had to be of great importance. Oh, no, she thought. Did he know of her trips to the cave? Did he plan to stop her from going there?

"Sarah," her father began hesitantly. She knew he was weighing his words: the hesitation, the white lines around his mouth, the way he tapped the fingers of one hand on the table.

"Father?" she asked, sitting back in her chair and facing him.

"Sarah," he began again, still hesitating. "This would be easier if you were a boy," he stated, "or betrothed."

Sarah looked at him questioningly, wondering what on earth was bothering him. She noticed how much he had aged since her mother's death, how many strands of white now showed throughout his normally black hair, and how tired his eyes looked of late. Oh, dear. He's ill, she suddenly thought, tensing. But, before her thoughts could overwhelm her, her father continued.

"I've asked Rosie, Mrs. Mitchell, to become my wife and she's accepted," he stated dramatically.

Sarah almost fell out of her chair, her surprise was so great! "Oh, Father!" she said. "I'm so happy for you," she commented, adding, "I was afraid you were ill." Instantly, her thoughts sprang to her cave, and the wounded Indian awaiting her return.

"No. Not ill, Sarah, happy, and I hope you are, too, about this?"

"Yes! Yes, I am! Mrs. Mitchell is a wonderful woman, a great cook and always so cheerful," Sarah exclaimed, quickly going to his side to hug him. "I'm very glad, Father," she stated exuberantly. "It'll be nice to have her here with us."

"Well, that's not quite the plan," he said, once again tapping his fingers nervously on the table. "That's what bothers me." Sarah sat back down and waited for him to continue. "We've decided to stay in town, Sarah. She's comfortable in her house, and I spend most days in town anyway." He hesitated and then went on, "We want you to come live with us."

She stared at him, astounded, her thoughts racing. "I . . . I can't," she stammered, thinking how little chance she'd have to go to the cave and to do as she wanted unobserved.

"You can't?" her father asked, a look of confusion on his face.

"I . . . Oh, Father. I'm so happy here. I don't want to leave," she stated. "*This* is my home." She watched his face. "I'll be fine here," she added.

He looked at Sarah, then down at the floor, a frown covering his features. "I don't know," he hesitated. Then a slight smile began as he looked around at their home, at its inviting warmth and coziness. "You can be proud of the home you've made here, Sarah. I always felt happy to come home from town." He hesitated, thinking thoughts that he had never voiced before, surprising both Sarah and himself. "And you are a good cook. Can shoot better than I. Know all the ways of surviving you learned from John Bruce." He smiled at her, seeing how pleased she was at his words. "And it won't be long, I suppose, before you and Tommy marry."

"No!" Sarah stated emphatically, seeing the frown return

once more to her father's face. "No," she repeated firmly. "I *won't* be marrying Tommy, Father. I . . . I don't love him. I don't *want* to be the wife of a storekeeper. I . . . I want a different life. A life . . ."

Interrupting her, her father got up and poured himself a cup of coffee, his frown deepening. "It's those books your mother always read to you," Samuel stated, "made you a dreamer. A . . . a . . . romantic." He shook his head. "Life's not like that, Sarah. Life's not like that."

She saw how concerned he looked and it touched her heart. "Father, I'm a grown woman. Most women my age are married and have a houseful of children by now. And church socials and sewing bees. And that's what their lives will be for the rest of their lives. I . . . I'm not like that." She rushed on, hoping he would understand the words that poured forth from her heart. "I love it here, not in town. And I can shoot, and hunt, and track. And, oh, Father, I can dress a deer and put up food for the winter, and run in the meadow with eagles soaring above me, and flowers around my feet. I'm happy here," she repeated, pleadingly, "and I can come to town every week and visit you and Rosie." She paused, watching him closely, "You'll be happy at Rosie's, Father, in town by your friends. My friends are the birds and animals and . . ."

Her father stopped her, placing his hand upon her shoulder. "All right. If you're so sure about this, Sarah, it's all right with me. But, if you ever change your mind, I want you to know you'll always be welcome at Rosie's. We both want you to know that. She feels motherly toward you." He patted Sarah on the shoulder then and cut himself a second piece of cake.

"When are you marrying?" Sarah asked, happy to realize she could have her way and he approved.

"At church, next Sunday," he answered. "No reason to wait at our ages," he added, smiling a contented smile that was so unusual for him. His mood was contagious, and Sarah moved to his side and hugged him once again.

"I'm so happy for you both!" she stated, realizing it wasn't just happiness for them, but also for herself, that filled her with joy. "Oh, Father. I'm so happy! For all of us!" she exclaimed. "We must make plans for your marriage. I'll go into town to see Rosie with you tomorrow morning. I'm so happy," she added once more. With that, she cut herself a second piece of cake, realizing that in just a week she would be on her own, and *freer* than ever before. She thought of her Indian. Now she could spend more time at the cave, nursing his wounds and exploring their new friendship. Her mind whirled with the magnitude of changes that lay ahead.

"You'll keep Glory, of course," her father stated, finishing the last bite of his cake, obviously savoring its rich chocolate flavor, its recipe handed down from Rosie's Irish grandmother. "She's a good horse, and there's plenty of feed for her and pasture." Satisfied, he stretched his legs and yawned, still thinking of Sarah's well-being. "And, of course, Pet. She's been a good cow, and will easily give enough milk for your needs and to fatten the calf she's carrying. She always did favor you milking her better than me." He hesitated, pulling off his boots, then continued, "You'll have plenty of eggs, apples from that old tree down in the glade, and lots of meat when we slaughter the pigs come late fall. And Rosie and I'll stop in often to see how you're doing." He brushed cake crumbs off his shirt, yawning again. "I think I'll turn in now, girl. It's been a big day." He smiled at Sarah. "You'll be all right. I'm sure of that. Goodnight, Sarah. Sleep well."

"Goodnight, Father," Sarah replied, blowing out the oil lamp and heading toward her room, already anticipating the endless possibilities that could lie ahead for her in the days to come.

When Sarah's father left early the next morning, Sarah went with him. It was a cool morning with a brisk wind blowing. She pulled her shawl tightly around her shoulders, and wished she had worn a scarf. Then she remembered the scarf was still at the cave. She wondered how the Indian had fared through the night, remembering how tenderly he had touched her. A touch that made her tremble, even yet, at the memory! She thought, too, of how he had leaned on her as they made their way to the safety of the cave, her arm lightly around him, and how difficult it had been to set his broken arm.

"You're awful quiet this morning, Sarah. Having second thoughts about the marriage?" her father asked.

"Oh, no. Not at all," she answered.

"If you'd rather live with us, Sarah, you'll be welcome. There's no need to worry if you've changed your mind," Samuel stated, watching his daughter closely.

"Oh, Father, I haven't changed my mind. I'm looking forward to being on my own. I could hardly sleep last night, I'm so excited about it. And about your wedding, of course," she added hastily, hoping to divert his attention from herself.

He smiled and shook the reins, making Glory step along faster. "I'll probably have to sit with the old-timers at Tommy's store while you and Rosie make plans," he joked, happily. This was a new side of him that Sarah had never seen before, and she laughed, too, enjoying their easy camaraderie.

Presently, he continued, "I'm sorry for always pushing Tommy at you, Sarah. I didn't know you felt so strongly about not marrying him. A father don't worry much about a son growing up in the world, but it's different with a girl. I don't care if you never marry, if that's what makes you happy, Sarah. I just want you to be happy."

Sarah felt a tremendous rush of love for him flood her heart. "Did you ever wish I'd been a boy?" she asked, realizing they had never talked of such things, or been as close before.

"That's sort of a hard question to answer, Sarah. I guess every man wants a son." He hesitated, thinking thoughts held inside for many years. "Being a cavalry officer when you were born, yes. Yes, I hoped for a boy, I guess. I felt I had more to offer a boy, could teach him things that I knew, things that interested me. I had no sisters and my mother passed away when I was young. I guess I wasn't all that sure how to raise a daughter: what to teach her, what she'd need." He was silent again, then continued, "Jenny wanted a girl. She sewed little dresses for you, and made you dolls and ribbons for your hair. She knew how to answer all your questions and you became her whole life, it seemed, after awhile. I was never sorry you were a girl, Sarah. I just felt I had more to offer a boy."

They rode on in silence for quite a distance, watching a hawk circle high in the sky, and a rabbit dart across the road and back track before racing once again out of sight.

"I've always been proud of you, Sarah. I hope you know that. With all the things John Bruce taught you, I guess I sort of got the son I wanted, in you." He laughed, and Sarah smiled, pleased with all the things they were sharing. "'Course, I'm sorta' jealous of him, you know," he stated. Sarah looked at him to see if he was joking. He wasn't. "I always felt I should have taught you those things, Sarah: hunting and trapping, and all, if anyone was gonna," he shook the reins slightly, then continued, "but, you seemed so happy around him. I'd see the excitement on your face when you spoke of him, and hear your laughter. I wasn't sure I could give you those things, somehow." He paused, "Sort of pawned you off on Rosie when your mother died." He shook his head, and then continued, "I love you, Sarah, more than I can tell you, girl. No boy could have meant any more." He patted her hand then, and they both had smiles on their faces as they arrived at Rosie's.

CHAPTER NINE

Sarah had a busy week getting ready for her father's wedding. She packed his belongings, tended the Indian, and did not only the regular chores, but also a thorough cleaning of the cabin. She dusted, scrubbed and swept, washed curtains and bedding, and even stuffed clean, wild hay in the ticking of her father's mattress. He wouldn't be taking it to Rosie's, so Sarah decided to clean it and sleep on it herself throughout the winter months that lay ahead. Her small room had always been cold with the door shut, and many a night she lay shivering, even though only her nose stuck out from under her quilt. Yes, she decided, that was what she would do. She would move to the big room with its warmth from the fireplace and the stove.

She thought of the day the stove arrived. Not many folks had both a wood stove and a large fireplace for cooking, but her father had saved up and ordered it special when they came to Hastings, saying Jenny should have had one, and Sarah would definitely not do without. Sarah was grateful for his thoughtfulness, as it made cooking much easier. It also made heating large quantities of water from the creek easier for a Saturday-night bath. Sarah enjoyed those hot, sudsy baths and the tremendous feeling of cleanliness she felt after using it. Sometimes, she even used it in the summer months, when it would have been just as easy to wash in the creek by the cabin or at the lake by her cave. She preferred a hot-water bath and looked forward to many once her father lived at Rosie's. It was an indulgence, she knew, but one she welcomed.

Samuel came and went everyday that week, leaving for Rosie's or business in town after their noonday meal. Then, Sarah would wrap up what was left and put it in her basket along with herbal concoctions, and what salves she had, for tending the Indian's wounds.

He was asleep the first day she entered the cave to care for him, and awoke as she came near. "I won't hurt you," Sarah said, slowly going closer and speaking softly. He watched her warily, at first, but soon seemed to understand, and let her change his bandages and spread the poultice across his wounds. She had never seen a man as bruised, nor touched one. Her hands shook the first time she did so. He groaned, but smiled slightly when she looked alarmed.

When she had finished dressing his wounds, she quickly unwrapped the food she had brought: a roast made of bear meat, tender and succulent, with potatoes and carrots, and a large piece of apple pie she had sweetened with honey. He tasted the roast tentatively and then ate it in large gnawing bites. She wondered when he had eaten last. He seemed so ravenous. She watched him, fascinated, as he devoured every last morsel. Then, she offered him the pie, but he gently pushed it away. Obviously, it was not to his liking.

"I'll be right back," she said and left the cave, still cautious and alert for danger. She walked to the lake below. There, she filled an old canteen of her father's with cold, refreshing water for the Indian to drink. He was looking at her when she returned, a curious look not unlike the way she looked at him earlier. "I can't stay long," she said, "but I'll be back tomorrow and bring more food. I hope you'll be all right." She looked anxiously around the cave. "The ointments should heal your chest," she continued, and then blushed slightly as she glanced at him. His dark eyes watched her closely, and she wondered what he was thinking. "I'm leaving my knife. It won't be much protection, I'm afraid, if a bear comes, but better than nothing." She reached into the basket and took out the knife, looking at him as she did so. She wondered for just a second if she was being foolhardy, but she thought of the eagle feather he had given her as a sign of friendship, and laid the knife near him. "I'll be back," she said, picking up the basket and stepping quickly away from him. She walked to the cave's entrance and left, stacking the pile of brush in front of the entrance like she usually did. She glanced around, cautiously, for signs of others or any danger, and then walked down the path and into the forest.

Birds sang in the branches overhead, and Sarah felt like singing with them, so great was her joy! He was alive and getting well. And, best of all, he was her friend. Just for a moment a shadow of concern crossed her mind at how angry her father would be. "I can't think of that," she admonished herself. "He's not like other Indians," she whispered softly. "Why, he doesn't even stink."

When she got to the meadow, she picked a basket of wildflowers that grew so abundantly, enjoying the sweet scent that emanated from them. She thought of the bouquet she had picked for Nancy and wondered if Nancy had any regrets now that she was married to Silas. Of course not, she thought. She'll just have to get used to living like I do. She smiled as she thought of Nancy learning to hunt and trap and shoot. Too bad Old John can't give lessons to all the women of Hastings, she thought, and had to laugh at such a silly notion.

To her dismay, her father was at the cabin when she got back, looking anxious and a bit annoyed. "Where have you been, Sarah? You worry me when you go off by yourself."

She smiled, keeping her voice cheerful and light. "I went for a walk to pick some flowers. Aren't they pretty?" she asked, showing him the basket full of flowers. Beneath them, she knew, were the plate, utensils, and medicines she had taken to the Indian. She hoped her father would not catch sight of them. Her stomach tensed as he glanced at the basket, then turned and walked to the stove.

"Where's the roast that was left, Sarah? I thought I'd have a bite of it," he stated.

She bit her lip as thoughts raced one after another through her head. "You'll spoil your supper," she answered. "I'm making a special meal tonight since we won't have many meals alone together after Sunday. It'll be ready soon. Why don't you have a cup of coffee and I'll get right at it?" she asked, her stomach churning uneasily.

"All right," he answered. "I want to sharpen the axe and chop more wood anyways, so you'll have a good supply. I guess I can wait."

Sarah breathed a sigh of relief as he went out the door to the barn, but felt horribly ashamed that not only had she lied to her father again, but seemed to be getting quite good at it. "Maybe I had better go to church more than just this Sunday," she stated, hurrying to get the evening meal cooking.

Sunday morning Sarah was up before the first light of dawn crossed the sky, milking Pet and getting things ready for the wedding. She quickly fixed sourdough biscuits and syrup for her father's breakfast, but was too excited to eat any herself. As he shaved and brushed his hair, Sarah whipped up a cake from the recipe Rosie had given her. It was her father's favorite, she knew, and she was certain everyone at the wedding would enjoy it. Her thoughts ran rampant. The excitement of the day must be catching, she mused, as Pet shifted nervously while she was milking her, unlike her usual placid self, and Glory stomped and whinnied in her corner of the barn. Sarah wondered if somehow they knew it was her father's wedding day, not realizing they were reacting to her own excited manner.

After she had placed the cake in the oven, she sat down with a cup of coffee, asking her father if he wanted to join her.

"No, Sarah. I'm going to pack up the last of my things, and turn Pet out to pasture. She should be okay while you're gone today. Looks like it's gonna be a nice day. Sun's already peeking through the trees."

He smiled at her, and she noticed a change had come over him in the past few weeks. He smiled often now, and she had even heard him humming something as he worked in the barn the other day. It was so unlike him, she thought. Already Rosie's company had brought a smile to his face and a spring to his step. Why, he even seemed younger somehow.

Someday, I'll be a bride-to-be, she mused, as her thoughts rushed back to the Indian at the cave. She had taken him a light blanket a few days earlier and helped him sit up, wrapping it carefully around his shoulders. The skin on his back and most on his shoulders still had great purple and black areas of bruising, and here and there a sickly yellow tone emanated outward from the bruises. She had reached out to pull the blanket up higher on his back, and just for an instant her fingers brushed against his skin. She held her breath, not realizing she was doing so, and gently placed her hand against his shoulder. He turned his head looking toward her, then down at the floor, closing his eyes, waiting to see what she would do. He enjoyed her touch. His hair, dark as a raven's wing, fell down his back and, as he turned, a strand or two skimmed her hand. She took a deep breath and quickly stood up, moving a short distance away from him, her heart beating fast in her chest, her feelings fluttery with emotions she was not used to having.

"Sarah, don't I smell cake burning?" her father spoke from the doorway.

"Oh!" she exclaimed, jumping up quickly as she rushed to save the cake. Luckily, it was not beyond saving. She shook her head and chided herself for almost letting it burn. For a sensible, able woman, she thought, I sure get addlebrained when it comes to men. She laughed at the thought and then turned her attention to the tasks at hand, forcing herself to dwell on what needed to be done.

CHAPTER TEN

After the regular Sunday service, Rosie Mitchell, Amanda Culpepper, Sarah and her father reentered the sturdy, whiteboard church. There was a hushed silence inside, and though it was small—one room only—Sarah felt a certain inner calm within its walls. Reverend Cole bustled about, having a few words first with Rosie, then with Samuel. Sarah smiled at the young preacher and he nodded at her, a smile changing his boyish face into an angelic countenance. I wonder if he knows something regular folks don't, Sarah mused, remembering a story her mother had told her of a young woman who received a message from Heaven and was later burned at the stake.

"Joan of Arc," Sarah said aloud, remembering the name of the young woman.

"Did you say something, dear?" Amanda Culpepper asked in a whispered tone from her seat beside Sarah.

"Oh, no," Sarah replied. "I was just thinking aloud."

"Doesn't she look beautiful?" Miz Culpepper noted, nodding toward her friend, Rosie Mitchell, who had taken her place beside Sarah's father in front of the minister. Rosie had on a light-green homespun dress that set off the radiance of her beautiful red hair to perfection. It was twisted into a braid, full and luxuriant, around her head. Her eyes seemed to twinkle, so great was her happiness. She took Samuel's arm as he leaned toward her, whispering something in her ear. They both laughed softly. Sarah was filled with a tremendous sense of joy as she watched them. Rosie was good for her father. Sarah knew she would bring joy to his remaining days. She smiled contentedly as Reverend Cole began to pray.

When the vows were spoken, and Rosie was Mrs. Samuel Justus, everyone hugged and kissed the happy couple, amid congratulations, handshakes, and a few tears of joy. Sarah hugged first her father, then Rosie, and had to laugh when Rosie teased her.

"Have ya' burned the weddin' cake, love?" she asked.

Sarah blushed. "Almost," she answered, knowing her father had told Rosie about it. She felt her face redden.

"No matter," Rosie replied. "'Tis a glorious day for a weddin', child, and cake or no, we'll be enjoyin' it." Sarah hugged Rosie again, and was glad to have this lovely friend as her new mother.

To Sarah's surprise, Rosie's small house was filled with people who had heard of the celebration and had come to congratulate their friends. The table was filled with food the women had prepared for the occasion, and the wonderful aromas mixed and mingled, making everyone's mouths water and stomachs rumble. Sarah visited with the women as she bustled about setting out plates and forks.

Lydia was there, though Lilly had sent her regards, staying home to tend their mother. Tommy and his mother, Mrs. Dawson, who rarely left the house any more, the O'Leary family, Johnathon Clark, and Doc Pearson and his missus were all present. Sarah greeted these friends of her father and Rosie. She was pleased to see Ophelia Denton arrive just then, and waved to her across the room.

As she returned to the kitchen to fix a second pitcher of

tea, she heard the back door open, and found herself face to face with none other than Moses Gentry.

"Hello, darlin'," he said in that irritating way of his that sent shivers up her arms and spine. "Thought I'd find you in here."

"Well, where else?" she retorted, already on the defensive since the mere sight of the man infuriated her.

"Now don't go gettin' all riled. I just meant that I knew you'd be tendin' to things, that's all," he drawled as he leaned against the door watching her. She moved past him, filling the pitcher with water from a bucket nearby. "You look pretty, Miss Sarah," he said, sounding sincere, she noticed.

"Thank you," she answered, stepping around him, deliberately avoiding looking into his eyes, which she knew would be filled with pure devilment. "Don't you have some 'sheriffin" to do?" she asked haughtily, lifting her face up, her chin raised defiantly, just like he had pictured in his mind since last seeing her at the Haverty wedding.

"Yup," he replied, "guess you're right." Then he added, "You sure do look pretty, darlin'." Before she could reply, the door closed and he was gone.

Sarah touched her cheeks, feeling the heat in them, and knew her face was red. Why does this . . . this *person*, irritate me so? she questioned silently. She just could not understand the effect he had on her. She never acted like this when Tommy was around. She felt perplexed by her reaction. Why, she never acted like this with her Indian! With him she felt tender and kind, and couldn't imagine being as furious with him. She shook her head and, taking up the pitcher, headed for the other room and the guests.

Later that afternoon, Sarah returned to her cabin. It seemed oddly discomforting that her father would not come home as usual. She unharnessed Glory and turned her out to graze. Pet sounded a greeting as she came near the cabin, her bag swaying gently as she walked. Sarah gazed around, realizing this was the first time she would be by herself. She entered the cabin, lighting the oil lamp on the table to dispel the unaccustomed emptiness that seemed to invade each corner of the room.

She put a pot of coffee on to heat and went to her room to change from her good dress into a skirt and blouse that had been her mother's. As she dressed, she spoke aloud to the silence, "Well, Mother, it's you and I now. Father looked so grand today. Did you see? I've never seen him look happier." She fastened her skirt and blouse and went to hang the dress in the tall cabinet in the corner. It was made of a lovely golden pine and had come by wagon from Virginia with her mother to the fort, and later to Hastings. She rubbed her hand along its smooth front, her thoughts returning to the day her mother died. "I felt so afraid," she said to the empty room. She remembered how her father had tried to comfort her, but his words were lost amid the grief that had enveloped her. She felt a tear course its way down her cheek. "I hope you're happy, Mother. I miss you so much." As she stood there, tears began to flow, tracing paths down her cheeks. "Rosie's good for Father," she said aloud. "She'll make him a good wife." She sniffed again, then hung the dress in the cabinet and looked slowly around her room.

The small bed she had slept in all her life stood in a corner, the bedding smoothed neatly in place, the washbowl and pitcher near it, clean and awaiting use. A round, braided rag rug covered the floorboards beside the bed, its colors faded and its fabric worn from years of being walked on. Sarah knew how much love must have gone into the making of it. Knew how many hours her mother must have sat in the empty stillness, before she was born, weaving each braid one over the other, tightening each precisely the same amount so it would lay flat upon the floor and last for years to come. "Thank you, Mother," Sarah whispered, drying her face with the back of her hand. "Thank you for everything." Then hearing the coffeepot begin to rattle, she left the room, closing the door and leaving many memories within.

That evening after she had put Glory in her stall, milked Pet, and fed them their rations, Sarah sat outside by the barn on the old fallen log, listening to the evening sounds. A loon cried somewhere in the distance, and the night seemed alive with sounds she had never heard before. A wolf howled and was soon answered by a bevy of calls, each echoing through the stillness. An owl hooted and bats crisscrossed the sky, hunting for insects, wings whirring as they dipped and rose above the trees.

Sarah enjoyed these new discoveries and was not afraid. She had always imagined that silence filled the stillness of night and was amazed to realize there were a million sounds filling the air. Nothing was still. She sat there listening in awe, entranced by this new awareness.

In time, the sky darkened as though covered by a soft velvet quilt, and stars shone like a million diamonds, sparkling and twinkling above her. A gentle breeze rustled the leaves on the trees, and a faint scent of pine wafted in the air, pleasing her senses. She inhaled deeply, at peace with her world, then stretched and went inside.

She dreamt that night, in her father's bed, of daring exploits and misty visions, of faces blurred yet oddly remembered, though neither recognized nor known. Branches whisked gently against the outer walls of the cabin. And a twig snapped sharply nearby, causing Glory to snort in her stall inside the barn, disturbing Pet, who had been standing with eyes closed, contentedly chewing her cud. Pet opened her eyes, momentarily stopped chewing to listen, then closed her eyes and resumed chewing. In a small stand of pine not far from the cabin, a doe nestled close to her fawn, nuzzling it tenderly, while Sarah slept.

CHAPTER ELEVEN

The next morning Sarah slept late, waking refreshed and reveling in the anticipation of her new life and all it might hold. She dressed in pants and blouse, and the Indian moccasins Old John had made for her years earlier, and then braided her auburn hair into one long braid that hung nearly to her waist, tying it with the piece of yellow ribbon Cassandra had given her.

She heard Pet moo, obviously displeased because she had not been milked yet. Truth was, she was near to being dried-up, yet still gave more than enough milk for drinking and cooking, and more than enough cream for Sarah's coffee. "I'm coming, Pet," she called, and picking up the pail by the door, went outside into the already warm weather to milk. She turned Glory out to pasture after petting her soft muzzle and neck, and then sat down on an overturned old, rusty bucket that had a hole on one side. She gently washed Pet's udder and teats with a clean piece of woven cloth, and dried them. Talking softly to the Jersey cow, she began to milk her. "Looks like it's going to be a hot day today, Pet," Sarah said as the warm, creamy milk hit the bottom of the pail with a steady rhythm. "I'll have to be drying you up soon, old girl," she stated, her hands working tenderly as she spoke. "Figure your calf's due in a couple weeks. Awful late, it'll start to be cold

not long after, but don't worry. We'll take good care of it."
She finished milking, the pail over half-full, and turned Pet
out to pasture.

Then she carried the pail into the cabin to skim the cream
off the top, once it rose. There would be enough cream to
make a jar of butter, if she didn't add so much to her coffee
every morning. She poured off the cream, strained the milk
into a second pail, and took it to the icehouse down the hill
by the creek. She marveled at how wise her father had been
to construct the icehouse, knowing without it they would not
have been able to store milk and meat safely through the hot
summer months.

When she was done, she hurriedly cleaned out the stalls,
filled a pail with fresh water from the creek, and went in the
cabin to wash. Then she had a bite to eat and noticed that
the flowers she had picked in the meadow only the day before
were already starting to droop slightly in the warm weather.
She made a mental note to pick fresh ones next time she was
there. She wanted to head back to her cave and Indian friend
more than anything, but knew she had to do some hunting
first. Taking the gun down from over the mantle and loading
it, she left the cabin, walking quickly and silently into the
woods in the opposite direction of the cave.

As the sun reached its highest point in the sky above her,
she spotted a flock of turkeys off to her left. The hens were
trailed by a dozen or so small chicks that ran quickly into the
bush, alarmed by her presence, though she had approached
them as quietly as possible. The two largest, which she knew
to be two males—one half-grown and one old—opened their
wings and strutted in a circle in hopes of frightening her away.
She took careful aim but, to her chagrin, missed.

Oh, well, she thought, at least John isn't here to tease
me. She reloaded and continued along on her hunt. It wasn't
long before a young buck came into view in a clearing just

ahead. Sarah raised her gun and shot, the shot finding its mark. It fell where it stood. Sarah was elated, knowing Old John would have been proud.

She walked over to the deer—stepping over a fallen log—and leaned her gun against the log, after reloading. If a bear, wolf, or cougar was nearby, she didn't want to have an unloaded gun. She knelt, slit open the deer's belly, and carefully pulled out the innards. The smell of warm blood and guts caused her stomach to roll slightly as she worked. It was a tiring job, and she knew she wouldn't be able to carry the animal the long distance back to her cabin. Even though she hated waste, she skinned the hide and cut off the hindquarters, shoulders and tenderloins, leaving the rest for foraging animals. She bagged the hide and meat in a large woven bag she had brought, and threw the bag over her shoulder, settling it as comfortably as she could for the trek home. Picking up her gun, she headed back toward her cabin.

The meat would be tender as the deer was young and would provide steaks, stew meat, and roasts to last her a couple months, she figured. Her stomach rumbled as she savored the thought of potatoes, carrots, and onions cooking in the venison juices along with a tender and succulent shoulder roast. Perhaps she would invite her father and Rosie to join her. She visualized hot sourdough biscuits fresh from the oven, and a pie for dessert, as she walked on carrying her load, smiling at her thoughts.

I may be an able woodsman, she thought, but I still think like a gal. As she thought that, the Indian crossed her mind, and she wondered how he had faired during the night. She was anxious to get back to him, and the cave, but she knew she'd have to take care of the meat and the hide before she could go to him. The hide had to be scraped and stretched so it could be traded for goods, or made into a coat or pants, or new moccasins to keep her warm this winter.

By the time she got to her cabin, her arms and shoulders ached from carrying the bag of meat and her gun. She was glad her journey hadn't taken her any farther from home. She was surprised to see a big bay horse tied to the tree beside the cabin. She put down the bag of meat and entered the cabin cautiously, still carrying her gun.

"Hello?" she said questioningly as she entered, and was surprised to see Moses Gentry sitting at the table, drinking a cup of coffee.

"Hello," he replied. "I made myself at home, Sarah, figured you wouldn't mind." A slow grin started across his face. "Been over to Black Dog Lake on business and thought I'd check on you on my way back. Didn't think you'd be gone long with your horse out to pasture."

"Doesn't surprise me," she replied, "that you'd make yourself at home." There was a note of challenge in her voice already. "What kind of business? A new saloon girl come to town over there?"

He gave a hearty laugh at her remark and coughed on his swallow of coffee, his eyes getting that old devilish look she knew all too well. "No, darlin', just sheriff business," he replied. "Been word of a gang from somewhere south of here checkin' out a few towns, makin' folks a bit jumpy. Thought I'd go have a talk with the sheriff over there. See what he knew about it."

"You want a piece of apple pie?" Sarah asked, washing her hands in one of the pails by the door and pulling on her apron from the nail near the door.

"I reckon I'd like that," Moses answered. "Heard you can cook pretty decent," he added, enjoying seeing her cheeks begin a slight flush.

She looked at him then, her own eyes taking on a glint of devilishness. "You ate enough of my pie, I hear, at Nancy's wedding, to be a good judge of it." She raised her eyebrows, challenging him to choose his words carefully.

He grinned, "Yup, that I did. It was fair, as pies go. Didn't know you were keeping such good track of me, though," he added, teasing her.

"Ha!" Sarah exclaimed. "I just heard you ate nearly all my pie. Heavens! I wasn't keeping track of you. Be a cold day in May before I keep track of *you*, Moses Gentry!"

He laughed at her words, noticing once more how she lifted her chin defiantly at his teasing. It pleased him. He finished the piece of pie and then stood up to leave. "You just be careful out here by yourself, Sarah. I know you know a lot about survivin' by yourself, but that's not to say you can't run into trouble." He looked at her in all seriousness, then put on his hat and walked to his horse. She stood in the door as he mounted the bay, and for just a fleeting moment she wondered what it would be like to be kissed by someone like him. Not him, of course, but someone like him. "You take care," he said, interrupting her thoughts, "and thanks for the pie, darlin'. It was mighty good." And with that he was gone. Sarah smiled a long time at his compliment.

It was too late to go to her cave once she had the meat put up and the hide scraped and stretched. It was all she could do to milk Pet, her arms were so sore. She finished the milking, fed Pet, put Glory in for the night and fed her. She strained the milk and carried it to the icehouse, then carried some buckets of water up to the cabin. She heated them and then dumped them into the old tin tub.

It was nearly dusk when she slipped out of her clothes and stepped into the tub, enjoying the heat from the stove and the hot water. Before long, she was sound asleep in the tub, her hair falling softly around her shoulders and into the water. As she slept, she dreamt dreams of dance-hall girls and a tall dark faceless man who held her close and kept her warm.

When the water cooled, she woke, at first startled and confused. Her body shivered in the long shaft of moonlight that spilled across the floor from the window on the far side of the room. She reached for a towel, stepping onto the cold wooden floorboards. Drying herself quickly, she ran to the big bed and snuggled under the quilt, not taking time to find her nightgown in the dark.

As her body heat began to warm the spot where she lay, her thoughts drifted to Moses Gentry, and her surprise at finding him waiting for her when she arrived home. He had ridden a long distance out of his way, she knew, to check on her. She snuggled further into the bedcovers and saw, in her mind's eye, the dark eyes that seemed so full of pure devilment, and his grin that irritated her so easily. "Moses Gentry," she said aloud, "I wonder just what it would be like to be kissed by you?" And a slight smile crossed her lips, as she drifted off to sleep.

CHAPTER TWELVE

For the next two weeks, Sarah was busy doing her chores, hunting and cooking, and visiting her cave nearly everyday. The Indian was much better now, and they both enjoyed their time together, it seemed. The weather had grown even hotter, and Sarah helped him down to the lake to wash himself and swim in the azure-colored water. Sarah waded near shore as he swam, wishing she could abandon all care and swim with him. It pleased her to see that his broken arm was healing nicely. He seemed in no hurry to leave the area, however, and she wondered if he had a family or where his people were. As she waded out from shore until the cool water deepened to her knees, she watched him swim, enjoying the sight of his smooth skin and dark hair as he glided through the water.

Suddenly, to her dismay, she stepped in a hole and lost her balance, slipping into deep water. She yelled out and then went under, the weight of her dress and petticoats holding her there. Frantically, she thrashed with her arms, trying to reach the surface and get a breath of air. At that moment, a strong arm encircled her waist, lifting her above the water. She coughed and sputtered, clinging to the Indian, her terror great! She knew if he had not rescued her, she could have drowned.

He picked her up in strong, sinewy arms and carried her

to the shore, her body shaking from fear. As her feet touched the ground, she continued to cling to him and he held her tightly, their bodies touching. It was then he bent his head and kissed her, as she knew he would. She also knew that she had wanted him to kiss her for a long time. She remained close to him, enjoying the tender softness of his kiss. Her heart pounded as he held her close, and her dress clung to her body, but her only thoughts were of the feelings building within her.

"S-stop," she stammered, at last, gently pushing on his chest to end the embrace that threatened to engulf all of her senses. The Indian stepped back hesitantly, looking at her as though as surprised as she. "Oh, my," she said, lifting her soggy skirts about her ankles and stepping further away from him. She was trembling, but unaware of it. He stood still, looking at her questioningly, neither of them knowing what to do next. She felt her face begin to redden and turned quickly, then ran up the path to the cave. He sat down on the big, flat rock, looking out to the center of the lake, giving her time to compose herself and giving himself time to consider the possible consequences of the kiss they had shared.

Sarah gradually calmed down, relieved that the Indian had not taken advantage of the situation. She was grateful that he had saved her, but embarrassed by the fact that she had not only welcomed his kiss, but had kissed him back. She bit her lip, wondering what she should do now, her wet dress uncomfortable against her body.

She looked at the quilt she had brought for him. She could remove her dress and wrap up in the quilt, hoping her dress would dry in the sun, but the thought made her uncomfortable. She had felt the stirrings of a woman when he kissed her. What if their kiss had also stirred feelings in him? Would she be safe wrapped in just a quilt? What would happen if he reverted to his savage ways, and raped or killed her?

She looked out of the cave, seeing that he still sat looking out at the lake, his back to her. Without another moment's hesitation, she quickly gathered up her soggy skirt and quietly tiptoed down the path, watching him with bated breath and hoping he would not turn. When she got to the edge of the woods, she plunged into its dense cover, running as fast as her legs could carry her to the safety of her cabin. She never looked back in her haste to get away, but she would have seen that he did not follow, if she had.

Bursting through the door of her cabin, she quickly locked it behind her and hastily removed her wet clothing. She was panting hard from the long run, and shivering from the chill she'd gotten from the wet garments. She wrapped a quilt around her, then lay down on her father's bed, her heart pounding and thoughts racing. "Oh, goodness," she gasped, "what have I done? What if he comes after me?" She felt confused and began to cry. "Oh, Mother," she questioned, "what have I done?" She rested there awhile, trying to gather her thoughts and make sense of the new feelings that stirred within her.

Sarah remained near the cabin tending chores for the next week, still upset by the feelings she had felt when the Indian kissed her. She had not expected those feelings and did not know they were a woman's normal response to a stimulating kiss from a man. Sarah longed to talk to her mother about these feelings, but since that was impossible she wondered if she could somehow broach the subject to Rosie.

No, that just wouldn't do, she thought sadly. Rosie would want to know who the man was, or, worse yet, assume it was Tommy Dawson. "Ugh," she groaned aloud. "Who can I ask about such things?" The wind rustled leaves on the trees, but no answer came to her. "Oh, Mother, if only I could talk to you."

Finishing her chores the following Friday afternoon, she decided to quit moping about and go to town to visit her father and Rosie. A visit would do her good, she figured, and get her mind off things. She saddled Glory and headed for Hastings. Her gloomy mood began to turn to one of cheer as she rode along, enjoying the warmth of the day, the fields abloom with all manner of wildflowers, and the steady rhythm of her mount.

She had on a pair of brown pants and a light-blue cotton blouse. Her hair was pulled back in a high ponytail that bounced and bobbed as she urged Glory into a canter. Her father would be surprised to see her in town dressed like this. He much preferred her to wear a dress, or skirt and blouse like the other women wore, but she was more comfortable in pants and found herself less restrained by them than long, heavy, cumbersome skirts or dresses. Her feet were clad in the moccasins Old John had made for her. She found them more comfortable than stiff boots or the fancy shoes she had worn to Nancy's or Rosie's weddings, though in a satchel strapped behind the saddle, she had brought her blue gingham dress and the dressy shoes of her mother's. If an occasion called for it, she would be able to dress properly, otherwise she would remain in her usual clothing. She had dried-up Pet, and would not have to hurry home, which pleased her.

An eagle soared overhead and she turned to watch it, once again causing a rush of embarrassing thoughts. What does my Indian think of me now? she wondered. Had he waited at the cave very long, once he realized I wasn't coming back? She wondered, too, how long she could stay away. Already she had begun to miss the serenity of the lake and cave. She urged Glory on, seeing in the distance the rooftops of Hastings.

She encountered Doc Pearson in his old, worn buggy as she neared town. "Hello, Doc," she greeted him as he pulled up upon seeing her.

"'Lo, Miss Sarah," he replied. "Nice day for a ride."

"Going to see my father," she said, "and Rosie."

"I'm on my way to see a patient," the doctor replied. "Got hurt in a fall from a horse he was trying to break. Best I get on my way," he said, giving Sarah a smile and tip of his hat, and was off in a small cloud of dust.

She turned to watch him and wondered who would ever replace him if he died. She remembered hearing that he had been a doctor for about forty years and knew at his age his years were numbered. She thought of the winter, years before, when he was down sick himself and couldn't get out for a month or so to tend folks in their needs. He had only been able to treat those who had managed to get into town to his home.

She turned Glory toward town and let her walk along, a sudden surge of excitement growing in her as she entered town. "Maybe I'm just lonely," she said aloud. "About time I came to town to visit."

She waved at Ophelia Denton, who had just crossed the street, and saw Amanda Culpepper sweeping the walk in front of Dawson's General Store. She pulled up and slid off Glory, hitching her reins to the rail.

"Why, hello, Sarah," Miz Culpepper greeted her, smiling. "Doing all right out there by yourself?"

"Hello," Sarah replied. "Yes, I'm doing fine. Sure is hot today," she stated, for indeed it had warmed significantly since she had left her home. They walked into the store as they talked.

"Yes," Amanda replied, "but I do prefer the hot weather. Never could abide the cold winters."

"Sarah," Tommy spoke, hurrying from the back of the store. "I didn't know you were here. When did you get to town?"

"Just rode in, going to stay at my father's for a couple days," Sarah ventured, already wishing, as she said it, that she had not volunteered so much information.

"Well, that's good," he replied. "Maybe we can get some time to . . ."

"Well, hello, Miss Sarah," came the deep-voiced greeting from the doorway.

Amanda gave Moses a quick, disparaging look. "Don't you be bothering this girl," she ordered, glaring at Moses, her hands on her hips.

Moses smiled his slow, easy smile, looking over Amanda's head at Sarah. "I'm not bothering you, Miss Sarah, am I?" he drawled, his eyes full of pure devilment.

"No," Sarah replied, surprising both Tommy and Amanda. "Hello, Sheriff. Heard any more news on that gang?"

"Nope," Moses replied, leaning against the doorframe, looking first at Sarah then out at the street.

Tommy turned and walked away, his delight in seeing Sarah diminished by her interest in Sheriff Gentry. He used to get angry when Sarah made him feel unimportant, but to his surprise he realized it no longer bothered him. He no longer fooled himself where Sarah Justus was concerned. She wasn't at all interested in him, and he didn't have to get hit in the head with a rock to realize it. Once, long ago, he had dreamed of a day when he would marry her, and they'd have a fine family: a strong son who favored him in looks, and a little girl with pretty red hair like her mother. But that dream had gradually died, along with so many of his dreams. No wagon train would he lead west. No gold bulging from his pockets. No large home in a new town, a town built by the very settlers he had taken west across mountains and plains, through Indian attacks, and gorges filled with rushing floods that swept everything in their path away.

No, he thought, I couldn't hold a gal like Sarah Justus, or dream dreams to suit her. Why, hell, I can't even dream my own dreams. And he tried to remember just when it was that he had given up on them. When did I let go of so many of my own hopes and dreams? He used to tell Sarah of his hopes and dreams, he remembered, and he looked back at her as she talked to Moses Gentry. When my father passed, I guess it was, and my mother quit getting out much to socials and needed me to see to her needs. When it was up to me to run the store.

He looked around at the things that surrounded him: kettles, barrels of flour, fine material from back east, sickles and saws, nails and such, bullets, guns, holsters and saddles, boots and bonnets, hats, britches, shirts, coats, and so many more things. He smiled at himself, knowing he had doubled the inventory since his father's death. He had succeeded in making his father's dream come true, if not his own.

He glanced once more at Sarah, surprised to see that Moses had left the store. He hesitated, and then went out in back to the storeroom to bring in more supplies. What I need, he thought, is a settled gal, a gal who doesn't have her heart in some fairytale from books. A gal who would be contented with me as I am now, who would be glad to share my life, and could appreciate what I have to offer.

He was surprised when he suddenly thought of the nice chat he'd had with Melinda Rose at the Pearly wedding. He thought of the way her hair had curled along her neck, little ringlets damp with sweat from the heat of the sun. How the fabric of her dress had pulled tightly across her belly, and he could see every movement the baby made inside her when it kicked. He blushed as he remembered how he had wanted to lay his hand on her stomach, so filled with life and promise, and feel each movement. He had wondered, just for a moment, how he would feel if it was his baby she carried and she was his wife. He shoved back his thinning brown hair with one hand as a trickle of sweat ran down his face. "Maybe there's a dream or two of my own still to be had," he said, and he smiled for the first time in a mighty long time.

Sarah walked down the street leading Glory, happy she

had come into town. Seeing other folks had been "good medicine," she realized, and she hummed as she walked along, waving at old acquaintances or offering a cheery "hello." She was actually pleased that Moses had come along when he did, cutting off Tommy's usual boring talk. She grinned as she realized that for once Moses hadn't irritated her. Why, he never even called me darlin', she thought, laughing at her discovery. He must be slipping, she said to herself and laughed again, happy to be in town among friends.

Rosie opened the door at Sarah's knock, surprised and pleased as could be to see who stood there. "Come in. Come in. Oh! 'Tis happy I am to see ya', child. Come in," Rosie greeted her.

Sarah hugged Rosie and sat her satchel on the floor. "Would you want a guest for a couple days?" Sarah asked

"Oh, yes, dear. Your father is over to the bank on business. He'll be so happy to see you, Sarah. We wondered how you've been gettin' along. Come sit and tell me all your news," Rosie chatted on, making Sarah feel very glad she had come.

"I got tired of . . . being alone, I guess," Sarah replied. "Not much news to tell," she paused, "dried up Pet, shot a small buck. I want you and Father to come to dinner soon. There's plenty of meat, so you can bring some home, too." Rosie bustled around her kitchen, mixing up a bowl of batter that Sarah knew would be one of her delicious cakes. "What's new here?" Sarah asked, as she licked the nearly empty bowl and spoon Rosie handed her after pouring the batter into a pan and putting it into the oven. "I see you have a new stove?"

"Oh, yes, dear. A gift from your father," Rosie exclaimed, her green eyes twinkling with joy. "Such a darlin' man, he is, Sarah," Rosie added, her face flushing red as she spoke. "He's a fine husband, he is, Sarah, and it's proud I am to be his wife."

"And it's proud I am to be your husband," Sarah's father spoke from the door, mimicking his wife, as he entered the comfortable house. "Hello, daughter." Sarah couldn't help noticing how happy he was, and how cheerful and inviting the house was. Delicate white doilies covered the tables, and pretty china cups were used, even by her father, not old cups like at her cabin. A dainty, lace-edged tablecloth covered the table and a tall pink vase sat in the center of it filled with tall red poppies, their blossoms and nearly transparent petals bursting forth in radiant color. She hugged her father, noticing at once the change that marriage had made in him. He laughed and talked with an ease and joy Sarah was so happy to see. "Can you stay awhile?" he asked, smiling at her.

"Yes, I'd like to," she replied and saw Rosie wink at him. She was glad she had come. They chatted on as Rosie prepared supper, then Samuel went out to put Glory up for the night. The horse nickered when she saw Samuel, in recognition of her old master.

"Yes, Glory. It's me," Samuel stated, beginning to brush the animal that had been his long before Sarah had gotten her as her own. "You been takin' good care of Sarah?" Samuel asked, brushing her flank as he spoke. The horse licked his hand as if in answer, and Samuel gave out a hearty laugh. "I have a new life here, a swell wife, Glory old girl," Samuel talked as he brushed. "Though I still miss you," he added, a soft smile on his lips. He was getting as romantic, he thought, as Sarah. Talking to a horse, no less.

He smiled and thought then of Rosie and how her bubbly spirit had changed his life in just the short time they had been man and wife. He thought of her ample body so welcoming at night as he lay beside her in their large feather bed. How she curled into him, soft and lovely, her beautiful red hair fanning out across the pillow, her warmth enveloping him. He thought, too, of her lovely accent as she whispered softly in his ear, enthralling his senses to greater heights of passion than he had ever known, until he lost himself within her in the glorious heat of consummation.

He patted the horse and gave her some grain and hay to eat. "'Tis lucky I am, Glory," Samuel stated, mimicking once again his wife's manner of speaking. He smiled as he spoke, "It's so lucky I am!" And then he left the barn and went into his home, a contented man at peace with his world.

"You must come to the social, Sarah. Everyone will be so happy to see you," Rosie entreated. "I don't know," Sarah stated, as Rosie continued, "I'll be baking pies and cakes to take, and there'll be many of your young friends there. How long's it been since you went to a church social?"

Sarah replied, trying to figure the years by the events of her life, "Almost twenty years, just before my mother passed away."

"Oh, child," Rosie said, coming to her and giving her a quick hug around the shoulders, "I didn't mean to bring sadness to mind."

"No," Sarah hesitated, "it's okay. Maybe I should go with you and Father," she replied. "Is it over at the church where Reverend Cole preaches?"

"Aye, that it is," Rosie replied. "There'll be services first, o' course, then plenty of good food and pleasant conversation." She laughed, continuing, "The young'ns'll take walks along the river and give each other the eye," she said, looking at Samuel as he sat in the other room reading his paper. She blushed as a rush of warmth enveloped her. Her eyes twinkled as she turned her attention back to Sarah and their conversation.

"Ophelia will be there, and the Benedict girls, and the O'Learys, of course." She took the cake out of the oven, tested it to make certain it was done, and went on, "And if we're lucky, perhaps Mr. Hart will sing us a song or two. Voice of an angel, he has."

"Would you like a cup of coffee and bowl of soup, my husband?" she asked in a soft voice that brimmed with love and caring. Sarah was filled with an immense respect for this lovely, warm-hearted Irish woman who so easily brought joy to those around her.

After the cake had cooled, and they had all finished their coffees and soup, Rosie showed Sarah to her room upstairs. Sarah felt a bit uncomfortable in such feminine surroundings. She noted the fine linens on the tall featherbed and a pile of pillows. Each encased in a white pillowcase edged in fine lace that Sarah knew Rosie had sewn herself. A mahogany washstand held a beautiful china pitcher and bowl upon which a bouquet of pink roses was painted. Lovely white linen curtains graced the long narrow window, each embellished with tiny colorful, embroidered flowers and small green leaves.

Sarah felt the slight breeze that wafted across the room, caressing the curtains with feathery embrace, cooling the room and bringing to it the lovely scent of the roses that grew so abundantly up the side of the two-story house to just below the window. Sarah hugged herself in happy abandon. I wonder if I will ever have such a lovely home, she thought, and she pictured her cabin surrounded by roses of the same blushing pink hue, and smiled at the thought.

Undressing in the soft light from the window, she slipped into the old faded flannel nightgown she had brought from home, and then slid into the soft bedding, pulling the quilt up to her chin. She thought of the cave and wondered if the Indian slept there, wrapped in her quilt and awaiting her return. Sadness enveloped her as she thought of him. She turned on her side, trying to focus on happy thoughts. It was a long time before she drifted off to sleep. A long time before dreams of cookies and cakes and phantom-like people filled her mind, and an even longer time before restful sleep welcomed her to its soft black-velvet embrace.

CHAPTER THIRTEEN

Sarah woke early the next morning, but lay in bed listening to the sounds of morning in Hastings. They were different than the sounds at her cabin: less birds chirping, and the occasional rumble of a wagon or buckboard as it passed. She smiled at the crowing of a rooster nearby, but missed the muted sounds from her own barn: Pet mooing, calling her to come milk, and the gentle answering whinny and occasional stomping sound of Glory in her stall. The rooster crowed again—not unlike the rooster at her home—and Sarah languished there, stretching out full-length on the bed, feeling her muscles expand and pull beneath the covers.

She heard Rosie moving about in the kitchen below her room and quickly got out of bed, surprised to find warm water in the pitcher beside the bed. She washed quickly, wondering when Rosie had brought it up to her. She had slept soundly, she realized, not hearing anyone enter the room. She smiled, knowing at home, alone, usually even the slightest noise woke her. She stretched again, noting how rested she felt and how easily her muscles responded to movement. She yawned then, shivering a bit as a slight breeze blew the curtains aside, momentarily chilling her.

She dressed quickly in her petticoat and blue gingham dress, thinking how this attire would please her father more so than the pants she had worn upon arrival. The dress hugged her breasts and waist, a thin edging of white lace surrounding the rounded neckline. It was her favorite dress and made her feel quite feminine, though the neck did seem rather low, and she wondered if her father would disapprove. She brushed her hand down the front of the skirt, smoothing the fabric, admiring the lace that also edged the sleeves at her elbow.

She brushed her hair, tying it back from her face with the piece of yellow ribbon Cassandra had given her, wishing she had a blue ribbon to match the blue of the dress. Pinching her cheeks and stepping into the soft leather moccasins, she left the room to go downstairs.

Rosie greeted her, speaking softly. Already another cake sat cooling on the table, and eggs and ham fried on the stove beside a bubbling pot of fresh coffee.

"Good morning," Sarah responded.

"Sit, sit," Rosie entreated. "Your father will be in from the barn any moment and breakfast is all ready." Sarah inhaled deeply, enjoying the aromas that filled the room, and smiled at the woman who so easily made them possible. "How did you sleep?" Rosie asked, while dishing up heaping plates of food and pouring coffee into dainty, gold-edged cups, each with a bouquet of pink-and-burgundy colored roses gracing the sides. The plates matched too, Sarah realized, as did the sugar bowl and cream pitcher in the center of the table.

Sarah thought of her own set of dishes at home: the faded design on the few good ones, and the cracks and chips of the others. She had never considered hers less than perfect. In fact, she had never given any thought at all to lace-edged table linen and napkins that matched, much less dishes that matched and were delicate and elegant.

Her father entered just then. "Good morning, ladies. And how does the morning find you?"

Rosie went quickly to his side, admonishing him to wash up quickly so his food would not get cold. She reached up, touching his cheek with a hurried but tender kiss, and Sarah was surprised to see him pat her playfully on her backside.

"Bossy woman," he protested, smiling at Rosie as if they were the only two people in the room. Sarah blushed, but felt immense joy in seeing their happiness. Rosie said grace, and they began to eat, savoring each delicious bite. It was true that Rosie was an excellent cook, and Sarah again thought of how lucky her father was to have her for his wife.

"Did you hear the O'Leary boy gallop through town earlier?" her father asked, not waiting for an answer. "Raced by like the devil himself was after him, yelled for the sheriff, and soon left with Moses, barely breaking stride."

"Oh, dear," Rosie replied, wiping her lips with the pretty white linen napkin, "I do hope nothing's wrong."

"Pretty obvious, something's wrong," Samuel replied. "I'll walk over later and see if anyone knows what happened."

"Did Moses . . . ah, Sheriff Gentry seem upset when they left?" Sarah asked, blushing slightly at her use of his given name. She saw Rosie glance quickly in her direction.

"Didn't look happy," her father replied, "sure was in a hurry."

"I do hope it's nothing serious," Rosie stated. "They're such a nice family. Don't have much, but close-knit and real good Christian folks, even if they are dirt-poor," she added non-judgmentally, her tone caring and sympathetic. She rose to get the coffeepot and poured a second cup for Sarah and Samuel.

"Don't worry, love," Samuel replied, "if it's serious we'll all help them. One nice thing about the folks in Hastings, we all stick together and help when one of our own has troubles." He wiped his face, pushing away from the table. "I'm going to be bursting out of my clothes, Sarah, the way my wife feeds me."

Sarah and Rosie laughed at his teasing remark, and Rosie blushed, her cheeks turning nearly as red as her hair. "You go on," she said, an embarrassed smile upon her face as she began to clear the table. Sarah rose and began to help, fully enjoying their tender banter, yet realizing sadly that there had been none between her mother and father when her mother was his wife.

Sarah finished the dishes just as Samuel returned. She could tell immediately that the news was not good. "What happened, Father?" she asked, noticing how the veins at his temple pulsed. She had seen it before when he was angry or terribly upset.

"It's Daniel," he replied, "Melinda Rose's husband. A bronc he was breaking threw him yesterday, tearing him up inside. He died early this morning."

"Oh, no!" Sarah and Rosie both exclaimed, anguished by such devastating news.

"Poor Melinda Rose," Rosie said, sitting down heavily at the kitchen table, her eyes filling with tears. Sarah stood still, waiting for her father to continue.

"Doc had to go over to Black Dog Lake right after Daniel died, so he sent one of the O'Leary boys to fetch the sheriff to go break the news to Melinda Rose. Doc will stop by to see her when he's done over at Black Dog. A sorry thing, her expectin' and all," Samuel lamented.

"Poor Melinda Rose. She's lost all those other babies, and this one's so close to birthin', and now her husband's gone," Sarah said, shaking her head sadly. "How will she ever get through this?"

Suddenly, Sarah knew what she must do! "She shouldn't be alone out there, that's for certain," she stated, determinedly. "I'm going out there to see if I can be of any help. Would you check on Pet for me, Father, and feed her until I get back? I'll leave immediately."

"Good idea," Samuel answered. "Consider it done."

Rosie offered to send some baked goods, but Sarah declined her kind offer, explaining there was no time, as she intended to ride as she was in her gingham dress, not taking any time to change. She hugged Rosie, kissing her quickly on the cheek, and then hurried from the house.

Samuel had just finished saddling Glory. Sarah swung up into the saddle, bending to kiss his cheek, and was in a full gallop when she passed John Bruce's cabin a half mile south of town. She stretched close along Glory's neck, urging her on, her thoughts turning to Melinda Rose's unborn baby and the impact Daniel's death could have on its survival. "Lord, please don't let her lose the baby, too," Sarah prayed. "She lost all the others, and now her husband. She needs this baby. How can she go on if she loses it, too?" She felt the wind streak across her cheeks as she raced along.

She guided Glory through a dense stand of trees and through a glen, never breaking stride. She wondered why God seemed to favor some folks and overlook others? She thought of her father and Rosie, how happy they were and the comfortable surroundings they lived in. What had they done to have so much, she wondered, while Melinda Rose had so little: a ramshackle cabin that looked about to fall down, threadbare clothes, faded and worn, and all those babies? Every one, so far, buried on the hill behind their cabin. Sure, Daniel loved her, *had* loved her, she amended her thought. Everyone knew how taken he was with Melinda Rose, always trying to please her, his eyes looking at her with so much care and concern that no one could help but notice his love for his wife. What would Melinda Rose do now? Sarah wondered.

She slowed Glory to a walk to cool her, patting her neck while still deep in thought. Who would help her when winter storms cut her off from town, and blizzards roared across the valley, freezing and burying everything in sight? She isn't strong like me, Sarah thought, remembering the old worn dress she had had on at the Pearly wedding. Her skin had looked so pale. She shook her head. And her feet had been so swollen. There was no way she could survive alone. Sarah was certain of that, and her heart was heavy with worry. *I should have been kinder to her at the wedding,* Sarah thought, feeling ashamed of herself.

She thought then, of her cave and the Indian. She thought of how she had left that day—had run from him—and she wondered if she would ever see him again. She shook her head angrily, speaking aloud, her voice filled with disgust. "How can I be so selfish?" she questioned. "How can I think of myself and the Indian, when Melinda Rose has lost so much, and may lose more?" She shook her head once more and, at that moment, saw Moses Gentry riding toward her at full gallop.

"Sarah!" he exclaimed, "am I ever glad to see you! I was coming for help. Melinda Rose is about to have her baby. Hurry! We've got no time to lose." And he wheeled the big bay around and raced back the way he had come, with Sarah and Glory close behind.

Dismounting soon after, at Melinda Rose's, she asked him if Melinda Rose knew about Daniel yet.

"Yes," Moses answered solemnly, "I told her." He looked at Sarah, his eyes showing the grief he had felt in telling Melinda Rose. He reached out, touching Sarah's arm. "She went dead white," he said, looking down at his feet, then back up at Sarah. "Just stood there trembling, her face getting whiter and whiter. I tried to get her to sit down." He paused, his hand still resting on Sarah's arm. "I could have comforted her . . . held her close or something, if she had screamed or cried out," he stammered, the muscle in his cheek tightening with tension. "She just stood there," he repeated, "then walked toward the door and . . ." She watched his face, realizing the emotion he was feeling. "I saw her start to sway," he said, his voice barely a whisper. "Caught her before she hit the floor. Saw the blood then, on the floor by her feet."

Sarah was shaken by seeing his immense feeling of anguish as he spoke. This was not the rogue who teased her mercilessly, whose dark eyes sparkled with pure devilment at her discomfort. She was moved beyond words by the pain she saw in his eyes.

CHAPTER FOURTEEN

A scream pierced the air! Moses and Sarah rushed together into the cabin, no longer caught up in their own feelings. Sarah saw the blood on the floor by the door and the trail of it leading into the bedroom. Moses looked at her questioningly. "Get water. Get it boiling," she ordered, "We'll need *lots.*" He grabbed two large pots off the stove and, giving her a quick smile, rushed outside to the well they had passed as they rode into the yard.

"I'm here," Sarah called, to the inert figure lying on the bed. "It's me, Sarah," she said. A feeling of tremendous dread engulfed her as she took in the pitiful sight before her. Melinda Rose lay there, pale as new-fallen snow, her eyes open, though vacant, staring at nothing. Blood soaked her skirt and bedcover. "Oh, Lord," Sarah intoned, her voice barely a whisper. She shut the bedroom door and began removing Melinda Rose's clothes, pulling off the old, faded, blood-soaked skirt, and the dingy gray petticoat beneath it. I'll give her one of my petticoats and skirts to replace these, Sarah thought, as she unbuttoned the faded blouse and pushed on Melinda Rose's shoulders, lifting her arms and trying to pull the clothing from under her.

She was surprised at how thin Melinda Rose actually was. Sarah had thought her much heavier when she saw her at

Nancy's wedding. She tried to roll Melinda Rose on her side and pull the garments free again, but it was no use.

Suddenly, Melinda Rose grimaced and her body tightened in a contraction. She screamed long and loud, sweat dampening her face and hair, yet her eyes remained open but unfocused. Sarah grabbed a blanket from nearby, covering Melinda Rose with it, and pulled off the blood-soaked undergarments that bound her legs. Then, she spread her legs to see if the baby was close. She saw nothing but blood. She felt a trickle of perspiration run down her forehead and brushed it away, going quickly to the kitchen.

Moses had water boiling in every pan Melinda Rose owned, it seemed, and he jumped as she entered the kitchen, nearly upsetting the chair he had been sitting on.

"What can I do to help, Sarah?" he asked. "Is it time?"

"No," she replied, "but you can help. I need you to turn her so I can get the bloody clothes off her." She washed her hands in one of the pails by the door and dipped a cloth into a kettle on the stove that hadn't begun to boil. "Come," she ordered, glad to have his help.

They entered the room where Melinda Rose lay covered by the old blanket. "Can you try to turn her?" Sarah asked. "Then I'll pull the clothes out from under her."

"Can do," he replied, smiling a gentle smile that seemed to warm Sarah and strengthen her at the same time. Soon, the clothing lay in a heap on the floor. Sarah took the wet cloth and washed Melinda Rose's face, alarmed that she seemed unaware of what was happening. "Now what?" Moses asked, while thoughts of a different time flashed unbidden across his mind.

"Bring a small pan of water so I can wash her better, please," Sarah replied and tensed as Melinda Rose's body contracted once more and another scream shattered the quiet. Moses searched Sarah's face, tension showing on his own.

"It'll be okay," Sarah stated, looking into his eyes. "It has to be," she added. He realized she was as frightened as he. "You'll need to get a knife ready, and sterilize it. We'll need it," she told him, "and find a lot of towels or soft cloth. There must be some somewhere." Moses left the room to do as she asked.

Sarah knelt beside the bed and began washing the blood from Melinda Rose's legs and feet and from between her legs, hoping she would be able to see when the baby was close to coming. She remembered a story she had heard of a woman who was in labor for days. She shuddered at the thought. Surely, Melinda Rose would die if this baby didn't come soon.

Oh, God, she thought, what if they *both* died? No! No! She would not think such thoughts. She noticed that the blood seemed less, and of a milky pale color, not red and thin like blood from any cut she had ever seen. "Lord," whispered Sarah, glancing at Melinda Rose's ghastly white face, "I don't know much about birthin' babes, only what I've seen of Pet's calves, but if You'll give me a hand, I'm sure I can do it all right." She paused as another trickle of sweat ran down her forehead. "Please, God," she pleaded, "I'm not much of a praying person. That's true. Don't go to church any more than I have to," she continued, "but I'd be mighty grateful if You'd help Melinda Rose . . . and help her baby to be born. Okay?"

Her knees hurt from kneeling, so she shifted, realizing tears had dampened her cheeks. "I've never asked You for anything before, God, 'cept when my mother got sick," she paused, remembering. "Guess You were busy then, or didn't hear me," she added, "but I'm asking You now, please help Melinda Rose and this baby. Please!" Growing weary, she laid her head on the side of the bed, sniffling and wondering if God really did hear her, or even cared.

As she stood back up, a strong hand covered her shoulder.

Moses had entered the room and sought to somehow comfort her. "It'll be okay, Sarah," he whispered, his voice sounding hoarse but steady, and filled with a tenderness that surprised her. She stood still, looking down at Melinda Rose, not realizing she had reached up and covered his hand with her own.

They stood there until the next contraction occurred, filling the room with a scream from Melinda Rose that seemed to jar their very souls. Moses left the room then, and Sarah grew worried as more of the pale-colored liquid gushed from between Melinda Rose's legs. She put a clean cloth between Melinda Rose's legs, covering her again with the blanket. Then left the bedroom, wondering what Moses was doing, and was surprised to find the cabin empty.

Kettles of boiling water covered the stove. Sarah walked to the shelves in the corner, looking at the meager quantity of food on them. She shook her head in dismay. There was no way Melinda Rose could manage here alone. No way she or the baby could survive. Sarah lifted a medium-sized kettle from the stove, setting it aside, then found a broom and swept the kitchen floor, glad to be doing something so as not to worry so much. She opened the front door and was surprised to see Moses coming from a lean-to with a pail in his hand.

She stood there, watching him approach, and smiled at how a strand of hair fell across his forehead. He smiled, too, surprised to find her watching him. "Milked the cow," he explained, gesturing toward the lean-to with his head, "looked like it was about to burst. Don't know when it was milked last. They'll . . ." he amended his words, "She'll have plenty of milk for the baby. Is everything okay?" he asked, seeing the sweat on Sarah's brow.

"I guess," she replied, "at least they can be thankful for the milk. Not much else in the house."

"Got a root cellar behind the cabin. I'll see what's in it as soon as I get this milk strained. Must be some jars around, can fill 'em and set 'em in the creek beside the chicken coop," Moses replied, sounding confident and empowering Sarah with a slight feeling of hope. She wasn't used to leaning on anyone, except for her father, but she felt safe when Moses spoke and not as worried.

"I'll cook us something to eat," she said. "See what you can find, while I wash up this floor. Okay?" She smiled at him and turned to go back inside.

"Sarah?" he said.

She turned back, looking at him. "Yes?" she replied as he stood there smiling at her, a smile quite unlike the old devilish one she was used to. "Yes?" she asked again, questioningly.

"Nothing," he said. He winked at her and went into the cabin to find jars and a strainer for the milk. Sarah stood there, a bit perplexed, then she also went inside.

After the milk was taken out to the creek, leaving only enough for their supper, Moses brought in a basket of potatoes, carrots, and onions and then left, getting on his horse without another word. Sarah felt panicky, as she watched him go, but soon realized what he must be up to. A few minutes later she heard a shot and knew she had guessed right. A prairie chicken dangled from his hand when he returned. He set about plucking and gutting it and then took it to Sarah.

"It's small," he said, a look of apology crossing his face. She thought he looked like a boy who had just shot his first game.

"It'll do," she said, smiling at him. She washed it off in a pail of water and then put it in a large kettle to cook, with the onions. Then she peeled the potatoes and carrots and put them on to cook, and found flour and other fixings and made a pan of biscuits to go with their meal. "Are there any eggs?" she asked, and Moses said he'd go check.

Then she went in to check on Melinda Rose. Her eyes were closed now, though her stomach still clenched as contractions continued, each spaced closer than the one before. "Melinda Rose, can you hear me? It's Sarah." She watched her friend for any sign of awareness. There was none. She dipped a clean cloth in the small pan of water that had cooled and wrung it out, gently wiping Melinda Rose's face. There was still no response. Sarah covered her mouth with one hand, wondering what to do next. She knew that the longer it took a calf to be born, the bigger the chance of it dying. She covered her face with her hands, took a deep breath, held it a few seconds, and then let it out.

"Sarah, is everything okay?" Moses asked from the other room, concern flooding his voice.

She walked out to him, shutting the door to the bedroom. "I don't know," she answered. "I don't know." Feeling helpless, she began to cry.

Moses bent to her, enfolding her in his arms. "Cry, darlin'," he said. "It'll relieve some of the strain." She laid her head against his chest, feeling the rough fabric of his shirt and smelling the manly scent of him, and cried softly a few moments. When she quieted, she stayed in his arms and he held her, neither caring to leave the comforting embrace. She shuddered as Melinda Rose gave another scream, this one much weaker than the ones before. Sarah took a deep breath and stepped away from Moses.

"I'll see to her," she said, blowing her nose on a hanky from her pocket. Moses stood still watching her. "Thank you," she said so softly that he barely heard her.

"For what?" he asked, looking at her as if seeing her for the first time.

"For . . . everything," she replied, turning and closing the door to the bedroom behind her.

There was no sign of the baby, and no pink fluid that she could see coming from Melinda Rose. Sarah wiped the sweat from Melinda Rose's face, wondering if Doc Pearson was ever coming. "Are You here, God?" she asked, whispering. "Are You going to help?" she questioned, shivering slightly at the magnitude of the perplexing uncertainty that faced her. "Please help," she implored, hoping God, or her mother, or "someone" heard. "This can't go on. She can't take much more, and I don't know what to do," she admitted, a tone of desperation in her voice. Melinda Rose's body clenched in pain as another contraction occurred. They were only minutes apart now, and Sarah feared if nothing were done it would not be long before both mother and child died. "Mother. Oh, Mother," Sarah whispered. Sarah felt weak with hopelessness, defeated. "First my mother," she said, her voice raising slightly in anger, "and now them," she added, motioning toward the figure on the bed. "Does it really do any good to pray?" she asked. She turned and walked out of the bedroom then, her heart heavy and hope gone.

Moses watched her from where he sat, seeing the futility she felt in her facial features and movements, as she came out of the bedroom. "I dished up, Sarah," he said. "Come and eat. You'll feel better." She was surprised to see food upon their plates, hot and ready to eat. She had always prepared the meals for her father, as her mother did before her, and now Rosie. She realized Moses lived alone, but it had never dawned on her that he could set a table and would dish up the food while she was in with Melinda Rose. She stood there, a look of wonder crossing her face as he pulled out a chair for her. "Come eat," he repeated. "You'll feel much better."

She crossed the room and sat down on the chair, looking at the meal before her. It had begun to grow dark outside, and he had lit an oil lamp and set it in the center of the table. Its warm glow changing the shabbiness of the cabin into a welcoming and comforting place. "Eat," he entreated and took a bite of his food. She looked at the food before her and sighed loudly, then slowly began to eat. She was surprised how hungry she suddenly felt and ate everything he had put on her plate.

"Better?" he asked, as they finished.

She smiled in response, shaking her head at him. "You surprise me," she said. She stared at him then shook her head again. He laughed and she found herself laughing with him.

"Looks like we're gonna turn out to be friends," he said, the devilish glint in his eyes once more.

She smiled at him. "Won't be long till you irritate me again," she replied. "I'm sure of that. You know what they say, something about a worm turning . . . Oh, my God!" she squealed, nearly causing Moses to overturn his chair, she surprised him so.

"What!" he questioned, startled by her outburst.

She jumped up from the table, rolling her sleeves up higher on her arms, and rushed to grab the bar of soap near the wash pail. "We're gonna have a baby!" she exclaimed, "I know what to do!" She was smiling from ear to ear.

"Have you gone daft, woman?" Moses asked, trying to figure out what had gotten into her. "What are you talking about?" he asked, thoroughly confused by her excitement.

"I know what's wrong!" Sarah exclaimed, "I'm sure of it." She scrubbed her hands and arms as high as her sleeves would permit.

Moses stared at her, wondering if he should slap her. Maybe she was hysterical, he thought, but he doubted a good slap would calm her. Hell, the way they usually got along, she'd probably slap him right back. What would he do then?

"Find some cord, Moses. Don't just stand there, and put more wood in the stove! If I'm right, we're gonna have a baby by the time you get more water boiling!" Then, being careful not to touch anything with her clean arms and hands, she walked hurriedly towards the bedroom.

Moses stood still—as though transfixed—beside the table, wondering just how hard he should slap her to bring her out of the hysteria, and when the best time would be. As he was trying to decide, she passed beside him. To his further astonishment, she quickly leaned forward and kissed him a resounding smack right on the lips, hurrying into the bedroom. "Well, I'll be," he said, as stunned by the kiss as by her sudden excitement, "I'll be!" He was smiling broadly as he went to put more wood in the stove.

She had been right, Sarah realized, as soon as she got her courage up and reached into the birth canal. The first thing she felt was the baby's buttocks. "Breech!" she exclaimed, feeling a wave of fear run through her. The baby was coming backwards and—like a calf that came breech—could not be born. Every time Melinda Rose had a contraction, it was futile, and each contraction only weakened Melinda Rose more and lessened the chance of both mother and child surviving.

Sarah felt the buttocks again, searching blindly to feel where the legs were and the cord that connected the baby to its mother. It was almost impossible to tell much, the birth canal being so small and the baby filling it so completely. Sweat trickled down Sarah's forehead, and once again she began to pray. "Okay, God. You gave me the answer, and I thank You, but what do I do now? I turned a calf, once, but You know how hard that was. How can I turn the baby?"

Melinda Rose groaned and another contraction began, her inside expanding around the child and Sarah's hand as she involuntarily pushed, to no avail. Sarah was sweating profusely now and reached in further, finding the cord beside the child and not around the baby's neck. "Thank God," she whispered, removing her hand and standing up, wondering what to do next. "Moses!" she called, "I need your help."

He came in an instant, a questioning look upon his face. He was relieved to see she was calm now, though he noticed her arm was covered above the wrist in blood and a viscous secretion. "Breech?" he asked, glancing quickly at the woman lying so still upon the bed.

"Yes," Sarah answered. "I'll need your help. I need you to hold her shoulders. Somehow, I have to turn the baby.

The cord is beside him, not around his neck," she rushed on, her words tumbling from her in a kind of staccato rhythm. "Can you help?"

"Yes, ma'am," he replied with a firmness that filled Sarah with a bit of renewed confidence. She smiled quickly at him and he moved to the bed, kneeling beside it. "I've got her, darlin'. Let's get that baby out of there."

Sarah glanced at him, knowing that devilish glint was in his eyes, even before she saw it. She smiled and knelt at the foot of the bed, reaching into the birth canal once more as the next contraction began. It was not as easy as she hoped, even with his help. Melinda Rose screamed with each following contraction, though her screams were growing noticeably weaker each time.

Afterwards, her head lolled to one side, her skin getting paler. Sarah was panting with exertion, frantically pulling and shoving the tiny body that seemed so firmly entrenched within its mother's womb. She looked at Moses in desperation, seeing he, too, was drenched with sweat. The look on his face unsettled her.

"Moses?" she pleaded.

"You can do it, darlin', I know you can," he answered. She heard the encouragement in his words, but doubted their validity.

"I'm . . . I'm tired," she whispered, her voice breaking under the strain. "I'm so tired," she repeated, though she continued to shove the small baby as another contraction occurred.

"Think of the *baby*, Sarah. Don't think of *your* feelings! You can do this! I *know* you can!" Moses rankled her with his words, and anger filled her.

"How dare you!" she exclaimed. "Do you really dare claim I'm only thinking of *my* feelings?" She hurled the words at him, furiously angry! "Why, you pompous bag of wind! You walk around town with those dark, devil eyes of yours, and that sinful smile, stirring up all the women's hearts. Damn you!"

Her fury grew with each word from her lips, and as it did the baby's tiny body turned beneath her hand, shifting into the proper birth position. Sarah realized this just as another contraction began, and she hurriedly removed her hand. Her look changed from one of intense anger to one of immense surprise as the infant's head burst forth from inside its mother. "Moses!" she squealed, catching the child as it slid into her arms, free, at last!

Moses rose, pulling the blanket up around Melinda Rose's limp body, a grin covering his face as he shook his head and began to laugh. Sarah looked up at him, with a look of tremendous relief as the child coughed twice and began to cry. She saw, to her disbelief, a tear run down Moses' cheek.

"We did it," she whispered, laughing and crying at the same time with relief. "We did it, Moses, we did it!" He put a hand over his eyes for a moment, overwhelmed by his own emotions, and she was touched. She wiped her eyes and laid the baby on the blanket beside its mother.

"Hey," she said, her voice soft and caring, "we're not done yet." And she proceeded to tie and cut the cord.

When the baby was all cleaned and wrapped in a small blanket, she handed him to Moses. To her surprise, he reached for the little one as if he were used to doing this, and snuggled the baby within his arms.

"It's a boy," Sarah told him, smiling at the two of them. "Take him out by the stove so he'll stay warm, please. I still have work to do here," she stated, glancing back at Melinda Rose.

"Yes, ma'am," Moses replied, smiling, and left the room.

She heard the baby cry—strong cries that filled the cabin— and to her astonishment, heard Moses' deep, gravely voice— slightly off key—croon a well-known saloon song, and the baby quieted. She smiled, shaking her head, and began to tend to Melinda Rose.

CHAPTER FIFTEEN

It was nearly midnight by the time Sarah finished cleaning up Melinda Rose and making her comfortable. She was concerned by the lack of response from the new mother, but figured it best to let her sleep. She had lost a lot of blood, and between the child's delivery and the shock of losing her husband, Sarah was certain sleep would be the "best medicine." She wondered if Doc Pearson was on his way, but knew she would stay however long it took until his arrival. In the meantime, it was best to let Melinda Rose sleep, as sleep was a known healer.

Sarah walked out of the bedroom, shutting the door quietly behind her. Moses was slumped in the rocker, his arms wrapped securely around the newborn babe. She smiled, stretching her arms and back, and went outside. Tomorrow she would clean the bedroom, she decided, exhausted from the tension of the previous hours.

She sat on the porch steps, resting her back against the post beside them, listening to the peacefulness that surrounded her. It seemed impossible that she had been in a life-or-death situation just inside, while outside all seemed calm and serene. She looked up at the moon, its brightness lighting the whole yard. She saw the slightly darker areas upon it and wondered if that was land, and if someone not unlike herself sat there looking down at the Earth. She brushed her hair back off her face, retying the ribbon that had slipped far down her head earlier. "Thank you, God, for letting them live. I'm so grateful," she said. Then she added, "You really *do* answer prayers . . . I'm so glad."

She heard the door open behind her and knew Moses had come outside. He sat down on the step beside her, his face clearly defined by the light of the moon. They sat there quite a while, saying nothing, listening to the crickets chirping and small nocturnal animals scurrying about. A coyote barked off in the distance, answered soon by others, and the shadow of a bird crossed the circumference of the moon. The night air was warm and, except for the sparkling glow from many tiny fireflies, there were no insects to pester them.

Moses broke the silence. "You okay?"

Sarah smiled. "Yes. You?"

"Just fine," he replied. "Nice little boy."

"Sure is," she answered. "Thank you for all your help."

"Couldn't have done it without you," he said, as he reached over and took her hand in his, holding it warmly and securely before he continued to speak. "Tonight meant a lot to me, Sarah. Brought back a lot of memories." He paused so long she began to wonder if he would say more. "Knew a woman, a long time ago, a lot like you. Young, pretty, a strong woman capable of whatever she set her mind to."

He was squeezing Sarah's hand tightly, but unaware of it. She turned her head, looking at him, his profile clear in the brightness of the moonlight. "She was a gentle person, but had a fiery temper when mad." He was smiling, Sarah could tell, and had eased his hold on her hand. She sat quietly, waiting for him to go on.

"Lived by herself, most of the time, in a little cabin outside of town. Could shoot, and ride, and . . ." His voice quivered slightly, and he cleared his throat before continuing, "fell in love with a young man who didn't have much to offer. A fellow who earned his pay at different jobs: Indian scout, trail boss, stagecoach guard." He cleared his throat again and then sat there, silence surrounding them. His fingers rubbed hers, though she knew he was deep in thought and not aware of it. She looked down at their hands, hers closed securely within his, and was pleased with the simple intimacy they were sharing. He cleared his throat again and began to talk. "He left her for long periods of time as these jobs required, not realizing . . ." he hesitated, "not realizing how precious time is. She was heavy with their child when he returned the last time. Looked beautiful when she ran to him, laughing so happily, as she threw herself into his arms."

His hand was squeezing hers tightly again, and she felt pain, but couldn't interrupt him. "They held each other that morning, lovin' and savorin' every moment, every blessing God had bestowed on them." He shook his head as if in disbelief then went on. "He promised to stay, to work at any job in town, to be there with her from that day on." He hung his head, sniffling loudly. "They went to town that day to buy things for the baby. She crossed the street to go to the store while he went to check on a job at the livery stable. It was a sunny day and she wore a pink dress that looked pretty with her red hair."

He ceased talking and looked up at the moon, then out into the darkness for a long, long time. "Didn't know there was a gang in town that day, robbing the bank. Two Mexicans and a young black fellow." He paused, as though seeing clearly back into the past. "They robbed the bank, then raced down the street."

He was squeezing her hand again, hurting her, but she endured it as she watched the anguished look upon his face. "It happened so quickly. The young Mexican reined in his fancy black horse when he saw her, nodded his head at her, and . . ." His voice broke, but he soon continued, "then he pulled out his gun and shot her in the stomach."

"Oh, my God!" Sarah exclaimed, horrified at his words.

"She died almost immediately . . . both of them," he said. He wept then, holding his face in his hands, his shoulders heaving as great sobs of long-pent-up grief pierced the silence around them.

Sarah wept, too, silently, her arms enfolding him, her head against his. She felt his pain, as deeply as if it were her own, and knew they would never be the same. They had shared so much, and it bound them together forever by its intensity.

Only when the baby began to whimper did they speak again, her arms still holding Moses, her head close to his. "She was your wife?" she asked hesitantly.

"Yes," he answered and turned his head toward Sarah. "Never told anyone before," he said. "Held it inside all these years." He looked away again at the moon and out into the darkness. "She was my wife. Her name was Sarah."

Sarah reached up with one hand and brushed back a strand of hair that fell across his cheek. "I'm so sorry," she said. "I'm so very sorry, Moses."

He smiled at her, a sad smile that only intensified the sorrow in his eyes. "You remind me of her," he said. He stood then, taking her hand in his, helping her to her feet. "Let's go see to that young'n, Sarah."

As she began to turn, he stopped her and turned her to him. Then he took her into his arms and kissed her.

CHAPTER SIXTEEN

Doc Pearson arrived early the next morning. He was surprised to find Sarah and Moses at the cabin with Melinda Rose and the new baby boy they had delivered. He checked the baby carefully, declaring him "fit as a fiddle," but was not happy with the condition of Melinda Rose. She lay in her bed, staring out at her surroundings with a blank stare, not responding to anything, including the new baby. When they sat her up and placed him into her arms, she would hug him to her and rock back and forth, back and forth. Tears trickled down her cheeks, though her eyes remained vacant and unseeing.

Doc said the strain of Daniel's death and the birth of the little one happening at nearly the same time had just been too much for her mind to handle. He shook his head sadly as he said it. "Some folks seem to have more than their share of grief, Sarah," he continued, shaking his head again.

She thought of Moses: how his wife had been gunned down so senselessly, killing her and the baby she carried within her. She trembled slightly as she saw again, in her mind's eye, his overpowering grief. She wondered how he was able to carry that grief the last ten years, telling no one until last night when he told her.

Doc was speaking, she suddenly realized. "I'm sorry. What were you saying?" Sarah asked.

"I've seen cases of severe grief in my lifetime. Cases where the woman never did come 'round and recover," Doc repeated, glancing toward the bedroom and shaking his head sadly. "We'll have no choice but to take her to town and get someone to tend her and the baby until," he paused, "until she gets her senses back . . . if ever. Sarah heard Moses whistling out in the yard as he came in from milking. There would be plenty of milk for the baby, though probably not as rich and good, she knew, as his mother's own milk would have been. Well, they'd find a way to see to it he survived, she thought, if she had to tend to him herself.

"Excuse me, Doc. I'll be right back," she said and went outside. She felt a bit shaken when she saw Moses' horse tied to a post, all saddled and ready to go.

"Morning," Moses said, coming from the direction of the lean-to. "Fed the cow and chickens, and milked," he said sitting the bucket on the porch.

"You leavin'?" Sarah asked, knowing the answer even as she spoke.

"Yup," he replied, looking off in the distance. "You'll be fine with Doc here and all," he said, turning to look at her. She smiled, forcing herself to do so, and he returned the smile. "I . . . loved my wife," he said, never taking his eyes from her. "Always will," he added, pausing. Sarah felt her heart skip a beat and waited for him to go on, not daring to interrupt. "If I could love someone new . . . it would be you," he said. As her eyes filled with tears, she walked into his arms and clung to him, crying quietly. They had shared so much, and because of it, both knew they now had a deep, unbreakable bond of friendship that would last the rest of their lives.

She pulled back from him when her tears stopped, wiping her face with the back of her sleeve. His hand still rested against her waist. He seemed as hesitant to leave her, as she was, to let him go. Quite unbidden and much to her surprise, she thought of her Indian and the kiss they had shared, and felt ashamed of herself for having these thoughts at a time like this.

"Moses?" she said, looking straight at him. She didn't know what to say, and he seemed to know it somehow.

"It's all right, darlin'," he said, in that old flirtatious voice she knew all too well. He smiled broadly and winked, his eyes taking on that devilish look that used to irritate her so. She sniffled and began to smile as he turned, walked to his horse, swung up into the saddle, and started to ride away.

He turned back, however, and rode over to where she stood on the step. "Can I ask you a question?"

"Why, of course," she replied, surprised.

"Do you always call all of your best friends . . . 'pompous bags of wind?'" And before she could reply, he whirled his horse around and was gone.

Sarah helped Doc Pearson with the baby and Melinda Rose the rest of the morning. Then cleaned the cabin and washed the bedding, along with cooking food for them to eat. Melinda Rose was in shock, Doc said, and though they tried to get her to eat, it was impossible. All she seemed able to do was stare off into a void. Sarah tried to talk to her, to tell her about her sweet little boy and how he needed her. Tried to tell her how beautiful the day was—hot and sunny—all to no avail.

Overwhelmed, and more and more tired as the day went by, she swept the floors and did up the dishes after their noonday meal, then walked outside. She sat on the porch step, appreciating the slight breeze that cooled her.

Her thoughts again of Moses and all he had told her. She realized now why he flirted so openly with saloon girls. A man had needs, after all, and Moses apparently satisfied those needs in the only way he could, with women who no doubt appreciated the time he spent with them, but did not expect a lasting relationship. She also understood now why she had attracted his attention so easily. She reminded him of his wife, whom he still loved, who had also been named Sarah. She yawned and stretched her arms out in front of her. It was funny how things happened in life. Just when you thought you had someone all figured out, things certainly had a way of changing.

She thought of the kiss they had shared, wondering if she had not had feelings for the Indian would she want more with Moses than friendship. Again the memory of the Indian's kiss crossed her mind. Why, she wondered, was it so natural to kiss Moses, and so frightening to kiss the Indian? She remembered his strong arms around her, lifting her from the deep water, holding her so closely. "Oh," she sighed, "I'd better see if Doc needs help." She rose and went back inside, confused by her thoughts and feelings.

Doc had managed to get Melinda Rose to not only hold the baby, but to suckle him, though she still did not seem aware of her actions. She simply held the baby tightly to her breast, staring vacantly and rocking relentlessly to and fro. The infant would wiggle and squirm until his mouth found a nipple, then nurse contentedly. At least he was eating, to their great relief, and no longer needed to nurse on cow's milk from a bottle. Everyone knew mother's milk was best for a newborn, and besides, to Sarah's surprise, milk ran from Melinda Rose's ample breasts each time she held the baby. It was a relief when she began to nurse him.

He was a cute baby with dark-blue eyes, a velvety-soft covering of blonde fuzz for hair, and finely defined ears that stuck out from his head like Daniel's had. Sarah wondered what Melinda Rose would name him when she was well. Probably Daniel, after his father, she thought.

The baby nursed like he was starving, nuzzling frantically all over Melinda Rose's breast until he found a nipple. Sarah wondered if she would enjoy this oneness with a child of her own someday. She smiled, watching them. Did my mother enjoy nursing me? she thought. Did she even have enough milk? She realized her mother had been much smaller than Melinda Rose.

There are so many things I'd like to know, Mother. So many questions I'd like to ask you, Sarah thought, gently taking the sleeping baby from Melinda Rose and laying him in the tiny wooden cradle that Daniel had built, years before, for their firstborn. She covered the baby, patting his small bottom gently, and then went back to Melinda Rose, covering her breasts. She eased her into a supine position, so she could rest, and stop the rocking motions that never ceased when she was sitting up.

"Melinda Rose, can you hear? Your little boy is so sweet. You must come back to him. He needs you," she paused, watching Melinda Rose's face for some sign of awareness. There was none. "He has soft blonde fluff for hair, Melinda Rose. Do you hear me? And Doc says he's a fine boy, healthy and very strong." Her words fell on deaf ears, and her heart was heavy with sadness for her friend.

"I need to get back to town, Sarah. Do you think you can manage her?" Doc asked later that afternoon. "Seems to be one thing happening after another lately. I'd better check on my other patients, see if anyone's ill or broken a leg or something," he said, a weary look upon his face.

She wondered how old he was, and how long he could keep up the pace, always on the go and tending to so many folks. "I'll manage, Doc. Don't worry," she replied.

"I'll have to find someone to come out here and bring Melinda Rose and the child back to town," Doc said. "Find some accommodations for her, so she and the boy can be tended until she's well. I'll see what I can arrange." Sarah realized he was thinking aloud as he said it, trying to form a plan.

To their surprise, a man's voice spoke from the doorway. "I'll take them into town, Doc. I have my buggy outside. My mother can care for them." Sarah turned, shocked to see

Tommy Dawson standing there, hat in hand, an intent look upon his face. He smiled shyly. "Moses told me about Melinda Rose. Thought I'd bring the buggy and take them home." He paused, "My mother is airing out one of the rooms upstairs, getting ready for them. It'll give her something to do besides mourn my father."

He stood there looking at Doc and Sarah. They looked back, their mouths open, both surprised that he was so intent on helping that he had taken the initiative in having his mother get a room ready.

"Tommy," Sarah replied, "that's a wonderful idea! Come in. Come in."

He smiled at her and Doc, asking softly, "How's Melinda Rose doing? Moses said she wasn't doing too good, getting the news of Daniel's death and all. Is she gonna be okay, Doc?"

Sarah couldn't help but notice how concerned he was about Melinda Rose, and she felt a strange mixture of pride in his so visible act of caring, and a little jealousy that he could forget *her* so easily. Yes, she thought, it sure was true. Every time you thought you had someone all figured out, it could change in an instant. What a day this had been! What next? Sarah thought, as Doc talked to Tommy about Melinda Rose's condition and what care she would require.

After Doc had left, insisting Melinda Rose and the baby not be moved until morning, Sarah took Tommy in to see Melinda Rose. He walked in nervously, looking into the cradle, first, at the small child it held. The baby's fists were drawn up and the tiny bow-shaped mouth sucked as he slept, as though nursing.

"A fine boy," Tommy whispered, smiling sheepishly at Sarah. He stepped past her and walked slowly to Melinda Rose's bed. He stood there, looking down at her, seeing her open eyes staring at nothing, her gown rising and falling with each breath she took. To her surprise, Tommy bent and kissed

Melinda Rose on the forehead, then knelt beside the bed and began to talk to her as though she were awake, as though she could hear.

Sarah watched in astonishment, wondering a million things at once. Why did he act like nothing was wrong? Like he could help her just by talking to her so softly and easily? Sarah stood there, listening to Tommy, whom she thought she knew so well: this boring fellow who had nothing to offer but some old store, this weakling who didn't have enough backbone to go after his dreams. She wondered, for the first time in her life, if she had ever known him at all—had ever *really* known him.

"Melinda Rose, can you hear me? It's Tom. I'm here. I know you can hear me," Tommy spoke softly, his eyes never leaving Melinda Rose's face. "Don't be afraid, Posey. I came as soon as I heard and I'm not leaving without you. You're not alone, Posey. Do you hear me? Mother's fixing up her big old room upstairs for you and your little one. He's a fine baby boy, Posey, a beautiful little fellow and he needs you, Melinda Rose. Can you hear me? He needs you."

Sarah felt like she was having a strange but lovely dream, and when she woke up everything would return to normal. Melinda Rose would be with Daniel, and big with child, and Tommy would be boring, as usual, watching her, and trailing after her like some pathetic lost puppy. She shook her head, wondering how reality had changed so completely. It had shifted so totally, like everything else in her life in the past two days, it seemed. She sat down in the rocker next to the crib, trying to sort out what she had thought to be true, and what she was discovering.

Tommy still knelt beside Melinda Rose's bed, his voice firm and sure, not wishy—washy as she always thought it. His manner was that of a man whom a person such as Melinda Rose, could lean on and turn to. Someone who would keep her safe and who could be . . . who *was* . . . strong and secure! A rock to cling to when things were rough!

She looked at Tommy. "It's me," he had said to Melinda Rose. "It's me, *Tom.*" Sarah shook her head in confused surprise. To her, he had always been Tommy, just Tommy, not Tom. Not a man, but a boy. A weak, indecisive boy who let life, or his mother, make his decisions for him. A boy who never made a choice, but let others make them for him. "Someday," he used to tell her, "someday I'll do this," and each time he said it, Sarah had become more discontented with him.

Sarah saw Tommy take Melinda Rose's hands and begin to rub her hands between his own as he spoke to her, on and on, encouraging her tirelessly to hear him, to not be afraid. He was here, and she'd be okay. Sarah quietly rose, glancing at the sleeping baby, and then left the room, these new realizations unsettling her.

She remembered that long ago when Melinda Rose was a young girl, her father had called her Posey. Sarah had asked her one day, "Why does he call you that?" And Melinda Rose had smiled a wide smile and answered, "Because I'm special! Father says I'm like a beautiful flower!" Sarah smiled at the memory and went to put on a pot of coffee.

After a while, Tommy came out of Melinda Rose's room, smiling shyly.

"Any luck?" Sarah asked hopefully.

"No," he replied. "Not yet." Tommy picked up the coffeepot and poured himself a cup of the hot coffee.

"Have you eaten?" Sarah asked. "I have a pot of beans and some biscuits, if you're hungry." She watched him straddle a chair and shake his head wearily.

"How long can she stay like that?" he asked, looking up at Sarah.

"I don't know," Sarah replied. "Doc says sometimes, if there's too great a shock, the mind never heals. I don't know," she repeated.

"Damn!" said Tommy, surprising Sarah by his outburst.

"She's never done nothin' to deserve this, Sarah! Always worked hard and never got nothin' much in return for it." Sarah listened, sipping her coffee, as he continued, "'Course Daniel was good to her, loved her, always tried to do by her as best he could." He took another swallow of his coffee. "Don't know what'll happen if she don't come back to her senses. The little one needs her." His voice drifted on, "Seems a shame, don't it, Sarah? A person goes through life workin', strugglin' to survive, to do their best to satisfy others, and one day he wakes up and realizes he's done his best, but it ain't made him happy. It's like those dreams you always had, Sarah. So many romantic dreams, and here you are, in Melinda Rose's house tending a sick woman and newborn child, and what'd all those dreams get ya? Dreams!" he repeated, "Darn fool dreams. Ain't no knight in shinin' armor gonna ride in here and take you in his arms and whisk you away from all this . . . any more than I'm gonna lead that darn wagon train I dreamt of all those years ago! No, Sarah, *this* is reality! You work hard, do your best, and someday you get tired of things the way they are . . . and you decide right then and there that you've gotta make your *own* dream! We've just plain gotta make our *own* lives count for somethin'!"

He quit talking then, and Sarah didn't know how to answer or what to say, so they both sat in silence, drinking their coffee. After a while, he continued, "Sarah, did you know I was sweet on Melinda Rose? Way back when we were kids, in school?"

"No," she replied, completely surprised.

"She liked me, too," he said, remembering back. "Then Daniel came to Hastings. He was everything I wasn't: strong, tough, able to ride and shoot, and had a way about him that girls liked. I guess Melinda Rose was just 'bowled over' when he took an interest in her. He never looked at any other girls once he met her, courted her, and then married her. He loved her, I'm sure of that. Almost as much as I did."

His voice drifted off as he sipped his coffee again. "I'm

not gonna lose her again, Sarah. I'm not gonna spend the rest of my life always dreamin' dreams that can't be. I'm a good man, Sarah. A solid, steady sort, and I . . . well . . . I'd make a good husband to someone like Melinda Rose, you know, and a good father for her baby. When she gets well, Sarah, if she'll have me, I'm gonna tell her how I feel," he paused, "how I've *always* felt," he said, his voice filled with determination

"I'm sure you would be good for them," Sarah replied, and went to check on Melinda Rose.

Sarah slept beside Melinda Rose that night, so she could hear any sounds the baby might make. She was exhausted and fell asleep almost as quickly as she lay down. It had been a long day full of surprises and she slept soundly, dreaming muddled dreams that were tangled in themselves, making no sense: some happy, some sad. Faces stared out at her as she slept: her Indian telling her not to dream, Moses reaching for her, a desperate look upon his face, and Tommy shouting at her, "I'm Tom, Sarah. Tom, Sarah, Tom." She rolled and tossed, waking with a start when the baby began to cry.

Tommy had taken a blanket and slept in the lean-to, though Sarah offered to make him a place in the main room of the cabin. He had laughed and refused, saying he wouldn't think of it. He didn't want to cause any of the old gossips in town to talk. Sarah laughed at that, knowing that they were far from town and most folks thought he and Sarah were sweet on each other, so she was certain they would talk anyways.

They had decided that in the morning, after the cow was milked and chickens fed, and after they had eaten and Melinda Rose and the baby were all ready, they'd load a scant few of her belongings in the buggy and go back to Tommy's house. Someone would come back later in the day, in a wagon, to get the rest of her things, tie the cow on behind, crate up the chickens, and close up her place until she felt better . . . if that time ever came.

Daniel's body was laid out at the ranch where he had worked, and folks from miles around came to pay their respects. News spread quickly of the double tragedy that had befallen Melinda Rose: first her husband dying, and then the shock of it affecting her mind. And even though she gave birth to a healthy child, strong enough to survive, how she could not care for him.

In the days to come, it was spoken of far and wide, by both the curious and the caring, that she was being cared for by Mrs. Dawson, and could not do anything to help herself. She only stared fixedly, seeing nothing. It was also common knowledge, though doubted by some, that Tommy Dawson himself had brought her home for his mother to care for. It was further noted that he opened the general store at 9 A.M. instead of the usual 6 A.M. and closed at 5 P.M. instead of 6 P.M. and someone said they also saw him go home for lunch two days in a row. They said Miz Culpepper had to eat her lunch at the store, because he took such a long lunch hour. The gossips were having quite a time.

CHAPTER SEVENTEEN

The next day, Rosie Justus went over to the Dawsons' house taking two loaves of bread, fresh from the oven, and spent the afternoon there helping to care for Melinda Rose.

The following day, Mrs. O'Leary—who never went anywhere without her large family—showed up at the Dawsons' with a lovely quilt and tiny shift for the baby, both embroidered with blue and yellow flowers. She stayed two hours, helping to give Melinda Rose a bed-bath and wash her hair. It was a bit messy and required the carrying of heavy pails of water all the way from the well to the upstairs. When she had washed and rinsed Melinda Rose's hair, she dried it, then gently brushed it, all the time talking softly to the woman she barely knew.

The following day, Amanda Culpepper stopped in, bringing a chocolate cake she had baked early that morning before going to work, and a tiny gown and small quilt she had made for the new baby.

Each woman who came to help tend Melinda Rose did so from the goodness of their hearts, knowing in the harshness of the times they lived in, if tragedy came knocking at their door, they could count on their neighbors to help them, too. For that's what neighbors were for. You stood by and did what you could, and when your turn came, others did for you.

Reverend Cole came everyday, praying for Melinda Rose

in a young, earnest voice. He often held the baby, talking softly to him of God's goodness and mercy. Usually he stayed long enough for a prayer with Mrs. Dawson, too. He couldn't help noticing how well she was doing. Being needed by Melinda Rose seemed to be the best tonic for the depression that had seemed to plague her since the death of her husband.

Sun up to sun down, she worked tirelessly, tending her charges and seeing to her everyday work with a smile upon her face. She often hummed as she worked. How long had it been, she wondered, since anyone had really needed her? She thought of her husband and remembered how hard it had been after he had gotten sick.

She shivered as she remembered the fear she had felt, and the revulsion, when she noticed that summer day—years before—that his toes had turned black and lacked any feeling. Then they were gone, cut off by Doc. Soon after, it was his foot, and then his leg. He died before it could spread further. He broke a glass while he lay in the very same bed Melinda Rose now lay in, and slashed his arms, while she hung out wash in the yard beneath his window.

Tommy came home early that day, bringing a book for his father: something to occupy his mind and help the time pass quicker. Tommy found him, his body still warm, the bedding soaked red with his life's blood. He shut the door and sat quietly beside him, after telling her to go tell Doc Pearson his father had taken a turn, and his help was needed.

She wiped her eyes as she remembered, a feeling of despair washing over her. It wasn't until days later, after he was buried, that a well-meaning friend had said how awful it was, him killing himself and all, that she had learned the truth. Tommy never talked to her about that day, about what happened. He simply bundled up all the bedding when she took to her bed that afternoon, consumed with grief, and took it to Melinda Rose, asking her if she'd clean it. He explained that there'd been an accident and his father was gone.

Six o'clock in the morning, the day after his father was buried, Tommy had opened the store just like his father had done for so many years, and still continued ten years later to do so. Mrs. Dawson often wondered why he didn't have dreams like other young men, or the hankering to venture west and seek his fortune in a different profession. She had asked him once, and he had looked at her with such a wounded look that she had simply dropped the subject and never asked again.

She looked out the window then, catching sight of a beautiful red bird sitting on a branch, and watched it until it flew away. I would have been free, too, she thought sadly, if only Tommy hadn't wanted to stay. If only he hadn't stepped into his father's shoes and ended all my dreams. For she had had dreams then, too, and would have flown away like the beautiful red bird . . . if only her son hadn't needed her.

She shook her head sadly and thought of Melinda Rose and the sufferings that had befallen her. "I should count my blessings," she said aloud. "How do I know if I would have enjoyed the life I dreamt? Women—good women—took care of their families, cooked and cleaned and set aside foolish dreams." She sighed.

Her thoughts continued as she prepared the noonday meal for her son. I would have been too old to change, probably. Too old to learn. Slowly, in spite of these thoughts, she walked to a tall cupboard in the far corner of the room. She reached far into it behind a china platter and large wooden bowl until her fingers found what she sought. She stood there, holding in her hands a sheaf of yellowed papers, their edges tattered and soiled from years of concealment. She touched them tenderly, running her fingers gently across the carefully penned words. Reading them, like she had so many times before, as she waited, first for Thomas, then for Tommy to come home from the store: *Miss Delila White's Manual on a Gentlewoman's Place in the Teaching Profession.*

She folded the bundle and carefully placed it back in the cupboard behind the china platter and wooden bowl. "I would have been a good teacher," she said, smiling at the thought. "Other women taught. Of course, they were single, like Miss Denton. They had to earn a living, after all, if there were no marriage prospects." But, of course, she had married, and her husband had provided. She pondered the thought. "But, oh, how I would have liked being a teacher," she whispered, "if only . . ."

She remembered the day her parents had told her of Mr. Dawson, and how she was to be his wife. "It is all arranged," her father had said, not listening to her as she tried to protest. "He's a good man, Christina. An honest merchant from a good family," her father had explained, his voice raised at her obvious reluctance to wed.

"But he's *old*," she had wailed.

"Seventeen years is not that much," her father said, his face flushing in anger. "It's all arranged. You *will* be wed!"

Her mother stood aside as he left the room, her face pale and eyes downcast. She, too, would have protested, she thought, but could not cause disruption and further discourse by speaking thus. "You'll do as your father says," she said finally. "Mr. Dawson is a good man. A bit old, perhaps, yes, but he will know how to handle you. And, God willing, daughter, he will be kind. We must prepare for your wedding day. Come, Christina."

At that moment, the back door opened and Tommy came in. "Mother," he said, going to her and giving her a quick kiss on the cheek, "how's Melinda Rose? Any improvement?"

"No, son. I'm afraid not," she replied.

He looked crestfallen, shaking his head sadly. "When will lunch be ready?" he asked, not noticing the look of despair on his mother's face.

"Soon," she replied flatly.

"Good. I'm hungry. Bring it upstairs, all right? I'll sit by

Melinda Rose,"he stated, "she needs to be talked to, needs to know someone cares." He rushed up the steps two at a time.

His mother stood there, stirring the pan of food. "We *all* have needs," she whispered.

CHAPTER EIGHTEEN

Sarah was happy to be home again. She enjoyed the restful silence of her little cabin after all the excitement of the past week. She brushed Glory before turning her out to pasture, and then stood quietly, surveying her surroundings. Long vivid rays from the sun shone between the slats in the barn. I'll have to fill the gaps before winter, she thought, so the cold winter winds won't rush in, chilling the animals.

Pet was dry now, her calf due anytime. Being such a late birth, her calf would not have an easy winter. Sarah walked over to Pet's stall, leaning on the gate and watched a tiny dark-brown beetle balancing precariously on a lengthy piece of straw. She wondered if the Indian had thought of her since her hasty departure from the cave. She turned, looking outside the barn door, and watched a gust of wind swirl dirt and leaves across the yard. Then she closed the barn doors and walked slowly to the cabin.

Her thoughts turned to Moses Gentry and the change that had come over her in regards to him, since all they had shared at Melinda Rose's. She felt completely different toward him now. A host of feelings filled her when he came to mind. Feelings somewhat unsettling as she remembered the soft warmth of his lips and the tender strength of his arms as he had held her.

She smiled, wondering what it would have been like to

have been his Sarah. She wondered, too, if anyone would ever love her the way he loved his wife. Ten years his wife had been dead and still he carried her in his heart. She shivered slightly at the thought. Ten years, and no one had replaced her or ever would. Sarah smiled, tiny chills running up her arms.

She thought of how he had angered her just before the baby turned in the birth canal, finally able to be born. She realized now that if she hadn't been so angry, she would have given in to her tiredness and the baby would never have lived. He had done it on purpose. He had known just what to say to get her so fired up and knew just what was needed to keep her going and save Melinda Rose's baby. How horrible it must have been to have not been able to save his own baby, or his wife. She shook her head and then went into the cabin to get supper cooking.

Her father and Rosie would arrive soon to sup with her and she had dallied so long she had no time to waste. She grabbed a pail and hurried to get water from the creek. As she started down the path, she suddenly became aware that she was not alone. It wasn't that she saw anyone. It was a feeling that came over her. No birds sang or flew above her. All was still; too still!

Sarah stopped walking, her heart suddenly pounding in her chest. She scanned the surrounding area. The only sound was the beating of her own heart. The gun was above the mantle in the cabin, the knife on the table. She took a deep breath to steady her nerves and continued to scan the area, her eyes darting back and forth to each side of the path. She was about to turn and race for the cabin when she saw him.

The Indian stood to her left behind some thick brush, his gaze unwavering, and his face grim. She stood still, glancing around, looking for others who might have come with him. Seeing none, she met his gaze. They stood still, looking at each other. Neither moved for ages, it seemed to Sarah, though she was certain only seconds had passed, before he stepped out into the path and came toward her. She smiled, watching him, and then heard the sound of a horse and buggy approaching her cabin. She turned to look, knowing it was probably her father and Rosie arriving early, and when she looked back he was gone, vanishing as though he had never been there. She set the empty pail down, disappointment washing over her, then turned and went to greet her folks.

"We came early, Sarah," Rosie said. "Thought I'd give you a hand with the meal. Give us more time to visit," she said, bubbling with joy, as was her way.

Though her heart was heavy, Sarah was glad to see them. "I'm running behind," she replied. "I slept late this morning. Hello, Father."

"Hello," Samuel replied. "Bet it feels good to be home after all the doin's with Melinda Rose and the baby, eh?"

"Yes," Sarah answered. "Have you seen them? How are they doing?"

"Bout the same," Samuel replied as he helped Rosie down from the buggy, taking the cake she was holding.

"Brought dessert," Rosie said. "Going to fatten you up a bit, child. I'll bet you haven't had a good meal since I don't know when." Rosie took the cake from Samuel, smiling up at him. Then she winked at Sarah, and they all went into the cabin.

Sarah glanced back toward the creek before going inside, and then remembered she had been about to get a pail of water. "I'll be right back. Make yourselves at home," she said and hurried down the path to where her pail sat. She looked where the Indian had been, then all around, trying to see him again, if only for a moment. There was no sign of him. She picked up the pail and walked to the creek. There in the soft earth beside the rapidly flowing water lay a gray-and-white eagle feather. She picked it up, joy filling her heart, bringing a smile to her lips. She looked around once more, for any sign of him, but he was nowhere to be seen. She filled the pail and went back to the cabin, feeling happy.

Samuel and Rosie visited while the meal cooked, telling Sarah of the church social she had missed, who had attended, and what a good time they all had.

"I wish you had been able to come," Rosie said, smiling at Sarah. "'Tis too lonely out here, I'm afraid, all by yourself."

Samuel stirred in his chair where he had been dozing. "Are you sure you want to stay here, Sarah, now that I'm in town?"

"Yes, I'm sure," Sarah replied, her tone firm. "I love it here, you know that. And besides, I enjoy the peace and quiet. Seems like there's always some commotion going on in town: a birth or death or such. I'm much happier here!" she stated emphatically.

"Speaking of deaths, Sarah, saints preserve us, I forgot to tell ya', Lilly Benedict's mother passed away yesterday. Now how could I forget that?" Rosie questioned. "Mrs. O'Leary told me Lilly went up to take her breakfast and found her already gone. Died in her sleep, peaceful as all get out, not a hair out of place."

"Best way to go," Samuel said, interrupting.

"Well, it was an act of God," Rosie ran on. "A charitable act of God, if ya' ask me. Making that poor girl wait on her all those years. Never had a chance for a life of her own, poor thing. And so pretty, too! Very few prettier than Lilly Benedict," she stated. "Why, she's been taking care of her mother and their place, and that Lydia, too, since long as I can remember. Practically raised her sister since birth, if I be remembering right. Pooh!" she snorted as Sarah looked at her in surprise.

"You don't sound like you care much for Lydia?" Sarah asked, curious as to why.

"Can't say as I do. Can't say as I do," Rosie repeated, staring at the fireplace, pondering her next words. "Always been taught to be neighborly to folks," she paused, "to show Christian kindness toward all," she continued pensively, "but that young'ns gonna come to no good, I'm afraid. I can feel it in my bones. Sad, too, 'cause Lilly's been a fine example to the girl, always putting others' needs before her own. Cooking, cleaning, and caring for her mother, while that girl . . . well, she's a wild one. Pretty, too, but got no prettiness about her ways. Selfish as all get out, always has been." Rosie grew silent, shaking her head sadly. "No good'll come to that one, I fear, mark my words, 'less she changes her ways."

Samuel stretched his legs, getting up. "I'm going outside," he said, "holler when supper's ready, love." He squeezed his wife's shoulder, smiling at her. Sarah hoped her Indian was far from the cabin.

To her horror, a few minutes later—as Sarah placed plates on the table—a shot rang out. She dropped the plate she was holding and raced outside. "Father!" she exclaimed, running around the cabin to the path that led to the creek. There was no sign of him. Sarah turned toward the cabin in time to see her father come around the side of the barn.

"Sarah, what's wrong?" he asked, seeing her look of anguish.

"I . . . I . . ." Sarah tried to answer but no words came, so great was her distress.

"Sarah, what is it, girl?" he asked again, coming to her. "I shot at a fox. Is that what upset you?"

"I guess . . . I was just surprised," she stammered, knowing how foolish her answer sounded. He patted her on the shoulder, "Never saw you so jumpy, girl."

"You just go on now," Rosie said, interrupting him as she pushed between him and Sarah. "We women can't explain our actions every minute," she added. "You men just wouldn't understand. Now go on. Go on, love."

Samuel looked at her, a perplexed look on his face, and then brightened. "Oh!" he replied. "Oh! I understand." His cheeks flushing, he quickly turned and walked away, going back toward the barn.

"Are ya' all right?" Rosie asked, taking Sarah by the arm and leading her back into the cabin. "I never saw anyone look so frightened, child. What is it, if ya' don't mind me asking?"

"I . . . nothing," Sarah answered, not looking into the kind green eyes of the woman she longed so deeply to confide in.

"Ya' nearly scared me to death," Rosie said, bending to pick up the pieces of broken plate from the floor.

"I'm . . . really sorry," Sarah whispered, looking at Rosie.

"If ya' need to talk, Sarah, if ya' ever need to talk, honey," Rosie offered, "I'll be glad to listen." She paused, watching Sarah's ashen face. "It'll stay just between us," Rosie emphasized, squeezing Sarah's hand, "though I think I already know what it is," she whispered, conspiratorially, startling Sarah.

"What? What do you mean?" Sarah asked, her eyes widening in surprise.

"A long, long time ago, when I was but a young girl, there was a certain young fella' who came courtin' me sister, Margaret Mary." She paused, a look of remembering in her eyes. "Now, me father did not like the young man's family. 'Low-life no-accounts' they was, that were always in brawls at our local pub. Margaret Mary, on the other hand, was a spirited gal who had a mind of her own. Pretty as a spring moon, and good-natured to boot, who could have had her choice of any of the young fellas in town. But—lo and behold—as is so often the case, the young man in question had stolen her heart." She laughed at a memory, then continued, "One day, the young man come a courtin', thinkin' Margaret Mary was home alone. Well, there he was, a bouquet in one hand, his hat in the other, and around the shed came our pa, gun in hand from huntin' rabbits in the field." She paused, her eyes twinkling, "Well, I know now, that Father would not have shot him, but Margaret Mary was too surprised at seeing his gun to rationalize." She giggled, "Besides, the lad had just stolen a wee kiss, and there was Father! Seeing the lad, and not taking time to think, he off'n shoots into the air. I'll tell you, Sarah—for I was watchin' at the window the whole while—the young man screamed, dropped both his hat and the flowers, and ran down the road, never to return!" She was laughing wholeheartedly now, her shoulders shaking, and Sarah began to laugh too as she imagined the ill-fated encounter.

As her laughter subsided, Rosie wiped her eyes with a hanky from her pocket and continued. "Was that look," she said, nodding her head in explanation, "Margaret Mary had the same look on her face that you had when you heard the shot and lit out the door." Sarah felt her face flush and looked away, not meeting Rosie's eyes. "Yes indeed, honey, it was the same look you had. I guessed the truth right away," Rosie said, patting Sarah on the arm and smiling kindly at her.

Sarah tried to think of something to say, but before she could do so Rosie spoke again, "The only thing that worries me, child, is why would a sensible man like your father use such little sense?" She looked at Sarah.

"What . . . What do you mean?" Sarah asked, confused by her words.

"Why, love, he may be older—and quite a flirt—if you don't mind me saying so, but who would have so little sense as to shoot at a *sheriff*?"

Sarah coughed in total surprise, covering her mouth with her hand. Rosie thought Moses had come courting and her father had run him off! A feeling of relief came over her as she began to laugh. "Oh, Rosie," she said, hugging the older woman, "you are priceless, but you're wrong!"

Rosie stepped back from her, looking into her eyes, "It's all right, Sarah. I saw you and our sheriff at the Pearly wedding, and later when ya' spoke of him after being at Melinda Rose's two days delivering her wee babe." She patted Sarah's arm again, her blue eyes twinkling like moonlight on snow. "I know that look, child."

Sarah knew it was useless to argue with Rosie, but tried once again to set her straight, "We're just friends . . . really. Just friends."

"Aye," replied Rosie, "and before I fell in love with your darlin' father, 'tis just friends we were, too."

CHAPTER NINETEEN

The next day, Sarah rose early, rushed through her chores, and then left for the cave. It was an overcast morning, the air heavy and warm. She wore pants and a light-blue shirt with short sleeves and tiny buttons down the front. Her hair hung loose, falling gracefully around her shoulders. She had to see him. There was no use putting it off, she thought. Her feelings for the Indian could not be denied.

She smiled as she walked, thinking of the conversation Rosie had with her yesterday. Rosie, Rosie, Rosie, she thought, and to think she was so sure I'm in love with Moses. If only she knew, she thought, stepping over a small carcass of some animal that had met its death quite recently. She walked on, stepping gingerly among the many flowers that filled the meadow. A hawk flew overhead in graceful dips and whorls. Sarah watched it, thinking how wonderful it was to be free of restrictions.

She began to run, her feet landing softly upon the ground in her comfortable old Indian moccasins. When she reached the stream at the edge of the forest, she stopped, stooping to scoop up some of the cold water into her hands to drink. Rays of sun filtered through the trees. A misty, golden haze radiated throughout the forest. She wiped her hands on her pants and entered the woods, alert at all times for any signs of danger.

Her knife rested against her side in a case she had fashioned from deerskin. Another pouch containing sourdough biscuits graced her other side. She patted the pouch gently, knowing she planned to stay at the cave all day, and the biscuits would taste good as the day grew long. Birds chirped overhead, and a rabbit scurried through the low undergrowth.

She walked on, anxious to reach her destination, filled with the hope that he would be there waiting for her. A large doe bolted out of sight when it realized she was near. She watched it leap again and again in its hasty departure, the white flag of its tail visible as it ran. Others joined it. Ahead, a patch of sky, golden with sunlight, beckoned her onward.

She entered the clearing surrounding the lake below her cave. Peering beyond cautiously, for any sign of danger, she stepped out into the clearing. Everything looked as it always had. No sign of the Indian or others. She hurried up the path to the cave, her heart pounding.

The brush pile blocked the entrance and she knew he must have piled it there, after she had left so hastily. She moved it aside enough to squeeze into the cave, looking first for any intruders within. Her sewing basket sat where she had left it, her old quilt folded neatly beside it. The quilt she was working on for her father lay nearby, also neatly folded. There was no sign of the Indian, and Sarah felt immense disappointment.

She sat down, picking up her sewing basket, taking up needle and thread and the quilt she was making for her father. I must finish this, she thought, knowing that keeping busy would diminish her disappointment somewhat. She threaded the needle and began a series of tiny stitches, securing another square of material to the quilt. Only eight more pieces and the quilt top would be finished. Her fingers moved quickly across the material with precise movements, her heart heavy, though she tried to ignore her feelings.

When the sun shone directly overhead in the sky, she finished. Setting the sewing basket and quilt top aside, she rose and stretched her arms and legs, a slight stiffness noticeable in her knees. She surveyed the area around the lake, enjoying the peacefulness that prevailed. Birds flew here and there or sat on branches calling to one another. She saw a woodpecker, its black and white markings and red crest showy among the leaves of the trees. A cardinal and its mate—the male a brilliant red with black mask and dark—orange beak, the female a blend of muted browns and a smattering of red, paled by the beauty of the male—flew close by.

Sarah's mother had taught her which bird was which, and she was pleased she could recognize so many different ones. She thought it strange that in birds and animals, and even humans, the male of the species seemed to stand out, whereas the female was usually more plain. Except for saloon girls, she thought, though everyone knew they painted their faces and lips to stand out, too. Why she had even heard tell that some of them powdered their bosoms, though she doubted it, a blush of embarrassment crossing her features.

She smiled as the thought of Moses, with his devilish look and mischievous grin, filled her with happiness. She was so pleased that they had become steadfast friends. "Moses Gentry," she said softly, closing her eyes and savoring the joy that filled her.

"Sa-rah," a male voice spoke quietly from the entrance of the cave. She jumped, startled, not recognizing the voice, the sun behind the man casting his features in darkness.

"Who . . . who is it?" she stammered, her hand going to her knife and her heart racing within her breast.

"Not be afraid," the words were spoken with hesitation, the voice soft and non-threatening.

"Who are you?" Sarah asked, backing away cautiously, her mind racing. The man was taller than she, and she turned her head slightly, trying to tell who he was and if she had cause for alarm.

"I am Gray Eagle," he replied. "I am friend," he said,

stepping into the cave and turning toward her so the sun shone on his features. Sarah stood with her mouth open, stunned that he was here and spoke English! "Your father say Sarah," he answered, "at cabin when you hear shot and run outside." He continued, "You think he shoot Gray Eagle." He paused, "You sad, yes?"

She took a deep breath to calm herself. "Yes," she replied looking into his eyes. "You speak English," she stated in amazement. Noticing the taut bow he held in one hand.

"Friend teach," he replied, approaching her. She looked into his liquid black eyes, so gentle and kind, then at his chest, the long scar white against his dark skin. He followed her gaze, smiling, "You healer," he stated, "heal Gray Eagle good." Then he flexed the arm he had broken when he fell. "Sa-rah good healer."

She smiled at his compliments, aware that he was looking at her blouse. She felt herself blush slightly and was momentarily startled as he reached out slowly and touched her hair where it draped over her shoulder and fell over her breast.

"Red Bird," he said, feeling the silky strand of long auburn hair between his fingers. She stood, aware of their closeness. Aware, too, of the warmth that pulsed throughout her body as he touched her hair. She closed her eyes. Her heart seemed to sing within her, knowing that she felt something for him that no man, not even Moses Gentry, could change.

"We talk," he said, rousing her from her reverie. They walked to the center of the cave. The buckskin pants he wore covered his long legs, his chest bare above them. She shivered at the sight of him, remembering the day he lay so near death among the fallen rocks, buckskin pants his only covering, then, too. She blushed, wanting to touch his ebony hair that hung down his back, as he walked before her. She looked at the quiver, full of arrows, that hung across one shoulder and the deerskin pouch at his waist.

Gray Eagle, she thought, and remembered the gray-and-white eagle feathers he had given her: the first affixed to Glory's mane, the second left beside the creek. She watched him sit down, easily crossing his long legs in front of him. She sat, too, wishing she had worn her light-blue gingham dress. It hugged her body above the waist, making her look more feminine. "Sa-rah brave," he stated, smiling at her. "White women stay near home," he added, nodding in the direction of Hastings. She smiled, happy at his compliment, the second in so short a time. "Sa-rah run like deer," he said. "What Sa-rah mean?" She looked at him, confused by his question. He tried to explain when he saw she didn't understand. "When young, find eagle nest. Mother eagle dead, one baby eagle in nest. Feed, till it able fly. Make friend of eagle. Can see enemies through eyes of eagle. It warn me they come. Name Gray Eagle, now."

Sarah wasn't sure exactly how he had gotten his name, but she said it aloud, "Gray Eagle."

He smiled at her. "Sa-rah, Red Bird. Gray Eagle. Same." He moved his hands like two birds flying. They looked at each other, smiling.

"Where did you learn English?" she asked slowly, hoping he could understand.

He thought a minute and then answered, "English? White man teach. Wolf Hunter teach."

"An Indian taught you English?" Sarah asked.

"Wolf Hunter teach," he replied, "friend. White man."

"Oh," she replied, not certain she understood. They sat there in silence, each wondering about the other, yet unsure of what to say.

Finally, Gray Eagle spoke, "My father Lakota Sioux. Mother white woman."

Sarah looked at him, a startled look upon her face. "Your mother's a white woman?" she exclaimed.

He watched her face, an uneasiness growing within him.

"Wolf Hunter marry sister of Gray Eagle many moons ago. She die," he said, pointing to his stomach and then making rocking motions with his arms.

Thoughts raced through Sarah's mind as she took in what he was telling her. His father was a Lakota Sioux Indian, his mother a white woman. Apparently, his friend, Wolf Hunter—who taught him English—had married his sister, who died in childbirth. She shook her head, a sad look upon her face.

"Where is your mother?" she asked, speaking slowly, hoping he would not mind her asking. "Mother die many moons ago," he replied, a pensive look upon his face. "Shot by white men who come to trade with 'The People.' They try take her back to white man's fort. She fight, then gun go off. She die." He looked down at the floor as Sarah sat silently absorbing his words. "White men die, too," he added.

She felt the hair on her arms rise, and a twinge of fear run through her. "They were killed?" she asked, her voice rising.

"Kill Mother. Must die," he said flatly. She got up, alarmed by what he had said, and walked to the entrance of the cave, looking down toward the lake. She crossed her arms across her breasts, thinking how foolish she'd been to come here and to hope he'd come. What did she know of Indians, after all? Hadn't her father warned her of their savage ways? She took a deep breath, then another, not hearing the Indian approach.

"Sa-rah," he said in a soft, yet questioning, voice. "Gray Eagle not hurt Sa-rah. Sa-rah great healer," he stated. "Sa-rah brave."

Yes, brave and foolish, she thought, and she stepped away from him, into the sunlight on the ledge, in front of the cave. He stood where he was, watching her. She looked back at him, seeing the tenseness in his face. She also noticed the gentleness in his eyes as he looked at her. What am I doing here anyway? she mused. Why can't I be more like the girls in town, satisfied with their lives, not needing knights in shining armor to rescue them from dull men like Tommy and lives of drudgery? She shook her head, took a deep breath, and walked around him and back into the cave.

He smiled, then, and they sat down again, side by side. "Father very wise. Know white man come someday. Send Bending Willow and Gray Eagle to Wolf Hunter. Teach English. Learn white man's ways," he said.

"But you look like an Indian," Sarah stated, watching his face.

"Gray Eagle wise Indian. Know ways of 'The People' and ways of white man," he stated, his voice raised slightly. "Sister look white, pretty like Sa-rah, not like Indian," he explained. "Wolf Hunter take her for wife. Happy many moons till die." He was silent then, staring out of the cave at the blue of the sky. "Now Wolf Hunter have new wife. Happy again," he stated. "In early spring baby come."

"Oh," Sarah replied, "how wonderful."

"Gray Eagle not want squaw for wife. Gray Eagle want woman like Mother. Good woman, wise and brave. Woman like Sa-rah."

Sarah felt her heart leap within her chest, and she could not look up and meet his eyes. This was too fast, not at all what she expected, not at all like it was supposed to be. A white man courted a woman a decent measure of time. She felt her face redden.

Gray Eagle reached out, turning her toward him. "Gray Eagle want Sa-rah for wife," he stated. Then, before she could get her thoughts in sensible order and answer him, he stood and walked quietly from the cave and down the path, disappearing into the woods, leaving Sarah to ponder his words and the surprising things she had learned.

CHAPTER TWENTY

Sarah rose early again the next day, rushing through chores and bathing in the tin tub. She tried to keep her mind on the day ahead of her and not on the Indian and the day before. She dried her hair and braided it, twisting it into a large bun at the base of her neck. Her dark-brown skirt looked trim and elegant, and her white pique blouse, with its high neck and dainty buttons down the front, seemed a proper choice. She was going to the funeral of Mrs. Benedict, Lilly and Lydia's mother, and wanted to look appropriately dressed.

It was the first week in August and already the leaves were starting to turn in the forest. Strange, she thought, way too early for them to change. Must be an early winter coming. She grabbed her shawl and then hesitated before hanging it back on the nail. Too hot today, she thought. Bad enough, I'm wearing a long-sleeved blouse.

She thought of her own mother and knew how devastated Lilly and Lydia must be feeling at the loss of theirs. Mrs. Benedict had been ill a long time, Sarah knew, though some folks said she didn't suffer from a physical illness, but from an illness of the mind. She had taken to her bed soon after the birth of Lydia, and Lilly had to take over the responsibility of raising her younger sister, tending their home, doing farm chores, and taking care of her mother from that day on. Mrs. Benedict never left her room after that, it was said, and Lilly not only had to bathe her, but to empty her chamber pot everyday. Lilly never complained, and Sarah admired her for that, but she also felt sorry for her.

Lilly was so beautiful. Many times, it was said, young men came to court her. But she sent them away and then sat by oil lamp, late into the night, figuring the cost of seed, labor costs, and profits gained, if any, in the running of their farm. Many young women would have grown old before their time, and bitter, by the weight of so many burdens and so little pleasures, but Lilly grew more beautiful as the years went by.

She developed a quiet, serene nature and grew into an elegant woman. She wore her hair pulled back into a large bun with soft, wispy tendrils framing her face. She was soft-spoken, though it was known she could be firm, when necessary, and demanded fair treatment when discussing prices for her crops. Everyone respected her, from the lowliest farm worker to the head banker in Hastings, Johnathon Clark. She was honest and thoughtful, many times going out of her way to bake a cake for a church social, then sending Lydia to have fun, though she herself could not go.

Sarah admired her, as did everyone else who knew her, but wondered if Lilly would grow old never knowing love or having a husband and children of her own. Of course, Sarah thought, after taking care of her mother nearly all her life, maybe she didn't want the continuing responsibility of a husband and children.

Sarah heard a buggy approaching and went out to greet her father who had come for her. "Hello, Father," she said as she stepped up into the buggy beside him. She kissed his cheek, asking where Rosie was.

"We'll pick her up on the way through town," he answered. "She wasn't quite ready when I left."

"Oh," Sarah replied, straightening her skirt so it wouldn't be wrinkled.

"How are things going, Sarah?" her father asked and shook the reins, hurrying the horse along so they would not be late.

"Fine," she answered. "Beautiful weather, isn't it?"

"Yes," he answered, "though I hear tell we'll have a hard winter."

"I hope not," Sarah replied, "the older I get, the more I dislike our winters."

"Me, too," answered Samuel. They rode on in silence then, each absorbed in their own thoughts.

As they arrived in town, they passed by Dawson's store and Sarah asked her father if Melinda Rose was any better. "I hear tell she is," he answered. "Seems that . . ." suddenly he was quiet, and then he continued, "I'm sorry. I don't know if it'll hurt you or not, Sarah, but . . ." He paused again.

"What is it, Father?" Sarah asked.

"Rosie said Tommy is spending a lot of his time at home, taking long lunch hours just to sit with Melinda Rose." He glanced at Sarah, noting how unaffected this news seemed to make her. "Said he talks to her the way a . . . a man would do if . . . if he was interested in a woman. Often sits rocking the baby, too. Sometimes, he sings to him and feeds him from a bottle. I hope this doesn't distress you, Sarah," he said softly, questioningly.

"It doesn't, Father. I told you, Tommy and I are just friends. That's all we've ever been."

Samuel nodded, a relieved look upon his face. "He'll be good for Melinda Rose and the baby," Samuel said. "They could use a steady, solid fellow like him." He glanced at Sarah again, "If she gets over her illness, that is, and the loss of Daniel."

Rosie was as bubbly as ever, talking cheerily as they rode along in the buggy on their way to the church in the valley. Sarah listened and commented when necessary, but her thoughts were on her mother and how badly she missed her.

They arrived at the church just in time to join the others around the grave. Lilly stood slim and still, her face pale, her arm around the shoulder of her younger sister, Lydia, who fussed and fidgeted while the minister spoke, then broke out in wracking sobs when he finished.

Rosie hurried over to try to comfort the young girl, but Lydia grabbed Reverend Cole's arm as he, too, moved to try to comfort her. Lydia turned her back to Rosie, spiriting the young minister off toward the church. She leaned against him, looking helplessly distraught.

Rosie came back to where Sarah and Samuel stood, her eyes flashing angrily. "I declare," she fumed. "The nerve of that child! No good will come to her if she doesn't change her ways. Heaven help Reverend Cole if she's set her sights on him," she said, turning to watch Lydia and the good reverend enter the church, Lydia being supported by him.

Sarah excused herself and walked over to where Lilly stood. "Lilly," Sarah said, "I'm so sorry about your mother."

"Thank you, Sarah," Lilly said, her face still pale, though composed.

"Is there anything I can do to help you?" Sarah asked as Lilly shivered slightly, in spite of the warmth of the day.

"I would like so much to talk to you someday, Sarah," Lilly spoke softly, looking intently at Sarah. "I . . . her voice faltered, "I admire you so, Sarah. You're so strong and courageous, living by yourself, so far from town. Always so sure of yourself." She paused as Ophelia Denton approached, voicing her condolences, as did Johnathon Clark, who walked beside Ophelia. "Thank you," Lilly replied, smiling at Ophelia and Johnathon. When they walked away, Lilly spoke, "I feel a great need to discuss some personal things with you, Sarah, if you have time, sometime. I could make lunch, if you'd like to come to the farm. Whenever it's convenient for you, of course."

"I'd like that," Sarah replied. "I'll be glad to come whenever you wish." For the life of her, Sarah could not imagine why

Lilly would feel a need to discuss any personal issues with her. Then again, she thought, Lilly has never been free of the burden of caring for her invalid mother. Perhaps she wishes to discuss how I manage my time alone.

Lilly touched Sarah's arm just then, excusing herself, and Sarah watched her walk over to the side fence where Jonas Hart stood, looking uncomfortable and nervous, an old hat in his hands. Sarah could not help hearing what Lilly said as she thanked Jonas for making her mother's casket. "It's so beautiful, Jonas," Lilly said, placing her hand gently on the big man's arm. "I can't tell you how much it means to me."

Jonas looked down at her, a nervous smile crossing his face. "I carved the roses on the lid," Jonas said, stammering in embarrassment as he looked down at the ground before continuing, his voice low. "They remind me of . . . of you, Miss Lilly."

He looked at her and was stunned when she rose up on her tiptoes and kissed him quickly on the cheek. "Thank you, Jonas," Lilly said, her voice kind and caring.

Sarah was surprised, seeing Lilly kiss Jonas, and she quickly looked away, wondering if there wasn't more to Lilly than met the eye. Why, I'll be, Sarah thought.

CHAPTER TWENTY-ONE

Moses Gentry polished his sheriff's badge with the sleeve of his shirt, while Jasmine LaRue sashayed over to talk to him at the Lucky Lady Saloon. "'Lo, Miss Jasmine," he drawled, his voice a deep, velvety vibration, as he looked her over from head to toe. "Mm-m," he intoned, meeting her smile with one of his own. "You're lookin' right pretty today," he said, as she leaned back against the bar, so he couldn't help but notice all of her many charms.

"How ya'll been, Sheriff?" she drawled in her soft southern accent, sending shivers up and down his spine.

"Never could resist a lady with an accent, Miss Jasmine," he said, grinning daringly at her. "I've been fine. Yourself?"

"Just fine. Been wonderin' if ya'll might come see me sometime," she cooed, licking her lips and smiling temptingly at him.

"Sheriff! Sheriff Gentry!" a young boy yelled from the door of the saloon. "Come quick, Sheriff. There's a gunfighter looking for you, says he wants to talk to the sheriff."

Moses looked at Jasmine, shrugging his shoulders, a sad expression on his face. "Duty calls, darlin'. I'll get back to ya'," he said.

"Hope so," she answered, watching him walk quickly across the saloon to the door. "I sure do hope so," she said again, to no one in particular, and headed toward a table where a well-dressed stranger sat dealing cards. Maybe she'd get lucky, yet, tonight.

Moses followed the excited boy. "At your office, Sheriff, says he'll wait there for ya'," the boy exclaimed excitedly, as two friends joined him, all of them anxious to see a gunfight. Moses could see the tall man leaning against the hitching rail. He glanced at the man, noticing the black shirt and pants he wore, and the black hat that hid his face. The man didn't look familiar from the distance between them, but Moses thought he recognized the golden palomino beside him. The saddle was fancy, with a lot of silver trim, and as he got closer Moses grew more certain of the man's identity.

"Well, I'll be," he said, his eyes taking in the aged features of the man he was approaching. From beneath the black hat, hair white as snow protruded here and there. Even his mustache was white. Moses was surprised how time had aged the tall man: the deeply carved lines in the bone-thin face, and the wrinkles in the skin covering his hands. Only his eyes looked the same. They were blue, like a bright summer sky. Alert, but no longer threatening.

As Moses came nearer, the man straightened, no longer leaning against the rail and turned slowly to face him. "Moses Gentry?" the man questioned, surprised, his deep voice just the same as Moses remembered.

"Amos . . . Pepper," Moses answered, watching closely for any sudden movement on the old man's part. "What can I do for you?" Moses asked, stopping about ten feet away, his hand still on his gun.

"You sheriff here?" the gunfighter asked, cautious of any moves on Moses' part, too.

"Yup," he replied, standing his ground, never taking his eyes off Amos Pepper. Years back, under circumstances he no longer cared to remember, Moses had known him. He also had known his reputation with a gun. It matched his own, back then, and he wondered if it still did. The young boy and his friends peered from beside the watering trough at the far side of the sheriff's office. Their eyes were bright with excitement. They recognized the old man's name and hoped, as young boys do, they were about to see a gunfight.

"Wanted to tell the sheriff I'm in town. I didn't know it'd be you," the old gunfighter said, rubbing the side of his hand across his mustache. It was an old nervous habit Moses had seen him do many times before. "Been pardoned by the governor," he stated, "too old to cause many problems now. Time to settle down and enjoy what years I have left. Got papers from the governor, if you want to see 'em?" He reached slowly into his shirt pocket for the papers.

Moses approached and took them, reading each line. When he finished, he handed them back, asking, "Why here? Hastings is an odd place for you to settle, isn't it?"

The old man looked at Moses a long time before answering, "My wife's here. I thought maybe you knew that."

"Your wife?" Moses questioned incredulously, watching as the old gunfighter refolded the papers and placed them back in his pocket.

"Yes," he answered, "my wife, Amanda *Culpepper*. I changed my name to Pepper to save her any embarrassment," he stated. Then he unhitched his horse and looked at Moses, "You got any problem with me being here, Gentry?"

"Not as long as you keep out of trouble," Moses replied, his voice firm.

"Too old for trouble," Amos Culpepper replied, a sad, faraway look on his face. "I've come home to Amanda, as I promised I would, long ago," he said, looking down the street as though looking back in time. "I've come home to die," he added, and then swung up onto the palomino. "Maybe we can . . . reminisce sometime, Gentry. Talk about some of the old days," he added, a look of wistfulness crossing his features.

"Coffee's usually on," Moses replied and watched him tip his hat and ride on down the street. The end of a legend.

It was dark as the old gunfighter dismounted in front of the small house. Inside, Amanda Culpepper sat reading her Bible by the light from an oil lamp. She heard footsteps cross her porch, and closed the book, taking off the glasses she wore just for reading. She smoothed the skirt of her dark dress. Once it had been black, but that was long ago. Now it was faded to a shade of dark-gray from repeated washings.

She glanced in the small mirror that hung in the hallway just as someone knocked on the door, causing her to jump. "I wonder who that could be?" she asked, used to talking aloud to herself from the many years she had been alone. The shadow of a tall man could be seen through the glass in the outer door. "Must be Mr. Dawson," she said. "I wonder what's wrong."

Opening the door, she stared at the man who stood before her. She opened her mouth to speak, but no words came. He smiled at her, as he had so very long ago, and still she only stood as if frozen in place, the rapid beating of her heart the only sound she was aware of.

She looked at the silver-white hair as he removed his hat, looking at her questioningly. In her heart, she saw the young man who had married her so many years before, then left to go west and seek whatever it was that drew him away from the wife who loved him so dearly. "Amos," she said at last, her voice a mere whisper. She blinked her eyes, smiling slightly, as tears began to trickle down her cheeks.

"I've come home, Amanda," the old gunfighter replied. He searched her face for the young girl he had left, so very long ago, when he had so little to offer, and thought riches lay to the west. "I've come home, Amanda," he repeated, when she didn't answer, "if you'll still have me?" He unfastened his gun belt and handed it to her, along with his guns.

Word spread like wildfire about the gunfighter and his wife, Amanda Culpepper. Heads turned when they passed by, and Tommy Dawson had to get somebody to help at the store, a week after the infamous gunfighter arrived. Some folks said he'd been in with a gang of bank robbers who'd killed dozens of men, while others claimed he'd robbed trains and rode with a gang from down by the Mexican border. Still others claimed he'd been a hired gun, who made his living killing folks for pay. Whatever the truth was, it was made worse by all the gossip, and he could do absolutely no good, whatsoever, as the stories spread from person to person, growing in deed and size with each telling.

On Sunday morning, when he and Amanda walked into church, all heads turned to look at them. Tongues wagged so fast that Reverend Cole had to shout three times before the talking stopped and the sermon could begin. The sermon was a good one on "loving your neighbor," and people snickered when the good reverend said that, making him blush. He wasn't certain if they were laughing at the thought of loving their neighbor *if* he was a gunfighter, or laughing at him, because of the way Lydia Benedict had maneuvered him away from her mother's funeral. He blushed, as he remembered.

"Excuse me, Reverend." The old gunfighter had stood up, his hat in his hand, the silver-white of his hair shining like a heavenly light atop his head. There was a sudden hushed silence.

"Yes, Mr . . . ah . . . Pepper," the reverend said, uncertain as to what to expect.

"It's *Cul*pepper," the handsome old man stated, looking at all the faces around him. "Excuse my interruption, Reverend, but I need to address the good people of Hastings, since my wife and I intend to stay here." There were a few whispered exclamations among the parishioners then, but soon silence followed.

"Go on, sir," the young preacher said, nodding at the man.

"I want folks to know that I've been pardoned by the

governor for any and all past deeds," he cleared his throat, holding his head high as he continued, "and I've come home, to my dear wife, after many long years of separation. As you can see, I no longer wear my guns, and don't intend to, ever again. I would be obliged if everyone would accept my word on this. I . . ." He hesitated, reaching down and taking his wife's hand in his, then continued, "I promised Amanda, many years ago, that when I came home to stay, I'd take off my guns, and I aim to keep that promise, as God is my witness." He looked around, taking in each and every face, noting each and every expression. "Thank you, Reverend," he said and sat down.

The congregation clapped then, and a few of the men walked over to Amos and shook his hand, welcoming him to the fold. Voices rang out with joy and excitement. Few were negative in nature.

"Thank you, Amos," Amanda whispered, squeezing his hand and smiling happily.

"I didn't do it for you, Mandy," he replied, a twinkle in his eye. "I did it for *us!*" And he patted her knee tenderly, happy to be home, at last.

CHAPTER TWENTY-TWO

Days passed rapidly as fall greeted the folks of Hastings with a fine array of colors throughout the surrounding woods. Bright orange, rust, green, and red leaves vied for attention among the yellows and deep scarlets. Folks were overheard commenting on the good Lord's "painting of the trees," though few liked to think of the winter that would follow.

The first week of September, Pet gave birth to a hearty golden-brown heifer that wobbled unsteadily around its mama. Its legs were as knobby as a gnarled tree branch, and it sucked greedily when it finally found a teat.

Sarah had been to the cave at least a dozen times, but found no sign of the Indian. No trace of anything that hinted he even existed. Her heart was heavy, first with worry for him, then worry for herself. "I've been so foolish," she lamented. "I should never have trusted him, or even cared." But the feelings, even the thought of him stirred in her, kept her hopeful that he was all right and would return.

In the days that followed, she went less and less to the cave, finding no solace there, only upset and anxiety. In time, her anxiety turned to anger, and she grew furious with herself that he had become the center of her thoughts. She vowed never to think of him again, and never to return to the cave.

Her father and Rosie stopped by to visit on a couple

occasions and were surprised at the sharpness in Sarah's voice at times, and how unsettled she seemed. Rosie shook her head, smiling, telling Samuel it would be all right, believing Sarah and Moses had had a lover's quarrel.

Fewer and fewer colored leaves clung to the trees, and a chill filled the night air; a harbinger of the winter ahead. Sarah kept busy, hoping to clear her mind of thoughts of Gray Eagle. There were chores to do to prepare for the winter months ahead: wood to cut, meat to dry and put up, and vegetables to store in preparation for the long, cold months. She had filled the cracks around the barn and cabin with a mortar made of mud and straw, and split wood till her arms ached.

On her last trip to the cave, Sarah brought back the quilt top she had made for her father. Often, she sat—in the evening—working on it, when chores didn't leave her too weary. She planned to give it to her father and Rosie on one of her future trips to town.

One particularly nice, sunny day, Moses rode out to see her and brought her a note from Lilly. She had finished the majority of chores needing to be done and was happy to get Lilly's note inviting her to lunch. The next Saturday, dressed in her light-blue gingham dress, with her hair done in a large bun at the base of her neck, she went to visit Lilly.

When she got to Hastings, she stopped at Dawson's General Store to see how Melinda Rose was doing. Tommy rushed from the back of the store when he saw her enter. "Hello, Sarah," he said, a smile upon his face.

"Hi, Tommy," she answered. "I just stopped by to ask how Melinda Rose was doing."

"A little better, I think," he replied, "and the little one is growing like a weed."

Sarah couldn't help noticing the happiness, not only in his tone, but also in his features. He no longer looked spiritless and dull, but alive and caring. There was an energy that flowed from him, an effusion of feelings that surprised her.

"You should stop at the house and see her," Tommy said, his eyes filled with a plethora of emotions.

Sarah was so taken aback by the change in him that she felt she had never truly known him at all. This was definitely not the dull man who lived day by day in the same old rut, a man who would bore a saint to death. Why, his whole countenance has changed, she thought. He even looks younger, somehow.

"Come on, Sarah." She realized he was speaking. "Come home and see her, say hello. She might react to your voice and come back to us," he pleaded, but not in the old whiny voice she was used to.

"I'm having lunch with Lilly," she answered. Then seeing how crestfallen he looked, she added, "But I suppose I could stop by, for just a moment."

"Great!" he exclaimed. "I'll lock up and go with you." He took her arm, grabbed his keys from his pocket, and, with nary a glance back at the store, rushed her along toward his home.

Sarah was amazed! Tommy was not one to walk out of the store at ten o'clock in the morning, even if the store was on fire. She had to smile at the thought. Why, he *lived* at the store, from nearly daybreak to sunset, and often skipped a noonday meal because the store "needed" him, as he used to say. This was definitely not the same old Tommy she knew!

He propelled her down the street, a custom also not common to him. He said little, and walked so quickly that Sarah could barely keep up. She was slightly breathless when they got to his house, and she had barely a chance to greet his mother, before he hurried her along to the upstairs bedroom.

Melinda Rose sat in a chair beside the bed, facing the window, her features devoid of any emotion or recognition of her surroundings. Tommy knelt down beside her chair, taking her hand within his own, his eyes widening in excitement as he spoke, "Melinda Rose, look who's come to see you. It's Sarah, Sarah Justus. She came to say hello." He watched her face, hoping beyond hope for any sign of recognition, for even the smallest sign.

Sarah walked closer to Melinda Rose and sat down on the side of the bed facing her. "Hello, Melinda Rose. It's me, Sarah," she said. She couldn't help noticing how thin she had gotten: her face placid and her skin drawn tight across her high cheekbones. Her thinness was pitiful to see, as she had seemed overly heavy when she was with child. "I haven't seen your 'little one' yet," Sarah said, looking over at the small cradle in the corner.

Tommy jumped up at once, going to it and picked up the tiny infant, and brought him to Sarah. "I call him Danny," he said, a softness in his eyes that made Sarah nearly want to cry. He laid Danny in Sarah's arms. She looked at the child, remembering all the events of his birth.

She was surprised to see how he had grown. His head was covered with a soft fluff of reddish-blonde hair, as were his eyebrows, though so light in color they were barely noticeable. His hands were wide across the base with pudgy little fingers. She touched one of his tiny hands and was delighted when he grasped her finger and held onto her as if he would never let it go. His eyes were blue, but she had heard that all babies had blue eyes, and wondered if his would change.

"Oh, he's so cute," Sarah said, smiling. As she spoke, the little boy smiled too, a wide smile that seemed to warm, not only Sarah's heart, but also the whole room. "Oh, look!" she exclaimed, "He's smiling." Tommy beamed at her, glancing hopefully at Melinda Rose.

Sarah tried to get Melinda Rose's attention, telling her how quickly winter was approaching, how many of the leaves had already changed from beautiful reds and yellows, but there was no response. Soon, she said she had to leave and handed the tiny infant, whom she and Moses had delivered, into Tommy's waiting arms.

"I think I'll stay with her awhile," Tommy said softly as he laid the baby back in the cradle. "Would you mind walking back to the store by yourself, Sarah?" he asked, a hopeful look upon his face.

"Not at all," she replied, and she bent down close to Melinda Rose. "I'll be back, Melinda Rose. I'll come again soon," she said, doubting if Melinda Rose would ever recover.

Tommy walked downstairs with Sarah, seeing her to the door. "She looks better, don't you think?" he asked, a pleading in both his voice and his eyes.

Sarah gave him a quick hug, not knowing how to answer, afraid of destroying what little hope he had. "I'll pray for her," she answered.

"Yes," Tommy replied, "do."

Sarah turned away and walked back to where Glory was tied. Her heart was heavy, even though the sun shone brightly and people greeted her cheerfully. She smiled when they passed, thinking of how changed Tommy was now, from the Tommy she had always known. Sarah remembered how hopeful he had looked as he knelt beside Melinda Rose's chair. He's so in love with her, Sarah thought, so deeply in love. She smiled, dispelling some of the gloom that had overcome her, only a moment earlier.

CHAPTER TWENTY-THREE

Lilly was sitting on the porch when Sarah arrived, dressed in a lovely pink muslin dress, her hair pulled back off her face, braided and wrapped loosely around her head in a softly feminine style. She had ivory skin and was much smaller boned than Sarah. There was a delicate slenderness about her that Sarah envied, and she was glad she had taken extra time with her hair and had worn her light-blue gingham dress, instead of the pants and blouse she had almost worn.

"Sarah," Lilly said, her voice light and cheery. "I'm so glad you could come. How nice you look," she said, hugging Sarah quickly, in greeting.

"I'm glad you invited me," Sarah replied. "I've been looking forward to our visit."

"We can sit on the porch awhile, if you like?" Lilly said. "Or go in, whichever you'd like?"

"Let's sit out here," Sarah replied, at once at ease and feeling as comfortable as she would have at her own home. They sat down in the charming wooden rockers, in the shade on one side of the porch. "Oh, how comfortable," Sarah said.

"Jonas made them for me," Lilly said, her voice so soft Sarah wasn't certain she heard correctly.

"Jonas?" Sarah asked. "Jonas Hart?"

"Yes," Lilly replied, a slight smile forming upon her lips. "He's a wonderful craftsman," Lilly added, "very talented."

Sarah rocked, looking at Lilly as she spoke. She couldn't help seeing the tender look that came over Lilly's face as she spoke of Jonas Hart. She remembered the quick kiss on the cheek Lilly had given him, in gratitude for the casket he had made for her mother. My goodness, Sarah thought, I do believe Lilly likes Jonas.

"How was the ride over?" Lilly asked, rocking as she spoke.

"Nice," Sarah replied. "I got to Hastings early and stopped at Dawson's store to ask of Melinda Rose. She's at Mrs. Dawson's. Did you know?"

"Yes," Lilly replied. "Lydia heard the news when she was in town. How terribly sad," Lilly commented, looking out across the field as she spoke, a pensive look upon her face. "It's so unfair," she continued, "losing her husband and being unable to care for their newborn." She rocked slowly, watching two birds swoop down toward the ground, one chasing the other. They banked quickly, then rose effortlessly, winging across the sky. "It's so unfair."

Sarah rocked in silence, her thoughts once more on the tiny baby she and Moses had delivered. "The baby is really growing," she said. "He has reddish-blonde hair and eyebrows, and the prettiest smile."

"I'll have to go see them," Lilly said, "see if I can help Mrs. Dawson in some way." She continued, "I haven't been able to get away, what with Mother, and farm chores and all."

"I'm very sorry . . . about your mother," Sarah said. "Are you managing okay?"

"I feel so . . . free," Lilly hesitated, watching Sarah's reaction intently. "Free for the first time in my life," she stated, adding, "I hope I don't sound cruel? Can you understand?"

"I understand more than you know," Sarah said, "and it's not cruel to enjoy your freedom. You mustn't feel it is. Look at all those years you've taken care of your mother, and the farm. If you hadn't, you probably would have been married long ago and had a whole passel of children by now."

Lilly laughed. "Maybe I should be grateful my mother needed my care," she replied, laughing softly. "I'm not sure I could handle a whole passel of children."

They laughed together at her comment, looking back out across the field. The warmth and radiance of the sun shone brightly down upon the rich black earth, infusing the light-blue sky with golden rays. "Let's go in now," Lilly said, "lunch is ready."

As they ate the hearty vegetable soup, brimming with pieces of carrots, potatoes, peas, corn, and tomatoes, and dipped pieces of golden-crusted bread into its rich broth, they continued to talk of many things. Sarah was surprised to learn of Lydia's deliberate dalliances to town and her refusal to help Lilly with any of the farm chores. She remembered how Rosie had said Lydia would come to no good and sympathized with Lilly, aware of the sadness and concern she felt for her younger sister.

"I've thought of sending her to a boarding school back east," Lilly said, "but she says she won't go, that she'll run away first. And I do believe she's hardheaded enough to do it." She shook her head, her features glum.

"I'm glad I don't have a younger sister," Sarah replied, "especially one with a mind of her own."

"It's more of a burden than you can imagine," Lilly stated sadly.

When they finished, they moved back out to the porch, a tray with tea and cookies, to suffice, for dessert. It was still, as no breeze was blowing, and the sound of birds filled the air, along with the creaking of a board, as they rocked.

"Sarah?" Lilly said, lowering her voice, though no one else was around to hear.

"Yes?" Sarah replied.

"Have you got a beau, if you don't mind me asking?

Remember when I spoke to you at church about needing to talk about personal things? I wonder if we could talk now." She looked at Sarah, her gaze serene, yet questioning.

"What do you have in mind?" Sarah asked, avoiding Lilly's question about a beau.

"I'm twenty-six, Sarah. Do you believe that's too old for . . ." she blushed, her face made even more lovely by the pink in her cheeks, "too old to hope . . . for a chance to marry?" she asked.

"Heavens, no!" Sarah replied. "I'm twenty-eight, Lilly, and . . . well . . . I believe that love can come along at any age. We're never too old to care for someone, or for someone to care for us. Now that you have more free time," Sarah said, "I imagine a regular line of fellows, from town, will come to court you." She smiled at Lilly and was surprised by her next comment.

"I hope not," she said. "I'm not one to sashay around town, or waste my time with frivolous activities." She paused, taking a sip of tea. "I've too many chores to do."

"Oh, but surely if the right man came along?" Sarah said laughing, and waited for her answer.

"The right man?" Lilly asked. "And how will I know if he's the right man?"

"Your heart will let you know," Sarah replied, thinking of Gray Eagle and his last words to her so many weeks ago. "You'll know when the right one comes along, Lilly. I'm sure of it. Your heart will tell you so. When he looks at you, you'll feel warm and happy. And when he speaks, you'll hear a song that fills you with joy."

"You've met the man you love, haven't you?" Lilly asked, looking compassionately at Sarah.

Sarah looked at her a few seconds, trusting her new feelings of friendship and closeness with the woman across from her. "Yes, I have," she answered.

"I'm happy for you," Lilly stated. It pleased Sarah

immensely that Lilly did not ask who it was she loved, or why. "I've always been so busy," Lilly went on, "with Mother's care and the farm to run. Sometimes, it's morning before I finish the books. Or, when Mother was alive, before I got her settled." Sadness filled her voice. "I'm not energetic like Lydia. She always bubbles over with enthusiasm. Most men would find me quite dull, I'm afraid," she lamented.

"Oh, Lilly, you shouldn't compare yourself with Lydia. She's young and enthusiastic, true, but she doesn't have your compassion or caring," she paused, "or your strength and substance. What would have happened to your mother or the farm, if you hadn't been the person you are? Do you think either would have survived under Lydia's care?" Sarah reached over and squeezed Lilly's hand. "She also doesn't have your beauty. Not the outer beauty, Lilly, *or* the inner beauty. Your caring and compassion has cloaked you in a beauty that everyone, but apparently yourself, can see. You've grown older, true, but you have a quietness about you that makes you easy to talk to, and a calmness and loveliness of spirit that surrounds you in everything you say and do. When the right man comes along, Lilly, he'll see these things and he won't walk away, if he has any sense at all." She thought for just a second of Moses: his devilish grin and flirtatious eyes. "You'll have to watch out for the rogues out there, though, I'm afraid," Sarah said, laughing, and Lilly laughed too.

"Oh, you do make me feel so glad that we had this chance to visit," Lilly said, "I've always been too busy to socialize, but often hoped that we would be able to sit and visit. I've always admired you, Sarah. I heard how you could hunt and track, thanks to that old fellow, John Bruce, and I admired you so." She paused. "And envied you. I know little of guns and hunting, though I could shoot, and have, when it's been necessary to put meat on the table. Usually, we've had our meat brought over by . . ." she hesitated, "by Jonas. He's always watched out for us, ever since my father . . . died. Three women alone, you know, on a farm this size." She waved her hand out in front of her, emphasizing the length and breadth of her land. "I don't know how we would have managed without him, especially through the winter." She offered Sarah a cookie and sat back, rocking gently, a peaceful look upon her face. "He brings us supplies from town and cuts our wood," she said, a smile crossing her lips.

Sarah grew more certain that Lilly cared for him as she watched her. "Does he love you, too?" Sarah asked, hoping she was correct in her assumption and would not offend her lovely friend.

Lilly jumped slightly, turning her head toward Sarah, a slight look of alarm upon her features. "I . . ." she began, her cheeks turning a bright pink in her embarrassment.

"I'm sorry," Sarah said. "I didn't mean to embarrass you, or make you uncomfortable, Lilly. It's just that you . . . you get a look on your face when you speak of him. Perhaps, I'm wrong." Sarah stated. "I'm sorry."

"You're not wrong," Lilly replied, her voice so soft that Sarah turned toward her to hear. "I've loved him for years, Sarah, ever since I was sixteen. He's so kind and gentle. He has such a good heart." A tear ran down her cheek, followed quickly by another. "I've never told anyone before. You know how the boys at school teased him when we were young. Always made fun of his shyness around girls, embarrassing him till he finally quit school and stayed home. I felt so sorry for him back then."

She looked out across the field before continuing. "They've never seen him carry his mother out onto the porch so she can see the sunset." Sarah couldn't help noticing the radiant look of love that shown in her eyes. "They've never seen him bury a kitten one of his horses stepped on, or the sorrow in his eyes over the small kitten's death. Oh, Sarah, he's such a good man!"

Sarah felt tears well up in her own eyes and smiled at Lilly. "He's so lucky, Lilly, to have someone love him so deeply."

Lilly wiped her eyes, a smile once more upon her face. "So how do I tell him?" Lilly asked, startling Sarah.

"He doesn't know?" Sarah exclaimed.

"He's so shy," Lilly remarked. "I didn't want to scare him away. Besides, I was always too busy to be courted, or even to hope for a life of my own," she whispered softly.

"Oh, Lilly, you're *free* now," Sarah stated emphatically. "You should get on your horse and race right over and tell him! If that scares him away, then he's a fool!" They both laughed happily then.

Sarah decided to stop at her father's when she got to town after leaving Lilly's. She was in no hurry to get home, having had such an enjoyable visit with Lilly. She wished they had visited years ago, but knew things would not have been the same when Mrs. Benedict was alive. She felt great delight knowing of Lilly's love for Jonas Hart. Whoever would have thought a woman like Lilly, dainty and delicate, would someday—if things worked out for them—become the wife of a great giant of a man like Jonas Hart. Sarah guessed it was true, as her mother's books had said again and again; "There was no telling where cupid's arrow would land."

Jonas and Lilly, she thought. Was that really any stranger a match than she and Gray Eagle? She shifted in her saddle as Glory walked slowly along, neither in any hurry. It's funny, actually, she thought, how similar Jonas and Lilly are. Both have farms they run with efficiency and success, both go to town only when necessary. Both have cared for their widowed mothers, though now, at long last, Lilly is free. And, best of all, both have a gentle quietness about them that seems rare in so many others.

She brushed a bug away from her face, and her thoughts turned to herself and Gray Eagle. What do we have in common? Let's see, she thought, he can hunt and survive in the wilds, and so can I. We both speak English. She wondered again who this Wolf Hunter was: this white man who had married Gray Eagle's sister, and taught Gray Eagle to speak English.

She turned back to the likenesses she and Gray Eagle shared. He can . . . he . . . ah, he wants to marry me, Sarah thought, and I . . . she shook her head . . . and I don't know enough about him to marry him, she admitted to herself. Was he kind and gentle, like Lilly said Jonas was? Would he carry his mother out onto the porch to enjoy a sunset?

Sarah giggled at the thought. "Since when do Indians have porches?" she said aloud, causing Glory to perk up her ears, as if listening. "Oh, Glory," Sarah said, leaning forward to pat the horse's neck, "maybe Father is right. Maybe I am too much of a dreamer and hopeless romantic." She nudged Glory into a cantor, suddenly anxious to get to town.

CHAPTER TWENTY-FOUR

Rosie opened the door and ushered Sarah inside. "You're just in time for a coffee, child, and a piece of fresh-baked apple pie," Rosie exclaimed, pulling out a chair and going to get another cup, plate, and utensils. "Your dear father is at the livery stable getting the buggy fixed, but he should be back soon," she said. "Have you eaten, Sarah? I have some beans on the stove, and cornbread, too."

"Yes," Sarah replied. "I ate lunch with Lilly Benedict. We had a lovely visit."

"How nice," Rosie said, pouring them both a cup of coffee. "How's she managing since her mother's passing?"

"Fine," Sarah answered.

"Not sure how to enjoy all her freedom, I suspect," Rosie said, smiling, "and about time it is, too." Sarah smiled. "Saw that young'n in town, flirting with Tommy Dawson the other day at his store. But, I'm pleased to say he gave her no mind at all, seemed too preoccupied with his own thoughts to even realize what she was about." Rosie cut them both a large piece of pie that smelled delicious.

"Mm-m," Sarah said, taking a piece of the pie into her mouth. "This is delicious, Rosie. You certainly can cook." Sarah wished she could cook as well.

"Thank you, honey. Your father seems to agree," she said, as they ate, savoring every bite. "Did you hear the news of Miz Culpepper?" Rosie asked, her eyes lighting with excitement.

"No," Sarah stated. "Is she ill?"

"Oh, heavens no, child, far from it!" she exclaimed, putting down her fork and wiping her mouth. "The other night, some boy ran into the Lucky Lady shouting for Moses. Said a gunfighter was in town asking for him." She reached over quickly and patted Sarah's arm. "Now don't go frettin', child. He's all right. Didn't mean to worry ya'." Rosie continued excitedly, "anyways, the sheriff was talking to . . . to someone at the Lucky Lady, probably setting some no account 'round proper," she added. "Anyways, these boys come running in, saying a gunfighter was at the sheriff's office, waiting for him. Well, Sheriff Gentry, he walks right over there, brave as can be, not even a worry showing on that handsome face of his, and—lo and behold—there was none other than Amos Pepper all dressed in black, with silver spurs and two big guns all shinin' and ready to fire! Well, Moses says, easy as all get out, 'You want to talk to me, Amos?' And Amos was surprised to see it was Moses Gentry addressing him. You know who Amos Pepper is, don't you? A real bad fellow, years back, rode with, oh . . . uh, I don't know how many gangs, killin' and robbin' and all."

She took a deep breath and rushed on. "Well, come to find out, Pepper pulls these papers outta his pocket and says 'Here, Gentry, read this,' ordering him around like he was in charge and Sheriff Gentry, not being afraid of him, but not wanting any trouble 'cause them younger boys were nearby and mighta got hurt if there was any shooting, took them papers and read 'em."

She clasped her hands to her bosom while she caught her breath, then began to expound upon the story. "Well, anyways," she said, "seems them papers were sent to Sheriff Gentry, by the governor, telling him that Amos Pepper was pardoned of all his crimes. Can you imagine? Well," she hurried on, her cheeks red from excitement, "the sheriff asks him, 'You staying around here?' and Amos answers right out, brash as all get out, 'You bet I am! My wife is here already.' And Moses says, 'Your wife?' And Amos Pepper says, clear as day for anyone to hear, 'My wife, *Amanda Culpepper!*'

"Why, I declare, Sarah, I almost fell over when I heard tell of it! All this time I was her friend, and her always pretending to be a widow. Never said she was, but that's what everybody assumed, her always wearing black, day after day, all those years. And now, she's going around in calicos, and cloth blue as the sky, and pink and such. Makes her look so lovely with her hair all soft and pretty." She paused as Sarah took in all she had to say. "Always wore it pulled back in a bun, you know, all tight against her head, looking so severe."

"And, they went to church that very first Sunday, and him with no guns and tipping his hat to the ladies that passed him, like he was a normal person. He got up in church, before everyone, and told young Reverend Cole that he was settin' everyone straight. That he was pardoned by the governor and wouldn't be wearing his guns ever again! Can you imagine? That he was going to live a regular life in Hastings with his wife, and his name wasn't Amos Pepper it was Amos Culpepper, and he said it right out, loud as could be, so there'd be no mistakin' it."

Sarah was nearly as breathless as Rosie after her long narration and shook her head, taking in all that Rosie had said. "Is she happy he's back?" Sarah asked.

"Happy ain't the word," Rosie grinned. "I hear tell they're like two youngsters in love, if you can believe it. Everywhere one goes, the other's there, too. And they smile and laugh like a courtin' couple! I've been thinking of inviting them over for coffee sometime, sort of a 'welcoming party,' if you will, but I'm not sure what your father would think of that, him being sort of unbendable when he sets his mind to things. What do you think of that, Sarah? Amanda was my friend for a lot of years. I suppose it'd be all right, don't you, if your father agreed, that is?"

"If I agreed to what?" Samuel spoke as he entered the house. "What are you cooking up now, wife?" he asked, a smile crossing his face as he looked at Rosie. "How are you, Sarah? How long you been here?"

"Long enough to have the best piece of pie, Father," she answered, "and all the latest news."

"Aha," her father replied, "so what do you think of our new resident?"

"Hard to tell," Sarah answered. "I'd have to meet him to get an opinion, I guess?"

"Well, why don't we do that, Rosie?" Samuel said, surprising both Sarah and Rosie. "Amanda's your friend, and I'm sure you've been missing her. Why don't you gals get all 'gussied up,' and, Rosie, you bake that good Irish cake your grandmother used to make, and let's meet Amos Culpepper!" Rosie beamed at Samuel, taking his arm and kissing his cheek.

"Great," Sarah said, cheerfully.

"You're a kind man, Samuel Justus, and it's proud I am to be your wife," Rosie replied.

Samuel winked at Sarah and patted Rosie on the backside. "I like to see you happy," he said, then sat and talked awhile to his wife and daughter.

Sarah enjoyed seeing the change that marriage had brought to her father. He smiled and joked, his happiness evident not only in his features, but in his actions. She thought again of the similarities of people who loved each other. Loving Rosie had changed her father from a reserved, placid man into a happy, cheerful one. What would her life be like, she wondered, if she was to marry Gray Eagle?

Chapter Twenty-Five

Not long after, all the leaves had changed in the area and only a few remained on the trees. A cold wind blew in from the north, and flowers bent their delicate heads, never to recover from its icy blast.

Tommy left work, holding his jacket around him. He felt low in spirit and wondered what good it did a man to hope when life seemed to always deal one blow after another. He thought of Melinda Rose, how she lay in her bed, her face purged of its fullness. Day after day, in spite of his words of encouragement, she became thinner and thinner.

Her eyes were sunken now, with dark circles in the soft skin beneath them. Her lips bled where they were cracked. Beneath the blanket that covered her, he saw, each day, her body grow smaller, and he knew she would not be able to go on this way much longer. Doc Pearson shook his head sadly after every visit when Tommy asked him what he could do, what he could say to help her, to save her, to bring her back. She was wasting away. He knew it and was beside himself with grief.

He walked slowly toward his house, not wanting to go there for the first time in his life. He felt like going to the Lucky Lady, and drinking until the pain subsided, then picking a fight with the meanest person in there, till there would never be pain again. But he wasn't a drinking man, or a fighting one, and knew that only losers solved their problems at the Lucky Lady. He also knew that when they woke the next day they usually had more problems than they had the day before.

He passed the bank and nodded at Johnathon Clark, who was just locking up. "Cold night," Johnathon remarked, and Tommy shook his head in agreement and walked on. He pulled his coat collar up around his neck as he passed Rosie and Samuel Justus' house. A light burned in their parlor and the glow from it seemed to freshen the pain in his heart.

How many nights can I go home, he wondered, to the despair that lingers there? How many nights can I trudge up the stairs, only to see Melinda Rose lying there, dying? For he knew in his heart now that she was, and he knew he could not go on if he lost her.

His mother tried to cheer him, tried to give him hope, but he saw the changes in Melinda Rose and his heart grew heavy. He no longer had the strength to give hope, either to her, or to himself. He no longer slept, but dozed fitfully in a chair beside her bed, afraid she would quit breathing and die alone. He ate little food, but drank cup after cup of coffee to keep going, its warmth the only warmth in his life, except for Danny.

He walked into his yard, but felt too defeated—too weary of spirit—to open the door and go inside. He walked to a wooden bench near the front door and slumped onto it. "Dear God, what have I done to deserve this? What has Melinda Rose done to deserve it?" A sob tore from his throat, and he put his fisted hand across his mouth to stifle the next one. "I love her, God. I love Melinda Rose. I always have. We're good people, God. We try to do Your will, try to do our best. I don't pray often, God, but I'm praying now. I'm asking You, begging You. Please, please, don't let Melinda Rose die! Please! We need her, Danny and me. We need her, God." And with his face cupped in his hands, Tom Dawson cried into the cold night air.

Sometime later, he entered the house, hanging his coat on a hook by the door and steadying himself a moment before going up the stairs to sit, once more, beside the woman he loved. His mother dozed in a chair beside the bed, and Danny lay in his cradle just inside the room. Tommy bent, kissing the baby gently on his head, and pulled the blanket up to Danny's chin, tucking it in around him. The room was warm except for a slight draft, and he didn't want Danny to catch a chill. The baby smiled in his sleep, and Tommy wondered if he was dreaming.

"Mother? Mother," he whispered, patting her on the knee softly so as not to startle her from her sleep.

"Oh, Tom," she said. "I fell asleep." She yawned, looking over at Melinda Rose. "There's no change," she said looking at him, her expression pained.

"I know," he replied. "I didn't expect any."

"Oh, Tommy," his mother said. "You mustn't give up hope, son."

"I already have," Tommy replied. "Go fix yourself something to eat, Mother. I'm not hungry. Go. I'll just sit here with her." His mother got up, wanting to say something to comfort him, but words failed her.

Tommy sat beside Melinda Rose, his heart torn by grief, drained of hope, bereft of comfort. He leaned forward, unable to sleep, so great was his weariness. Taking her hand within his own, he held it gently, his head bent low against it. "Melinda Rose?" he whispered, unable to say more.

He sat there in silence, unaware of the wind howling outside, unaware of time passing, minute-by-minute, aware only of the pain in his heart. "I love you," he said, speaking softly in the dark. "I love you, Melinda Rose. Please don't leave me. I know you've been through too much, what with Daniel's death and all, and I know it wasn't easy being alone when you were with child." He sighed, "I know how you grieved when your other children died. Life hasn't been easy,

Posey, but you can't give up on it. You've got Danny now. He's strong and he's healthy, Melinda Rose, and his smile lights up the room."

Tommy sniffled and then continued, "And you've got me, Melinda Rose, if you want me. I'm not handsome, and I'm not rich. I'm not a strong man like Daniel was, but I love you, Melinda Rose, I always have. And I'll take care of you the rest of my life, you and Danny." A sob tore from him. "I love you, Melinda Rose. Please don't leave me. I need you." He cried then, his shoulders shaking, until he suddenly realized her hand had moved from his. He inhaled sharply, holding his breath to listen.

Then, in the darkness, she slowly reached out, touching his face. "Tommy," she whispered, her voice weak, but clear. "Tommy . . . I need *you*, too."

Dawson's General Store remained closed the next day, and folks all through town passed along the good news that Melinda Rose had regained her senses, and with good food and further care, she had a fine chance of recovering completely.

Doc Pearson had hurried over in the middle of the night when Tommy pounded on his door—yelling like a madman— to wake him. He nearly pulled his arm off, hurrying him down the street to check on Melinda Rose. Lights went on all along the street, as one oil lamp was lit after another, and people hurried to their windows to see what the commotion was all about. Voices yelled up and down the street, "Melinda Rose is awake! Melinda Rose is awake!" And Tommy Dawson was only one of the many people who gave thanks that night in Hastings when they said their prayers.

CHAPTER TWENTY-SIX

Moses rode out a couple of evenings later to tell Sarah the good news. He had missed her, if truth be known, and was happy for an excuse to go see her. He thought again of the time they spent at Melinda Rose's: the birth of the baby, and what they had shared on the porch later. He had never told another soul about his wife. Never could. But it was good that Sarah knew about "his Sarah." He wanted her to know. Wanted her to understand.

He thought about the life he had led after the death of his wife and baby. As it always did, a cold chill went through him and then lay like an icy blanket around his heart. He rubbed his chest to dispel the feeling, and urged his horse on. His thoughts besieged him, however, as he remembered the turns his life had taken those nine long years between their loss and his arrival in Hastings.

Hell, he wouldn't have settled in Hastings either, he supposed. He would have gone on the way he was, if old Sheriff Davis hadn't gotten himself shot and died in his arms, telling him it was two Mexicans and a young black kid who'd done it, and they were planning to come back and rob the bank.

Moses had followed them from town to town for nine long years. Two Mexicans and the kid. The Gonzalez Gang. The men who killed his wife, and the baby inside her. Nine years he had drank and followed them, and drank some more. Some days he remembered who he was, others he didn't.

He got a reputation with a gun, but wasn't sure if he had earned it fair and square, or if lady luck rode by his side those years. The only thing he was certain of was that someday, somewhere, if it took the rest of his life, he was going to find those three men! Find, and kill the "animals" that had killed his wife, shooting her down for no reason as she stepped into the street to go to where he waited, her stomach large with child, her lovely face smiling happily as she started across to him.

Moses saw the scene as clearly as if it was happening again, and groaned in remembrance. They had just robbed the bank and raced down the street. The old Mexican rode a spotted horse, the kid a bay. The young Mexican, dressed all in black, rode a large black horse that pranced and pawed as he drew up to where she stood, surprise showing on her face, but no fear. The young Mexican halted his horse in front of her. He tipped his sombrero at her in a kind of salute, then pulled his gun and shot her in the stomach, before racing off after his companions.

Moses had tried to move; had tried to walk, then run. He remembered picking her up in his arms, her face serene as though she slept, her head resting against his chest. He called her name, again and again, as the bright red stains grew larger, spreading across the front of her soft pink dress.

He remembered burying them, and he remembered waking up a week or two later in a shed behind some saloon, trying to get his feet under him, trying to get his bearings. For nine years he had lived like that, getting through each day as best he could. Then, old Sheriff Davis had died in Hastings, and he had put on the sheriff's badge and went back to decent living, waiting, and never forgetting.

"Moses," Sarah called out as he rode into the yard. She was in the barn cleaning out the stalls of Pet, her calf, Emmy, and Glory. She had on her father's old pants, cinched at the waist with a piece of rope, an old faded shirt, a size or two too big for her, and the moccasins John Bruce had made for her. Her hair hung down in a long braid, and Moses had to grin at the sight of her. He dismounted and stood just inside the barn, out of the cold wind. "What are you doing way out here?" she asked, leaning on the rail in Glory's stall.

"I came to see you," he answered. "Got some news to tell you."

Her eyes widened in expectation. "Good news, I hope? Hold on. I'm just finishing up. We'll go in for a coffee then."

"Great," he answered, watching her pitch a forkful of manure out the back door of the barn. Some gals looked pretty in fancy dresses, he thought, with their faces all painted up like dolls, but Sarah was pretty even in dirt-stained clothes with straw in her hair. His Sarah had been like that, too, had a natural prettiness that didn't take paint and fancy clothes. His Sarah—he had to stop thinking of her, had to bury her again in his heart and mind, so her memory wouldn't tear at him until it drove him crazy.

"Let's go in," Sarah said from beside him, and he jumped, not realizing she had come up next to him. He helped her shut the barn doors, and then they walked side by side to the cabin. "So what's the good news?" she asked, smiling at him.

"Melinda Rose is awake," he answered, "and should be good as new before long." Sarah whooped, hugging him in her excitement. He was surprised and hugged her in return. "Got coffee made?" he asked, looking toward the stove.

"Yup," she said, "pour us both a cup while I get decent." And she went into her old room and shut the door. He heard her moving about, splashing water, opening a cupboard door, then shutting it, and the icy cold memories squeezed his heart again, nearly taking away his breath. His Sarah—lying on their bed all soft and naked—her stomach a large mound that moved every so often, his hand upon it, feeling the movement of the child within. He coughed and sniffled, then took out his hanky and blew his nose. He had to stop the memories—had to stop them or he'd go mad!

He got up and went outside. The sun was setting, casting the sky in red and yellow hues, and off to his left he heard a coyote yip. She's brave, he thought, being out here alone. Sarah . . . his Sarah, would have been afraid out here. She liked to be in town—said it was "the only place to live, the safest place to live." He shook his head sadly. The safest place to live, and it had killed her. He looked up at the sky, finding no solace in its endless display of rapidly disappearing colors.

"Moses?" Sarah called from inside. He turned and went back into the cabin.

"You look much better," he remarked, and she smiled at him and went to pour their coffee.

"You hungry?" she asked. "I've got a good stew all made, and sourdough biscuits. Want some?"

"Sounds good," he answered, realizing he hadn't eaten all day and was suddenly very hungry. "Sarah?" he said, looking at her as she moved around the stove dishing up their plates.

"Yes," she replied.

"I mean it, you look pretty," he said.

"Why, thank you," she said, knowing something was bothering him. "What's bothering you, Moses?" she asked as she sat the plate before him.

"Nothin'," he replied. "Everything's okay."

She watched his eyes as he answered and knew the truth even though he denied it. "I'm glad you came to see me," she said and smiled at him, wishing his bad mood would end, figuring it was memories that laid him low.

"You're a good cook," he said, eating all the stew on his plate.

"Thank you. Let me get you more," she said. He ate

two large platefuls and three biscuits, and then washed it all down with the cup of coffee.

When he finished that, she poured him another cup and sat in silence while he told her about Melinda Rose's recovery. She was happy for Melinda Rose and the baby, but even happier for Tommy. She knew he would do everything possible to please Melinda Rose, and in doing so, would be happy himself.

"Oh," Moses said, "Tommy named the boy Danny while Melinda Rose was ill, and now she's made it official. He's now Daniel Thomas. Daniel after his father and Thomas after Tommy, of course."

Sarah was delighted. Tommy might not have been the man for her, but she had no doubt that he could and would be all the man Melinda Rose could ever want or need. "I'm so happy for them," she said. "They'll have a good life together." For just one fleeting moment, Moses thought again of his wife, then shut his mind to his sorrow and long-dead dreams.

It was late when Moses left for town. He had stayed longer than he intended, soothed by the comfort and warmth of her home, and the enjoyment of Sarah's company. They talked a long time, Moses in her father's rocker in front of the fireplace, and her in her mother's smaller one as she stitched on a quilt and listened to him.

He told her he'd been born down near the Rio Grande. That his mother had been short and feisty. His father, Frank Gentry, was tall like him, a clerk in a general store a lot like Dawson's. He had two younger brothers, Lou and Billy. Lou had died of a rattlesnake bite, and Billy had drowned in the river behind their house, not long after. Their dad had taken to drinking when the last boy died, and their mother had taken in washing and sewing to keep food on the table.

"I was away working on a cattle ranch when Billy died," he said. "We were close and I still miss him. Never did get to spend much time with Lou. I was away a lot of the time he was growing up. He was a good-lookin' kid, lots of blonde curls and the prettiest blue eyes you ever saw on a boy."

Moses stretched his long legs out toward the fireplace, enjoying the warmth from it. "I sent money home from wherever I worked," he said, smiling. "Sent it in my paw's name, never knowing till years later that he used it to buy his booze, and Maw never saw any of it."

"How sad," Sarah replied. "Are your parents alive?"

"Nope. Got no one now," he answered, his tone melancholy. "Maw died a few years after Billy," he stated. "Later, Paw drank himself to death. I planned to go back, to visit their graves, but never did." He stared at the log, crackling in the fireplace, his thoughts subdued. "Got no one now."

"You've got *me*, Moses Gentry," Sarah stated, "and don't you ever forget it!"

CHAPTER TWENTY-SEVEN

Days dragged on as the remaining leaves dropped from the trees, and soon after Hastings got its first snow. It was a heavy, wet snow that began during the night and stopped just after dawn. It fell quickly to the height of a man's ankle. When it stopped, cold wind blew the lighter top snow up against the windows.

Lydia lolled in her bed, the covers pulled tightly up under her chin, her legs drawn up beneath her long white gown. She hated cold weather and vowed, as she had every year, that someday she would live in the far west. She'd heard tell it was warm all year round. You could even swim on Christmas Day without catching a chill.

She was warm beneath her many covers, warmer still when she thought of her mother's funeral and her snaring of Reverend Cole. Oh, it's true he didn't know it had all come together as she had planned, not yet anyway. But that was of no concern to Lydia. She had learned many ways to entice and entangle a fellow, especially a preacher. They were the easiest of all to turn inside-out until you could lead them where you wanted, with a smile or a tear.

She smiled, running her hands over her slightly rounded stomach and small firm breasts. "Reverend David Cole, you sure got caught in my trap," she whispered, "like a fly in a spider web." She snuggled down further beneath the bedding and closed her eyes as waves of warmth enveloped her. She was now Mrs. David Cole and free of Lilly's rules! Free of that stinking farm! She hated the farm nearly as much as she hated the cold weather.

Lilly might not mind being an old maid, spending her nights figuring bills and the cost of seeds, but that isn't the way I want to spend my nights, Lydia thought, no siree! A couple months ago, in the woods behind the schoolhouse, she had tasted what a man had to offer, and loved every minute of it! She knew Lilly would be shocked if she knew. Why, if she had found out she surely would have sent her away to that boarding school she talked about, without a second thought!

Well, the man was long gone—as were a few others— back to his wife and kids, knowing if he breathed a word to anyone about their afternoon in the woods, his wife would be told, forthwith, and she would claim he had taken her against her will. She moaned as her hands moved faster, each breast responding, the nipples tingling and becoming harder beneath her fingertips.

She thought of her mother's funeral: how she had maneuvered the good Reverend Cole, with his boyish charms and so decent intentions, into helping her to the church while the others stayed at the grave giving Lilly their condolences. She laughed as she remembered how she had whispered, making her voice sound weaker as she spoke, that she felt so alone now that her dear mother was gone. Then she stumbled, knowing Reverend Cole would grasp her around her waist, his slim but adequate arms supporting her.

"I'm afraid I'm . . ." she had paused as long as she dared, "going to faint," she had said, going limp in his arms as soon as they were in the church and away from prying eyes. He picked her up and carried her to the closest bench, as she knew he would, then held her hands, saying her name over and over. She had lain there, fluttering her eyes so she could see his expression, trying not to laugh at the serious look upon his boyish face.

Then she whispered, "Can't breathe, David. You must loosen my bodice a bit or I shall perish." She had repeated, "Can't breathe," one more time for good measure and, after just a moment's hesitation, he had undone her bodice to the waist, his hands shaking so much that she was certain he would never succeed in undoing it. She had moaned then, taking in a large breath of air, making her breasts swell and push up at him. Then, she waited.

Just when she thought her scheme had not worked, forcing herself not to peek to see the look on his face, she felt his hands encircle her breasts, gently clutching at them. She began to moan and move against him, until she heard him groan and felt his lips crush down upon hers. It was then that she opened her eyes in shocked disbelief, pretending to cry and scream, knowing she could not, with his lips pressed tightly against hers.

She pulled back as best she could, exclaiming, "What have you done? Oh, no! Oh, no!" And she grasped her bodice to her, forcing tears to come. Young Reverend Cole looked about to cry, himself, and she had all she could do not to burst into gales of laughter.

"Oh, God!" he had exclaimed. "Lydia, you said to loosen your bodice." He looked ill. "You said . . . you couldn't breathe," he stammered, his face red, his eyes wide with fear and upset, and Lydia had enjoyed every minute of it! Except, of course, for stopping him from further advances.

"You've ruined me," she had hissed at him. Then burst into tears again, holding one hand out in front of her, as if to ward off his evil person.

"I'm sorry," he had choked. "I'm so sorry! I don't know what came over me, Lydia! You said . . . I . . . I should have known better," he rambled on, trying to right his grievous wrong and comfort her.

"Now I can never marry," she had said, a forlorn look crossing her face. "I shall die," she whispered, making her voice quiver and her body shake. "I can't live now."

He had groaned at her words, then as suddenly, took her hands in his. "You can *marry* me!" he exclaimed. "You will forget my unforgivable behavior in time, Lydia. We will have a good life here, in the service of the Lord. No one has to know of my shameful conduct today."

She had looked at him a long time, pouting and sniffling, as a tear ran down her cheek. Then, in a small, sad voice, she had replied, "All right, David, if you insist. But just so you won't get into trouble." Then she fastened her bodice, smoothed her skirt, and they walked outside, a sweetly innocent smile on Lydia's lovely face.

CHAPTER TWENTY-EIGHT

Lilly finished the inside chores she had begun late the night before. She had worked all night and was satisfied with her accomplishments, knowing the blankets she mended were sorely needed now that cold winds blew fiercely outside. The farm books had been brought up to date, and heavy chores outside would be done by the man she had hired, on Jonas' recommendation, two years before.

She smiled as she thought of Jonas. How would she ever have managed, if not for him? She thought, too, of her visit with Sarah Justus a month earlier. She had told Sarah of her feelings for Jonas, expecting a shocked reaction, or at least mild disbelief. Sarah had seemed to understand, however, even to the extent of commenting on the heart telling a person when the right person came along.

Lilly had wondered later who it was that Sarah loved. She had admitted there was someone, but now looking back on their visit, Lilly realized Sarah had been careful to change the subject, not divulging the fellow's identity.

She sat at the kitchen table, pushing aside the farm books, tired of figures and charts, as thoughts assailed her. I know it's not Tommy Dawson. Everyone believed they were a couple over the years, but Sarah had always insisted they were just friends. His recent actions regarding Melinda Rose certainly gives credence to that.

Poor Melinda Rose, she thought, thinking how unfair life had been to her. Lilly sighed, wondering why life delivered such devastating blows to some folks, while others seemed to breeze through with no worries. She thought of her own life, too.

God had been good to her—had blessed her with the necessary strength and fortitude to bear the load that circumstance had heaped upon her young shoulders. She had carried that load for almost twenty years: the care of Lydia and the running of the farm, once her father was gone. She had run the farm according to the plans he had so diligently prescribed, sitting alone through the long hours before dawn, again and again, reading the notes he had left her.

Folks around Hastings believed her father had gone south to purchase a special seed-crop, and had died in a storm that ripped through the town he was staying at, his body never being recovered to be brought home and given a decent burial. Lilly had never told anyone the truth behind his disappearance, for indeed he had disappeared long ago, when her mother took ill.

An occasional letter had come, his only contact, one-sided as it was, for there was never a return address where she could write back. The last letter had arrived four years ago, almost to the day, and she finally stopped expecting another, believing in her heart that he was indeed now dead.

She rose from the chair at the kitchen table and went to stand by the window. She thought of Lydia, so beautiful, but headstrong, and so terribly unsettled. Dawn was breaking as she stood there, the sky touched with a suffusion of color to her right and diminishing darkness to her left.

A rooster crowed, welcoming the light, and she stretched her body. She had grown stiff as she sat sewing throughout the long night. She thought how good it was to have a friend like Sarah: a friend who understood what it felt like to be alone, yet strong. A friend who understood what it felt like to be free, free at last, and yet to continue to feel yoked to the oppressive servitude so long her lot in life.

"I'm going to see Sarah," she spoke aloud, suddenly making up her mind. "I feel such need for her counsel and friendship. She's the only person who would understand."

She thought of her mother then, a chill passing through her. "I must tell Sarah the truth," she said and turned, walking quickly to her room to dress, feeling a spark of hope begin to burn within her.

Sarah was surprised to see Lilly gallop into her yard as she hung up wet clothes on a rope strung between two trees. "Lilly, is everything all right?" Sarah asked, realizing she had never seen Lilly on a horse before or wearing pants.

Lilly slid off her horse. "Hello, Sarah. I see you're busy. Would you mind some company?" she asked.

"I'd love some," Sarah replied. "Have you eaten?"

"No. I was up all night, mending and doing the books. I just decided on the spur of the moment that I needed some 'girl talk,'" Lilly stated, her face taking on a momentary look of sadness.

"I'm glad you decided to come. Come on in. I'll cook us some breakfast. The coffee is already hot, if you'd like a cup."

"Wonderful," Lilly replied.

As they ate, the two women talked of winter and how quickly it had arrived, of quilts made, and chores still to do. Sarah was glad Lilly had come. It was nice to have the company of such a pleasant friend. She hadn't realized, until now, how much she missed having someone to talk to. "More coffee?" she asked.

"No, thank you. Maybe later," Lilly replied, going to sit in one of the rocking chairs in front of the fireplace. Sarah sat in the other rocker, glad she had put more wood on the fire when she got up much earlier that morning. Last night was one of those nights when she felt too restless to sleep, and she had gotten up long before dawn. Not one to laze around, she had heated water and got right to washing her dirty clothes, wondering what she would do the remainder of the day.

"Sarah, can I talk to you?" Lilly asked. "I don't mean to burden you, but if I don't talk to someone, I think I'll go mad. You're the only person who might understand, us being close in age and alike in so many ways." She looked at Sarah, her eyes betraying the turmoil within her.

"Nothing you say will go any further," Sarah replied. "Of course you can talk to me. That's what friends are for, Lilly, and I'm very glad we're friends."

"I am, too!" Lilly stated emphatically. "More than you know, Sarah, more than you know. I don't know where to begin. I'm not used to telling my problems to others, Sarah, but I can't hold them in any longer or I'll go crazy." Sarah smiled gently, settling more comfortably into her rocker. When Lilly looked at her, saying no more, she realized her friend was under great duress.

Finally, choosing her words carefully, Lilly began to speak: "Sarah, I don't know if you know this or not. Lydia is married. She had a quick ceremony about a month ago," she replied, shaking her head slowly.

"To whom?" Sarah asked, very surprised.

"Reverend Cole," Lilly replied. "Oh, Sarah, it's all so horrible. Reverend Cole was such a nice fellow: enthusiastic, purposeful. He wanted to be a preacher ever since he was a child."

"*Was* such a nice fellow?" Sarah questioned. "He's dead?"

"Oh, no!" Lilly exclaimed. "Worse! Worse than dead!" she paused. "He came to see me, Sarah, a couple days ago." She struggled for words, "He was beside himself with grief. Said Lydia had tricked him into marriage the very day of Mother's funeral. Said she had seduced him in the church when we were just outside and had, only moments before, laid Mother to rest."

Lilly pulled a hanky from her pocket, blowing her nose. Sarah remembered seeing Lydia burst into sobs, and then go into the church on Reverend Cole's arm. She had no doubt the story was true, and she spoke softly, not wanting to further upset Lilly, who continued to cry, but felt the need to comment. "I saw them go into the church," she said. "Poor Reverend Cole."

"Yes," Lilly sniffled, "poor Reverend Cole. Oh, Sarah. He told me that Lydia was so cruel to him. I can't believe she would be so cruel. But it's worse than that." She paused a long time. "He woke in the middle of the night soon after they were wed, only to find her side of the bed empty. He thought perhaps she had taken ill, and quickly got up to see if she needed his help." She began to cry again, her shoulders shaking as her sobs filled the room.

Sarah leaned close, patting Lilly's shoulder, comforting her as best she could. "It's okay, Lilly. It'll be okay," she said, feeling tremendous sympathy for her friend.

After a while, Lilly gained control and went on. "He found her behind their little house, in a buggy . . ." She shivered, her eyes revealing torment and grief. "She wasn't alone," Lilly said, covering her face with her hands, as shame washed over her. Sarah was stunned, and she grieved for Lilly. "It wasn't the first time, Sarah. She told him that, threw it in his face, told him there were . . . *many* others! Oh, Sarah! I failed her! I failed her!"

Lilly began to cry again, and Sarah let her, for a while, and then spoke. "Lilly! Lilly! Listen to me. You did *not* fail Lydia! She failed, not you! You're a decent woman, respectable. I can truly understand your shock and upset, truly I can, but, Lilly, you did *not* fail Lydia! She's the one who failed. She's the one who hurt you, and Reverend Cole, and brought shame down upon herself."

Lilly looked at Sarah, dabbing her eyes, then shook her head and stared into the fire in the fireplace, as though looking back through time. "I tried to be there for her, Sarah, but she wouldn't listen to me. She hated the farm once Father had left, hated having an older sister telling her what to do, hated the fact that Mother . . ." She paused, glancing quickly at Sarah then back at the fireplace, "that Mother was ill." She sat there, shaking her head, overwhelmed with sadness. "I couldn't be there for everyone, Sarah. I tried, but I just couldn't do it. And now I realize how horribly I failed her."

"You did *not* fail, Lilly! You must not blame yourself," Sarah insisted, hating to see her friend so distraught. Sarah rose. "I'm going to reheat the coffee, Lilly," she said, not knowing what to do to comfort her friend. Hoping to give her time to compose herself. Sarah felt such sadness for Lilly— felt like strangling Lydia! She thought how right Rosie had been all along about the wayward Lydia, and now she had hurt not only her sister, but Reverend Cole. As the pot began to heat, Sarah sat back down, patting Lilly's hand gently.

"Lies," Lilly said softly. "It's all lies." She looked forlorn as she continued, "It's all lies, Sarah, and I can't carry them anymore!" she stated emphatically.

"What do you mean, Lilly?" Sarah asked, watching her friend, empathizing with her sadness and grief.

Lilly hung her head as she continued. "Mother. Father. It's all lies," she lamented. "Mother didn't have a . . . a problem with her memory, Sarah. She was . . ." she paused a long time before continuing, "she was mad, Sarah. Mad! Doc Pearson told Father that, the very first time he came to see her. He gave us pills for her, but they didn't help. She ranted and raved, and from the beginning had to be restrained." Her voice was a mere whisper now, and Sarah saw that she shivered noticeably every so often.

Sarah rose, taking the blanket off her bed, and wrapped it around Lilly as she went on speaking, seemingly unaware of Sarah's actions. "She raged at me when I tried to help her, throwing the trays of food, spitting it at me, slapping me if she got the chance." She shivered, in spite of the blanket around her. "One day, she was quiet, laying there, her face normal," she grew silent, remembering. "I untied her, Sarah. I hated keeping her tied like that, so I untied her. I talked to her like when I was young, before she became ill. I felt so happy." Lilly paused, and Sarah became aware of the coffeepot bubbling on the stove and went to move it.

Lilly continued as Sarah sat down, "She hit me with the vase that I kept by her bed. Always tried to keep fresh flowers there to cheer her, you know? She hit me, knocking me senseless. It was cold out—had snowed the night before—an early snow," she shivered. "That's what saved her, Jonas said. He heard my screams, and ran up from the barn. We found her footprints in the snow and followed them."

She stared into the fireplace, seeing the horror of that earlier time. "Jonas found her, her nightgown soaked through, her body blue with cold. He carried her up to her bed. And all the time she . . ." her voice broke, "she screamed at him! 'Big dumb oaf! Get away from me! Put me down, you stupid brute, you fool!'" And then she saw me, and her hatred turned to me, "'She loves you. Take her! But beware! She'll tie you up, lummox, if you're not careful! She'll turn on you, too!'"

Lilly started crying then, great convulsing sobs, and Sarah felt such tremendous sorrow for her friend. Quieting, Lilly continued, "I wrote letter after letter to father, entreating him to come back, but there was no return address on his letters to mail them to." She stopped talking suddenly, staring at Sarah, then hung her head. "He's alive, Sarah, or at least he was. He couldn't take her . . . her madness. She'd bite him and dig his face. He wouldn't tie her up, but couldn't sleep. She tried to kill him. We couldn't trust her. Finally, he went away. We were left with her, Lydia and I, but only I knew he was alive. All these years, Sarah, I knew. He wrote to me. Jonas brought the letters when they came. They stopped some time ago. I don't know if he's still alive or not. There was never a return address." Sarah reached over to pat her arm, stunned by all she'd been through. "Oh Sarah, I've failed them all: Lydia, Mother, and Father! Reverend Cole left town for a position elsewhere. Told Lydia she could go with him, cried when he told me she had laughed in his face. Told him he was 'too boring' for a woman like herself. Oh, Sarah, whatever will she do now? She refuses to even see me," she cried. "And how can I tell Jonas I . . . I love him? He knew all along of Mother's madness. Do you think he'd want to marry me? What if I'm . . . what if it runs in *me*, too? I couldn't do that to him, couldn't put him through the horrible things my father went through. Sarah, I've done my best, and failed them *all*, miserably!" She sat quietly then, her face pale, devoid of tears.

"Lilly," Sarah said, taking her hands in hers, "My dear, dear friend. I had no idea all you suffered. I'm so sorry, Lilly, so very, very sorry! But *you* didn't fail them, Lilly. *They* failed you! How strong you are to have survived it, all by yourself." Sarah was stunned by her friend's revelations, even more stunned by her assumption of guilt. "Lilly, you can't change Lydia. She has a mind of her own, and right or wrong, she's not going to listen to you. She never has! And it's too bad about Reverend Cole. He apparently wasn't very wise to the wiles of certain young women who are used to going after what they want. But he'll survive. He did do the honorable thing after all, asking her to go with him. I admire him for that. As for your mother, I never realized the extent of her illness. Oh, Lilly, dear, dear Lilly, your father should have stayed," and she realized the impossibility of that as she spoke, "or at least he should have taken her . . . somewhere. Had Doc do something. You shouldn't have had the burden of caring for her, Lilly, caring for her, and the farm, and Lydia."

Sarah was overwhelmed with sorrow by the burdens Lilly had had to bear alone, for so many years. Then she thought of Jonas. "Lilly, Jonas knows of your mother, of her illness.

There's nothing to hide from him. He also knows about your father. Still, he makes it a point to always help you. And he made you those lovely rockers. He's shy, Lilly, you said it yourself the last time we visited. He's shy around females, but he's always there for you. I think you must tell him how you feel, Lilly. Trust him. He's not Reverend Cole. He'll be honest with you. I know he will. He's a good man, Lilly, gentle and caring like you've said again and again."

She paused, her thoughts running on, "And you know he's taken care of his mother and his farm for years, Lilly, just like you have yours. I imagine he's as lonely as you are. You must talk to him. You must!"

"Oh, Sarah," Lilly replied. "You're such a good friend. I feel like a huge weight has been lifted from my shoulders." She stood, walked to the window and looked out, and then turned to face Sarah. "I am going to tell Jonas," she replied. "I'm free at last. If he loves me like I love him, we can face whatever lies ahead. If not, I'll just have to cross that bridge when I get to it, as they say." She hugged Sarah then, smiling, and both of them fervently hoped that Jonas also loved Lilly, and wouldn't be too shy to tell her.

CHAPTER TWENTY-NINE

The next snow fell early in November, covering everything in a thick coat of white. Sarah was glad her cabin was tightly chinked, as was the barn. If this snow held, she knew it would be a mighty long winter. She made a list of last-minute things she needed to get from town and wrapped the quilt she had made for her father, having finished it the evening before. Dressing warmly and tucking her pants into her boots, she saddled Glory and headed for town. She wished she had made the journey before the snowstorm, hoping her cabin would still be warm when she returned.

The ride was difficult, with the snow and wind blowing directly at her all the way. Her cheeks felt frozen, even though she had wrapped her scarf twice around her neck and face. She wore another wool scarf on her head, which at least kept her ears warm. Her fingers felt stiff, even in mittens. She rode most of the way with her hands stuffed into her pockets, her eyes often shut because of the wind and cold. She was glad that Glory was such a good animal, and needed little handling.

Few folks were out and about in town, she noticed, waving to Johnathon Clark as she passed the bank, and Jay Bullard as he came out of the barbershop. They smiled and waved back. The snow began to let up as she dismounted at her father and Rosie's house, and Sarah hoped the sun would break through and melt most of it before she headed back home.

To her surprise, her father opened the door at her knock, saying Rosie was in bed with a cold. Sarah kissed her father on the cheek, stamping snow off her boots, and brushing it off her coat and scarf before entering. She handed Samuel the package containing the quilt she had worked so diligently on. "A present for you, Father, you and Rosie now, though when I started making it, you were still at home at the cabin and not yet wed. I hope you like it," she said.

He opened it, smiling when he saw the quilt in its various shades of reds, blues, yellows, and greens. "Why, Sarah," he said, sounding genuinely pleased, "thank you so much. I appreciate your thoughtfulness and all the work that went into this. Thank you. Now come in by the stove and get warm. You must be chilled clear through."

"I am," she replied, shivering, "but the sun tried to break through a moment ago, so maybe it'll warm up and the snow will melt away soon." She rubbed her hands together, trying to warm them, but it only seemed to make them burn and tingle more. "I'll be so glad when spring comes," she said, and they both laughed, since winter was coming and it'd be a long time till spring came again.

"I'll see if Rosie's awake," Samuel said, "so you can show her the quilt. Pour yourself a coffee, Sarah. I'll be right back."

"Don't wake her. She'll feel better if she sleeps," Sarah said.

"She'd never forgive me, if I let her miss a chance to say hello," he remarked, leaving the room.

Sarah stood close to the stove, holding her hands out to the heat. It seems the older I get, the more I hate the cold, she thought, as she had so often of late.

"Sarah," Rosie said. "I won't kiss you, child. You might get my cold." Rosie looked sweet in her ruffled pink-and-white dressing gown, and heavy wool socks that Sarah knew were her father's.

"You shouldn't have gotten up," Sarah said, turning her face away as Rosie coughed an awful-sounding cough.

"Oh, I'll be fine," Rosie said, looking flushed. "Sit down, child, drink some coffee. Oh! What a lovely quilt!"

"It's for you and Father," Sarah said, and Rosie beamed, thanking her.

"Oh, Sarah, did you hear the news," she asked, "about your friend Tommy Dawson? Well, it's really about Melinda Rose, I guess," Rosie exclaimed, getting more excited as she spoke.

"No. What is it?" Sarah asked, hoping it was good news.

Rosie continued, "I heard she's recovering nicely, is even well enough to help him out at the store, in fact. Course, he doesn't let her do much, no liftin' or carryin' of boxes that even you or I could manage." She smiled at Sarah and then began to cough again.

"Anyway," she continued as soon as she could catch her breath and speak, "my friend, Amanda Culpepper, was in the store the other day, and she told me later . . . of course, Amos Pep . . . uh . . . *Cul*pepper was with her, but that's another story."

She rushed on excitedly and Sarah wondered how her father could stand so much chatter after being used to the relative quiet at their cabin. "Anyways, Amanda was at the store. She used to work there, you know, and there was Melinda Rose looking pretty as a picture! She had on black, of course, being so recently a widow and all. Terrible thing, just terrible," she lamented and then brightened, "Amanda said her face had filled out real pretty like, too, not fat like before, and not so thin as when she was sick."

She began coughing again, and Sarah thought of how thin Melinda Rose had looked the day she stopped at the Dawson's to see her, and how bloated she had looked at Nancy Pearly's wedding: her feet bulging within her shoes, her stomach barely held within the tightly stretched seams of her faded old dress. She shook her head sadly at these thoughts.

Rosie continued, "Amanda said she looks healthier than ever now, and Tommy dotes on her like ya' can't imagine, always by her side, askin' if she needs anything, if she wants to sit down, or go home and rest. I must say, I never thought he'd turn out to be such a caring man," Rosie remarked and then got up to put a kettle on the stove.

"I'll heat up this stew for lunch," she said, "and some good sourdough biscuits. Your father will be getting hungry soon. Anyways, Amanda said Melinda Rose looked real pretty, her cheeks all rosy and pink, and her hair all done up in a bun at her neck, and Tommy fussed around her and the young'n like an old 'mother hen,' mind you. He carried him to Melinda Rose, looking like Danny was his very own. And, oh, child, the sweetest thing . . . ya' know Tommy was the one who named him Danny, after Daniel, o' course." She chuckled happily before continuing, "Well, Melinda Rose named him Daniel *Thomas*. Thomas after Tommy! Isn't that the nicest thing?" Rosie sniffled then, and Sarah realized she was on the verge of tears. "Imagine, Melinda Rose working right there alongside Tommy," Rosie stated, sniffling once more, a tender smile upon her face. "And Danny has the softest fluff of red hair, Amanda said, and his eyes are turning a deep brown. A pretty child. Smiles all the time," Rosie said. "I'll have to go see him, when I'm over this cold. Made him a blanket," Rosie continued, as she went over to stir the stew, its succulent aroma beginning to fill the air and make Sarah's stomach rumble with hunger.

They ate the delicious stew and sourdough biscuits, then her father excused himself, saying the snow had let up and the wind had quieted, and even though it was still a bit brisk out, he thought he would walk over to Amos Culpepper's and visit. He gave Rosie, then Sarah, a kiss on the cheek and left.

Sarah was surprised that her father would want to spend any time around the likes of Amos Culpepper.

"Oh," Rosie exclaimed, "was gonna tell ya' about Amanda and Amos." She began clearing the table as she spoke, bustling around the kitchen as she always had, reminding Sarah of long ago, when she stayed at Rosie's, and had been amazed at her endless energy. "Your father—bless his heart—knowing Amanda and I were the best of friends, decided we would invite them over. A 'welcome home,' of sorts, after what Amos had said in church about changing his evil ways and all. When a person like that decides to go straight, you know, the least folks can do is to encourage him."

"Anyways, your father decided to have them over, and right away Amos accepts." She coughed a bit before continuing, "I was beside myself almost, happy for Amanda, but also a little angry that all these years she'd never let on she was married. Ya' know, always wearing black like a widow. Well, in they come, Amanda in a real pretty light-green dress, and her hair all soft and pretty. Never seen her look so nice. Or so happy. And him!" she exclaimed. "Why, he's the most handsome fellow! Of course, not as handsome as your dear father." Rosie smiled, pouring them each another cup of coffee. "He comes in, so tall and good lookin'. Has a shock of white hair and a white mustache, but it's his eyes, I guess, that makes him so nice to look at. They seem to sparkle when he looks at ya'." She paused, stirring her coffee. "Well, he takes my hand ever so gently and says how pleased he is to meet Amanda's best friend. Made me feel so happy, knowing she'd told him of our friendship. Then we ate my grandmother's special Irish cake, while Samuel and Amos talked, and Amanda and I caught up on all the latest news about town. Ya' know, your father says Amos is one of the smartest men he's ever met, and kindly, too. Can you imagine, for a gunfighter, that is?"

She coughed again, and Sarah tried to visualize the tall,

handsome Amos, a gunfighter, with Amanda Culpepper. She could not. Her only image of Amanda was the one she had known for years: an old woman who wore her hair pulled tightly back against her head, making her look quite severe, especially with her black outfits. Sarah could not imagine Miz Culpepper in colored frocks with her hair all soft and pretty.

"Seems Amos has been all over the country," Rosie went on, "to Californie and even to Mexico, your father says. And he's done all sorts of things, besides gunfightin', that is. Dug gold in Californie, surveyed some land in a place called the O-ray-gon Territory, way out west." She smiled and Sarah could tell she was very impressed with Amos Culpepper, even if he had been a gunfighter.

"Best thing of all, your father says that he can read! Can ya' imagine? And can quote Shakespeare, whoever that is, or was. I've never been much of a reader." Rosie continued, "Oh, Sarah, I'm real happy for Amanda. Happy too, that your father feels friendly toward her husband, even if he *is* a gunfighter."

Sarah smiled, wondering if the day would ever come when Amos Culpepper would *not* be thought of as a gunfighter.

CHAPTER THIRTY

Sarah entered Dawson's General Store after leaving her father and Rosie's. She wanted to get the supplies on the list in her pocket: a new coffeepot, a length of rope, and rice, which she cooked often. She was glad it was plentiful. She also wanted more candles for the long winter ahead.

She was looking at a length of heavy woolen fabric when a woman behind her spoke. "Sarah, how nice to see ya'."

She turned quickly, recognizing the voice, but surprised nonetheless. "Melinda Rose," Sarah replied. "How are you?"

"Much better, thanks to Tommy," she said, as he came to stand beside them.

"Hello, Sarah. Doesn't she look great?" he asked, smiling down at Melinda Rose, who was decidedly healthier and positively glowed when she looked at him.

"Yes, she does," Sarah answered, "and where's Danny?"

"Daniel *Thomas*," Melinda Rose replied, as Tommy grinned at her, taking her hand. Sarah had never seen two people so in love, she thought, and was so very happy for them. "Come, he's over here," Melinda Rose said, leading the way to a large woven basket on the counter. Inside, snuggled peacefully among a blue cotton blanket and a thicker blue-and-white quilt, lay little Daniel Thomas.

He looked up at the faces above him, smiling, as his tiny

hands waved around, grasping at nothing in particular. Sarah reached down, and instantly his tiny pink fingers closed around one of her slender fingers. "Oh," she said, "look! Isn't he sweet?" The baby smiled, as if he understood her words, and the two women laughed.

Tommy came over to stand beside Melinda Rose, gazing down at the red-haired little boy. "What do you think of Danny?" he asked Sarah, as he reached into the basket, stroking the baby's soft red fluff of hair.

"He's sweet," Sarah answered. "A wonderful, little fellow." Tommy beamed at her words.

Melinda Rose asked then, "Do you know, Sarah, that Tom asked me to marry him? I know it's quite soon . . ." she paused, "after Daniel's death." Tommy put his arm around her shoulder, comforting her, as she continued, "But we thought with Danny and all . . ." She grew quiet for a moment. "We're getting married next week." She smiled tenderly, a smile that seemed to say more than mere words could. "We have so much to be thankful for."

"Congratulations," Sarah said, hugging first Melinda Rose, then Tommy. "I'm so happy for you," she exclaimed, "all three of you!" And they all laughed happily, relieved that the troubles of the past months now seemed behind them, at last.

Melinda Rose took Sarah's hand then. "Thank you, for what you and the sheriff did," she said. "Without you, Danny and I wouldn't be here." Sarah smiled at her words then paid for her purchases, glad that everything fit in one bag. She wished Melinda Rose and Tommy good luck and walked outside.

The sun shone brightly on the newly fallen snow, which she was glad to see was melting quickly. Maybe it'll all melt, she thought as she saw Moses come out of his office across the street. She waved and suddenly heard a loud noise from further down the street. She stepped to the edge of the walk in time to see two men run to their horses, leap onto their saddles, and race down the street in her direction. A third man joined them.

"Hold up! Hold up!" she heard someone yell from that direction, realizing the noise she heard had been a gunshot. The men had obviously just robbed the bank. She looked across the street at Moses, saw him drop the papers he had been holding, and begin to reach for his gun just as the two men—an old Mexican and a younger black man—thundered by, their guns firing. Sarah was so startled she could not move.

"Sarah! Sarah!" she heard Old John call her name, and it seemed she turned her head in slow motion to where he ran in her direction from down the street. She saw Moses fire his gun, and the old Mexican fell from his horse. It was then Sarah turned back, realizing the young Mexican had pulled to a stop in front of her, his sable horse prancing and dancing before her.

He's going to tip his hat and shoot me, she thought. He's going to shoot me! She knew, in the far recesses of her mind, that these were the same men who had killed Moses' wife and unborn child. She looked into the handsome young Mexican's face as he smiled, tipping his hat.

"Sarah, don't move!" she heard John Bruce shout a short distance behind her. Then she heard a shot. One shot, two? Or was it three? As if in slow motion, she saw the young Mexican start to fall forward over the neck of his horse, the blade of Old John's Bowie knife buried deeply in his chest! His gun still firing as it turned away from her, and toward Moses, who looked as stunned as she!

Sarah looked down at her clothing. There was no blood, she realized, touching her stomach, a feeling of relief coming over her. She saw her bag of supplies scattered at her feet and heard Tommy and Melinda Rose's voices behind her, as they rushed out of the store. She turned to where John Bruce had been running and calling to her.

"John?" she said, and to her horror, saw him lying against

the building, his hand outstretched toward her and one side of his beard and hair a bright red. "No!" She heard someone scream "No! No!" as she ran to her old friend's side. She was unaware that the screams had come from her own lips. She knelt down, lifting his head up against her breast, cradling him in her violently shaking arms. "John!" she cried, "John! John! Oh, my God! No! No!" But she knew her cries went unheard.

She heard someone say something about getting Samuel Justus, heard sounds that seemed to skitter just out of reach of her understanding, as tears coursed their way down her face. She laid John Bruce's head down, reaching out to gently close the blue eyes that would never look at her again with laughter and love filling them.

"Sarah," she heard Moses say, and felt his hand touch her shoulder tenderly. She rose, still shaking, her mind reeling in pain and shock. She turned toward him, looking into his eyes, startled to see him grimacing in pain.

"Moses?" she questioned, seeing how pale his face had gotten. It was then that she saw the blood spreading down his side, his shirt soaked. "Moses!" she cried in alarm and saw more blood dripping from his hand, coloring the snow at their feet. "Oh, my God! You've been shot!" she cried.

He whispered hoarsely, "Just a little, darlin'," and slumped forward against her, as she tried to hold him, screaming for someone to get the doctor!

Doc Pearson worked all night, sweat covering his brow, as Sarah waited just outside the room. Her father and Rosie were there, trying to comfort her. Rosie was much quieter than usual, as Samuel paced, stopping often to peer out the window, and then continued to pace, a worried look upon his face.

Sarah sat still, a blanket wrapped around her shoulders. She couldn't remember who put it there, her mind numb with grief. John Bruce was dead. Her dear, dear friend was dead! Her mind kept repeating it. She shook her head, and a sob escaped from deep within her, causing Rosie to rush to her side and her father to look quickly at her, a pained expression upon his face.

And Moses? She thought, What if *he* dies, too? She saw again the rush of blood soaking his side, his hand dripping a steady output of blood from his fingertips. She shivered, listening for any sounds from the room where Doc was working on him.

She stood, but was too shaky to walk and reluctantly sat back down. Her mind kept picturing the man on the large black horse, seeing the horse prance and dance in front of her, seeing the smile upon the Mexican's face. He was handsome, about the most handsome man Sarah had ever seen. He didn't look like a killer. He didn't even look dangerous, at first glance. But you knew what he was capable of when you looked into his eyes! They were menacing, cold, totally devoid of feeling! Handsome, yes, she thought, in his black shirt, pants, and boots. The silver trim like bright flashes of light against the black of his outfit, and the ebony-black of his horse. He was handsome, yes, but so very deadly. She was glad he was dead.

She shuddered, as she remembered her thoughts as he paced before her in the street. He's going to tip his hat and shoot me, she had thought, and it would, indeed, have been true, if Old John hadn't run up at that moment, throwing his Bowie knife, just before the Mexican fired.

She remembered, too, the shots—two, three—she couldn't remember how many. She heard again their sharp retorts and shivered, her mind seeing it all once more.

One shot must have hit Moses, she thought, or two. She groaned at the realization, and Rosie began to cry softly. Samuel hurried to her side, gently rubbing her shoulder, a strained expression upon his face. Sarah put her head down into her hands and also began to cry, quietly at first, then louder, unable to stifle the grief that flowed from her very soul.

CHAPTER THIRTY-ONE

The door opened slowly, just as dawn broke, and a very tired Doc Pearson walked into the room. He glanced at Samuel, a look of uncertainty crossing his face. "He's alive," he said, and then looked at Sarah, "It's up to him. I did the best I could."

Sarah pushed the blanket from her shoulders. "He'll live?" she asked hopefully.

"I don't honestly know, Sarah. He's lost a lot of blood," the doctor replied as Samuel walked over to stand by his daughter. He had walked Rosie home during the night. She was feeling ill and no longer able to take the strain of any further upset. Now, he put his hand on his daughter's arm as she began to shake.

"He's alive, Sarah, that's good news. He's a strong man," Samuel told her.

At that moment, Tommy Dawson entered the doctor's office with the new preacher, a Reverend Higgins. "Sarah, is there any word? How is he, Doc?" Tommy asked.

"Fine as can be expected," Doc answered, "lost a lot of blood."

"I brought the new preacher, thought you might want him here," Tommy said, adding quickly, "Didn't figure prayers could hurt."

"Thanks," Sarah replied, then walked over by the doctor,

noticing the spots of blood on his pants and shoes. "Can I see him, Doc? Please?" Doc Pearson looked at her, seeing the worry in her eyes, knowing she'd been through an awful lot, what with John Bruce's death, her almost being shot, and Moses being wounded. "I need to be with him," she stated, her voice firm and unwavering.

"He's in bad shape, Sarah. The bullet hit him in the side, splintering a rib or two. Not much I could do about that except get a few sharp pieces out. Might be more inside, deeper, but that's not the worst of it." Sarah looked at him, afraid of what he might say next. "The second bullet went into his arm just above the elbow and tore up the muscle. I got the bullet out, but . . ." He watched her take in what he was telling her. Suddenly, she understood.

"Which arm?" she asked.

Doc looked at her, a compassionate look on his kindly face. "His gun arm, Sarah. It'll be a miracle if he can use that arm anytime soon."

Sarah felt as though the wind had been knocked out of her and sat down in the chair closest to her. She knew a man like Moses Gentry would be devastated if he lost the use of his gun arm. She heard her father ask Doc something, and tried to concentrate on his reply, "Lost a lot of blood, had to dig out bone fragments and the bullet, it'll take a miracle . . ." Sarah felt sick to her stomach.

Oh, Mother, she thought, this is my dear friend. Please help him heal. I lost one best friend, John Bruce. Please, don't let me lose Moses, too. Silently, she added, Oh, I wish you were here with me, Mother. Suddenly, she realized Doc was speaking to her. "What?" she asked.

"Go on in, if you want, then go home and get some rest. He'll probably sleep all night and part of tomorrow."

"No!" Sarah exclaimed, "I'm staying with him, Doc. I have to! He's my best friend. I lost one best friend already. I'll not leave his side!"

Doc patted her arm. "Go in then, child, but let him sleep. Sleep is a good healer."

Moses woke early the next morning to find Sarah asleep in a chair drawn up next to the table he lay upon. She was leaning forward, her head resting against his undamaged arm. His other arm and side hurt worse than anything he had ever felt, but he raised his head, trying to see where he was. The room was cloaked in darkness, and it was difficult to make out objects. As his eyes adjusted, he saw the cabinets and doctor's equipment and realized he was at Doc Pearson's office.

He shifted, trying to reach with his injured arm to touch Sarah's hair, but grimaced in pain, nearly yelling out loud. Instead, he groaned and then lay still, remembering the recent events. He had shot the Mexican who killed his wife. He remembered seeing him fall forward out of his saddle, all the while firing, as he fell.

He shot me, Moses thought, once, maybe twice. Then he remembered Sarah's face as she stood there, like his wife had, too frozen with shock, or surprise, to move. He lay there, noticing the sweet scent of her hair as she rested so close to him. Rage boiled up in him as the image of his wife came— once again—to mind, standing there so long ago on another street, in another town, at another time. His Sarah, who had died where she stood, his unborn child within her. A deep sadness filled him, crushing his heart until he moaned aloud under the weight of it. First *his* Sarah, then *this* Sarah, he thought.

"Moses?" Sarah quickly sat up, looking at him and leaning in close in the darkened room. "It's okay," she said softly. "It'll be okay," she reassured him, taking his good hand in one of hers and brushing back a strand of his hair that had fallen across his brow, with the other. She began to weep softly, laying her head against him, her shoulders shaking.

"It's all right, darlin', don't cry," he crooned, hoping to

comfort her. "Oh, my God!" he suddenly exclaimed, causing Sarah to jump in alarm.

"What is it? Do you hurt?" she asked, her concern for him stopping her tears.

"I hurt like hell," he answered, his old rogue's grin that she liked so much momentarily crossing his face. Then his features changed to concern as he looked at her. "I just . . . remembered," he paused, taking her hand within his, "about John. I'm sorry about John, Sarah. I know how close you were to him. He was a good man, an honorable man."

Sarah felt new tears well up. "Thank you," she whispered softly. "I'm gonna miss him so much." She saw again, in her mind, John Bruce's snow-white hair and large blue eyes that seemed to twinkle when he was happy, saw him doff his hat to the widows and old maids, making them blush. She remembered the Indian moccasins he had sat up late at night making for her when she was young. She shuddered, overwhelmed at her loss.

"Come here, darlin'," Moses whispered. "Come closer. We both could use some comfortin'." He groaned as he tried to pull her closer with his wounded arm, and then lay still, very aware that Hastings' sheriff was out of commission, and *would be* for some time to come, by the looks of it. She nestled her head against him, her arm resting across his chest. She felt safer than she had since the horrible events of the previous day, and so thankful that this "best friend" was still alive. "Did you say something?" Moses asked, looking down at the top of her head as she rested it against him.

"I was thanking God," she answered, "for keeping you alive." She spoke softly and her words pleased him.

That afternoon, they buried John Bruce. It was cloudy and bitter cold as the wind blew, whistling and howling, around the mourners. The whole town turned out for his funeral. The new preacher hadn't known John, but he had no trouble getting anyone to say a few words about him. Though he had been a loner, it was obvious he had been well thought of and respected. The fact that he had died protecting Sarah Justus, made him a hero.

Sarah was filled with an abundance of wonderful memories, and to her surprise, instead of sobbing hysterically—as she was afraid she would—she was able to keep her composure, bidding her old friend goodbye in a dignified manner. Only after all the others left did she begin to cry. Walking closer to the grave, she whispered softly, "Goodbye, my dear friend. I hope someday we will meet again." She wiped away her tears before adding, "Thank you for everything, John. I love you."

She turned away then, closing the door on a treasured part of her life, knowing how deeply an impact losing him would have on her life, but never guessing just how important he would *always* be to her.

Sarah stayed in town, rarely leaving Moses' side, her father more than willing to go to her cabin to feed the animals and see that all was well. She felt sorely shaken by Old John's death and would not leave Moses until she was certain he was on the mend. He insisted on getting up and walking that first day, but was too unsteady to attend the funeral. Every attempt to move left him pale and shaky, and he clenched his teeth to augment the pain. Moving his arm hurt as much as could be expected, but moving his body was pure agony.

Sarah sat by his side everyday, talking quietly with him, cheering him, if necessary, or just listening to his even breathing as he slept. She saw to it he ate nourishing meals, coaxing him to eat more. Rosie came to Doc's everyday, bringing Sarah and Moses hot, delicious meals: stews, roasts, biscuits and gravy, and, of course, pieces of her grandmother's prized cake.

"Sweets for the sweet," she giggled, her face flushing as red as her hair. Moses smiled at her, winking and teasing right back, until they got to laughing so hard that he ended up nearly howling in pain. Sarah was glad to see him be his old self and knew it wouldn't be long before he was good as new.

A week later, with Moses able to do more and more for himself, Sarah decided to go home. It was still hard to leave him, but she knew he was getting better, and she was anxious to sleep in her own bed, instead of a chair at Doc's, or in the bed at her father's. Anxious, also, to wear other clothes, instead of the outfit she had worn to town, or the outfit Rosie had taken in for her. Truth was, she hated to impose on her father and Rosie's hospitality, any longer, and missed the comforts of her own home.

Yes, she thought, it will soon be Christmas, and I'm ready to go home. She kissed Moses on the forehead, one cold, blustery day, telling him to stay out of trouble or he'd answer to her. Then bid her father and Rosie goodbye and turned Glory toward home, hoping to put her sorrows behind her.

CHAPTER THIRTY-TWO

Lilly had finally made up her mind! She had had plenty of time to think it over, unable to get to sleep till hours after she went to bed each night. Days, she caught herself pacing and pacing. If this keeps on, I'll end up sick, she thought, sick or crazy. Well, I'll just take the chance, she decided, and tell Jonas what I feel, no matter the outcome.

She dressed in her long petticoat and dark-brown wool skirt. She donned her favorite white blouse with the high lace collar, then her heavy socks and warm boots. Her hair was pulled softly back from her face, but hung loose down her back. She pinched her cheeks, put on her dark-brown riding cape and mittens, and went out to the barn.

It was snowing quite hard: large thick flakes that stuck to her cape and face. She thought it was beautiful, how the snow covered the branches of the trees, as if outlining each one. The path to the barn was slippery. Twice her feet slipped, though she caught herself before she fell.

The ranch-hand, who worked for her, greeted her with a cheery "good morning." Then he saddled her horse and helped her mount. She rode sidesaddle, because of her petticoat and skirt, but would have felt more comfortable in pants and astride the horse, especially with the snow making the ground so slippery.

Oh, well, she thought, better to have Jonas see me looking

my best, than done up like somebody's brother in pants. She hadn't ridden sidesaddle in a long, long time and balanced precariously, feeling very uneasy, as she urged the horse out of the barn and down the road. As they went along, she adjusted to the position and the horse's rhythm, letting it walk along at a leisurely pace, thinking of just what she would say to Jonas.

The sun came out, making the ride much more enjoyable, as its bright rays brought a crisp sparkle to the snow and a feeling of encouragement within her. She had no reservations any longer. It was time for her to "lay her cards on the table," an expression her father had often used.

She smiled at the thought of him, wondering as she often did, if he was alive and would ever come home. She missed him: his gentle laughter and kindly ways. Missed the way he talked: his voice soft and sweet to her ears. He was a gentle man, easy to talk to, easy to please. The farm and his family had been his life. Then her mother took ill, little by little becoming more violent. She shivered, as she remembered.

He wasn't strong enough to stay. She understood that and never hated him for leaving. She was the strong one. She had no choice. She simply put her back into the load heaped so unexpectedly upon her and did the best she could. Now here she was, free at last of her burdens, free to have a life of her own with the man she had loved as far back as she could remember.

She smiled at the thought of Jonas and waved to the new preacher, Reverend Higgins, as she passed the small white church on the hill, its snowy outline a beacon calling lost souls to "come, come and be fed, come and be accepted, no matter who you are or your lot in life." She felt happy now as a feeling of hopefulness flowed within her, and she urged her horse to go faster. She was anxious to see Jonas and tell him of her love for him. Even if he didn't feel the same and laughed at her, something she could not imagine him doing, she was ready to let him know how she felt. Again, she urged the horse on, as they came to the long buggy path that led back off the road to his farm.

As she neared his house, she saw him coming out onto the porch and waved, turning her mount directly toward the house and off the path. A small hill rose in front of her, and she knew she could reach him quicker by cutting across it. She saw him wave in return, but could not make out the look of surprise, then concern, on his face. She urged the horse on, heedless of any possible danger in her way.

She saw Jonas hurry down his front steps just as her horse came over the crest of the hill. She did not see the rabbit that bolted at the sight of the horse, causing it to shy to one side, unsettling her and tossing her off its back in a fluff of petticoat, skirt, and cape. She hit the ground with a thud, knocking the wind from her, and lay in a snow-covered heap, unable to get her breath. She heard the horse continue to run toward the house and tried to get air into her lungs, gasping frantically. Then she lay still.

Suddenly, she was lifted up into strong arms, keeping her eyes closed as dizziness overtook her. "Lilly?" Jonas said, "Oh, God. Lilly!" He held her close, looking into her face, his breath coming in great gasps from running. "Lilly, oh, my sweet, sweet Lilly," he said, rocking her in his strong arms, "don't die! Please don't die!" She felt his heart beating thunderously against her body, felt his warm breath upon her cheek. She tried once more to get some air, but she could not! Not because she was injured, but because he held her to him so tightly, crushing her breath from her in his attempt to help her.

He was running now, taking great strides, his arms holding her securely. His words were music to her ears amidst his puffing and panting, "I love you, Lilly. I'll get help! Don't die, my sweet Lilly!" She opened her eyes, finally able to get a breath, the world righting itself once more as her dizziness abated.

He rushed into his home, laying her gently on the couch, his arms still around her as he knelt beside it, his eyes frantic with worry. "I'm . . . I'm all right, Jonas. Got . . . the . . . wind knocked out . . . of me," she had to pause between words to try to breathe. She saw the look of fear on his face and the tremendous worry that showed so clearly. She reached up, placing her small hands on either side of his face, her mittens lost in the sudden fall from the horse. Cradling his face in her hands, she looked at him questioningly, "Jonas, did I hear you correctly? Did you say you love me?"

He bowed his head, not answering. She waited for him to speak as a feeling of uneasiness enveloped her. He withdrew his arms from around her, though he remained kneeling. "I . . . I didn't mean . . ." he began, his voice barely a whisper.

Lilly's heart sank inside her, watching the look of sadness that came over his face. "Jonas?" she said, but he only knelt there, his head bowed, no reply from his lips. It was a long time before either spoke. When Lilly's breathing returned to normal, she could stand the silence no longer. Watching his face she said, "I came here today . . ."

He looked up, interrupting her, "Is something wrong at your farm?"

"No," she replied, disheartened. He stood then, as she sat up on the couch, straightening her garments around her. He eased down beside her, but continued to look away from her. "I've made a mistake," she said, feeling tears well up.

"Shouldn't have ridden fast in the snow," he replied, his shoulders slumped as he continued to look straight ahead. "Are you sure you're all right?" he asked, turning to look at her, seeing her beautiful dark eyes so close to tears.

"I'm fine," she replied, wondering what she should say or do, now that he had told her he didn't mean to say he loved her. She sat still, unsure of her next move. Suddenly, she made up her mind. She had come all this way in blustery weather and had nearly broken her neck in her foolish hurry to tell him. Well, she *would* tell him, she decided, regardless of the fact he didn't want her!

She turned toward him. "Better take that cloak off," he said, "it's damp. You'll get chilled." She stood, and he did, too, taking her garment and hanging it on a hook by the door. She sat down again, more confused than ever. He remained standing.

He spoke then, his voice soft and deep, and suffused with pain. "I didn't mean for you to . . . to hear me. I thought you were unconscious. I've always . . . loved you, Lilly, since the first day I met you." He spoke so softly now that she could barely hear him. "Been a fool," he stated, his voice rising slightly. "Big clod like me . . . a dummy that couldn't get up the courage to . . ." he cleared his throat, "to say what I felt. What I *feel*," he amended.

"Jonas," she said, going to stand beside him, wanting to stop his foolish words and tell him of her feelings.

"No, Lilly. I saw the fellows from town who came a courtin'. I watched them. Saw their fancy clothes and fine manners. They were everything I'm not," he said, looking out the window, seeing those days of long ago and feeling the pain once again inside of him. "I saw you in your pretty dresses, looking like a beautiful bird, so small and sweet." He cleared his throat again. "Wanted to throw every one of them fellows off your porch. Big, clumsy fool of a man. Your mother was right. I couldn't tell you, knew I couldn't measure up."

He looked at her, aware of her beauty: her hair, as it cascaded over her shoulders, her small nose, and tiny bow-shaped mouth. He closed his eyes, as he had so many times before when she was near, and his love for her overwhelmed him. "I have nothin' to offer you, Lilly. I have nothin'," he said, looking into her lovely brown eyes.

"Jonas," she said, reaching up to cradle his face between her hands, "Oh, Jonas. Dear, dear Jonas," she replied, starting to cry. "I don't want fancy dressed fellows or fancy talkers. I don't want anyone!" she exclaimed. "Anyone, but *you*! I love you, Jonas. I have *always* loved you, since I was young, the very first time you came to the farm to talk to my father."

She watched his face, as her words registered. He looked down at her, a broad smile spreading across his face, his eyes lighting with joy, dispelling the pain and doubt that had been in them. "You love me, Lilly? Oh, Lilly, I've prayed so long that someday you could care for me." He picked her up in his great, strong arms, kissing her with all the tenderness and love she had ever imagined, and then danced her around and around the room. Two people, who deeply deserved the love they knew, at last, they shared.

CHAPTER THIRTY-THREE

On Christmas morning, Sarah had barely finished chores and put on a pot of coffee, when her father and Rosie arrived. The snow glistened in its sparkling wrap of silvery diamonds, as the early morning sun caressed it, covering the countryside in pristine whiteness. Tiny flakes floated gently down, barely discernable to the naked eye.

Rosie was her usual bubbling self, filled with enthusiastic bursts of laughter, joy, gossip, and reverie. Samuel seemed slightly preoccupied, but laughed and visited with the women. Sarah had knitted a pair of socks and gloves for her father, and a lovely wool shawl for Rosie. They presented her with a bolt of soft pink cotton fabric, perfect for a summer dress. They had also brought a bottle of homemade syrup that she knew would make a tasty addition to the pancakes she often made during the long winter months.

As breakfast cooked, and later still as they ate, Rosie filled the cabin with all the latest news of town, bringing Sarah up to date. Sarah was extremely pleased to hear that Jonas and Lilly were being married, that very afternoon, in a simple ceremony at his farm. "*She* proposed!" Rosie exclaimed, her face flushing in excitement. "I heard tell from one of the ladies at church that she went over to see him, racing her horse on the snowy ground, paying no heed to how foolish that was—mind ya'—and her horse side-stepped and she fell.

Well, Jonas was on his way to the barn and saw her fall and ran, yelling, to where she lay."

Rosie paused to get her breath and Sarah bit her lip, afraid to ask if Lilly had been hurt. "Knocked the wind out of her, I hear tell," Rosie continued, "but here he comes and scoops her up in his big arms, and tells her he loves her. Why—lo and behold—when he gets her into the house, she tells him she loves him, too! Can ya' imagine? That dainty girl with that big fellow, and them both being stuck, caring for their mothers, all those years and unable to have a life of their own!"

Sarah shook her head, thinking to herself, I'm so glad they're not waiting any longer to be together. I know they'll be happy. She smiled, remembering her talks with Lilly, happy that the sadness from the past was finally over for her.

"And that's not all. Seems they're going to have a baby!" Rosie blurted out.

Sarah's mouth dropped open in surprise. "What?" she asked, staring at Rosie.

"Yup. That sister of hers drove poor Reverend Cole away by her wild ways. I heard tell she bragged to him about seeing other men, if ya' can imagine."

"Rosie," Samuel interjected, "that's best left unsaid."

"Well, it's true!" she exclaimed. "I always said that young'n was too wild for her own good. Well, anyways, now it seems she's in a 'family way,' and it ain't the reverend's. Guess she don't rightly know whose it is. Anyway, she up and asked Lilly, since her and Jonas were gettin' hitched, if they'd take the baby when it was born. Guess she's got better things to do and don't want no baby tying her down. Can ya' imagine?"

"Yes, I can," Sarah answered. "So Lilly said she'd take it?"

"Sure as can be," Rosie answered, "and she told Jonas, and he up and agrees, too. He said they got plenty of love to go round. Now ain't that something? I used to think . . . well, never mind. Sure funny how first impressions can be wrong about a big fellow like him." She shook her head. "Ain't life surprising? Ya' think ya' got it all figured out, and then everything changes—sometimes even for the best." Rosie smiled, pouring a cup of coffee, and took it to Samuel.

"By the way, Sheriff Gentry says he'll be stopping round to see you today, Sarah. Seems that black man that . . . well, you know . . . the one who got away in the bank robbery? Well, he just might be hiding 'round Black Dog Lake and the sheriff has to check it out," Samuel said, glancing at her.

"Oh! I almost forgot!" Rosie exclaimed. "You know Amos Pepper . . . I mean, Culpepper? I just can't get used to calling him that. Well, Moses went over to see him right after you came back home. Told him he couldn't use his gun hand—wouldn't be able to for awhile—and asked him to be his deputy. Don't that beat all! Amanda just sat there, still as death, when the sheriff was asking Amos, never sayin' a word. Then he looked at Amanda a long time before he says, 'No, I can't. Thanks for asking, but I promised Amanda I'd never put on my guns again, and I don't intend to break my word to her.'"

"Well, Amanda gets up, never sayin' a word, and left the room. So Moses finishes his coffee, then gets up to leave and here she comes, carrying Amos' gun belt with the guns still in it and says, 'Do what ya' gotta do, Amos. I'd rather have ya' on *this* side of the law, than the other,' and hands him the belt. He just smiled at her, knowing how hard that was for her. Then she says, 'Just don't get shot or I'll shoot ya', too!' and winked at Moses. I don't know as I'd do that if your father was Amos and I was in Amanda's shoes. I'd be worried to death, I tell ya'." Sarah looked at her father, and they smiled, knowing how true her words were.

Rosie helped Sarah clear the table and do up the dishes, while Samuel went outside to see how the animals were faring. The women talked and laughed as they worked, enjoying each other's company. Sarah was glad her father had married Rosie—glad they were so happy together They were more compatible, it seemed, than her mother and father had been. Sarah missed her mother, today, on Christmas, especially, and wondered if she would have been happier, here in Hastings, than she was at the fort.

Rosie sat in the small rocker, holding her chubby feet out to warm before the fireplace, humming a cheery tune. Sarah smiled at the sight of her, though in her heart she wished it was her mother sitting there, for just a day, an hour, a moment. She turned away quickly to dispel her wishful thoughts and got out a long red scarf from her sewing basket, taking it to show Rosie. "Rosie, see what I made Moses for Christmas?"

Rosie's eyes lit up, and a big smile broke out across her face. "Oh, that's pretty," she replied. "He'll sure like that, honey. You'll have him all 'tied up' then," she giggled.

"Rosie, Moses and I are just friends," Sarah stated, "nothing more, nothing less."

"Well, of course ya' are," Rosie stated, with a mischievous look in her green eyes.

"Really, Rosie, we talked," Sarah hesitated, not wanting to say too much and add more gossip to Rosie's already abundant accumulation. Rosie looked at Sarah, waiting anxiously for her to go on. "We're the best of friends, like John Bruce and I were. I love Moses dearly, but it's not like you think." She tried to find the right words, "I feel love for him, true, but not like . . ."

"Sarah!" Samuel shouted from outside the cabin, interrupting her words, his tone of voice startling both women by the upset in it.

Sarah opened the door and saw her father standing out by the barn, his hands on his hips, as he looked down at the ground. "Father," Sarah replied, "what is it?"

"Come here," he ordered, bending now, his eyes searching the snow around his feet.

Sarah grabbed her coat and pulled on her boots, hurrying to his side. "What is it?" she asked again.

"Moccasin tracks," her father replied, "I wasn't sure at first, but here's a full print. Not that old, either."

Sarah felt her heart leap in her chest. "I wear moccasins. It's probably my print," she said, hoping to divert his attention from the possibility of it being an Indian's footprint. Gray Eagle! she thought. He was back and had come to see her. Her heart leapt with joy. She had a hard time containing the immense burst of happiness that flooded her body.

Her father continued to examine the footprint, shaking his head. "Thought I saw one by the door of the cabin when we first arrived," he said. "I don't like the looks of it, Sarah."

"Well, Father, if it was by the door, it was definitely my print. I wore my moccasins out to feed the animals this morning," she explained.

"Looks fresher than that," he stated, his eyes searching the woods and field surrounding them, for any sign of Indians. "I don't like it, Sarah."

"It's okay, Father. They're my prints, I'm sure of it. And I'm always cautious. I take the gun when I'm outside, so you don't have to worry," she added. He looked at her, and she lowered her eyes, hoping he could not tell she was lying. She felt ashamed, lying to him again, when he couldn't help how he felt about Indians and only had her best interest at heart. "Oh, Father. Let's go in, it's cold out here," she said, as he followed her reluctantly back into the cabin.

It was a while before he relaxed. Though he had an uneasy feeling, he was certain Sarah would not lie to him and had probably made the footprints in the snow herself, as she had said. After all, he did see her moccasins drying by the fireplace.

Rosie chatted on merrily about their plans for the rest of the day. If the weather didn't get worse, they were going over to the church in the valley for evening services. She liked the new preacher, Reverend Higgins, even preferred him over Reverend Cole.

"I think it's because he's older." She smiled, shrugging her shoulders. "Reverend Cole was so young, enthusiastic, yes, but still so young. And to be taken in by that Benedict girl," she shook her head, continuing, "well, he was as innocent as a newborn babe, next to that one, Sarah, but . . . well, I prefer our new preacher. You should meet him," she said. "He's single, ya' know. Not bad looking, and a real strong speaker." Sarah had to laugh at her obvious matchmaking attempt, all the while praying that Gray Eagle would stay around until after they left.

"We'd better get going," Samuel said, glancing out the window. The snow was falling very fast, and Sarah was surprised to see that, since she and her father had come back into the cabin, at least an inch of new snow now covered the ground.

As they left the cabin, Samuel looked around at the ground for any new footprints. Sarah looked too, knowing her father would insist she accompany them back to Hastings if he saw even one sign of Indians. She was relieved that the new snow had covered the old footprints she was sure belonged to Gray Eagle.

Rosie gave Sarah a quick hug and a kiss on the cheek, thanking her for the generous gifts. Then Samuel hugged his daughter. "I wish you were back in town with us, Sarah. I can't shake this feeling." Again, he glanced around the surrounding area, his view blocked by the density of the falling snow.

"I'm fine, Father. Please don't worry. I like it here. I'd be miserable in town. You know that." She kissed his cheek. "You had better get going. This snow doesn't look like it's about to let up."

"Well, all right," her father said, looking uncomfortable

and hesitant to leave her. He gave her a quick kiss on the cheek and then turned, walking briskly to the waiting buggy. He slid in beside Rosie, who waved happily in Sarah's direction, and pulled an old wool blanket across her and Samuel's laps. Sarah smiled and waved as she watched them ride off. Alone at last, she thought, anxiously awaiting the return of Gray Eagle.

CHAPTER THIRTY-FOUR

Sarah had barely taken her coat off and settled into her rocker in front of the blazing fire, a hot mug of coffee in her hands, when she heard a horse neigh and Glory's answering whinny from the barn. She jumped up, setting her coffee mug on the table, and hurried to the door. She hoped it was Gray Eagle, but guessed it was Moses who had arrived. She opened the door at his knock, not at all surprised to see it was him, but slightly disappointed.

"Merry Christmas, darlin'," he purred, his voice the deep, melodious rumble that had so completely irritated her in the past. He grinned at her, his dark eyes twinkling with mock devilment.

"Merry Christmas to you, Moses. Come on in," she replied. "Looks like we're in for quite an accumulation." She nodded toward the snow as he stamped his feet and brushed the snow off his hat and coat, as best he could, using only his good arm. She noticed the slight grimace of pain as he took off his coat, and how he favored his wounded arm and side.

"How are you doing?" she asked, nodding toward his arm and side.

"Fit as a fiddle," he replied, smiling, "a broken fiddle." She would have worried about his words if he hadn't smiled at her in his usual devilish manner.

"Seriously," she said, handing him a hot mug of coffee, "how are you?"

"'Bout as good as can be expected," he replied, his smile fading. "It'll be a while before I get my gun arm back." He looked slightly worried. "But I will," he stated, determinedly.

"Oh, I'm sure of that," she said, her voice decisively firm.

They drank their coffee then, in the usual aura of contented compatibility that always seemed to surround them, now that they had become heartfelt friends.

"Passed your pa and Rosie on my way here," Moses said, laughing. "That Rosie really brightens up a snowy day. She told me you were waiting and I'd better not poke along, then winked at me. Your pa just shook his head and shrugged his shoulders," he added.

"Rosie's an incurable romantic," Sarah replied, "and nothing's going to change her, not even the truth." They both laughed, then, and Sarah was truly pleased he had come. "Want something to eat?" she asked. "Got a roast and cornbread on the stove."

"Sure, sounds good," he replied.

Sarah wondered where Gray Eagle was and if he had eaten. Also if he was in out of the cold. She looked out the window as she dished them both up a plate of the succulent roast, noticing a brilliant ray of sunshine burst through the thinning snowflakes. "Looks like the snow's letting up," she said, "Maybe it won't be as bad as I thought."

"Never can tell this time of year," Moses replied, taking his plate from her, and sitting down. She smiled at him, glad they had become such good friends.

When they finished eating, Sarah cleared the table, and Moses went to sit by the fireplace in her father's large rocker. He rubbed his stomach, a satisfied look on his face.

"Want more coffee?" she asked, a feeling of contentment filling her.

"No, thanks," he replied. "Come sit by me, Sarah," he ordered softly, pulling her smaller rocker over closer to the one he sat in. She sat down, and the two of them looked at the red and gold flames in the fireplace, a rich silence between them. He reached over, taking her hand in his. The leathery feel of his hand as he rubbed her hand tenderly, with just the tip of his fingers, sent a tingling feeling through her. She smiled and closed her eyes, enjoying the deeply satisfying bond of friendship they now shared.

"Sarah," Moses said, interrupting their closeness, "I have something for you." He reached into his pocket, taking out a small, shiny box. "I saw this at Tommy's store and thought of you. I wanted you to have it. Merry Christmas, Darlin'," he said, as he handed her the box.

Sarah took it, wondering what it could be. No man, other than her father and John Bruce, had ever given her a present before. She rubbed the top of the satiny-smooth box, smiling at him. "Thank you, Moses," she said, her voice barely a whisper as she opened it. Inside was the most beautiful comb she had ever seen. It was a rich brown color with muted, golden yellow highlights. Sarah knew it was called tortoiseshell. "Oh, Moses!" she exclaimed, taking it from its container, "It's the most wonderful gift ever!"

"I thought it would look pretty in your hair, Sarah. Every time you wear it, I hope you'll think of me, and the friendship we have," Moses said, "that we'll *always* have."

Sarah eased the comb through her hair, wondering if he knew just how much his gift really meant to her. She reached up with one hand, and touched the new comb, so pleased to have it. Then leaned over and softly kissed him on the cheek. "I'll wear it *every day* as long as I live," she said, her eyes sparkling with happiness!

Moses smiled at her words, remembering how his wife had reacted the same way when he gave her gifts. But she wasn't his wife, and he was determined not to ruin Christmas with the painful memories from his past. "I'm glad you like it, darlin'. Now, how about another cup of coffee? I sure could use it," he said, trying to quell sad thoughts that threatened to engulf him.

"As you wish, my dear friend," Sarah answered, squeezing his hand and going to the stove. As she made a fresh pot of coffee, she thought of all the changes the past year had brought: her constant embarrassment at the hands of Moses, "the rogue"; of Gray Eagle's appearance at the cave, and his fall, and how she tended him; of how she grew to love him, in spite of her father's hatred for Indians; of the night she and Moses delivered Melinda Rose's baby, Danny; and of the death of her friend, John Bruce.

She looked at Moses, who sat with his legs stretched out in front of him, his sore arm cradled across his lean stomach. His head lolled to one side. "He's asleep," she whispered, "Bless his heart."

She walked to the window, looking out at the clear blue sky, happy to see the snow had let up. She knew he planned to go to Black Dog Lake, Rosie had said as much, but she hated to wake him—hated to have him leave. "Rest was healing," Doc Pearson had said, so she decided to let him rest.

She sat at the table, thinking of the bond between them and the friendship that had grown into a special kind of respect and caring. Oh, Moses, she thought, if we had met first, if there hadn't been your Sarah, or Gray Eagle, what then? She watched as he shifted in the rocker. "I do love you, my friend," she whispered softly, so only she could hear.

A short while later, Moses woke, stretching his long, lean frame.

"Good afternoon, sleepy head," Sarah said, as he stood, easing up to his full height. "Want that coffee now?"

"Sure," he said, his voice sounding drowsy. "How long did I sleep?"

"About an hour," she answered, handing him the cup of coffee. "Want anything to eat?" she asked. "A piece of Rosie's chocolate cake, maybe?"

"No, thanks," he answered. "You trying to fatten me up?"

"Wouldn't hurt to put a little meat on your bones," she said. He smiled, testing the temperature of his coffee with a careful sip. She walked to her sewing basket, then came back to sit across from him. "This isn't much," she said, "especially after your gift, but I made it for you." She handed him the long, red scarf.

He took it, smiling happily. "You made this?" he asked.

"With my two little hands," she teased.

Sensing her playful mood, he teased back, "Then I shall *never* take it off! *Ever!*" He wrapped it, twice, around his neck. The bright red color, looked striking against his dark hair and mustache. "Thank you, Sarah. I really appreciate it."

He quickly finished his coffee. Then walked over to the door, reaching for his hat and coat, grimacing as he pulled them on. "Thank you, darlin'. You take care. I should be back this way in the next couple days, if you've got the coffeepot on."

"Be careful, you hear me. Please be careful, Moses," Sarah pleaded. "And thank you for the lovely comb. The coffeepot will be on whenever you're near."

He smiled, kissed her on the forehead, and then left, grinning that old devilish grin she knew so well. You rogue, you. You dear old rogue, she thought, as she watched him ride out of sight.

CHAPTER THIRTY-FIVE

Moses pulled his collar up higher on his neck and settled into the saddle, his thoughts on a myriad of things that churned over and over in his mind: Sarah, his Sarah, and the Gonzalez Gang. He rode the satin-black horse that had been Antonio Gonzalez's. Spoils of war, he thought, urging the horse on faster, but not wanting to jar his arm or side.

The sun shone brightly, but a crisp chill filled the air, in spite of it. The horse that he now called Midnight, stepped quickly along the trail, surefooted in the soft snow. The trail wound left, then right. Then it wound back again among the trees, and up and down hills covered with pine, sycamore, and tall clumps of prairie grass, dead from winter.

Moses stretched, trying to work a kink out of his side. It was healing good, Doc had said, but he had sharp shards of broken rib floating around inside him, giving him stabs of pain if he bent wrong or slumped in the saddle. He straightened his back, his thoughts drifting, unbidden, back to the day he was shot.

One to go, he thought. I won't rest till the third one is dead, too. Animals! Well, we'll see how brave he is "one against one." And he'll have the advantage with my gun arm in such sorry shape. He thought then, of Sarah, as he came out of his office that day. She had stood frozen in place, a look of surprise and fear on her lovely face. Just like her, he thought. Just like *my* Sarah. He moaned in pain as much from the memory as from the sudden misstep of the large black horse.

"Steady, Midnight. Easy," he crooned, enjoying the way the horse perked up its ears, listening to its new master. Moses looked ahead at the changing landscape they were approaching: an area with large boulders. Snow glistened on the huge rocks that stood taller than a man on horseback, their gray sides streaked with mottled red and brown. A few had brush growing out of them: short, stubby branches still green beneath the newly fallen snow.

Moses shifted in the saddle, trying to ease the ache that grew steadily worse on his injured side. He was beginning to realize he was not up to this ride to Black Dog Lake, and wished he had taken Doc Pearson's advice and stayed off his feet a few more days. But it was too late now! He was too far from Sarah's to turn back, and had to keep going.

The sun was already low in the sky, and snow had begun to fall with a fury. Large, wet flakes quickly blocked the trail from view, making it dangerous for both horse and rider. "Made this trip to Black Dog Lake in a few hours easy, last year," he muttered aloud. "It'll be a blessing to get there tonight."

The horse nickered as if in answer to his voice. Then suddenly, to Moses' surprise, he sidestepped, snorting and rearing in panic, as a cougar hurled itself through the air at the frightened animal and its rider. Moses let out a yell, lost his balance, and fell headlong over the horse's neck. He reached out with the hand on his injured side, to break his fall. It was a reflex action, one that didn't take into consideration the wounds that were just beginning to heal on that side. He heard the horse scream in fear, and the cougar yowl, just before he hit the ground. Pain coursed through him and he welcomed the blackness that quickly blanketed his world. He lay face down, blood running from his cheek into his mustache. Another stream of it began to soak the side of his shirt. He lay unconscious, the densely falling snow quickly covering him. Only Sarah's red scarf stood out: a bright-red beacon in a world of white. Then time stood still.

Sarah had just finished chores for the night, hurrying back into the cabin and out of the heavy snow that fell relentlessly, blocking all but the closest things from view. She even had difficulty locating the cabin in the swirling whiteness, and was glad she hadn't waited any longer to go outside to do the chores.

She took off her coat and boots and began to heat the water she had brought in earlier. Going to the corner shelf, she picked out a book to read. It was one that Ophelia Denton had loaned her, and she was anxious to see what it was about. She was content with her day and ready to settle in for the night. Her only disappointment was that she hadn't gotten to see Gray Eagle.

As the water heated and steam began to rise from the pot, she carefully ladled out enough to fill her washbasin. She dipped her finger in it, quickly pulling it out. "Ouch!" she said, "It's too hot. Now I'll have to wait." She picked up the book, waiting for the water to cool, while she sat by the fireplace, enjoying the warmth within her cabin.

CHAPTER THIRTY-SIX

A horse whinnied and someone yelled her name. He yelled it repeatedly, pronouncing it in two syllables, "Sa-rah! Sa-rah!" She knew immediately it was Gray Eagle, and her heart leapt with joy.

She ran to the door, throwing it open. She was barely able to make out the man, but she saw two horses. "Gray Eagle?" she questioned, peering into the dense whiteness.

"Sa-rah, help! Hurry!" he yelled. She could just make out Gray Eagle stumbling toward her, a large shape draped over his shoulder.

"What is it?" she called, as he entered the cabin. Then she saw the bright red scarf and her heart sank, as fear gripped her with its icy fingers. "Is he dead?" she asked, realizing she was shaking. "Gray Eagle! What happened? Is he dead?"

"No. Not dead. Hurt bad," Gray Eagle rolled Moses off his shoulder onto the bed, straightening to look at her. "Man Sa-rah's friend."

"Oh, Gray Eagle, help me get him out of these wet clothes, please," Sarah asked. Gray Eagle removed Moses' snow-dampened coat, while Sarah removed his boots. Her hands trembled and she felt her heart pounding frantically within her breast. Don't let him die, God. Please, don't let him die! Mother, tell me how to help him. Please, show me what to do! Please! Please, don't let him die, she pleaded soundlessly.

She heard Moses groan as Gray Eagle removed his wet clothes and covered him with the blanket on her bed. Sarah hurried to his side, as Gray Eagle threw his clothes in a heap, beside the bed. "Man lose plenty blood," Gray Eagle told Sarah. She was dismayed to see how much fresh blood already stained the blanket. It was on the same side where the Mexican had shot Moses, weeks earlier.

She hurried to get a cloth, wringing it out in the hot water on the stove, and then rushed back to Moses. She wiped the blood away, trying to determine the extent of his injuries. He groaned again, and she looked at him, shocked to see the trail of blood that trickled across his cheek, into his mustache, and down his neck.

"Oh, Moses," she said, trying to wipe up the blood before it went any further. His face was pale, and she feared he had lost too much blood and might die. Her heart was heavy with grief and worry for him. She looked at Gray Eagle, who stood watching her, his face not betraying his thoughts.

"I need to stop the bleeding. Tear that material into pieces, would you?" she asked, pointing to a muslin shift in a basket by her rocker. Gray Eagle did as she asked and then put them on the bed. Sarah folded a piece of the cloth and gently laid it against the gash on Moses' cheek. She took a larger piece and held it to his side, amazed to feel sharp pieces of bone just beneath the skin's surface. Moses moaned and then lay still.

It took all the cloth pieces to stem the flow of blood from his side. She prayed as she worked, asking for guidance, and for God to help her help him. Gray Eagle helped, too, as she requested, but did not interfere or get in her way.

When the bleeding finally ceased, Sarah pulled the blanket up to Moses' chin and looked at Gray Eagle. "Where did you find him?" she asked.

"Sa-rah's friend at Big Bear Pass. Gray Eagle on way back to Wolf Hunter's. Cougar attack. Horse jump. Man fall. Gray Eagle kill cougar."

"Are you all right?" she asked, suddenly realizing that he could have been hurt.

"Gray Eagle not hurt," he said, smiling at her.

She smiled back at him, reaching up to touch his face. "I'm so glad," she whispered.

"Gray Eagle love Sa-rah. Sa-rah be Gray Eagle's wife soon," he replied.

Hesitantly she rose up on her toes and kissed him. Gray Eagle's arms slipped around her in a warm embrace that lit a spark within her, bringing feelings like none she had ever felt before. She relaxed against him, placing her arms around his neck. She felt the silky texture of his long black hair and the warmth of his breath against her neck. "I've missed you," she whispered, her voice husky with the new sensations that coursed through her. She thought of her father's words "stinkin' Indians,"and inhaled softly, smelling the clean, fresh scent of him. She was happy her father was wrong. Moses groaned then, disturbing their embrace. "I need to find some material to bandage him and see what medicines I have," Sarah said as she smiled and stepped away from Gray Eagle's strong, muscular arms.

"Gray Eagle put horses in barn," he said, wrapping his long buffalo robe around him, and then he went outside. Sarah searched through her cupboard, gathering all the medicinal supplies she could find. She found her mother's book of remedies and glanced through it, wondering what she could do to help. She looked nervously at Moses, who lay still as death, his face gray from pain and loss of blood.

Soon, Gray Eagle reentered the cabin. He stood looking at her, his dark eyes showing no hint of what he was feeling. Sarah, on the other hand, felt tense and nervous because of his closeness. She looked at him, admiring his chiseled face, his smooth skin stretched tightly across high cheekbones and his dark-brown, almost black, eyes. A necklace of bear claws circled his neck, on his buckskin shirt, and an eagle feather hung from his long ebony hair. He would have seemed menacing if she hadn't already known him.

"Sa-rah heal friend. Friend live?" he asked, looking at Moses.

"I'll try," she answered. "I hope he'll live."

"Sa-rah good healer. Heal Gray Eagle." She smiled at him, knowing Moses' injuries were much worse. "Sa-rah have medicine?" he asked.

"I'm not sure if what I have will be enough," she replied, with a worried look upon her face.

"Gray Eagle go to Wolf Hunter. He have good medicine. Wolf Hunter help," he offered. Sarah smiled, as a million questions went through her mind about this Wolf Hunter and his medicines. Gray Eagle came to Sarah, taking her into his arms. "I go," he said, holding her close, "Return soon." She touched his face, looking up into his eyes, her heart skipping beats as he held her against him. "Sa-rah Gray Eagle's woman. Love Gray Eagle?" he questioned, a serious look upon his face.

"Yes," she replied, "I love you."

"Gray Eagle love Sa-rah, too," he said, turning quickly, wrapping his long robe around him. With nary a glance back at her, he opened the door and was gone into the darkness of the night.

Moses began to cough and groan in pain. Sarah rushed to his side, worried that he might be bleeding inside. She called his name, as she checked his bandages, but got no response. She picked up his clothing and emptied the pockets, then hung them on the back of a chair. As she set the contents—his sheriff's badge and a small packet of papers—on the small table next to the bed, a picture fell from them. She knew, before she even looked at it, that it was a picture of his wife.

She picked it up, turning it over in her hand. The photo was of a woman with an engaging smile. Long hair curled softly around her face, and she had a small nose, and well-defined lips. Her cheekbones were high. Her chin, above the lace collar of her dress, looked petite. Somewhat similar to my own, Sarah thought.

Her eyes were what caught your attention, though. They seemed to be filled with an abundance of joy. Sarah understood, now, why he felt such a bond with her. There is a tremendous resemblance between us, she thought, tucking the cherished photo carefully back in amongst his papers, careful not to damage it.

She looked at Moses, lying in her bed, so pale and still. She thought of all they had been through together, and how their friendship had grown over the months into an unlikely, but unbreakable, bond. She knew, deep in her heart, she loved him. A love built on trust and respect. Yet she couldn't help the feelings Gray Eagle stirred within her when he held her. She also had no doubt she loved him, no doubt about wanting to be his wife.

She wondered what it was that determined whom a person loved. She wondered how it could be that a woman could love two men at one time. "Oh, Mother," she whispered, "I need you. I need to talk to you. I have so many things I need to ask you."

She yawned, stretching her arms out to her sides, and then went to dump the bloody water she had used to clean Moses' wounds. She rinsed the bowl and pieces of cloth, filled it with clean water, and returned it to the table beside the bed.

Carefully, she washed Moses' face, rubbing gently where the blood had dried around his mustache. He groaned and stirred as she worked. She pulled the blanket back, exposing his chest and the curly black hair that covered it, and moved his arm to get a better look at his side. Her face blanched as she saw the raw flesh and large black-and-blue area surrounding it. A trickle of blood still seeped from the wound, and she quickly stifled it, praying he would not lose any more blood.

His face was deathly pale, and the skin had begun to bruise around the gash on his cheek. Gently, she brushed the hair back from his forehead, noticing as she did, that his skin seemed cool to the touch. She pulled the blanket back up to his chin and went to get a salve to put on the wound on his cheek. She hoped she had everything she needed to make a poultice for the wound on his side. She had often seen her mother use poultices and heard Rosie tell of their healing properties, especially against infection. She washed her hands and took the jar of salve to his bedside. She pulled the blanket up again, then spread the salve across the wound on his cheek, barely touching the raw area, not wanting it to begin bleeding. Then she began to make the poultice to put on his side, hoping it might help. He moaned when she touched him, but lay still. She wished there was a way she could contact Doc Pearson, but knew it would be nearly impossible for the elderly physician to find his way to her cabin in the dense snow. She shuddered when she realized she was Moses' only hope. Like him, she too, was trapped by the storm.

She sat there, looking at him. His cheek was swollen now, making the contours of his face decidedly different. "Oh, Moses," she said, "my poor friend."

She walked to the window, seeing it was blanketed with snow, blocking everything from sight. Her thoughts turned to Gray Eagle, and she feared for his safety, having no idea how far he had to travel or when he would return. She only knew how grateful she felt because he had saved Moses' life.

CHAPTER THIRTY-SEVEN

For four days, Sarah tended to Moses. More and more, she found herself going to the window to peer out, worried about Gray Eagle. The snow had stopped falling around noon, the day after he left. Now, the sun shone brightly, though the air felt crisp. The wind blew in gusts, chilling a person to the bone.

Sarah was freezing when she went to feed and water the animals. She hurried into the cabin, quickly shutting the door so Moses wouldn't catch a chill. He lay as she left him. She hung up her coat and hat and laid her mittens in front of the stove, along with her boots, to dry. Then she turned, backing up to the stove and enjoying the warmth.

She smelled the chicken she had cooking on the stove, the succulent aroma causing her stomach to growl. She had had little luck getting the rich broth into Moses. She had lifted his head, placed two pillows beneath it, and turned his face toward her, spooning the broth into his mouth and praying he would not choke. She hoped what he didn't drool down the side of his face, or cough out at her, would give him enough nourishment to sustain him.

The gash on his face looked much better, though now it was black and blue with yellow undertones. She was certain he should have gained consciousness by now. She remembered Rosie talking about a man in a . . . coma? Yes, that was the word.

That man had never regained consciousness, and she feared the same fate for Moses.

She brought a cup of water to his bedside and tried to spoon some of it into his mouth. He coughed and choked, sputtering loudly. She spoke quietly to him, assuring him that he was safe and would be all right, but got no response.

A horse whinnied in front of the cabin and she ran to the window just in time to see Gray Eagle slide off his horse, a brown-and-white "paint". He had no saddle, and the bridle was different than Sarah was used to seeing.

She met him at the door, her heart bursting with joy at seeing him alive and well. He carried a large deer-hide pouch and smiled when he saw her. Sarah embraced him, and he dropped the bag, kissing her with a hunger that surprised both of them. She felt a warmth begin to build within her, and was overwhelmed by the intensity of the feelings that flooded her being.

It was Gray Eagle who pulled back, a groan escaping from his lips. He wanted her, and his body had responded to her softness and beauty. Yet he could not forget he was an Indian, and among "The People" there was a high moral code. The Sioux believed it important to show honor. Gray Eagle believed, as his people did, that dishonor would bring a shortage of buffalo at the next hunt. It was hard to control the feelings that coursed through him when Sarah was in his arms, though, but he knew he must.

He also remembered, all too vividly, the way Sarah had run away the first time he kissed her, by the lake, the day she nearly drowned. At first, he thought she had given her heart to another. The man in the bed, he suspected, but his suspicions were laid to rest when he saw how happy she was to see him. He had watched in silence, as she tended her friend, to see where her heart lay. "I love you," she had said: music to his ears that made his heart sing.

"Wolf Hunter send medicine," Gray Eagle said, breaking the mood.

"I'm so glad. I hope it helps. Be sure and thank him for me when you see him again, please."

"Sa-rah's friend better?" he asked, looking at Moses.

"I don't know," she answered. "The wound on his cheek is healing, and the ones on his arm and side no longer bleed, but I'm worried because he hasn't come to, yet."

"Great Spirit make man sleep. Heal," he said. Sarah was amazed by his words, having never realized that to an Indian everything had a sacred meaning.

"Have you eaten?" she asked.

"Eat plenty," he answered, rubbing his stomach. Sarah laughed, taking the provisions out of the bag. "These will help, I'm sure," she said, "thank you, Gray Eagle." He smiled at her, glad that he was able to be of help.

Gray Eagle remained at the cabin, helping Sarah with the chores, and assisting her as she tended Moses. Every time they moved him he groaned in pain, and Sarah kept an anxious eye on the pieces of bone still so near the surface of his skin. She thanked Gray Eagle for all his help, nearly beside herself with exhaustion, from staying by Moses' side both day and night, and sleeping very little.

"Sa-rah sleep," Gray Eagle told her. "Gray Eagle watch Sa-rah's friend."

Sarah looked at him in surprise. "You would do that?" she questioned. He nodded, going over to the rocker beside the bed. "Thank you," she replied. "I'm so tired. I'll only lay down a few minutes. If you need anything just call me." She went into her old bedroom, lay on the bed, still in her clothes, and was instantly asleep.

When she awoke three hours later, she was surprised to find her quilt covering her. She stretched, listening for sounds from the other room, but all was quiet. She got up, padding softly into the main room. Moses slept peacefully, but Gray Eagle was nowhere to be seen. Sarah walked to the window and peered out. There was no sign of him.

She put some water on to heat so she could wash, not happy at finding Moses alone, but more curious than anything as to Gray Eagle's whereabouts. Fresh coffee was on the stove, she noticed, and she poured herself a cup. She felt more rested than she had in days.

When the water was hot, she filled the basin in her room, shut the door, and quickly washed up. She longed for a tub bath, but knew that was out of the question. She dried herself and dressed in a yellow blouse that had been her mother's, and an old pair of brown pants. She put on heavy socks and her old, comfortable moccasins, then brushed her hair, combed it, and tied it back with the yellow ribbon Cassandra Winthrop had given her. She smiled, as she thought of her, and prayed her family had made it safely to California and not been caught in a blizzard in the mountains.

Moses groaned loudly. She opened the bedroom door and quickly went to check on him. "Moses?" she said, brushing his hair back off his forehead. His eyes opened, a hazy, unfocused look at first, followed by a hint of recognition.

"Sarah," he whispered, then groaned in pain and was silent. She felt his forehead and thought she detected a slight rise in temperature. She hoped he was not getting a fever, knowing he would have less chance of surviving.

The door opened and Gray Eagle came in, stamping snow off his moccasins. He smiled as he saw that Sarah was awake and looked fresh and rested. "Sa-rah sleep many hours," he said, "feel better. Gray Eagle feed animals. Bring in more water. Sa-rah look pretty." He walked over to stand beside her.

She turned to face him. "Thank you," she whispered.

His arms enfolded her, holding her close against him. "Sarah not need thank Gray Eagle. Gray Eagle love Sa-rah," he replied.

"I love you, too," she answered, as a feeling of joy spread quickly through her.

They sat at the table, then, and talked, getting to know more about each other. She told him she was twenty-eight and was surprised to learn he was nearly five years older. She told him that they had moved from a fort far north of Hastings, that her father had been the officer in charge, and that her mother had died when she was ten. She told him how deeply she valued her father's opinions, everything but his hatred for Indians. "Sadly, he will never accept my marriage to one," she told him.

"Sa-rah happier here with father?" he asked. "Forget Gray Eagle? Be friends with Gray Eagle?"

"No!" she exclaimed, looking to see if she had wakened Moses. She lowered her voice and continued, "I love you, Gray Eagle. I want to be your wife."

He smiled, taking her hand from across the table. "Marry soon," he said, "go far away."

She answered with a smile, wondering for the first time, if she *could* go far away. Far from her father and Rosie and Moses. Far from all those she loved here in Hastings. She looked at Gray Eagle, knowing that she loved him, and yet going away would not be that easy. She had enjoyed her life here, and had many friendships she treasured.

She thought of Lilly and their newfound friendship, and of John Bruce and the friendship they had shared, as he taught her how to track and shoot. She remembered his laughter when she fell in a pond, long ago, while trying to follow him across it on a fallen log. She remembered how he had whooped with joy the first time she shot a whole row of bottles off a fence, without missing even one. She remembered how he had lain on the walkway, the day he died, blood running through his soft white hair. How he had saved her from being shot by the young Mexican. Tears began to well up in her eyes.

"Sa-rah?" Gray Eagle questioned.

"I was just remembering my old friend," she replied, wiping her eyes and sniffling. "His name was John Bruce. He was my friend from the day I moved here until . . . until he died, saving my life." Her voice was as soft as a whisper now.

"Gray Eagle know Sa-rah's friend," he stated.

"You *knew* him?" She exclaimed, surprised by his words.

"He visit Wolf Hunter many moons ago. John Bruce called 'Spirit Dancer' by my people. Very wise man," Gray Eagle said, as Sarah sat still, astonished by what she was hearing. "'Spirit Dancer' friend to Indians and whites."

"Oh, Gray Eagle. I can't believe you knew him. He was like a father to me. Taught me to hunt and shoot." Sarah's words tumbled from her as fast as her thoughts. "He taught me to track and make a fire with a stick and rock."

"Indian ways," Gray Eagle interrupted.

"Yes," she replied excitedly, "and to clean a hide and make moccasins."

Just then Gray Eagle rose and walked to his robe. He took a pair of knee-high moccasins from the large pouch that hung near it. "Gray Eagle forget. Bring for Sa-rah," he said and handed them to her. "Gray Eagle make for Sa-rah."

"Oh, how beautiful," she said. She quickly pulled them on, feeling the thick rabbit fur inside them. "Oh, they're lovely," she exclaimed, "and warm! Thank you!" She walked back and forth in them, enjoying their softness and warmth.

"I have something for you, too," she replied and walked to her room, then quickly returned. In her hand was a leather sheath, and in it was John Bruce's Bowie knife. "This was given to me when John . . . when 'Spirit Dancer' died," she said, liking the name the Indians had given him, "because I was his best friend." She looked at the handle of the knife, encased in its sheath. "I want you to have it, to keep you safe."

Gray Eagle took it, smiling at her in gratitude. "Thank you. It will bring Gray Eagle much protection," he said and bent to kiss her. "Gray Eagle go now," he said, stepping away from her, "return soon."

"Oh," she replied, not wanting him to leave.

He smiled at her, seeing her disappointment. "Marry soon, when warm rains come," he said, looking at her in a way that made her cheeks flush. "Gray Eagle love Sa-rah." He wrapped the buffalo robe around him, opened the door, and left.

"Me, too," Sarah replied, flexing her toes within the warm moccasins he had given her. "Me, too."

CHAPTER THIRTY-EIGHT

Sarah was awakened, in the middle of the night, by a loud noise. She sat up in her bed, listening. "Sarah!" she heard Moses yell, surprising her. "Sarah, they're gonna shoot! Look out! Look out!" he shouted. Sarah jumped from her bed, taking no time to grab her robe, and hurried to the table, barely able to see in the darkness. Only the light of the moon guided her, as she lit the oil lamp. Moses groaned and thrashed about in the bed. "Sarah!" he yelled again, his voice hoarse.

"Moses," she replied. "I'm here. It's okay." She saw that the small table beside the bed had been overturned and realized that was the noise that had wakened her. "Moses, lay still. It's me. It's Sarah. You'll bleed again if you don't stay still," she pleaded.

He looked at her, his eyes trying to focus. "Sarah," he whispered, "Sarah."

She sat on the edge of the bed. "I'm here. It's okay. You'll be all right," she said, pushing gently on his shoulders to get him to lay still.

He reached up with his good arm, touching her cheek. "I love you," he said. "I love you, Sarah." Then his arm dropped down, and he moaned. He lay still, his eyes closed, once more. His hand rested against her, the threadbare gown all that lay between his hand and her breast. She glanced at him quickly, knowing he was not conscious, and back at his hand, his fingers curled against her. She looked at his face, at the childlike expression of innocence as he lay there, so helpless, his lips slightly open. She took his hand in hers, bending her head to it and holding it to her cheek. "You love *her*, Moses, your wife, not me," she whispered.

She laid his hand gently upon his chest and reached up to brush his hair back from his forehead. She was startled at the tremendous heat radiating from him. "Oh, my!" she exclaimed. "You're burning up with fever!" She hurried to get a cloth and the pail of water Gray Eagle had left by the door. She dipped the cloth into the water, placed it on Moses' forehead, then bent, to right the table and pick up the things that had fallen.

Moses began to thrash about, groaning as he did so. "Lay still," she ordered firmly, hoping he would do as she said.

"Sarah," he yelled. "Sarah! Look out!" She had all she could do to keep his flailing arms from upsetting the small table again.

"It's all right, Moses,"she said, trying to hold him down with the weight of her body. Her hands held his wrists, fighting to prevent him from hurting himself further. She was amazed at his strength and hoped she could hold him, afraid he was already bleeding from his side.

"Get out of the way, Sarah!" he yelled. Then his head rolled to one side and he was still once more. She took the warm cloth from his forehead, wrung it out in the pail, and placed it back across his forehead. He groaned, but continued to lay still. She pulled back the blanket and looked at his side. To her dismay, the bandage was red with blood. She wondered how much more he could bleed, and still live. She rose, hurrying to the kitchen table, and searched through the herbs and medicines. When she found what she needed, she began to mix a poultice in her mother's large bowl. She heard him groan in pain and worked faster, her hands trembling slightly. Taking a wide piece of cloth from her sewing basket, she tore it into strips, a worried expression upon her face.

She remembered the pieces of bone she had felt under the skin on the wounded side and knew they were probably causing him to bleed, as he thrashed about, piercing the skin. She went back to him and gently pulled off the old bandage, now sopping wet with blood, and, very carefully, ran her hand across his wound. She groaned as she felt the sharp ends protruding from the skin. A poultice wouldn't help this.

"Oh, Moses," she sighed, sitting on the edge of the bed. "Oh, Lord, help me." Moses opened his eyes and looked at her, a dazed look upon his face. "Hello, darlin'," he said, his voice deep, his speech garbled. She was about to answer, glad to see he recognized her, when he reached up and pulled her tightly against him, his lips finding hers.

She pushed against the bed with both hands, trying to turn her head, but she could not. She felt his hand slide across her back and down her side, and struggled harder. "Moses!" she exclaimed, pulling her face away from his.

"Sh-h! Darlin'," he said, "I won't hurt the baby."

She froze, looking at him, shocked by his words. His hand slid toward her stomach then, and she screamed "No!" as his body shuddered and, once again, he passed out. Sarah jumped away from him and slid off the bed onto the floor. She was trembling now and wrapped her arms across her breasts, crying silently. Then she pulled her knees up under her gown and wrapped her arms around them. Too many feelings were surfacing, at once, for her to understand.

He was her friend, her *best* friend, and he thought she was *his* Sarah! Why did that make her feel so angry? No, not angry—she searched her mind for the right word to explain her feelings—hurt . . . I feel so . . . hurt, she thought, fresh tears falling on the soft fabric of her gown, near the smudge of blood across the front of it.

She got up from the floor and hurried to her room to change her clothes, wondering what Gray Eagle would have thought, if he had come in the door when Moses was holding her. "Well, Moses Gentry," she said to herself in the solitude of her small room, "we're gonna have to set you straight on which Sarah you're with, before you go getting yourself scalped!" She smiled, then thought of Gray Eagle and the way she felt when he kissed her. She couldn't understand why she felt so sad, though, when Moses kissed her, believing her to be his Sarah.

She returned to the other room, intent on the tasks ahead, and changed the dressing on his arm, glad that it looked better. She took the cloth from his forehead and brushed his hair back, noticing he was still burning up with fever. Then, looking closely at his side, she knew she had to get the pieces of bone out, in order for him to heal.

She placed a thick piece of fabric under his side, and went to get her sharpest knife and needle and thread. She threaded the needle and then went into her bedroom. In the back of the cupboard, she found the bottle of whiskey her father had kept for medicinal purposes. Moses would surely need it if she were to open his side and remove the fragments of bone, she thought.

She went to the kitchen and began heating water on the stove, reading through her mother's medical book while she waited. When the water was ready, she washed her hands and cleaned the blade of the knife. It was then she prayed, asking God to help her, to show her what to do, and—for heaven's sake—to keep him alive! Please! As was her way, she also spoke to her mother, asking for her guidance and help.

Thus finished, she went to Moses, calling his name and lifting his head as she dribbled the whiskey into his mouth. He coughed twice, spraying her blouse and face, and opened his eyes, smiling that old devilish smile she knew so well. He raised his good arm, reaching up to the bottle, swallowing a goodly amount of the liquid. She had to smile, as he tried to focus, while swigging down more than half of the whiskey.

"Let's stay home, Sarah. I don' wanna go to town today," he said, his words thick and garbled, his breath strong with the scent of liquor. She knew he thought he was still with his wife, reliving the day he lost her. She shook her head, determined to ignore that fact. Determined to help him, if she could, in spite of it!

Oh, we're going to town, darlin', she thought, and you're not going to like it. She sat the bottle next to the bed and picked up the knife. Biting her lip, she cut a small slit beside the protruding bone in his side but was unable to do more, as Moses yelled and struck out with his good arm, hitting her a resounding crack across her cheekbone. She staggered back, landing with a thud, on her butt, on the floor. Pain shot through her face, and small stars seemed to bounce before her eyes in a sky of black. She lay back then, too dizzy to sit up, clutching her face in her hands.

She had no idea how long it was before her senses cleared and she could get up. The knife lay beside the bed, its tip red with blood. The cloth beneath Moses was pooled with blood as it ran from the fresh cut. She grabbed the clean cloth she had torn earlier and sopped up the blood, watching for his hand, not wanting to end up with two sore cheeks.

Then she caught hold of the end of a piece of bone and pulled gently, pleased, as it popped loose from within him, followed by another small piece. She pushed carefully on his side and saw yet another sharp piece of bone protrude. Moses moaned and tried to reach his side, but she blocked his hand, pushing his arm away. He said something, but it was too muddled for her to understand. She tried to grab another piece of bone, but it slid back under the skin. Her fingers were too slippery, with blood, to grab it. She held the cloth against his side as his head rolled back and forth and he moaned softly.

"Sarah," he said, squinting up at her, "hursh like hell." He tried touching his side.

"Here," she said, pushing his hand away and picking up the bottle. She lifted his head. "Drink this, you devil, before I slug you." She smiled as his mouth searched for the bottle, the same way an infants would. He closed his lips around it, swallowing steadily. When she pulled the bottle away from him, he tried to reach for it, but ended up howling in pain. She pulled back quickly, but not before his arm gripped her around the waist. "Moses!" she exclaimed, trying to get out of his reach and not spill the remaining whiskey.

She shoved against his chest, her feet slipping out from under her, and fell with a thud across him. He yelped in pain, at the same time she yelled out in surprise. His arm fell across the back of her legs, his hand resting on her buttocks. "Oh, for heaven's sake!" she muttered, trying to figure out how to get off him without hurting him.

"I love ya', ole Sarah girl," she heard him say. Then she heard a loud intake of breath! She turned, looking at the door, and her heart stopped! Gray Eagle stood stock-still in the doorway, his mouth wide open, seeing his intended as she *never* intended!

"This isn't what it looks like," she said, rolling across Moses, no longer worried about his wounds. She rolled onto the floor with a thud and then got up, trying to straighten her blouse with her free hand. Her other hand held the almost empty bottle of whiskey. Her hair straggled around her shoulders, not quite covering the swelling of her cheek, and her steadily darkening eye. She sat the bottle on the table and tucked in her blouse, one of her moccasins half off her foot.

"Oh, God," she said, seeing the stern look on Gray Eagle's face. "I was trying to help him," she explained. "His bones were . . . I mean, the bone was sticking up . . . Oh, God. You must let me explain . . ."

It was at that moment that Moses chose to speak, "Sarah, 'mere, honey. I love you, Sarah."

Sarah looked at Gray Eagle, who continued to stand perfectly still, his hand upon the door. "Oh, damn!" she exclaimed. "Sarah's his *wife's* name. He thinks *I'm* his wife," she blurted out. A mixture of alarm and despair crossed her face. Gray Eagle watched her, his eyes filled with a menacing look she had never seen before. Then he turned away.

"Don't go! It's not what it looks like!" Sarah cried out. And to her relief, he shut the door, shutting himself inside. She stood there, relieved, hearing Moses begin to babble. "Shut up! You polecat! Don't make things worse!" she yelled toward the bed.

She looked back at Gray Eagle, who had begun to smile. Then she went to him, wrapping her arms around his waist. "Sa-rah need help?" he asked.

"Sarah loves Gray Eagle," she said, looking pleadingly into his eyes. "Not that polecat!" He touched her cheek, causing her to wince and pull back from him.

"Piece of meat help," he said.

"No, I'm not hungry," she said, completely missing his meaning, "I have to get another splinter of bone out of that old rogue, before he dies."

"What is 'rogue'?" Gray Eagle asked.

"A . . . a polecat," Sarah said, reaching up and kissing his cheek. "Would you help me, please? I need you to hold him down."

"Gray Eagle help Sa-rah *and* Sa-rah's friend," he answered.

"He's no friend of mine!" she exclaimed, "Just a polecat!"

Sarah had to make a small crosscut incision in Moses' side, to remove the last piece of bone. But this time Gray Eagle held his arms so she wouldn't get hurt. Moses had had enough whiskey, by then, that he groaned as she made the small incision, but seemed oblivious to the pain, otherwise. The last piece of bone slid through the cut quite easily, much to her relief, and she cushioned his wound with the large cloth pad to stifle the flow of blood.

She looked at Gray Eagle and smiled. He knew how lucky he was that she loved him. He also knew how beautiful she was, even with a swollen black eye. "Sa-rah good healer," he said, pleasing her with his praise.

"If he doesn't die," she remarked.

"Sa-rah's friend strong," he stated. "Gray Eagle ask Wakantanka make him well."

"Who?" Sarah asked, curious to learn more.

"Wakantanka," he replied, "Great Spirit. Can heal all wounds."

Sarah smiled at him, awed by the discovery that even Indians had a god. "I'd like to know more about your . . . Wakantanka, your 'Great Spirit,'" she said, as she stitched Moses' side.

"Great Spirit like white man's God," Gray Eagle told her.

"You know about God?" Sarah asked, very surprised to learn this.

"Mother teach Gray Eagle about God and Great Spirit. Gray Eagle remember best Great Spirit's ways. Believe like Father's people," he explained.

"I hope you'll teach me more about your people."

"Gray Eagle teach Sa-rah," he answered.

"Sarah!" Moses yelled. "Look out, Sarah!" Then he lay still.

"Moses' wife was named Sarah," she explained, "She was killed. I look like her."

"Moses care for both," Gray Eagle replied, looking over at Moses.

"Yes," Sarah answered, "but he *loved* his wife."

"Gray Eagle understand. Love. Friendship. *Same* between man and woman sometime. Gray Eagle understand," he repeated, and Sarah knew, that indeed, he did understand and didn't feel threatened by the bond she and Moses shared.

All that day, and the night that followed, Moses drifted in and out of consciousness, as the fever raged, then abated. Gray Eagle tended the outside chores and helped with the care of Moses, while Sarah slept. Later he slept, while she tended Moses.

Snow began to fall again, and Sarah knew in her heart that Gray Eagle would leave soon. She was pleased at all that he had told her about his people, and after they ate a delicious supper of chicken and rice and saleratus biscuits brimming with butter, she walked out to the barn with him while he prepared to leave.

She was pleased to see John Bruce's Bowie knife strapped securely to his side. "This is Glory," she said, going up to her horse to pet her velvety soft muzzle.

"Glory," he repeated, patting the horse.

"And this is Pet and her calf, Emmy," Sarah said, rubbing Pet's nose as the calf skittered away, kicking its legs in the air, playfully. "On the other side of the barn is Midnight, Moses' horse." Midnight tossed his head and snorted as they came near.

"Good horse," Gray Eagle said, "plenty afraid, but strong." He talked softly to the horse, in the language of his people, as Sarah listened, enjoying the rhythm of his words even though she couldn't understand them. "Gray Eagle call him Night Racer, if he Gray Eagle's horse."

Sarah smiled, looking at Gray Eagle's horse. It was smaller than Midnight, yet sturdy and strong, white with large russet spots all over its body. "Gray Eagle call horse Sun Racer. Runs fast," he answered, patting his horse and brushing his hand across its flank.

"I wish you didn't have to go," she said, a feeling of sadness running through her.

He put his arms around her, pulling her to him, and bent to kiss her. "Marry soon. Be Gray Eagle's wife. Sa-rah help friend, Moses," he said. "Gray Eagle return soon." He let go of her then, and turned, walking his horse out of the barn. He smiled at her and leapt onto his horse's back. Then he rode off into the snow that quickly covered the ground and tree branches with a coat of white. Sarah closed the barn door and walked slowly back to the cabin, turning to look into the snow, once more, before she went inside.

CHAPTER THIRTY-NINE

You old rogue, Sarah thought, giving me a black eye. Moses lay still, sleeping, as she felt his forehead. He was still burning with fever. She wrung out the cloth in the pail of cool water, folded it in two, and placed it across his brow. He shivered slightly, as she checked his arm and side, then she pulled the blanket up to his chin and went to pour herself a cup of coffee.

A branch hit the window on the backside of the cabin, causing her to jump. She got up and looked out, but all she could see was snow as it filled the air, making her feel trapped and alone. Oh, Mother, she thought, do you even know what's going on in my life? Can you see me? Do you know I love an Indian? She filled her cup with coffee. I love him, Mother, so much. And he does know God, ours, and the god of his people.

She swallowed a sip of the steaming brew. "And do you know that I love that old rogue, too, Mother?" she asked aloud. "Two men, and neither like Tommy Dawson," she whispered. "These two are like the 'knights of old' in your books, Mother. Though Tommy has become a real surprise. He's become strong, now that Melinda Rose is in his life." She smiled as she thought of Tommy and Melinda Rose, and then sipped more of her coffee.

"There's so many things I'd like to talk to you about, Mother. About my dear friend, Moses, and the man I intend to marry. About the feelings I have when Gray Eagle kisses me. They're not like anything I've ever felt before. Do all men cause feelings like that? Or is it because I love him?"

Moses groaned then, and she went to him, stooping to change the cloth on his forehead. He still shivered, yet felt hotter to the touch than before. She wished her father and Rosie were there, or Doc Pearson. Wished she could get help for him, but knew he could die if he got pneumonia from being outside. Besides, she couldn't lift him. She felt frustrated by her lack of knowledge and ability.

"You better not die, Moses Gentry!" She ordered, watching him shake. "I'll never forgive you if you do." She covered him with another blanket, put two large pieces of wood in the fireplace, then paced beside the bed, wondering what else she could do.

By nightfall, she knew Moses was in trouble. His teeth chattered and his body shook with a fierceness that terrified her. She had every blanket on him that she possessed, and still he was cold. He would mumble and rage in his delirium, then lay still as death, only his teeth chattering loudly in the silence of the cabin. Once, he called out, "Sarah! Sarah, Melinda Rose is having the baby! Help me, Sarah!" and she knew he was thinking of the night they delivered Danny, and she was beside herself with worry.

In the dark of the night, not knowing what else to do, she slipped beneath the covers, holding him close to her, his back against her, her skirts covering his shaking legs. "Dear God," she prayed, whispering softly, "please don't let him die. You took my friend, John Bruce. Please don't take Moses, too. I couldn't stand it, if You did."

Sarah woke about midmorning to the sun shining brightly through the cabin window. She stretched and then suddenly remembered where she was. She was looking up toward the ceiling of the cabin, and realized she was laying flat on her back. She also realized that Moses' head lay against her shoulder and he was no longer shaking. He also no longer had his back to her, but was turned toward her, one leg thrown heavily across her, pinning her legs.

"Moses!" she pleaded. "Get off me!"

She felt him lift his head off her shoulder as he turned to look at her. He shook his head, stretching, wincing from the pain in his side, and then blinked, trying to get his bearings. A contented look upon his face. "Sarah," he said, as he rubbed his eyes. Then he gasped in surprise! "Sarah!" he exclaimed, pulling away from her. "Sarah! Oh, God! What's going on?" He tried to move, to sit up, and howled in pain. His eyes were wide with disbelief. "Where are we? Are you all right? My God, Sarah! How did this happen?"

Sarah lay still, at first amazed by his reaction as he discovered her beside him in bed. Then as she realized how upset he was, she had all she could do not to burst out laughing.

"I didn't mean to. I mean, I'll marry you." His words tumbled over one another in his haste to right the grievous wrong he thought he had committed. He looked around, trying to figure out where he was, as she lay still, delighting in his discomfort. "Oh, God," he groaned, "What the hell happened to my side? Hurts like fire." He tried to sit up to look at it. "This is your place," he said, recognizing her cabin. He shook his head, trying to remember how he had gotten into such a predicament.

"How do you like my black eye?" She asked, her voice whisper-soft compared to his. She turned her head so he could see.

A look of disbelief clouded his features. "Who did that? I'll kill him," he declared. "Tell me who hit you!" he ordered.

She had all she could do not to laugh at him. "Why, *you* did," she whispered.

"Oh, my God!" he moaned, "I've *never* hit a woman! I wouldn't." Sarah pointed to the whiskey bottle on the table beside the bed. "Oh," he groaned, taking his face in his hands.

He looked at her then, as she started to giggle. "Sarah," he said. "It's all right. It'll be all right," he repeated, a stunned look on his very pale face.

Sarah began to laugh, unable to stop herself. She laughed out loud, a pealing laughter that soon filled the cabin and made the bed shake as she lost all control! Tears ran from her eyes as she held her stomach and roared!

Moses lay stark still, believing she was hysterical because of the liberties he had taken. He tried to think of what to do to calm her. Rolling onto his good side, which hurt nearly more than he could bear, he suddenly remembered. A slap. That was the remedy for hysterical fits in women. He raised his hand, wondering how hard he should hit her. Then, just as he moved to slap her, she turned to face him, and he hit her in her good eye, stopping her laughter and causing her to yelp in pain! She slapped him a crack in return, jarring his whole body.

"Damn!" he sputtered, trying to grab her, as she rolled onto the floor from the bed. She tried to get away, but he held her skirt.

"Let go of me, you . . . you polecat!" she screamed. "First you blacken one eye, and now you hit me in the other." She jerked her skirt out of his hand, and he mumbled something and then lay back on the bed. "Oh, Lord," she thought, suddenly realizing he was probably bleeding again. She got up off the floor, looking at him. His face was white and he grimaced in pain.

"Moses?" she said. "Are you bleeding again? Let me see." She hurried to him, peering down into his face. His teeth were clenched and he groaned, frightening her by the intensity of it. "Moses, let me see your side," she said and began to lift the blanket, meaning to pull it down to his waist.

Before she knew what was happening, however, he reached out and grabbed her wrist! "Let me go, you brute," she screamed, but he held tightly, waiting for her to calm down. She was furious! She struggled to get lose, trying to free her hand so she could scratch his eyes out! How could she explain *two* black eyes to Gray Eagle, she wondered, or for that matter, to anyone who saw her in the next few days? What if her father and Rosie came to check on her? She moaned, overwhelmed by the gravity of the situation.

"There, there," Moses crooned, trying to soothe her. She quit struggling and began to try to figure a worthy explanation to tell folks. At last her heart quit racing, and she sat still, on the edge of the bed. "I know this looks bad," Moses said, "but we'll just go to the reverend and tell him we had a lover's quarrel. Tell him we want him to marry us, 'quiet like.'" He smiled at her, glad that she was listening to him and no longer hysterical.

She looked at him, her eyes flashing, but didn't answer him, wondering just how long he would go on. "I know you were a . . . um . . . pure, Sarah," Moses said, clearing his throat, "and it was beastly of me to . . . to . . . you know, but I never . . . *never* forced myself on anybody before." He grew quiet, growing more and more ashamed, as he thought of what he'd done. "It . . . it must have been the whiskey," he said, "I just hope you'll forgive me, Sarah. I've always cared for you, you know that. I'd be proud to be your husband."

She sat still, unable to help herself, enjoying his apology. He sat looking at her, waiting to see the effect of his words on her. "Why, you pompous son of a skunk! You think you can blacken both my eyes, take me to your . . . no . . . to *my* bed, and then just marry me?" Moses was shocked at her angry words. He pulled the blanket up higher, not sure what to say to comfort her.

"Moses Gentry," she said, suddenly beginning to smile, to his surprise, "you don't even know what happened, do you?" He wondered why she was smiling—wondered if some virgins were like this, wondered if he'd have to try to slap her again. She was positively grinning at him now.

"No, ma'am," he replied. "I don't remember. I'm sorry, darlin', but it's the God's truth." He looked at her pleadingly, wondering what else he could have done. "Tell me," he said, looking both forlorn and contrite.

"You didn't do *anything*," she said at last, when she could not stand to torment him any longer. "You were here on Christmas, remember? Then left for Black Dog Lake. On the way, you were jumped by a cougar and fell off your horse, hitting your wounded side and gashing your face on a rock. A friend of mine saw what happened and brought you here. I've been doctoring you for almost a month."

She paused, watching his face as he began to remember. He stared at her, his mind a whirl of thoughts. "But . . . but how did you get the black eyes?" he asked. "And why were we in your bed?" He looked more confused than ever.

"You gave me the black eye, when you hit me, after I cut open your side to remove some bone splinters," she replied, raising her eyebrows at him and pursing her lips.

"Oh, God. I'm sorry," he said. "Did I hurt you?"

"Of course, you hurt me! You gave me a black eye, you lout!"

"But when did I get drunk and . . . you know?" he asked, motioning to the bed.

"Last night," she answered. "You've had a fever, on and off for days, and last night it was at its worst. I kept putting cold cloths on your head, but you kept shivering and your teeth kept chattering. So I finally crawled in beside you to try to warm you with my body heat. You weren't drunk then. Well, maybe a little. I poured the whiskey down you before I cut on you, to get the pieces of bone out, so they'd stop hurting you. I figured if you lost much more blood, I'd have to bury you. And I didn't much fancy that." She smiled at him. "Losing one best friend was enough. I didn't want to lose you, too."

He smiled at her then, the old rogue's smile, shaking his head at the wonder of all that had happened. "So . . . I don't have to make an honest woman of you?" he asked, sheepishly grinning at her with pure devilment in his eyes.

"No. I know you *too well* to marry you," she replied, and he wondered exactly how she meant that.

"I hope you don't mean that like I think . . ." he began.

"Moses Gentry!" she exclaimed, "I've worked for a month to keep you alive. Do I have to wash your mouth out, too?" He laughed with her then, glad that their old friendship was once more secure.

CHAPTER FORTY

Moses lay in bed, trying to sort out the events that took place since leaving Sarah's on Christmas Day. He remembered giving her the tortoiseshell comb he had bought for her at Tommy's store. He remembered taking a nap, and Sarah giving him the red scarf before he left. He was sure of that. He could see the scarf hanging by the door, and Sarah was wearing the comb in her hair. He just wasn't all that sure of the rest. Suddenly, he thought of something Sarah had said.

"Sarah, who was it who saved me? Someone from Hastings? I'd like to thank him," he stated, watching a concerned look cross her face.

She hesitated, not sure what to say, then decided they had a strong enough friendship to bear anything. She just wasn't sure where to begin. He looked at her, knowing she was hesitating. Strange, he thought, most of her friends are also my friends. Seems odd she'd be so hesitant . . . "Sarah?" he questioned.

"Before I tell you who it was, you have to promise me something," she stated, watching him intently.

"Anything, darlin'. You saved my life, so I'm yours." He smiled.

"Moses, this is serious," she said, twisting her hands together, more nervous than he'd ever seen her before.

"I promise, Sarah. Whatever it is, you can count on me. I give you my word."

"I don't ever want you to mention me ... ah ... warming you, last night, like I did," she pleaded, a look of desperation in her eyes.

"Sarah," he said, affronted to think she thought she had to ask for his silence. "Of course, I promise." His voice sounded a bit harsh.

"There's more," she replied. "I didn't help you alone, after you hit me ... by mistake, of course ... I had help."

"Your friend?" he questioned.

"Yes, my friend." Her voice was so quiet he could barely hear her. "My friend ..." she hesitated, searching for the right words. "He's a friend of John Bruce, but I didn't know that until ... until we talked while we took care of you." She wrung her hands, unsure of how to explain. "I know you probably won't ..." Her words drifted off as they heard a horse nicker in the yard outside of the cabin.

Sarah glanced at the door, without moving, then back at Moses, her face paling. "I think you're about to meet him," she said, her voice sounding tense. She smoothed her clothing and ran her hands through her hair, wondering if both her eyes were now blackened.

"Sa-rah," called a male voice from the other side of the door, as Moses ran a hand through his hair and tried to look presentable. Sarah stood still a moment, looking back at Moses, then opened the door. An Indian brave in a buffalo robe stepped in, taking Sarah into his arms, kissing her as Moses had kissed his Sarah, many years earlier.

Moses looked at the Indian, not really knowing how to react. Sarah wasn't fighting him off. Good thing, he thought, because I'm in no shape to help. He saw the bear claw necklace around the Indian's neck and the eagle feather that hung from his long dark hair. Sarah pulled away then, taking the Indian's hand and leading him over to the bed, her face pink with embarrassment. Or excitement? He wasn't sure which.

"Gray Eagle, I'd like you to meet my dearest friend, Moses Gentry," she said, smiling up at him with a look Moses remembered on his own Sarah's face. "Moses, this is my . . . my husband-to-be, Gray Eagle of the Lakota Sioux." Gray Eagle reached out to shake Moses' hand. Moses hesitated, his thoughts whirling.

Then he reached out and took Gray Eagle's hand. "Looks like I owe you my life," Moses said. "I thank you for saving me."

Gray Eagle smiled broadly. "Gray Eagle happy save Sa-rah's friend. Make Sa-rah happy." He smiled down at Sarah, his arm around her waist.

"I . . . I didn't expect . . ." Moses stammered, "I'm at a loss for words."

"Gray Eagle kill cougar. Bring Moses here to woman who heals."

Sarah smiled at him and then at Moses. "I'll make a pot of coffee,"she said, feeling happy because of Gray Eagle's return, and Moses' improving health.

"What happen to other eye?" Gray Eagle asked, and Sarah and Moses both began to laugh.

"My friend hit me again," Sarah replied, when she could finally stop laughing. Gray Eagle looked at Moses, a dark glint appearing in his eyes. "Now take it easy," Moses said. "I was out of my head with fever. I didn't know it was Sarah. I don't hit women as a rule. Until now." He laughed then, as he held his side, and Sarah smiled at him, noticing a slight smile begin to cross Gray Eagle's face, too.

"So how did you two meet?" Moses asked, curious to hear the details.

"Meet far from here," Gray Eagle told him. "Gray Eagle hurt. Sa-rah heal him. Gray Eagle love Sa-rah. Marry soon."

"What will your father say?" Moses asked, seeing Sarah's worried look.

"I don't know," Sarah said, once again ringing her hands nervously. "I love Gray Eagle, Moses, and you know how Father feels about Indians."

"Sure do," Moses replied. "He'll not take kindly to it, Sarah."

"I know," she answered sadly.

"Gray Eagle talk to father. Tell him love Sa-rah. Tell him Gray Eagle's mother white," Gray Eagle said, looking at Sarah.

"No," Sarah stated, "that'll make it worse." She moved to stand behind the chair Gray Eagle sat in, next to Moses' bed, and placed her hands on his shoulders. "I'll hurt him terribly, Moses. He'll never understand."

"When are you to marry?" Moses asked, feeling an odd twinge of sadness.

"We go to my people in spring, when rains come," Gray Eagle told him. He reached up to take Sarah's hand in his, holding it tenderly. Moses was glad to see the closeness they shared, but he knew the trouble they faced if Samuel Justus discovered their plans. He shifted carefully, easing himself into a more comfortable position, trying to figure a way to help them. Silence filled the cabin as all three mulled over the situation.

Finally Moses spoke, causing Sarah to jump, "I owe you my life, Gray Eagle. And I owe Sarah even more for nursing me back to health and putting up with me while I recovered. Also, for being the best friend I've ever had." He cleared his throat before going on, "I guess the least I can do is be the one to break the news to Samuel. I'll tell him you've gone and that you're happy. Try to make him understand that life really don't amount to much without love in it." He looked at Sarah then, and a feeling of deep understanding passed between them. "I don't know if I can reach him or change his opinion. He's been set in his ways a long time. Maybe he had some reason when he was at the fort, but if men are ever gonna live as brothers, well, we have to start somewhere. I'll explain to him as best I can," Moses said, with determination in his voice. "It's the least I can do."

"Oh, thank you," Sarah said, "I'd hug you for saying that, but I've run out of eyes for you to blacken." They all laughed at her teasing remark, and Moses was glad to see her look happy again.

They talked then, Moses and Gray Eagle, getting to know each other better. Moses had heard of John Bruce's friendship with the Indians but wasn't aware of his Indian name, Spirit Dancer. He asked why they had named him that, and Gray Eagle explained that he had been found nearly frozen to death and then came back to life, when a weaker man would have died. Moses agreed that Old John had truly earned his Indian name and it fit him.

The subject turned to Sarah, and Moses told Gray Eagle he was lucky to be getting a wife who could shoot, track, and hunt as good as any man. Sarah blushed at his compliments, and Gray Eagle smiled happily, agreeing with Moses about his good fortune.

As the evening progressed, Gray Eagle tended the animals, while Sarah changed Moses' bandages, telling him he had come close to dying and had been unconscious many days. She showed him the gash on his cheek, with her mother's small hand-mirror, and explained how she had to cut his side to remove the sharp bone splinters that kept cutting into him, causing him to lose more and more blood.

"I got you drunk before I cut," she said, her voice softly apologetic.

"Not drunk enough by the look of your eye," Moses replied, and they laughed together, enjoying the camaraderie they shared.

"You'll have to stay and rest up more before you go back to Hastings," she explained. "You've been sick almost a month. It won't do to have you get an infection or a cold."

"You're the doc, darlin'," Moses answered, taking her hands and looking into her eyes. "Are you sure about this?" he questioned, motioning in the direction of the barn.

"Yes," she replied.

"He seems like a good man," Moses said. "I just hope you know how different your life will be." He watched her, still holding her hand, feeling happy to be doing so.

"I only know I love him, Moses. I have since the first day I met him, I think."

"Well, he sure isn't Tommy Dawson," Moses replied, and Sarah laughed, agreeing wholeheartedly.

"My father says I'm a dreamer. Always has said it," Sarah spoke softly, gazing at the fireplace as if seeing into the past. "My mother taught me so many things: to read and to write, and to have faith in God and myself. I was only ten when she died, Moses, but she left me all her books. Books that told of heroes and heroines, of knights and their ladies, of men, like yourself, who had a mission in life. Men who felt great suffering and pain, yes, but men who also knew great love."

She grew quiet for a few minutes. "I don't want a store clerk for my husband, Moses, or a cavalry officer filled with hatred for people whose only crime is that their skin is red and not white. I wish I could explain better." Sarah looked into his eyes pleadingly, wanting him to understand. "All my life I've believed in those books of my mother's. And I've believed in God. Believed too, that a person was on a path in life, and if they did their best, God would lead them where they should go. I don't know why my path is to go with Gray Eagle, to a people I know nothing about. But I have to trust God, Moses, and I have to trust what I feel, so strongly, in my heart."

He smiled at her, thinking how lucky Gray Eagle was. "Be happy then, darlin'," he replied. "I'm happy for you." He reached out then, giving her a quick hug, never realizing how very much he would miss her.

CHAPTER FORTY-ONE

Moses walked around in Sarah's cabin. Strength was returning to his limbs. His side no longer ached when he inhaled or stretched his arms over his head. Bending no longer caused him to cry out in pain. It was the end of February. He had been at Sarah's for nearly eight weeks. Eight weeks, he thought, amazed that time had rushed on, though, in truth, it seemed to have stood still.

He no longer felt caught up in the daily rush of life, having been ill so long. Truth was, he liked being at Sarah's. He liked her company and enjoyed the many hours they shared. He enjoyed watching her cook and do her daily chores. He felt satisfied, deep within his soul. Felt as though what had been taken away had somehow been returned to him.

A smile lit his face as he thought of Sarah. Of course, she was not his Sarah, how well he knew that! But she was as close to her as he was ever going to get, and he knew that, too. He walked over to the large rocker and lowered himself carefully into it.

"Need anything?" Sarah asked, her voice soft and comforting.

"No thanks, darlin'," he replied. It was useless trying to remember not to call her darlin'. It just came natural now.

Sarah looked at him: his long, lean frame and his dark hair. It glistened in the light from the fireplace. She rolled out dough for biscuits, humming softly—a tune she had heard, a long time ago—at church services at the fort.

Gray Eagle had been gone over two weeks now, and she hoped he was all right. She was glad Moses was there to keep her company. The snow lay nearly waist-high outside, and though it was not the worst winter she had seen, it was close to it. If she had been alone, she knew she would have been anxious and more than a little apprehensive. As it was, with Moses and occasionally Gray Eagle's company, she did not dwell on the severity of the storms or the accumulation that seemed to increase daily.

"One of these days I'm going into town to see Father and Rosie," she said, "when the weather gets better, that is."

"Good idea," Moses replied, getting up from the rocker and walking slowly to the window. "I should be getting back to town, too." His words sorely lacked enthusiasm.

"Oh," Sarah answered, looking at him, a slight tone of disappointment in her voice.

"If I was Gray Eagle," he said, "I'd have thrown me out a long time ago."

Sarah laughed as she put the biscuits to bake, and then walked over to straighten the quilt on the bed. "Father usually comes to check on me every couple weeks. I wonder why he hasn't come in so long. I hope everything's all right," she said, sitting down in her rocker and taking up her mending.

She was mending Moses' shirt, and he watched her. His thoughts drifted back in time to when his wife had sat in her rocker, in their home, making a small rainbow-hued quilt for their expected baby. He had watched her, too: the soft auburn curls that caressed her slender neck, her ivory skin, so clear and smooth, a delicate blush of pink on her cheeks.

"Moses?" Sarah turned to look questioningly at him.

"What?" he asked sadly. "I was a million miles away."

"I know," she replied, turning back to her mending. "I

asked if you had given any thought to what you'll say to my father," she hesitated, "when I leave with Gray Eagle?"

"No," he answered. "I'll just do the best I can when the time comes." He laughed, adding, "He'll probably shoot me."

Sarah shook her head sadly and sighed, continuing to work on the tear in his shirt. Moses was wearing a shirt of her father's and it was an ill fit. The sleeves were too short, and if he stretched out his arms, she was certain it would rip right down the middle of the back. She smiled, as she remembered him trying to cover himself with it, when she came inside one day from doing chores. As if she hadn't seen his chest before, and a whole lot more of him, to boot! She felt her face flush.

Such thoughts had a tendency to bring Gray Eagle to mind, and she closed her eyes as she remembered the way he had kissed her before leaving, stirring all sorts of feelings within her. As though reading her thoughts, Moses asked, "Gray Eagle should be back soon, shouldn't he?"

"I think so," Sarah replied, a hopeful note to her voice.

"Good thing your paw *hasn't* come to visit! They'd probably have run into each other," Moses observed.

"I know. I thought of that," she replied. "I hope that never happens."

Snow swirled around the cabin in large, soft flakes that blocked out any view of the barn and surrounding area. The sun had long ago disappeared behind the dense white veil of snow, and the grayness of the sky seemed to invade Sarah's very being. "I'd like to live where it's warm all year long," she said. "I don't care much for the long, cold winters."

"Me neither," Moses replied. "Seems my bones ache more every year in winter." She smiled, thinking how ruggedly handsome he looked.

She was about to speak when a noise was heard outside, and someone hollered, "hello." Sarah hurried to the door with Moses close behind her. She hadn't recognized the deep, rich voice, but welcomed any friendly visitor to break the long, dreary sameness of the winter.

A barely discernable figure dismounted, the dense white shroud of snow enveloping him. He approached the cabin, stamping and brushing away the snow that coated his hat and dark coat. Sarah stepped back, throwing open the door, still unsure of her visitor's identity. Moses stood still, watching closely, as the man entered, taking off his hat. "Amos?" he said. "What are you doing out here?"

"Gentry?" Amos replied, more than a little surprised at seeing Moses Gentry at Sarah's. He looked from Moses to Sarah and back again.

"Now don't go gettin' any wrong ideas," Moses said, looking Amos Culpepper straight in the eye. "I got hurt on the way to Black Dog and ended up here. Would have died if Sarah hadn't been so good at doctoring."

"Don't go jumpin' to conclusions 'bout what I'm thinkin'," Amos said. "I was just surprised to see you. The whole town figured you were dead!"

"Dead! Why would they think that?" Moses exclaimed, his voice rising.

"Why not?" Amos replied, equally loud. "You head out in a weakened condition to chase down that guy from the Gonzalez Gang. Then there's no word of you reaching Black Dog and nobody's seen you. What would *you* think?"

"Okay! Okay," Moses calmed, walking over to the table.

"Come in, Mr. Culpepper. It's awful weather to come this far in. Would you like a cup of coffee?" Sarah asked.

"I'd be pleased to have one, Miss Justus, to take the chill out of these old bones," Amos replied, taking off his coat and hat and smoothing back his silver-white hair. "But please, call me Amos."

"Amos, it is," Sarah said, getting another cup. "Have you seen my father?" she asked. "I thought he'd be coming to visit one of these days when the weather cleared."

"Well, that's why I'm here. You see, your father's been real sick. Got a chill about Christmastime and it turned into quite a bad cold." He paused to sip his coffee. "He seemed to get over it, but it came back even worse. Doc says its pneumonia now." Seeing Sarah's eyes widen and her face pale, he continued, "Now don't go frettin'. Doc's got it under control, and Rosie's making him stay in bed, this time. He'll be back on his feet in no time. He just got worried about you being out here all alone." He looked at Moses. "He asked if I'd come check on you, Miss Sarah. See how you were doing. Of course . . . *none* of us, knew you had company."

"Of course," Sarah said. "I do thank you for coming so far in this weather, Mr. Culpepper . . . Amos. Everything's just fine, though I do wish it would stop snowing. It looks pretty, but makes tending the animals rather difficult."

"Speaking of animals, would you mind if I put my horse in your barn?" Amos asked, stating, "Like me, he's not young anymore and the cold weather's hard on him."

"Of course," Sarah said. "I'll go out with you."

"That won't be necessary, missy. Best you stay in and keep warm. I'd like to get back to town before dark, so Miz Culpepper don't worry, so I won't be staying long."

Sarah smiled at the tall ex-gunfighter, thinking he was quite an impressive gentleman, and not that bad on the eyes either, though he had wrinkles around his eyes that made him look older.

"So, what's the news from town?" Moses asked, holding his coffee in one hand and pulling out a chair, from the table, with the other. He sat down opposite Amos.

"Well, let me see," Amos answered. "One of the O'Leary boys fell off their roof when he was patching a hole in it and broke his leg. Been keeping Doc busy what with all the colds and pneumonia going around. And the boy falling."

"Which one was it?" Sarah asked.

"Oh, I don't know," he answered. "They've got a whole

passel of 'em, you know." He rested his chin on his hand a moment, deep in thought. "Was there one that limped? That's the one, from what I hear tell."

"Yes. That would be Patrick," Sarah replied. "Poor Patrick."

"Bit of a rascal from what I hear," Moses interjected, thinking back to how he, too, had fallen off a barn roof as a young boy.

"You got that right," Amos replied, taking up his cup of coffee again. "This coffee hits the spot, Miss Justus, especially on such a blustery day."

"Thank you," she replied. "And how do you like being home, if I'm not being too bold by asking?"

"Like it just fine," he answered, looking at her with a gentle smile on his face. "Amanda and I thank God we have some time together. I should have come home sooner, but without the pardon, it wasn't possible."

"I'm sorry," Sarah said, not knowing what else to say.

Amos turned to look at Moses as Sarah went to get the pot of coffee and refilled their cups. "Don't suppose you heard. Word came about that Will Deeks fellow, from the Gonzalez Gang. He was shot over by Tanner's Trading Post in a holdup. Killed him outright."

Sarah saw Moses stiffen, his expression one of suppressed anger for just a moment or two. Moses nodded and then asked, "Anyone hurt?"

"Nope. Shot up the place a bit. Young pup. No sense of style," Amos replied, a faraway look in his eyes. "I remember back in . . . well . . ." he paused, looking at Sarah apologetically. "I guess it ain't a fit story to tell with a lady present. Forgive me. Sometimes I get to rememberin' and . . . well, stories of my . . . ah . . . younger days don't set good with Miz Culpepper."

"You can say what you please here, Amos," Sarah replied. "I don't blush and faint, like most of my gender."

Amos looked at Moses questioningly as a sudden laugh burst out of Moses quite unexpectedly. "She may not faint, but she sure does blush," he remarked. Both men looked at Sarah, who felt her face begin to redden. Sarah looked down, shaking her head, hoping to avert further flushing, as a slight smile crossed her lips. She was glad her eyes were no longer black.

"I'll let you two talk," she offered, "while I make us something to eat. You shouldn't leave without a good hot meal to warm you."

"Why, thank you," Amos replied. "That would be mighty kind. I'd better go put up my horse, though, before I get comfortable. That coffee warmed me up just fine." He shoved back his chair and stood up, smiling at Sarah. "You've got a nice place here. Real comfy." His words softened. "A lot like the first home Miz Culpepper and I shared after we were married, many years ago."

"Did you ever go back?" Moses asked. Sarah was surprised by his words.

"No," Amos replied, a finality to his tone.

"Me neither," Moses stated. "No reason to after Maw died."

"You knew each other, before coming to Hastings?" Sarah asked incredulously.

"Grew up together," Moses answered. "Not much to tell though . . . we *weren't* friends."

"A lot of time has passed," Amos replied, his voice deepening. "She was happy with you." Sarah listened attentively, looking from one man to the other, more than a little surprised by what they were saying. She felt the sudden tenseness in the room and kept silent.

"Might still be alive," Moses answered, "if . . ."

"No! I don't believe that!" Amos stated emphatically. "Things have a way of working out . . ." he hesitated, speaking softly, "though we don't always understand the good

Lord's plan, I do believe He has one." Amos Culpepper cleared his throat. "Time we put this behind us, Gentry, once and for all." He reached his hand out across the table toward Moses. "The best man won," he stated firmly.

Moses stood, looking at Amos with a foreboding look. "And ultimately lost," he replied, reaching out to take Amos's hand. Sarah watched, not fully understanding the tremendous reconciliation that had just begun to take place between the two men.

Amos was the first to pull away. "Better see to my horse," he said, a slight smile upon his face. "If you'll excuse me."

Moses shook his head, an easy smile now upon his lips. "I'll walk out with you," he said. "Been dawdlin' around inside, long enough." He glanced at Sarah, ordering jokingly, "Get cookin', darlin'. You've got two hungry men to feed." And with that, the men bundled up and went outside into the winter's fury.

CHAPTER FORTY-TWO

Amanda Culpepper bustled around her cozy kitchen, humming her favorite tune from church. Amos had ridden out, earlier that day, to check on Sarah, and Amanda was happily preparing his favorite dessert. She had everything to sing about these days. Her handsome husband had given up his gun fighting and was home, at last, much to her immense delight. She had lived alone, nearly twenty years, awaiting his return. But she had not wasted those years in suffering and regrets. She had taken care of her folks until they passed, making their last days as easy for them as any daughter could, tending to their needs to the best of her ability. She never regretted those years, accepting it as her due. They had been good to her, seeing to her needs and care, from her birth into adulthood. When they could no longer care for themselves, she naturally felt it only right she return their love and care, in kind.

Her father had objected to her marriage to Amos Culpepper, but she had remained steadfast in her determination to marry him. It was the only time she had gone against his wishes. She smiled, remembering back to the day, so very long ago, when Amos had come upon her by the old millpond as she sat on a fallen log, composing poetry and watching a family of ducks swim along the water's edge.

She had never had a boyfriend. Why, she had never even

been asked to dance at any of the socials or barn dances she had attended. Then, that day at the pond, Amos had come riding along, all filled with fire and fury, asking her if she'd seen Sarah Mathews or that Moses Gentry! She was frightened by his unbridled anger. She had never seen anyone so mad. Her father was a peaceable man. In fact, there were very few times she could remember him being angry. If ever he had been, he had kept it to himself, except, of course, when she decided to marry Amos. But that was quite awhile after that day at the millpond.

Amos had dismounted, she remembered, swinging his long leg over his horse and walking over to where she sat. She had heard about Sarah running off with Moses, but she said nothing. She sat there quietly, while he paced and raged, until at long last his anger was spent. Then he lay down on the grass and looked long and hard in the direction of the sun. It was beautiful, she remembered, all red and gold, as it sunk lower and lower in the sky.

She slid off the log and walked to where he lay, sitting down quietly beside him. She had always liked him, and wished more than once, to be taller and prettier so he would notice her. All he saw was Sarah Mathews, however, and she knew she had no chance . . . until then.

He lay there on his side, staring out at the water, his eyes fixed on things she dared not ask him about. So she sat still, enjoying being so close to him: close to the handsome boy with the long black, wavy hair and beautiful blue eyes whom she had dreamt of so many nights. She wondered what it would be like to be kissed by him. She had never been kissed. The sun sank slowly, as he laid his head upon his arm and closed his eyes.

Lost in her memories, Amanda poured herself a cup of tea and then sat at her kitchen table, sipping it with little awareness. She was young again, in her mind, remembering . . .

She didn't know how long they had been there, Amos

laying on his side, breathing easily in sleep, his hair falling across his arm, touching the grass. She had inched closer to him as if she had no power to stay away, and gently, with no forethought, reached out and began to touch his hair, stroking it softly, feeling its silkiness beneath her fingers.

He had rolled onto his back, then, a surprised look upon his face, and she slowly pulled back her hand. He looked into her eyes with a look unlike any she had ever seen before. He sat up—their shoulders touching—and gently reached out, turning her face toward him. Her heart beat furiously in her chest and she was afraid she would faint. He bent, touching her lips with his. They were soft against hers, pressing into hers gently, at first, then taking her breath away as his tongue slid into her mouth and his arms encircled her. She gasped in surprise, pulling back, as feelings coursed through her body. She felt herself melt within his arms and was overwhelmed by these new feelings. Then she felt the hardness of the ground against her back as his weight covered her.

It was then that they heard her father calling her name, his voice anxious as he searched for her. Amos pulled away from her, standing quickly, and straightened his shirt and pants. Then he helped her to her feet. Still she said nothing, though she knew he felt her trembling.

"I'm sorry," he said, brushing off his pants. "I'm really sorry, Amanda. It is Amanda, right?"

"Yes," she had answered faintly. And, as her father came closer, she whispered as she had so often to him in her dreams, "I love you." Amos had stared at her then, as if seeing her for the first time.

"Amanda?" her father said, interrupting their closeness. "What's going on? Are you all right, daughter?" He looked sharply at Amos Culpepper. "You best not be bothering my girl!"

"No, sir, we were just talking," Amos had told him nervously.

Amanda's father looked first at Amos, then at Amanda. "Well, it's late. Never knew you to stay out so late. Time we went home, isn't it?"

"Yes," she answered softly, then smiled at Amos and turned away, her heart skipping beats at what they had shared.

A week later he came to see her, wearing his best Sunday clothes, his hair slicked back, every strand in place. She nearly dropped the bowl she was washing as she saw him ride up to her home. She dried her hands and quickly took off her apron, smoothing her hair in place and trying to quiet her racing heart. She opened the door as soon as he dismounted, shutting it behind her so her parents wouldn't hear.

"Amanda," Amos said, "I thought I'd ride out. See how you were doing." She smiled, twisting the fingers of her hands together, nervously. "Can we sit awhile?" he asked, looking toward the chairs on the porch. She nodded shyly. She was at least a foot shorter than he, her hair a soft chestnut color that she wore pulled back off her face and tied with a light-blue ribbon that matched the dress she wore. They moved to the porch, both sitting quietly, as though waiting for the other to speak.

At last, she could stand the silence no longer. "I'm glad you came," she said, her voice barely a whisper. He nodded, looking uncomfortable.

Then he spoke, his words surprising her. "Why did you say . . . you know . . . what you said?" He looked at her curiously.

She looked down at her shoes and then forced herself to look up into his eyes. "Because it's true," she replied.

He looked out in the yard at a dirty gray mongrel dog running toward the barn, dust rising around its feet. "Why? Since when?" he questioned, looking back at her.

"Since just about forever," she answered softly, smiling. "Since I first saw you, I guess, years ago."

"I never . . ." he hesitated, wanting to be honest, yet

chose his words carefully, knowing the pain they could cause. "I never noticed . . . you."

She looked off into the distance, biting her bottom lip. "Didn't much matter. I always knew how you felt about . . . her . . . Sarah," she answered, not looking at him.

"But still you . . ." he began.

She interrupted, finishing his sentence, "Loved you? Yes." She spoke with sincerity, straight from her heart, her voice firm and unyielding.

He felt confused. He reached over then, and took her hand, holding it within his own. He noticed the delicateness of it, and he rubbed his finger over it, feeling its ivory smoothness. "The other day at the millpond," he said, looking at her, "if your father wouldn't have come . . . well, I wasn't sure . . . I mean, I didn't know . . ." he stammered, not certain how to say what he meant.

He had always known where he stood with Sarah. Or so he thought, until she ran off with Moses Gentry. He knew what to expect when he kissed her—knew what he could do and where she drew the line. Amanda had thrown him signals that didn't add up. She had seemed willing for him to kiss her, even said she loved him, but he had no idea what she expected of him and it made him darned uncomfortable.

He had never seen her with any other fellows, never heard any talk about her. Was she so innocent that she didn't understand the message she was sending? What if her father hadn't come looking for her the other night? He shifted uneasily in his chair, disturbed by the thoughts running through his head.

"I . . . I felt bad about the other night. Shouldn't have kissed you . . . like that," he said, watching her and hoping to understand her better.

"I've never had a fellow . . . kiss me before," she said, her voice so quiet he could barely hear her.

"Oh, Lord!" He sat up straight in his chair, the pulse in

his neck beating rapidly. "You should have slapped me!" he exclaimed, then lowered his voice, "What if your father hadn't come for you just then?"

She sat still—her heart pounding in her chest—unable to answer, knowing how she felt and wanting him to understand. "I wanted to comfort you," she said at last. "I knew you were hurting. I only wanted you to . . . to know you weren't alone."

"I'm sorry I . . . you know . . . kissed you like that," he stated, looking at her the way she had dreamed of so many, many nights.

"I'm not," she said, smiling gently at him. He wondered why he had never noticed her before. "I have to go in now," she said, placing her hand on his arm. "I'm glad you came." Her smile brightened as she rose and went inside.

He stood there a few minutes, surprised at how good he suddenly felt. Then he ran to his horse and rode away, thinking as he went, of how small her hands were and how nice her smile was, and most of all, how good she made him feel. He was all the way to his house before he thought of Sarah Mathews.

Two weeks later, he asked her to go to a dance and she accepted. She wore a pretty pink dress of homespun cotton, and her hair hung down around her shoulders. He couldn't help noticing how it glistened in the light from the oil lamps, or how sweet it smelled when his head was close to hers. He noticed, too, her small breasts and dainty feet, and the way she looked at him . . . like he was someone special.

On the ride home, she sat close to him—their shoulders touching—and he felt taller and stronger, even protective of her. At her door, he bent to kiss her cheek and she rose up on her toes, kissing him firmly on the lips. "Amanda," he said, his voice deep with emotion.

"Thank you, Amos. I had such a nice evening," she whispered in his ear, then pulled gently away from him and went into her home.

He wrestled with himself all the way home. Not only with the feelings she stirred within his body, but with the strong sense of joy and hope that always seemed to prevail when she was near. He shook his head, amazed at what he was discovering. "I'll be!" he exclaimed. "I like her. I really do like her!"

Amanda smiled, happy with her memories. "Well, Amos, my love, I always knew someday you would grow to love me," she spoke aloud into the empty room. "I thank God for answering my prayers and bringing you home, at long last. Not much time left, my dear husband, but I have waited faithfully, and would again, if I had to do it over."

She glanced up, then, at the two portraits hung side by side on the wall. One was of her handsome young husband, the other of herself as his bride. "I would have waited for you forever, my love," she whispered.

CHAPTER FORTY-THREE

The cabin seemed dreadfully empty after Moses left. Sarah was anxious to go to town and see her father, but she stayed there, waiting for Gray Eagle to come back. She threw herself into her chores and other activities to somehow try to fill the void. At first, she seemed to hear every sound that invaded the stillness. She would tense up, listening, a mixture of apprehension, verging on fear, enveloping her.

"I'm becoming a ninny," she said after one particularly uneasy spell, "just like the women in Hastings." Unlike them, however, Sarah was well aware of just how distant she was from her family and friends, and even Doc Pearson if, God forbid, an accident or illness laid her low.

The snowfall had ceased its continuous blanketing of the area. High winds, a few evenings earlier, had whipped the snow into tall drifts, leaving many bare and icy areas. One such bare area lay near the barn. Sarah was careful, crossing it daily to tend Glory, Pet, and the little heifer calf that playfully bucked and kicked her feet high in the air, when she came near. Approaching cautiously, the calf suckled her fingers greedily, looking for a teat.

Sarah enjoyed the company of the animals, as it assuaged her feeling of loneliness. She was glad she had caulked the barn the previous fall, finding it warmer than outside, simply because of the animal's body heat. She stroked Glory, humming as she did so, glad for the ensuing comfort of the little barn and the company of the animals within.

She was in the barn the day she heard Gray Eagle call out to her. Her heart leapt with joy as she ran out to greet him, hastily fastening the barn door closed behind her.

"Gray Eagle!" she called, running to him over the icy path, overjoyed to see him and know he was safe. He slid from his horse, turning to greet her, just as she caught her foot on a piece of rope that had frozen into a loop on the ground, and fell forward unable to catch herself. She reached out to break her fall, but the momentum was too great and her forehead hit the large snow-covered log where she often sat, in summer, shucking corn or shelling peas, or listening to the evening sounds. She gave a short yell as she began to fall, then everything went black as her head hit the log, and she lay still.

Gray Eagle dropped his horse's reins and ran to her side, rolling her over quickly, calling her name. There was no response. Carefully, he reached under her inert body, lifting her into his arms. He carried her into the cabin, aware of the rivulet of blood running across her brow.

"Sa-rah?" he called, laying her on her bed. She lay still, her body limp. He undid her coat, rolling her from one side to the other to remove it. Then he went to find a cloth to stem the trickle of blood. He found a dry towel hanging near the tin tub and wet one small corner of it, wiping away the blood. Sarah's face was pale, her body still.

"Sa-rah," he called softly, a feeling of anguish obscuring his usual rational response to an accident. "Sa-rah," he called a bit louder, touching her face tenderly, glad to see a steady pulse beating in her slim neck. He noticed the thin gold chain and tiny gold cross laying in the hollow of her neck, against her delicate, ivory skin. Warmth spread through his body at the mere sight of her.

She moaned then, beginning to stir, "Oh!" She opened

her eyes, a look of pain crossing her features. "My head." She reached up to touch where it hurt. "Ouch," she cried out as she felt the lump that was quickly forming, her vision becoming hazy. Then her hand dropped limply onto the bed, her head lolled to one side, and she lay still again.

Gray Eagle was beside himself with worry. He removed her wet moccasins and pulled the quilt out from under her, placing it gently over her. He stood up, taking off his buffalo skin robe and hung it by the door. Then he paced, back and forth, in the cabin.

If Wolf Hunter was here, he thought, he would know what to do. Many times he had cared for those who were ill or hurt. He realized it would do neither him nor Sarah any good, if he panicked. He sat down on the side of her bed, forcing his mind to be still. He concentrated on the prayer that suddenly came to his lips, saying it aloud: "Great Spirit. Wakantanka. You hear men's hearts. You guide the waters and bless the earth, trees, and birds of the sky. Hear my words now. Make well Sa-rah, Red Bird. Gray Eagle's woman." He opened his eyes, then, and looked at Sarah for some response. There was none.

He felt helpless, a feeling he was not accustomed to. Finally, he pulled the large rocker over beside the bed Sarah lay in, and sat motionless, watching her for any sign of change. After an uncertain length of time, he got up and moved to sit beside her on the edge of the bed, calling her name. She remained as still as death.

Gray Eagle had not eaten since early two evenings before, when he had set out from Wolf Hunter's cabin to come to Sarah's. He walked to the stove, dishing up a bowl of stew, and took a biscuit from the basket on the cupboard nearby. If she did not revive by the time he was through eating, he decided, he would ride to Hastings and find Sarah's friend, Moses. He knew Moses was the sheriff in Hastings and would know what to do. And knowing how Sarah's father felt about

Indians, he hoped he would be able to reach Moses without her father becoming aware of his involvement. He ate quickly and then went to Sarah, patting her hand and speaking softly, trying to awaken her. She groaned, but, otherwise, did not respond.

Throwing on his heavy buffalo robe, he looked, once more, at the inert figure on the bed, glanced at the fireplace to see that the fire would last until his return, and went out the door, shutting it securely behind him. He leaped up onto his horse and rode off as fast as possible toward Hastings.

It was nearly dark when he got to the edge of town. Staying off to one side of the road, in the brush, he quickly slid off his horse. He tied him to a tree where he would not be noticed, by anyone, either coming or going on the road, and slipped stealthily into town, running from one building to another, ever alert for any approaching danger.

Behind the saloon, a man leaned against its hitching rail, vomiting and cursing. Gray Eagle slid into the shadows beneath some stairs, watching, intent on using this time to catch his breath. The sheriff's office was only a few buildings away, and so far there had been no close calls. The saloon patron wiped his mouth on his sleeve, still mumbling to himself, and attempted to stand erect. His body wove from side to side in his drunkenness. He spit, wiping his mouth a second time on his sleeve, then slowly and unsteadily found his way back to the saloon door and went in.

Gray Eagle moved out of the shadows and began to hasten across the open space between buildings. Just then, to his dismay, a man's voice called out, "Who goes there? Stop or I'll shoot!" Gray Eagle froze in place, his heart racing. He had to get to Moses. He had to! "Well, what have we here?" the man said, from directly behind Gray Eagle. "Got me an Indian, by the looks of it." He paused, walking around to face Gray Eagle. "You just stay steady, son. I've got no call to shoot you, but I will, if I have to. Do you understand English?"

There was a moment of silence. Gray Eagle had heard no anger in the tall white-haired man's voice, only concern. He was a fair judge of men—Indian and white—and he saw no hatred or malice in his eyes, or actions, no malevolence in his attitude. "Must see Moses. Sheriff Moses," he replied, watching the flash of surprise cross the tall man's features.

There was only a moments hesitation as the man sized up the situation. Realizing the Indian had asked for the sheriff by name, he realized he must know him. "All right, son. He's at the jail. Let's go." Gray Eagle walked ahead, his head up and shoulders back, thankful that this tall elderly white man was a decent man.

The door creaked as they entered, and Amos called out, "Moses. You've got a visitor. Better wake up."

Moses came out of a side room, pulling on his shirt, his hair tousled and his eyes heavy with sleep. He started, when he saw the Indian. "Gray Eagle, what is it?" he asked, hurrying across the room as he buttoned his shirt, not yet totally believing Gray Eagle was standing in his office. Amos Culpepper stood to one side, holstering his gun, curious as to the relationship between the two men. His curiosity was soon to be quelled.

"Moses, Sa-rah hurt. Fall. Hit head. Gray Eagle not able wake up. Need healer."

Moses' face paled at his words. He sat down on a nearby chair, talking fast as he quickly pulled on his boots. "I'll get Doc Pearson. Can you get out of town okay?"

Amos cut in, "I'll see to it he does." Gray Eagle and Moses both said "thanks" at the same time, and then all three hurried out the door, Amos going first—to see that the way was clear for the Indian—as Moses raced across the street in the opposite direction, to wake Doc Pearson.

As they got to the edge of town, Gray Eagle turned toward the tall white-haired man. "I am Gray Eagle. You good man. Friend to Gray Eagle. Thank you."

"You're welcome," Amos said. "I'm Amos Culpepper. Glad to be your friend, son." And with that, Gray Eagle disappeared into the tall brush and was gone, leaving a very surprised, but pleased, Amos Culpepper smiling in the stillness of the brisk night air.

A few moments later, two horses raced by, heading out of Hastings, and Amos knew it was Doc Pearson and Moses Gentry. "Well, what do you make of that?" Amos whispered into the silence around him. "Samuel Justus, an Indian-hater, and Sarah, obviously, a friend of one. Will wonders never cease?" Then he turned and walked down the street, whistling a tune he used to whistle, a very long time ago, to his first sweetheart: a pretty gal, with long auburn hair, whose very presence seemed able to light up the sky and chase away the chill of winter.

CHAPTER FORTY-FOUR

Moses burst through the door, followed close behind by Doc Pearson. Sarah lay supine upon her bed, a quilt wrapped around her from her feet to her chin. The fire burned low in the fireplace, though the cabin was still comfortably warm.

Moses hurried to the bed after stamping snow off his boots, as did Doc Pearson, who sat his satchel on the small table next to the bed. Taking Sarah's wrist between his fingers, he checked her pulse.

"Sarah? Sarah?" Moses said, his face clouded with anxiety. "Darlin', it's me, Moses. Can you hear me?" Sarah moaned softly. "Come on, darlin'. Wake up. Open those pretty eyes," Moses challenged, brushing her hair back off her forehead.

Doc Pearson went about his business, more than a little aware of the words Moses spoke. He knew Moses had been laid up nearly two months at Sarah's and wondered what, if anything, had happened between them. "Wring out a cloth in some cool water for me. Will you, Moses?" Doc asked, as he began searching through his medical bag.

Moses hurried to the bucket by the door, grabbing a towel from the back of a nearby chair, and dipped an already damp corner of it into the bucket.

A slight movement, outside the window, caught his eye as he turned back toward the doctor, and he knew Gray Eagle was standing in the darkness, keeping silent vigil over the woman he loved. Moses felt the wrong done to Gray Eagle by this enforced separation. It was Gray Eagle who should be helping Doc, Gray Eagle who should be inside holding Sarah's hand, whispering words of hope, not him.

His thoughts dissipated as he heard Sarah cough, and Doc enjoined her, "Take it easy. You're all right, Sarah. It's me, Doc Pearson. Just take it easy."

Taking it easy was about all Sarah could do. Her head hurt something fierce and her eyes refused to focus as they should. She could barely make out the figures beside her bed. Her mouth felt cottony, and she felt dizzy and confused, unable to remember at the moment, what had happened.

"Smelling salts. Works nearly every time," Doc Pearson said, turning back to his well-worn black leather satchel. He took out a roll of gauze like cloth and lifted Sarah's head, winding it around her head three or four times, then secured it on one side. "Mild concussion," he said. "Be all right in a few days, in all probability. You gonna be able to stay with her, Sheriff, or should I send Rosie and Samuel out here? I'll have to tell them, you know."

"Of course," Moses answered firmly, knowing if they came, Gray Eagle would get very little time with Sarah before their arrival. "I'll stay, Doc. Can you get back to town okay by yourself?" Moses asked, realizing what a long, hard ride it had been for the old fellow.

"'Course I can," Doc replied rather sharply. "Been traveling all over this area for years. Not getting any younger, but I'm not about to quit yet."

"Good," Moses replied. "I'm grateful to you, Doc, real grateful. Is there anything I should be doing for her, until her folks arrive?"

"You might want to check her if she falls asleep. Wake her every so often, talk to her. Make sure she's making sense. Try to get some broth into her. I'll leave some medicine for pain, in case she needs it."

Sarah opened her eyes, her vision still blurry. "Doc?" she called. "How did you get here?" she questioned. "How did you . . . ?"

"Don't you worry, darlin'," Moses interrupted, hushing her and patting her hand, "We're here. That's all that matters."

Doc Pearson put on his coat and hat, wrapping a long green wool scarf around his neck, then picked up his satchel and moved to the door. As he turned back to Moses and Sarah, a quick movement outside the window made him stop, his mouth dropping open in surprise.

"What's wrong, Doc?" Moses asked, already more than aware of what he had seen.

"Well, I'll be," he replied, walking over to the window and trying to see out into the darkness. "I thought I saw an Injun outside," Doc hesitated, still trying to peer out into the night.

"Probably a bush, making shadows," Moses stated calmly. "You want me to go check?"

"Might be a good idea," the doctor replied. "These eyes of mine might be old, but they've always been keen. I'll stay in here with the girl. Watch yourself."

Moses winked at Sarah, who still looked confused, then buttoned his coat and walked around to the back of the cabin, making sure he walked in the tracks Gray Eagle had made.

"Moses," Gray Eagle whispered, from behind some bushes, not far from the window.

"Stay there," Moses ordered. "Doc thinks he saw an Indian out here. I'm just checking. Then he'll be on his way back to town." Moses smiled at his own words.

"Gray Eagle not see any Indians," Gray Eagle replied seriously, from where he crouched behind the bush, and both men grinned at their remarks. "Sa-rah awake?" Gray Eagle asked then, no longer any hint of joking.

"Yes," Moses answered. "Come in when Doc leaves."

And, at that, he turned and stomped his own footprints clearly into the snow beside the cabin.

"Well?" Doc asked as soon as he entered.

"No sign of Indians. Must have been shadows, like I thought," Moses replied, hanging up his coat.

"I'll go now, then," Doc replied, bidding Sarah be well and to take care, and out he went into the darkness. As his horse began the long journey back to Hastings, only the light of the moon to distinguish the trail, Doc tugged his old black coat closer around him and pulled the long green scarf up to where it kept his nose warm within its folds. His horse ambled on, knowing a warm bed of straw and an extra helping of oats awaited him at journey's end.

It was then, in the stillness of the night, that Doc asked aloud, "Now, how did Moses find out Sarah had fallen?" He wondered about it as he rode. Then, as he had done many times before, he shut his eyes and trusted his old horse to take him home.

As soon as the doctor left, Gray Eagle rushed into the cabin, going anxiously to Sarah's side. "Sa-rah," he said, taking her hand in his.

"Gray Eagle," she whispered, a slight smile crossing her lips. "My head hurts so bad," she continued, squeezing his hand. "How did Doc Pearson get here? I don't understand how he could have known," she stated, as the pain continued to throb in her head.

"Gray Eagle get Moses," he answered, sounding proud. "Moses get doctor."

"I hope no one saw you," Sarah replied, laying her hand against his cheek.

"Only new friend, Amos Cupper," Gray Eagle stated, smiling.

"*Cul*-pepper," Moses corrected, from the table where he sat drinking coffee.

"Cul-pepper," Gray Eagle repeated.

"Amos Culpepper!" Sarah shrieked, grasping her head in both hands, looking even more ill.

"Yes," Gray Eagle replied, "new friend."

"My *father's* new friend, too," Sarah wailed, shaking her head from side to side. "My father's new friend," she repeated, a sound of hopelessness in her voice.

Gray Eagle looked at Moses, who sat quietly, remembering back to long ago, to old memories not forgotten. "He won't say anything," he said at last. "He'll figure out the situation, but he'll keep quiet," Moses stated, his voice firm.

"But how can you be sure?" Sarah questioned, in the wailing tone of a child caught doing a misdeed.

"Because I know him," Moses stated. "He can keep any secret that propriety demands of him."

Sarah looked at him, seeing only a blurred outline of him, then at Gray Eagle. "Well, I hope he doesn't tell Amanda. She's Rosie's best friend!"

"He won't," Moses repeated, his tone unshakeable. "He's an honorable man and good at keeping secrets now."

Sarah wondered what he meant, but the warmth of the quilts and the pain medicine made her feel drowsy. She closed her eyes, welcoming sleep.

CHAPTER FORTY-FIVE

Strong March winds rattled the doors and windows of Sarah's cabin and barn, lashing, with a fury, anything that stood in its way. The animals were spooked when it shook the barn. Their eyes and nostrils were wide with fear. Sarah felt uneasy, though she knew she was being foolish. "I wish I was braver," she said, talking to herself in the empty cabin. "I'm getting just like those ninnies in town."

Moses had left for Hastings not long after Doc Pearson. Gray Eagle had stayed for another hour, always on the alert for her father's arrival. Then seeing that Sarah was up and about, and no longer having constant blurry vision or bouts of dizziness, he said his farewells. He did not want to cause trouble by being found there by Samuel Justus.

Sarah was glad he was so sensible, but she missed him and wished, greedily, for his quick return. The lump on her forehead was large, the size of a small egg, over her right eye. She laughed when she saw it in the mirror and promised herself she would move the log farther from the cabin, away from the path to the barn, the first chance she got. She knew, in all actuality, she would probably have to enlist more than one person's help to move it. But one thing was certain, it had to be moved! She could not take the chance of another accident like the one that had just occurred. If Gray Eagle had not been there, she knew she would have frozen to death.

It was only by the grace of God that he had been. She shuddered to think of the grief her father would have felt by her untimely death.

He and Rosie had been expected the day after Moses left, and she grew anxious, when another day went by and they still did not arrive. She worried, at their absence, and even considered saddling Glory and riding into Hastings. But common sense prevailed. She had just had a minor concussion, and it would not do to take the chance of collapsing on the road, and again putting her life in peril. Instead, she worked on making herself a quilt, from all the old pieces of cloth both she and her mother had saved over the years.

As she worked, she thought of all the events that had taken place in her life since crossing the meadow to go to her special place, on her birthday, almost a year earlier. She remembered her surprise, the day she first saw Gray Eagle, standing high above her cave on the cliff. She shuddered, as she thought of the earth giving way beneath his feet, the fateful day he had fallen. Remembered how his body had plummeted toward the earth far below, amongst the rocks and debris. Remembered too, how it crashed onto the ground, lost from sight within the billowing clouds of dust. She shook her head, shivering involuntarily, at the thought.

Picking out a piece of fabric the color of a newborn fawn, she remembered the first time she had touched him, pressing on his chest, while leaning across him to see if he had a pulse. She remembered how she had sniffed his chest and hair, to see if what her father said was true: that all Indians stink. Nimbly, her fingers stitched on, as she quietly laughed at herself and her naiveté. She had believed he would stink, because her father had always said Indians did.

She felt sad knowing there was such anger and hostility toward other people within her own father, whom she loved so dearly and who had always been so loving and kind to her.

She wished she could tell him how wrong he was, how mistaken his belief. She had no idea what made him so filled with hate for Indians. He had always been a fair-minded man when it came to others. He had given them the benefit of doubt, had helped the downtrodden, and encouraged those whose lives were not as comfortable or stable as his own.

The only difference, Sarah realized, was that those folks were also white, like her father and herself. Never were they Indians, or Negroes, or even Chinese, like the slightly-built man who worked in the boardinghouse kitchen. Sarah felt a wave of sadness run through her. She had never realized before that her father was unfair. She had unquestioningly believed everything he said, as she grew up, never doubting his opinions or beliefs, adopting many as her own: him being older and wiser, and of course, being her parent. I must remember not to burden my children with wrongful opinions, she thought, especially opinions that hurt other people.

She sifted through her basket, taking out a piece of red material, the color of the bird that hovered near her cabin. It was bright red in color with some black on it, and she often talked to it, sharing her innermost thoughts with it. The last time it had come, another one had come with it, just as red, though somewhat smaller. She began to stitch the red piece of material to a blue one, her stitches small and evenly spaced.

She blushed, as she thought of her dear friend, Moses Gentry, and how relieved she had been when he began to recover from his wounds. Not only from the wounds when the cougar attacked, but also from the wounds suffered when the Gonzalez Gang robbed the bank. She saw once more, the vile look in the eyes of the handsome Mexican as he drew up on his horse before her that day. The memory, so painful still, as she realized he had meant to kill her. Her thoughts turned then, to the similar horror Moses must have suffered, watching from across the street, remembering how, years before, the same man had pulled up in front of his wife and gunned her down. Her, and the child she was carrying within her.

Sadness overwhelmed her then, as she thought of John Bruce. She saw, once more, his crumpled body laying on the walkway near Tommy's store, his outstretched hand, the red of his life's blood quickly draining away, coloring his soft, white hair and beard, as it spread. She shook her head to stop the memory, tears beginning to run down her cheeks in quick succession.

"Oh, John," she said, to the empty room, "you gave your life to save mine. How can I ever repay you?" Tears raced down her cheeks, her heart breaking anew at the realization of her loss. "I'm so grateful to you, John. You were always there for me, always taught me so much." She wiped her eyes with a handkerchief taken from her apron pocket. "Maybe someday, somehow, I can repay your kindness by helping others and teaching others, as you taught me." She sniffed loudly, then wiped her eyes and blew her nose. She picked up the quilt piece she had been working on and continued to sew, as new thoughts assailed her.

She thought of Lilly Benedict, how devotedly she had taken care of her mother the majority of her life, never complaining and never faltering under the daily strain of her mother's illness and mistreatment of her. All those years, Lilly had gone on, the immensity of her burden taken in stride, her own hopes and dreams set aside indefinitely. Sarah felt such tremendous respect for Lilly. I wish I was as strong, she thought, shaking her head in amazement, at the suffering Lilly had endured. Suffering in silence, too, with the deep love she carried within her heart for Jonas Hart, and yet had never spoken of, because she was not free to act upon her feelings and had no idea when, if ever, she would be. Sarah thought, too, of the day Lilly had spoken to her of her fear that Jonas might not feel the same, might, in fact, be deterred from loving her because he knew, first hand, of her mother's insanity.

She smiled, then, remembering how things had turned out, remembering that Rosie had said they were to be married at Christmas. These thoughts made her feel a sense of hope and joy for Lilly and her large, very shy husband who had been blessed with a voice as sweet as heaven itself. "Oh, Lilly," Sarah whispered, "I hope you are so very happy!"

She set aside her quilt, having grown tired of working on it, and rose to stir the large kettle of bean soup on the stove, smelling its delicious aroma. Glancing out the window, she was pleased to see it was a bright, yet slightly cloudy day, with streaks of sun breaking through to warm the earth and melt the snow. If this continued, the snow would be gone in another month, or sooner, she thought. She knew it would not be long, then, until she left with Gray Eagle to begin their life together as man and wife. She smiled at the thought, as hope and anticipation soared through her.

CHAPTER FORTY-SIX

Sarah pulled on the fur-lined moccasins Gray Eagle had made her, and a heavy coat, and went outside. The snow glistened in the sun's rays, and she could feel its warmth upon her face. She walked, carefully, down the path beside the cabin. She paused when she heard the cry of an eagle, but her hope stilled as she saw the bird drift smoothly overhead and realized it was not Gray Eagle, signaling her of his return.

She turned, walking over to the barn, and opened the barn doors to allow the brightness of the day inside. She was certain the animals felt as closed-in as she did, and she decided to turn them loose to gambol and frolic outside awhile. Glory welcomed her with a whinny and Pet rose, as did her calf, as she entered the barn. Their breath blew out in puffs of hazy air as they got to their feet, and the calf raced around its mother, in happy abandon, at the sight of their visitor.

Sarah smiled, enjoying their company as Pet walked slowly to the side of the pen nearest her, reaching her head over the rail, attempting to lick Sarah with her long, rough tongue. "Oh, Pet," she said, "sweet, sweet Pet. How shall I ever leave you, my old friend?" She laid her head against Pet's soft golden-brown cheek, feeling the cow's warm breath on her neck and shoulder. She pulled back as Pet's tongue licked her coat, pulling a few strands of her hair, at the same time. Opening the barn door in back, she let them out.

Just then, Sarah heard the sound of approaching horses and wondered who would be such a distance from town. She hurried from the barn, just in time to see two riders dismount up near her cabin. One was very tall, the other much smaller. They were bundled-up in heavy coats, hats, and gloves, with thick scarves covering their necks and lower parts of their faces. Only their eyes showed above the scarves. They dismounted, and Sarah was surprised to see it was Lilly who stood before her, and to her side, her husband, Jonas Hart. "Well, I'll be," Sarah said, running to hug Lilly, delighted to see her again. "Come in. Come in," she said. "I'm so happy to see you. I was just thinking of you this morning. How are you? Oh, and congratulations!" she exclaimed. "I heard you were married. I'm so happy for you!"

"Thank you," Lilly replied, her eyes dancing with a joy Sarah had never seen in them before. "We had to go to town to sign some papers, so I asked Jonas if we could come a little farther and see you." Jonas smiled sweetly at Lilly's words. "Of course, he agreed," she said, her voice bubbling with happiness. "So, here we are!"

"Come in," Sarah said, opening the door and ushering them inside the cabin. When they were settled at the table, coats hung by the door and fresh coffee in hand, Sarah asked them what was new.

"Well," Lilly said, "I've moved to Jonas' farm, of course. Though I do go with him when he goes to help Father. Oh! You don't know, do you? Father's home again!"

"No!" Sarah replied. "That's wonderful!"

"Yes," Lilly remarked. "It's still hard for him to face the townsfolk who thought he was dead. But once he learned of Mother's death, he returned. Was at our wedding, in fact. Though I didn't realize it, until later that afternoon, when Jonas told me."

"My goodness!" Sarah exclaimed. "How did he find out about your marriage?"

Lilly reached across the table, taking Jonas' hand, smiling at him tenderly. "Jonas made it a point to find him," she answered. "He was the one who saw to it I received Father's letters, you know. And he kept the work going smoothly, according to Father's instructions. Anyway, he managed to find Father and tell him of Mother's passing, and of our plans to wed. I don't know how I would have managed without him."

"Oh, you would have, I'm sure," Sarah replied, knowing—for a fact—how strong in spirit her friend was, and able, besides. "Jonas, would you like more coffee?" she asked, noticing his cup was nearly empty.

"Yes," he answered. "Thank you."

"I was just going to make ice cream, and I have soup cooking. You will stay and eat, won't you?" Sarah asked.

"Yes," Lilly answered. "I'll help you make the ice cream."

"Good," Sarah replied. "We'll need to get a large pail of snow."

"I'll get it," Jonas answered, a shy smile upon his face.

"Don't get chilled," Lilly said, stretching up on her toes to kiss his cheek. His eyes twinkled in response, Sarah noticed, and she remembered another whose blue eyes had smiled at her like that, not that long ago.

"Sarah?" Lilly asked, noticing the faraway look in her eyes. "What is it?"

"I was just remembering John Bruce," Sarah's voice softened. "Whenever I did something to please him . . . shoot straight, or learn the lesson he was trying so patiently to teach me, his eyes would get that same look, like your Jonas."

"I heard about Old John, Sarah, and how you were almost killed by that bandit. I'm sorry about your friend. I'm sure glad his aim was true, so glad he saved you," Lilly stated. Sarah was silent. "How is Moses . . . Sheriff Gentry . . . doing? I heard he was wounded real bad that day, too."

"He was in horrible shape, for a while," Sarah answered,

as she stirred the soup. "Not so much from the wounds when he was shot, but later. He stopped here to see me on his way to Black Dog Lake, Christmas Day, not giving himself near enough time to heal. Then after he left here, a cougar jumped him over by Big Bear Pass. He fell on the rocks on his wounded side and was near death. A . . ." she paused, choosing her words carefully, "a friend of mine found him, killed the cat, and brought him back here. He was unconscious for days and I didn't think he'd live." Sarah looked pensive as she continued, "After he was here almost two months, he did recover. And now he feels nearly 'fit as a fiddle' he says."

"Do you see him often?" Lilly asked, smiling, a look on her face that implied, possibly, a relationship between them.

Jonas returned then, with a pail heaping with snow. "Thank you, Jonas," Sarah replied, taking the pail from him. He smiled and then went to sit in the large rocker by the fire. Lilly walked over to him, leaning down to kiss his cheek. He covered her hand with his, where it lay upon his shoulder, and Sarah couldn't help wondering where Gray Eagle was, and if he'd be back soon. Lilly turned, repeating her question.

"No," Sarah answered. "I see Moses when he comes this way, that's all."

"Oh," Lilly replied, looking at her friend with a sad expression on her face. "I thought perhaps . . ."

"No," Sarah stated. "Moses and I are the best of friends, the very best of friends." She glanced at Jonas, who slumped in the rocker, his breathing steady. Sarah realized he was sound asleep. "Lilly, remember our talk, the day you came to visit?"

"Oh, indeed I do!" Lilly replied. "If it hadn't been for that talk and your encouragement, I'd still be at my farm, going along day by day, and missing so very much happiness." She looked at Jonas, then back at Sarah. "Why do you ask?"

"I'd like to . . . to confide in you, as you did me," Sarah replied. "I have no one to really talk to about things of . . . well, you know . . . matters of the heart."

Lilly's face brightened. "Oh, Sarah. You've fallen in love, too!"

"Yes," Sarah stated, "but it's . . . it's imperative that my father not find out. I must ask you to promise not to speak a word of what I tell you, even to Jonas. Please?"

"I promise, Sarah. I'll not breathe a word!" They sat at the table, their voices a mere whisper, as the conversation continued.

"He's tall, and has dark eyes that seem to see all the way to a person's soul," Sarah expounded. "And he's so kind, Lilly, and gentle. And when he looks at me," she paused, "I feel feelings I never knew before, feelings I never knew were possible!" Lilly smiled at her friend's excitement. "He fell, and I nursed him back to health."

Lilly listened, happy that Sarah, too, had found love. "How did you know he fell," she asked, "if it was so far away? I don't understand."

Sarah tried to make sense of what Lilly was asking. "What?" she asked, confused.

"How did you know Moses fell, if he was so far away? Didn't you say a friend found him?"

Sarah looked at Lilly, her confusion even more apparent. Then, suddenly, she understood and began to laugh. "Oh, Lilly, I've confused you and gotten confused myself. Moses isn't my intended. My friend found Moses and saved him. It's my friend that I . . ." She blushed now, her cheeks becoming flushed with color. "My intended is . . ." Right then, as if on cue, a sound was heard not far from the cabin. "I'll be right back," Sarah said, grabbing her coat, "You might get a chance to meet him." And before Lilly could say a word, the door shut and she was more confused than before.

In a matter of minutes, the door opened and Sarah entered, her face flushed and her eyes sparkling with a happiness that Lilly could not help noticing. "Is Jonas still asleep?" Sarah whispered, excitedly.

"Yes," Lilly answered. "He's a heavy sleeper."

Sarah entered, and to Lilly's complete surprise, an Indian followed. Lilly screamed and Jonas jumped to his feet! He took one look at his wife and then saw Gray Eagle standing behind Sarah. Jonas charged, like an angry bull, toward the startled couple by the door! Gray Eagle shoved Sarah out of the way, afraid she would be hurt by the large man coming at him with a menacing look on his face.

"No! No! You don't understand!" Sarah screamed, just as Jonas reached Gray Eagle. The momentum behind the big man sent the two men out into the yard where they landed in a snow bank! Gray Eagle was knocked flat, by the weight of his attacker, and felt the wind go out of him.

Jonas raised his fist, but suddenly, to his surprise, found Sarah's hands encircling his arm, as she screamed, "No! No!" Lilly, thinking Sarah was hysterical, tried to grab her around the waist, knocking Sarah off balance, and both women tumbled into the snow beside the men. Jonas was so surprised by Sarah's actions, and the fact that the Indian wasn't fighting back, that he forgot to hit him and sprawled atop his breathless victim, who every so often tried, in vain, to breathe.

Suddenly, amid the confusion and upset, Sarah began to laugh. "He's my friend," she said, her peals of laughter so infectious that soon all three—Sarah, Jonas, and Lilly—were laughing. And between gasps for air, Gray Eagle was smiling.

When at last they gained control, they took turns helping each other up off the ground. Sarah made introductions, all around, and they went back inside the cabin. Jonas apologized for knocking the wind out of Gray Eagle, explaining that he was asleep when Lilly screamed. When he saw an Indian standing behind Sarah, he thought they were being attacked and reacted accordingly.

Lilly apologized for screaming, first to Jonas, Sarah noticed, for scaring him and causing the melee. And then, to Gray Eagle, for reacting like a silly twit, explaining that she had never seen an Indian before, especially a friendly one.

The rest of the afternoon was spent, in a convivial manner, enjoyed by all. Jonas and Gray Eagle discussed horses, finding they had a lot to learn from each other. Lilly and Sarah talked of Sarah's plans to leave Hastings and go live amongst Gray Eagle's people. Neither woman knew much about Indians, but Lilly had no doubt that Sarah would, and could succeed, if she put her heart into it. Only once did Samuel Justus' hatred of Indians come up, but the subject was quickly changed.

They ate the soup, made just that morning, and thick, soft slices of homemade bread, slathered with butter. Then the men went out to round up and tend the animals for Sarah while she and Lilly made the ice cream. Lilly told Sarah the latest news of Lydia, her younger sister, and how she and Jonas had agreed to take the child Lydia was carrying and raise it as their own. Sarah admired their compassion and caring, and told Lilly so.

"Oh, Sarah, you make me feel so good whenever we talk," Lilly stated. "I wish we had found the time, long before this, to get to know each other."

"Me, too," Sarah replied. "You always cheer me up, too." They hugged, then, and got to laughing at the memory of Lilly's gentle Jonas charging at Sarah's strong Gray Eagle, and both men sprawling, one atop the other, in the snow. Before long, they were both holding their sides and laughing at themselves, remembering how they, too, had ended up not very "ladylike" in the snow, beside the men. Tears rolled down their cheeks, as they laughed uproariously, unable to contain themselves.

When the two men reentered the cabin, everyone had a heaping bowl of the snow ice cream, and all too soon, it was time to say their goodbyes. Sarah hugged Lilly, wishing her unending happiness. And Lilly hugged Sarah, wishing her strength and love. The women's cheeks were damp with tears when, at last, Jonas lifted Lilly onto her horse, then mounted his own. Jonas and Gray Eagle shook hands, each having had a fine time discovering their shared interests and the compatibility of their new friendship.

After Lilly and Jonas rode away, Gray Eagle shut the door and took Sarah into his arms, kissing her tenderly. He had enjoyed meeting her friends and felt happy that they had not only accepted him, but liked him.

CHAPTER FORTY-SEVEN

Sarah's father arrived two days after Lilly and Jonas had come to visit. Gray Eagle had left that same evening, and she was glad to see her father. She was surprised to see he came alone. He had not been well since late December, and she could tell just by looking at him. His face was pale, and he moved slowly. Sarah was surprised to see he had lost a lot of weight. She knew Rosie was an excellent cook, but obviously it had not helped the situation.

"Oh, Father. You look so pale," she said, upon first seeing him.

"Just a little tired," he replied, walking to his favorite old rocker, pulling it up close to the fireplace, relishing the warmth.

"Can I get you a coffee?" Sarah asked. "Or a bowl of vegetable soup?"

"Yes," he replied. "Soup sounds good, but just a small bowl."

She hurried to dish it up, and they sat in their rockers eating. It was unusual for them to eat there, but she knew her father welcomed the warmth from the fireplace.

"Are you feeling better?" he asked between bites.

"Yes, no more dizzy spells or headaches. And no more blurry vision," she answered.

"I'm glad," he stated, finishing his coffee and setting his bowl of soup aside.

She noticed it was more than half full. "You should eat that, Father. It'll give you strength."

"Had enough," he replied. "Seems you've had a busy winter," he said after a few minutes. "I hear tell Sheriff Gentry stayed here quite a while."

"Yes. He was hurt in a fall and unconscious a long time. I nursed him back to health," Sarah replied.

"He . . . ah, he was a gentleman, I take it . . . during his stay?" Samuel asked, watching Sarah as she answered.

"Of course!" she replied, laughing at his insinuating tone of voice. "Except for my two black eyes."

Samuel's mouth dropped open in surprise. "What!" he exclaimed, his face flushing more than Sarah's had.

"Oh, Father. He didn't do it on purpose." Sarah laughed at the memory. "I gave him some of the whiskey you kept in Mother's cupboard for medicinal purposes before I cut him to remove some bone splinters that were protruding from his side. Guess I didn't give him enough." She laughed before continuing, "He felt me cut, and before I knew it, I had a black eye. The other black eye was also an accident."

Samuel shook his head, a relieved look upon his face. "I heard something about black eyes. Wondered just what went on. Thought it best I ask you if he . . . ah . . . stepped out of line."

"No," Sarah answered, "not at all." She rose then, asking her father if he'd like another cup of coffee.

"No thanks. I feel bad that I couldn't get out here to see you, Sarah. I was laid up with a cold first, then pneumonia."

"I know," Sarah replied. "I heard. Oh! I had other visitors recently. Lilly and Jonas Hart came to see me. We had such a nice visit. They stayed all afternoon, said they were so happy . . . as if I couldn't see it!"

Samuel got up and walked over to the window. "How's Glory and Pet and her calf? You got enough feed to last till pasture's in?"

"Yes," Sarah replied. "I'm a little low on meat, but I'll get out one of these days. There's always plenty of deer in the meadow, and other game. Easy shots."

"Glad you can manage so well," Samuel remarked. "I wouldn't have been much help this winter. It really laid me low."

"Well, I hope you're on the road to recovery," Sarah said, walking over and hugging him. "How's Rosie been? Did she end up sick with pneumonia, too?"

"No," he replied. "She's been busy as can be, tending me and doing for the church. Reverend Higgins stops by about twice a week now. Told him if he was trying to get me to attend his church, he was barking up the wrong tree."

"Father!" Sarah exclaimed, looking at him in surprise. "Why would you say that?"

"Oh, I get tired of hearing him talk about 'every man's your brother' or some such foolishness. He says we gotta love our brothers. Hmpf! I told him right out, I love my wife and my daughter, but I ain't got any brothers. No sisters, either." He chuckled at his words and then coughed a horrible, croupy cough that worried Sarah. "Rosie's always telling me how the good preacher says, 'someday, we're gonna be at peace with our "brothers," whether they're black, brown, or—God forbid— even red!' I told her she'd never see me in that church. No siree! Be a cold day in . . ." he coughed again, before continuing, "be a cold day, before I get *me* some Injun brother!"

Sarah felt terribly saddened by his words, but didn't know what to say. He was set in his ways, and no amount of talking or preaching—even from Reverend Higgins—was apparently going to change him. She put another log in the fireplace, then picked up her sewing basket and went back to her rocker. As she arranged the quilt pieces in the pattern she intended to make, she asked if anything else was new in town.

"Well, let's see," Samuel answered. "Old Doc Pearson took sick, not long after coming out here, when you were hurt. They say his missus is telling patients to go over to Black Dog if they need doctoring. She won't let him so much as step out of bed. Must be sorta frightening for her, I guess." He paused. "Forty-some years he's been doctoring folks and never had a sick day. And now, what is he? Sixty? Seventy? Now, he takes sick. Probably be the death of him, if he don't get to feeling better soon."

"Oh, I hope he didn't get sick from the long ride out here, and back, to tend me?" she lamented. "It was so good of him to hurry right out."

"How did he find out you had fallen?" Samuel asked, a curious look on his face.

"A . . . a friend I met, awhile ago, found me and went and got Doc," Sarah answered, trying to keep her voice steady. Her hands trembled, as she continued stitching.

"I'd like to thank him," Samuel replied, "for saving my daughter. You could have frozen to death."

"I already thanked him," Sarah said, then hurriedly changed the subject. "Father, you haven't seen Emmy yet, Pet's calf. Do you feel like walking out to the barn?"

"Well . . . sure," Samuel answered, and Sarah sighed silently with relief, glad to have the subject changed.

Samuel stayed another hour, seeing the animals and eating a piece of pie Sarah had made earlier that day. Then, after warning her to be careful, he got on his horse and headed back to town.

A great sadness overtook Sarah after he had gone. Not only had she lied to him about the friend who had gone for help when she fell, but she knew she would be leaving soon and might not see him ever again. She walked slowly into the cabin, laid her head in her arms on the table, and began to cry. At first, she cried softly, but her grief grew as she thought of never seeing him, and soon she was sobbing.

She longed to tell him . . . to somehow make him understand that Gray Eagle was an Indian, yes, but also a decent man who loved her as she did him. But it was useless, she knew, to try and change her father. When at last her tears subsided, she sat at the table in the ever-deepening shadows of the approaching night, thinking of the changes about to take place in her life.

True, she could hunt and track and knew many skills to survive in the wilds, thanks to Old John's teachings. But what did she know of Indians, and their ways and beliefs? What did she actually know, of the way they lived? Would she have a cozy cabin, as nice as her father had provided? She had seen the tepees around the fort. Surely Gray Eagle didn't expect her to live in a tepee. Or did he?

She wondered if his people would accept her and be friendly, or if she would be an outsider, in a distant land, with people who had strange customs and habits. Surely, Gray Eagle's people would accept her when they learned she was his wife and that she was a good person, eager to belong and fit into their lifestyle.

"I have so much to learn," Sarah said. "But, with God's help, I can make it work. I can and I will!" And with those words, she got up from where she sat and began planning her activities for the next day. There was hunting to do, and the usual chores. Not to mention, putting up the meat she would bring home, and tanning the hides for later use.

She pulled on her coat and boots and went out into the very cold, starlit night to feed Pet and Glory and look in on Emmy. She hurried, careful not to fall. She was anxious to return to the cabin, dress in her nightgown, and read one of the books Ophelia Denton had loaned her. It was a new book, written by a woman who left her home and family in the East, to go west with her new husband, and the adventures that had befallen them.

"Who knows?" thought Sarah. "I may learn something that will be of help in my own life's adventure. And, if nothing else, it will help pass the time until Gray Eagle returns."

CHAPTER FORTY-EIGHT

Sarah finished the quilt she'd been working on, happy with the way it had turned out. The weather had begun to improve. The snow was nearly all gone, though now the all-ensuing grayness and rain seemed enough to drive a person crazy. She felt an uneasiness that bordered on depression.

When the quilt was done, she worked on the letter she had been writing to her father. A letter, she hoped, would somehow explain not only how dearly she loved him and wished to thank him for his love and care over the years, but also how she had come to know and love Gray Eagle. She wrote and rewrote, tearing up page after page, wanting it to convey just how much she loved him. It was difficult explaining just how and why she must go to a land far away with a man her father did not know, and would not accept. A man her father hated, because he was an Indian.

She told him Gray Eagle was a decent man, this man she had chosen for her husband, and she wrote of the hopes she had for their future. She explained that she had prayed, long and hard, asking God for guidance, protection, and strength. And even more so, for Samuel to understand.

When the letter seemed just right, she placed it in an envelope. She did not seal it, though. She wanted Moses' opinion of it and would take it with her when she went into town. If he thought it was all right, she would leave it with him, she decided, and he could give it to her father, at the same time he told Samuel she was gone. It was a lot to ask of a friend, even one as dear as Moses had become to her. But she could see no other way to handle the situation.

She felt an extreme sadness pass over her. Everything she looked at, she looked at with leaving in her heart. She felt set apart from things that had meant so much in the everyday scheme of her life. She touched things, with a sense of finality, like the stove her father had provided, a generous gift few others had. She cried, as she lovingly felt each article of clothing that had been her mother's. Not to mention, the tall cupboard that had come all the way from Virginia with Jenny.

Hardest of all, she knew she must leave Pet and her small, frisky calf. She rubbed Pet's neck and the top of her head, tears running from her eyes as she did so. Pet mooed softly, as if asking her what was wrong. Sarah was certain the old cow knew she was sad, and that a change was about to occur. Animals sensed things . . . moods in people, like grief or elation. She had read that somewhere, or heard someone tell of it. She couldn't remember which. But she had no doubt it was true, as she looked into the large brown eyes that seemed to question her.

"I'm sorry, Pet," she said. "I'm so sorry. But I have to go. I have to! Father will take good care of you and Emmy. And you'll have a newer barn to stay in right near town." Pet lowed, watching Sarah, and then turned to lick her calf.

Sarah walked over to Glory, patting the horse's muzzle. "Well, Glory old girl, it won't be long and we'll be off. No more warm barn for you, or very easy life, I'm afraid. You'll have to learn to survive in the elements like the Indian ponies do. I hope you can do that." The mare nuzzled her hand, her long black tail swishing back and forth.

Sarah walked out of the barn, her thoughts many miles away. It wasn't just Glory who would have to get used to the changes ahead. She, too, would have a lot of adjusting to do. She shivered as she began to walk toward the cabin, reaching out to touch the log near the barn. It glistened from the rain that had just begun. Sarah entered the cabin, wiping her feet on an old rug by the door. Gray Eagle would be here soon. He had said he would come when the snow had melted and the spring rains came. It had been raining now, on and off, for nearly a week.

Sarah looked out the window at the gray sky, a sense of gloom settling upon her. "I have to stop this," she said aloud. "I have to say my goodbyes and get ready to leave. No more moping around." She straightened her shoulders, settling the unrest within her, once and for all. She loved Gray Eagle and wanted to be his wife. She had no doubts of either her feelings for him, or of his for her.

She had prayed for God's guidance, and trusted Him to lead her on the right path. She had felt, from the very first day, that Gray Eagle was the right one for her. She couldn't explain her feelings. Words couldn't explain the intense pull she felt, as though she was being swept along to her rightful destiny, in spite of herself. Cassandra Winthrop had called it "following your heart." It was an apt description of the unbidden course her life seemed to be taking since the day she first saw Gray Eagle, standing on the cliff above her cave.

Yes, she had doubts about her course of action. What bothered her most was the unknown: the monumental changes she would soon be facing. Change was never easy for Sarah.

She put a few things into her satchel, along with the letter to her father. Then she bundled-up, against the cold and damp, and went out to saddle Glory. She felt determination flow through her—felt ready to face her future.

She fed Pet and Emmy, then stepped into the stirrups to mount Glory, pulling herself up by the strength of her arms. She would go to town and say her goodbyes, though no one could know she was leaving. Only Moses knew what she planned. Only he would know she had come to say goodbye. Tears welled up in her eyes, but she wiped them away, as she eased Glory out of the barn. It was time to stop her crying. Time to move forward to whatever lay ahead. Time to embrace her destiny.

CHAPTER FORTY-NINE

The main street in Hastings was one long, deep mud puddle. Sarah eased Glory to the outer edge, as close as she could get to the hitching rail. Women's skirt hems were sodden and mud-coated, as high up as their knees, from crossing the street. Young boys jumped and played, clothes covered and faces spattered, with the dark-brown mess. Their mothers would not be happy with them when they got home.

Sarah walked to the jail, hoping Moses was at his desk. Instead she found Amos Culpepper sitting there, wanted posters laid out before him. "Hello, Amos," she said, reaching out to shake his hand.

"Miss Sarah," he answered, a smile breaking forth across his face. "What brings you all the way to town? Is everything okay?"

"Yes. I came to visit my father and Rosie. Thought I'd say a quick hello to Moses while I was here," she replied.

"I believe he's out to the O'Learys' or Old Man Pearly's. I'll tell him you're looking for him when he gets back," he said, adding quietly, "I met your friend, the young man who came to get help when you fell."

Sarah felt her face flush and looked at the jail cells before replying, relieved that no one was in there who might have heard. "Yes, I heard."

"Nice young man," Amos said, but, sensing her uneasiness, said no more.

"Well, I'd better go. I'd be pleased if you'd tell Moses I'm in town," she stated.

"Will do," Amos answered, and she thought of the tough choice the other Sarah must have had: choosing Moses over Amos. They both were tall, rugged, strong, and charming, and not at all that bad on the eyes either, though Moses had the advantage, being a few years younger.

Sarah left, leading Glory over to Dawson's General Store. She glanced at the walkway, seeing in her mind's eye the body of her dear friend, John Bruce, lying dead, his arm outstretched. She missed him so much and wished that she could see him, just once more, to tell him of her decision to leave with Gray Eagle and ask his advice on making such a change. She looked away. He was dead; he had died saving her life. She would take all that he had taught her, and do the best she could.

She turned and walked into Tommy's store. "Well, hello, Sarah," Tommy greeted her as she entered. Melinda Rose sat in a rocker beside the old stove, near the back of the store, young Danny in a basket by her feet. His face was filling-out nicely, and his hair had begun to cover his head in a soft reddish-blonde fluff.

"Sarah, how are you?" Melinda Rose said, standing and hugging her.

Sarah smiled, patting Danny gently on the head. "I'm doing fine, just fine," she answered. "My, how Danny's grown!"

"Yes," Melinda Rose said. "Got me a healthy one this time. Doc says no need to worry."

"That's wonderful," Sarah replied.

"What can I get for you, Sarah?" Tommy asked, coming over to the two women. He bent down, tousling Danny's hair and speaking softly to the baby. Sarah was amazed at the changes that had occurred since Danny and Melinda Rose had come into Tommy's life. He seemed calm and secure, and above all, content.

Sarah smiled at the three of them, wondering if she would ever be part of a close—knit, happy family, with Gray Eagle. "I just came in to say hello, Tommy." She looked slowly around the store, wondering if this would be the last time she would see it, the last time she would shop in a regular store. "But I would like a handful of those pretty beads you've got over there by the wall, the brightly colored ones."

Tommy laughed, "You plan on doing some trading with the Indians?"

Sarah started at his words, wishing she had not mentioned the beads. "No. I just think they're real pretty," she replied, keeping her back to him.

"You must really like living out there all by yourself," Melinda Rose commented. "I hated being out of town, was too lonely and afraid."

"No need to be afraid, or lonely, ever again, honey," Tommy assured her. "Danny and I don't plan to let you out of our sight." They all laughed, and then Sarah paid for her beads. When she left the store, she looked back, one last time, glad that these friends had found each other and life was good for them.

Sarah knocked on Rosie's door, happy to see her father answer it. His face was a bit flushed, but he looked better than he had at her cabin. "Father, hello. Would you mind a guest for the night?"

"Why no, not at all," he replied. "Rosie, Sarah's here. She's going to stay the night."

Rosie hurried into the room, ushering Sarah into the house and bustling around in her usual quick manner. "'Tis glad I am that you've come," she said, smiling. "Come in. Have you eaten?"

"Earlier," Sarah replied.

"Well, I've got some soup cooking and some delicious

bread cooling. Come, child, let me look at ya'." She stood back, glancing a time or two at Sarah. "So, what's new?" Rosie looked at her, her green eyes twinkling mischievously, "Had any handsome sheriffs land on your doorstep, lately, needing care?"

"Oh, Rosie. No, not lately." She laughed at the older woman's words.

Rosie dished up a steaming bowl of soup for Sarah, its rich aroma causing her stomach to rumble. Then she cut her a thick slice of fresh bread and pushed a knife and plate of butter toward Sarah. "Go ahead, Sarah. Help yourself. Eat it while it's hot."

"Aren't you and Father eating?" Sarah asked, wondering why her father went into the parlor, instead of sitting down to eat and visit.

Rosie dished up another bowl of soup and cut three more slices of bread, giving a second slice to Sarah and putting two on her own plate. "Samuel hasn't gotten his appetite back, I'm afraid." A worried look obliterated her earlier bubbly demeanor. "I try not to worry. Doc says it's normal, him being down sick so long." She paused, looking anxiously down at her plate. "I keep praying he'll get his appetite back," she said, her voice filled with caring.

"I'm sure he will," Sarah said, hoping she was right.

"So . . . you'll stay the night?" Rosie asked.

"If you'll have me?"

"Of course, child. It's happy I am to have the company. It's been a long, hard winter."

As they ate, Sarah longed to confide in Rosie—longed to tell her of her plans and seek her advice. Instead she said, "Tell me of your adventures, Rosie, when you came to America."

"Oh, child," Rosie replied, "'twas so long ago. I fear I hardly remember." She took another bite of bread, her eyes getting a far-away look, as she thought back to her journey to America. Sarah waited patiently.

Before long, her patience was rewarded. "Well, let me see," Rosie began, her eyes looking, once more, at distant scenes from long ago. "I was a mere child, younger than yourself." Sarah listened as Rosie recounted the ship's grueling journey, the frightening moments when a violent storm raged around them, nearly capsizing them and sending the ship to rest on the bottom of the ocean floor.

"After the storm, me sister, Margaret Mary, became ill. At first I thought she'd make it," she paused, pulling a hanky from her apron pocket and dabbing at her eyes. "But, 'twas not the good Lord's will."

"I'm sorry," Sarah said, patting Rosie's hand.

"Well, 'tis not for us to know the plans He has for us," Rosie replied. Sarah finished the last of her soup, waiting for Rosie to go on. "Then me brother, Michael, got the chills and fever. Michael and his friend, Shawnessy, and one of the O'Toole lads, all come down with fever and chills, at the same time." Rosie dabbed at her eyes again, continuing, "I was always a hearty lass. Took care of 'em, best I could, trying to get the fevers to break, and trying to get a wee bit o' food into 'em. Some they wouldn't lose over the side, that is, or in the large oaken buckets. I hated emptying them buckets. 'Bout made me sick when I got a whiff of what was in 'em." Rosie and Sarah sat in silence, each seeing the picture she was painting with her words.

"Only meself was left when we got to America. And scared I was, all alone with only a couple of dollars to me name and a wee trunk of clothes me mother and I had sewn for the journey. I felt like I was so alone, Sarah. And yet, there was a feeling of adventure . . . like all the pain was behind me now and only good could happen." She got up, getting two cups out of the cupboard, pouring them both a cup of coffee. "And good it was, that followed, all things considered. Sure, I was lonely and missing me mother and those that we'd lost, but somehow I felt like life would get better. That . . . well, you know how a rainbow follows the rain? That's what I was feeling, ya' see? Like there's hope just around the bend. As long as there's life, Sarah, there's hope! I try to always remember that. Life doesn't always go as we'd have it, but as long as we're livin' and believin' in the goodness of our Maker, we just have to hold on . . . and look for the rainbow."

When their coffees were gone, the two women went into the parlor to visit with Samuel. He was asleep in the big overstuffed chair in the corner, his head drooping against his chest. "Samuel," Rosie said, going to his side and gently touching his shoulder.

"Hm-m?" he said, taking in a deep breath and rubbing his eyes. "Guess I dozed off. What have you two been up to?"

"We were talking about Rosie's journey to America," Sarah replied. "I love to hear her tell of it, though there's so much sadness."

Rosie smiled sweetly at Sarah. "Remember the rainbow," she said. And Sarah smiled back at her, knowing that when her life got too rough or too sad to bear, she would, indeed, try to remember Rosie's words and look for the rainbow.

CHAPTER FIFTY

There was a knock on the door, and Rosie went to answer it. Sarah heard Moses' voice and got up, going out to greet him. Rosie's cheeks glowed fire red and a grand smile was on her face.

"Hello, darlin'," Moses said, when he saw Sarah. He realized too late that he had called her "darlin'" again.

"Hi," Sarah replied, enjoying Rosie's reaction to Moses' usual term of endearment.

"Well, you just come right in, Sheriff. Have ya' eaten?" Rosie asked.

"Yes, I have," Moses answered. "Amos told me you were in town, Sarah. Thought I'd stop over and say hello."

"I'm glad you did," she answered.

"Come into the parlor. Samuel's in there. He'd welcome your company, I'm sure," Rosie said, leading the way.

"Hello, Sheriff," Samuel said, as Moses entered. "Been chasing some robbers or Injuns?"

"No," Moses replied, his voice steady. "Just keeping the town safe and secure."

"You're lucky Hastings is so far from where we came from. Nothing but one crazy, mean Injun after another, there." Samuel said.

"Samuel!" Rosie replied, noticing the embarrassed looks

on Sarah and Moses' faces. "Couldn't we talk about something else? Please?"

Samuel looked at her, not saying a word for a noticeable amount of time, then rose from his chair. "Guess I'll get me a cup of coffee," he said, his tone sharp.

Sarah was surprised, but she said nothing. When he left the room, Rosie followed, and they could hear her apologizing to him. "I'm sorry," Sarah said, looking at Moses. "Rosie says Father hasn't been himself, since he was sick, this past winter. I don't know what's gotten into him. It's so unlike him."

"It's all right," Moses replied. "It's his house. I guess he has a right to speak his mind in it." They sat there in silence then, each wondering about Samuel's hateful outburst. "Want to take a walk?" Moses asked, at last.

"Yes," replied Sarah, "I'd like that." And they left the parlor, telling Rosie and her father they'd be back in awhile.

The night air was crisp as they walked along, their breath a foggy mist when they exhaled. Sarah placed her hand upon Moses' arm, thinking how peaceful it was in Hastings. She enjoyed the comfortable feeling that enveloped her as she strolled along at his side. If she had been his Sarah . . . if he had met her first . . . She took a deep breath, dismissing these thoughts from her mind, enjoying his closeness and the deep friendship they now shared. "I'm leaving soon," she said, her voice soft.

"I know," he answered. "I figured as much." She stopped, clasping his arm with both her hands, feeling suddenly unsure, and slightly afraid. "I'm proud of you, darlin'," Moses stated, his voice filled with warmth. "You'll do just fine. Gray Eagle is a good man and he loves you."

"I know," she replied. They walked on, only their footsteps breaking the silence of the night.

"Want a coffee, at the jail?" he asked.

"Sure."

"Looks like the street's pretty muddy," he said. "Here,

let me carry you." And before she knew it, Moses had lifted her up into his arms as easily as if she were a child, and carried her across the street. As he set her down on her feet, he looked into her eyes and she felt tears well up in hers. "If you ever need me, Sarah, you just get word to me, and I'll come running, I promise," he said.

"I'll hold you to it," she answered, sniffling and smiling at the same time. She took his arm again, and they walked along, both of them feeling an overwhelming amount of sadness, knowing this was goodbye. As they reached the saloon, the loud music and voices were coarse and abrasive, in the surrounding stillness.

Suddenly, a man, too inebriated to walk, fell across the walk in front of them, cursing loudly, as he tried to get to his feet. Moses lifted him up, commenting on his language in front of a lady, and sat him on a bench beside the saloon door. The drunken man said something Sarah could not understand, and she realized it was Nancy's father, Old Man Pearly. Moses took her arm, shaking his head, glad to resume their walk.

"He's gonna have one heck of a headache in the morning," Moses said, laughing.

"I'm glad Nancy doesn't have to put up with his drinking any more," Sarah said, taking his arm again and walking on in silence.

Moses opened the door to the jail and lit the oil lamp on his desk. Sarah walked around, glancing into the empty cells, reading the wanted posters that hung on the wall near the desk. "I hope you stay safe," she said, looking at him pleadingly.

He smiled, pleased to hear of her concern for him. "I'm always careful, darlin'. Always watch my back. It's the ones you *don't* expect that usually get you."

She looked alarmed. "You be careful, Moses Gentry! You hear me? Please, be careful." He smiled, pouring them both a cup of coffee.

He read the letter, then, that she had written to her father, telling her it was a fine letter, in his opinion. She asked if he would see to it that Pet and her calf were tended to, until her father could get out to the cabin to get them.

"I'll do better than that," he replied. "I'll have the oldest O'Leary boys go look after them. If Samuel and Rosie don't want them, I'll see to it they go to the O'Learys. They're barely surviving out there. I'm surprised they haven't starved to death, or moved on," Moses stated.

"That'd be good," Sarah said. "Pet gives the best milk and lots of cream. And the calf is a heifer. She'll provide them with milk and cream and butter, too, once she's old enough to have a calf of her own. Moses? You will talk to my father, won't you? I know it's a lot to ask." Sarah watched his expression as she spoke. "He's so filled with hate for the Indians. I don't understand. Seems he's getting worse, as time goes by."

She stared into her coffee, remembering her father's outburst at her cabin about "loving your brother," and then again, at the house, just tonight. "His hate seems to be building, seems to be growing by leaps and bounds. I just can't understand it. He's always been a fair man," she paused and then added, "except where Indians were concerned, that is."

Moses nodded, having no words to comfort her. After awhile, he asked, "Are you all ready to leave?"

"I guess," she answered, standing and beginning to pace back and forth across the floor. "Sometimes I feel ready. Ready to get on Glory and head out immediately. Then other times, like now, I have trouble even thinking of leaving. I get so . . . afraid. I don't know much about Indians, Moses. Don't know how they live, what they eat, what they think. It's easy to love Gray Eagle and think of being his wife. But what if I don't fit in with his people? His family? What if they don't like me?" Sarah stopped talking then, realizing she had been rattling on for quite some time. She looked at Moses, shrugging her shoulders helplessly. "Am I making a mistake, Moses? What if I am?"

He stood up, walking around the desk, to stand before her. She leaned her head against his chest, feeling the steady, rhythmic beat of his heart as he put his arms around her, looking into her eyes. They were damp with tears. "If you love Gray Eagle, Sarah, it's not a mistake. You're just afraid, that's all. And that's natural. You're leaving everyone you've known for years, and a way of life that you were born into. It's comfortable here. You know what to expect here. You're a strong woman and you know how to survive. Very few women know the things Old John taught you, or have the skills you have. If anyone can make a go of it with Gray Eagle and his people, Sarah, it's you."

They held each other then, two very dear friends, who— if circumstances had been different—would never have walked away from what they felt for each other.

Moses walked Sarah back to her father's, kissing her tenderly on the forehead one last time. "Be happy, darlin'," he whispered, as her eyes filled with tears, once again.

She smiled at him, her heart heavy. "Thank you, Moses," she said, her voice soft, "for everything." She watched, as he turned and walked away. "Goodbye, my friend," she whispered, as tears rolled down her cheeks. "You'll always be in my heart."

CHAPTER FIFTY-ONE

"Oh, you're back. Thought the sheriff would come in and have a bite of cake," Rosie said, as Sarah entered the house.

"He . . . he had work to do," Sarah said, forcing a smile.

"Well, come sit a spell, child. I'll cut us a piece of cake, all right?"

"Thanks, Rosie," Sarah nodded, asking, "Where's Father?"

"Oh, he turned in early. Said to tell you he'd see ya' in the morning. Just hasn't been himself since the pneumonia," Rosie replied. "Tires so easily. He'll be up at the break of dawn, though. You can have a hearty breakfast together. I know how glad he is to have ya' here." She hesitated a few moments, before asking, "Sarah, I know 'tis none of my business, but I can't help noticin' that ya' seem a bit upset. Is something bothering ya', child, something I could help ya' with, perhaps? You seem like me very own child, ya' know, and if there's anything you'd like to talk about, I'd be pleased to listen."

Sarah took the plate of moist chocolate cake from Rosie and wondered what she could say in answer. She longed to tell her about Gray Eagle and her decision to leave with him. Longed to get another woman's opinion of her intended undertaking, especially Rosie's opinion, with all that she'd been through. "How did you find the courage to . . . to come west with Reverend Mitchell when you didn't even know him that well . . . or even love him?" Sarah looked at Rosie, an almost pleading look upon her face. "How could you be so sure of yourself?" she asked.

"Oh, sweet child. I knew it was things, such as these, that was bothering ya'." She reached out and patted Sarah's hand, a distant look in her eyes as she chose her words carefully. "Can't say I was all that courageous. Don't think courage had that much to do with it. Ireland is a beautiful country, but poor. Me family was barely makin' a livin' from the land and lots o' troubles there were, thereabouts."

She paused, looking back in time, as memories assailed her. "We'd heard o' the opportunities in this great land. Heard o' the richness of the soil and the grand abundance to be had. No, it wasn't courage that spurred us on, 'twas necessity . . . necessity and possibility. Oh, Sarah, when ya' got little to eat and no prospects for better'n the conditions ya' see all around ya', possibilities pull at ya' like quicksand. They drag at ya' till there seems no other way to go! 'Course, I s'pose crossing the ocean took a wee bit of courage, to be sure. But once we sailed away from Ireland—wavin' our hearts out to those on shore—what could we do? There was no turnin' back, then. No changin' our minds. No wishin' we would open our eyes and find ourselves—all snug and safe—sittin' at our sweet mother's feet, afore the fireplace in our own wee cottage. No, there was no goin' back."

She got up and put the pot of coffee on to boil, then continued, "As for going west with Emory . . . Reverend Mitchell, well, I never felt that took courage either. I'd noticed him about town, when I was runnin' errands for the missus, where I worked. Was aware of his 'calling' and the kind, caring man he seemed to be. Liked his appearance, and the way he laughed, sorta soft, gentle-like. Didn't take courage to go with him, really, either. I guess the answer is the same to all these things, Sarah. What it really took was hope. Hope that things could and would be better here than they were in Ireland. Hope that we'd arrive here safely, and that we'd prosper, and make a good life in this new land."

Rosie got up and went to get them a cup of coffee, then sat back down. "It also took trust, or . . . I guess I should say, faith. That's the best word, faith. You gotta have faith, child, faith in yourself—in your inner feelings—but most of all, faith in the good Lord, that He has a plan for ya'. Faith that He'll show ya' where He wants ya' to be, and what He wants ya' to do. It's like that little voice ya' hear when you're about to do something you're unsure of. You have to have faith in that little voice. 'Tween that little voice, and faith that God always leads us in the right direction to fulfill His plan for us, we just can't go wrong."

Sarah sat quietly, savoring Rosie's words. "If you really feel you're making the right decision, then you have to do what you feel is right?" Sarah asked.

"Sure do," Rosie replied, adding, "Most of all, have faith that the good Lord will always be there to help ya', through the good times and the bad, Sarah, and you'll do just fine."

Sarah stood up and walked to Rosie, bending down to hug her stepmother. Rosie had always been the kindest woman. Sarah knew she would miss her something awful. "Thank you, Rosie, for being such a dear friend. I'm so glad you came into my life, and Father's. I love you," Sarah stated, hugging her and kissing her cheek.

"I love ya', too, Sarah. Always have . . . since the first day I met ya'."

Seeing Rosie yawn, Sarah stated, "Guess I'll be turning in now. I'm awful tired."

"Me, too," Rosie replied. "Me, too. In the morning ya' can visit with your father, child. I know he'd like that. Goodnight, sweet dreams."

"Goodnight," Sarah answered. She hugged Rosie again

and then walked slowly to the narrow stairs that led to the bedroom above.

Dreams flooded Sarah's sleep that night, dreams of strange places and unrecognized faces. At dawn's first light she woke trembling, her heart pounding loudly in her ears! She sat up, fighting to still her racing heart, trying to piece together the tormenting shards of what she had dreamt. It was so disturbing it had awakened her.

She hugged herself, as she envisioned the scenes from her dream. Gray Eagle had stood before her, tall and handsome, smiling at her, a look upon his face of caring and love. Then, he had looked away from her, his head turning, as if by measured degree, until he looked beyond her. She watched his expression turn to shocked surprise, it seemed. Though she couldn't see herself, she knew she, too, had turned her head in the direction he was looking. Through shadows that seemed to ripple and recede as she watched, a lone figure approached. It was a menacing figure. The closer it came, the more threatened Sarah had felt. She stared as it approached, realizing it was the figure of a man: an Indian with piercing eyes that seemed to glow bright yellow, against the dark black shadows surrounding him. She heard the sound of drums then, beating louder and louder, each beat growing stronger and quicker. She turned back toward Gray Eagle, then, only to discover he was gone, and in his place stood Moses. He was yelling at her, his facial expression frantic! And as the drums pounded wildly, she saw the knife in Moses' hand—Old John's Bowie knife! Its blade, red with blood! And the beating drums continued, becoming the rapidly hammering beat of her heart as she had awakened from the dream.

Rubbing her temples, she tried to make sense of the unsettling dream. She walked back and forth across the small room, glad that morning had dawned clear, and full of promise. I'll feel better once I get past my uncertainties, she thought, once Gray Eagle and I are on our way. She dressed quickly, hearing movement downstairs. Father's up. One more goodbye to get through. She walked down the stairs, her chin raising as she steeled herself for the hardest task she felt she would *ever* face!

"Mornin', Sarah," Samuel greeted her as she entered the kitchen.

"Morning, Father," she replied and sat down in the chair closest to him.

"How'd you sleep?" he asked.

"Lots of dreams," she answered, wondering why he had asked.

"Heard you call out, when I first came into the kitchen. Something bothering you?"

Sarah bit her lip. "No, not really. Is the coffee ready?" she asked, hoping to change the subject.

"Just made it," he answered. "I'll pour us a cup."

"No! Let me," Sarah said, rising quickly, before he could protest.

"This time of year always gets to me, too," Samuel stated, stirring his coffee. "Guess it always will." Sarah looked at him questioningly. "Your mother's birthday's tomorrow."

"Oh, yes," she replied, sadly. "I'd forgotten."

He glanced at her curiously. "Not like you to forget, Sarah. I thought that's why you came to visit. Always made us both sort of introspective. 'Course, time changes things, distances us from things like that. Painful things. Regrets." His voice drifted off.

Sarah looked at him. At how sallow his skin had gotten with his recent bout of pneumonia. How the lines had deepened at the corners of his eyes. How he seemed shorter or smaller, as if he was shrinking a bit, between her visits. "Why did you say regrets?" she asked him.

He put down his cup, looking into the dark-brown liquid, as if to see the answer within its depth. "Regrets plague a lot of people," he replied. "That's part of life. Guess God gives them to us so we can learn from them. Lessons, you know?" Sarah waited for him to go on, noticing the sadness in his eyes. "I have lots of regrets . . . where your mother is concerned," he said, at last. "She never said much. It wasn't her way to complain. But I could tell. She seemed so sad, sometimes. I thought she was missing her family back East. Asked her if she wanted to go back to Virginia for a visit." He shook his head, sadly, at the memory. "She cried and ran outside, never answering. I had to get back to my troops. Thought she was being foolish and childish. Told her we'd talk when I got back. Then I stormed out. Never even kissed her or tried to comfort her."

He closed his eyes as more memories came to mind. "She pulled away from me from that day on. We never talked about it again. She just seemed to draw into herself, after that. Only laughed when *you* did something that pleased her. Dedicated every minute to you, teaching you things, reading to you. I tried to draw her out, to tell her I loved her. But she was closed to my words. Grew to hate the fort and all that it stood for. Sometimes I . . . thought she even hated me."

He sipped at his coffee, again, and then leaned his elbows on the table. "Oh, yes. I have regrets . . . more than you know. Guess hindsight always brings some regrets. She was so pretty when I first saw her. She was standing on the front steps of her parent's home, in a yellow dress that seemed to float around her, like the wings of an angel. She was laughing, as I approached, a soft laugh that reminded me of bells. I can still see the tiny black slippers she wore on her dainty feet. I'd been invited to a dance that evening at her parent's home, by her cousin, Jared. We were in training together and had become friends."

He rose and walked to the window, gazing out as a buckboard rolled by, and then returned to his seat at the table. "She was the loveliest woman I had ever seen. I think I fell in love with her the first moment I saw her, standing there, laughing gayly with her sisters." He shook his head again. "Yes, I have regrets, Sarah. But, it's too late to erase 'em. Guess I'll carry them to my grave. Should have paid more attention, listened to her. Spent more time with her. Should have noticed her sadness. I loved her. God knows I did, but I got wrapped up in other things . . . my job, my position as an officer, and, later my hatred of Indians. If you love someone, Sarah, you have to let them know . . . have to keep them *first*! Life's hard enough without regrets."

"She loved you, Father. I'm sure she wasn't that unhappy," Sarah said, as she got up to fix breakfast.

"You made her happy, Sarah, and I'm thankful for that. But I've no doubt she was very unhappy with me those last years. I always thought we'd have another child, a boy perhaps, but she told me there'd be no more children. No more 'closeness' between us. I knew then, it was too late to change her. Too late to reach her. I've often wondered . . . if she died of a broken heart."

"No, Father!" Sarah exclaimed. "She often told me how much she loved you. Told me happy stories of your time together."

Samuel sighed, before replying, "Just be sure you keep your eyes on the goal ahead, Sarah, when you fall in love. When you're certain of your love for a man, do your best to be the wife he needs. Don't let *anyone* interfere with that! Not your friends, or your family. Not even me! When love comes into your life, set your sights on your mate, and don't let *anyone* or *anything* turn your head or become more important!"

Sarah dished up a plate, for both of them, and then sat down to eat. "I love you, Father," she said. "I'll always remember your words."

"If you do," he replied, "you'll never regret it."

They ate in silence then, Sarah mulling over the advice he had given her. Once again, she had shared with her father things between her parents that she had never understood before, and it made her feel even closer to him. She also felt more secure in her decision to marry Gray Eagle, more determined. She knew she loved him and felt ready, now, to stand beside him. Ready to put him first, and as her father had said, "not let anyone interfere with their relationship . . . not even him!"

When she left, later that morning, she hugged her father to her, laying her head against his shoulder, smelling the scent of him, and feeling the texture of his skin against her cheek as she embraced him. She didn't cry, but it was difficult not to. "I love you, Father, with all my heart."

"And I you, daughter," he replied. "Always have, always will."

She eased slowly from him, saying she'd better get going, and swung up onto Glory. She did not glance back until she reached Dawson's General Store, far enough down the street that her father would not be able to see the tears that coursed a path down her cheeks. He looked so alone standing there, watching her. She waved, and as she did, Rosie joined him, wrapping her arm around his waist and laying her head against his shoulder.

Sarah pulled up on Glory, looking back at them as they stood there together, waving. She felt happy that her father was no longer alone, happy that he had found love again. She was certain he would have no regrets concerning his life with Rosie. She waved again and smiled, then turned Glory toward home, urging her on. Glancing at the jail, as she passed, she saw that Moses was nowhere to be seen.

"Time to get on with my life," she whispered. "Time to live the adventure God has planned for me. Giddy up, Glory! Giddy up, girl!"

CHAPTER FIFTY-TWO

Amos Culpepper continued on as Moses' deputy, finding they worked together like teamwork, when the situation demanded. Amanda didn't seem to mind and dropped in often, bringing venison stew and biscuits, and other delicious meals. The men ate together, or in shifts, depending on what needed tending to in and about Hastings. Sometimes they sat, talking quietly, late into the evening. Then Amos would walk home to his waiting wife and Moses would curl up on the cot, in the spare room, at the jail.

Though neither would admit it, they had become fast friends. They never spoke of the secret that lay between them. It was best *not* spoken of, they both knew. They went about their business, content with their lives, and no longer as shackled to the past.

Moses thought of Sarah and Gray Eagle, as he drank his morning coffee across the desk from Amos. He knew they had left over a week earlier to go to his people. He stretched his legs out to full-length and yawned, awake, but not yet up and about.

"Looks like a good day," Amos commented. "Sun's coming up and not one cloud in the sky."

"Yup," replied Moses. "I enjoy weather like this: not too hot, not too cold."

"I can certainly agree with that," Amos said. "I'll be nearly fifty on my next birthday. Nearly fifty! I never thought I'd be around to see myself get so old."

"Looks like you'll make it," Moses answered. "Unless we get some kid in town who thinks he can make a name for himself by taking down the 'infamous Amos Pepper.'"

He grinned at Amos who replied, "Hardly a chance of that anymore, I'd say. Too darned old to have some kid gain much of a reputation by beating me."

"Let's hope you're right," Moses replied. They sat in silence then, enjoying a cup of the strong coffee that Amos made that morning, as he did every morning.

Moses dreaded telling Samuel that Sarah had left with Gray Eagle. But, if truth be known, he would have walked through fire, if it meant her happiness. He knew what hurt was, as well as any man, and he hated having to hurt Samuel. But he had given Sarah his word that he would speak with him, and that was exactly what he meant to do.

He paced back and forth, at the jail, checking his hair twice, in the mirror. Then he dallied over a second cup of the strong coffee, going over in his mind, the possible questions Samuel might ask, and the probable answers he would give in return. He would be truthful, of course, but not say anything that could possibly be misconstrued or tarnish Sarah, or her relationship with Gray Eagle. How well he understood their predicament!

On the other hand, Samuel had been a fort commander. Moses was well aware of that, and he realized that in his course of duties, Samuel had probably only seen the worst Indians, and the horrors they wrought. He put on his hat and straightened his shirt. He was procrastinating, though he knew that it would do no good to prolong the inevitable, any longer. Finally, garnering all his courage, he went to see Samuel Justus.

As he walked down the street, Melinda Rose waved to him through the large window of Dawson's General Store, but he had to look away as she lifted young Danny up and kissed him on the cheek. He was happy that Tommy Dawson had found the woman who would be a helpmate to him. And, more importantly, who wouldn't be bored with him.

He smiled, his thoughts turning to Sarah at Nancy Pearly's wedding, and how frustrated she had become when he "rescued" her from Tommy, as he had hurried toward her across the yard. Moses knew she had chosen the "lesser of two evils," as he liked to think of it, and had chosen to walk with him, instead of being bored to death by grimly persistent Tommy. He laughed aloud at the memory, his mind free for a moment, of the burden at hand.

He remembered too, how she always raised her chin, defiantly, when angry or when she felt threatened. Her small bow-shaped mouth looked so cute when she pursed it, when he teased and antagonized her. He nodded at Mrs. O'Leary and waved at Johnathon Clark, the banker, as he went by the bank. And shortly thereafter, arrived at Samuel and Rosie's.

He had purposely arrived early, before Samuel would be out and about his usual business. Rosie greeted him at the door, ushering him in, her surprise at having him on her doorstep so early, extremely evident. She called Samuel, who came hurrying into the room, his eyeglasses in hand, a worried look upon his face. "Is it Sarah? Has something happened?" he asked, with all the loving concern a father could have.

"Sarah's all right," Moses answered. "I need to talk to you." He tried to keep his voice calm and unwavering. They sat in the kitchen, Rosie stating, "It's warmer in here, with the stove and all." He noticed how Rosie wrung her hands, in nervous anticipation of the news he brought. An uneasy silence prevailed. Then Moses reached into his pocket and withdrew the letter that Sarah had, so painstakingly, written to her father. He laid the envelope on the table before Samuel, explaining that it was a letter from Sarah. "She asked me to talk to you," Moses said, keeping his voice steady. Samuel stared at the envelope, while Rosie twittered beside him.

"Maybe you better tell me what it is you have to say, first," Samuel stated, looking at Moses, solemnly.

Moses cleared his throat, praying silently that he would say the right thing. "A while ago—about a year ago—I guess it was, Sarah . . . ah, met a man. He was hurt at the time and she nursed him back to health." Rosie smiled then, believing it to be himself he was talking about. "She grew to love him and he feels the same." He hesitated, as Rosie continued to smile and Samuel looked guarded and stolid, only the pulse in his neck giving evidence to the emotion within. "They left, five days ago, to be married and live with his people." Rosie gasped, but Samuel remained still.

"He's a good man who truly loves Sarah," he added, hoping Samuel would say something or react in some way. But there was no reaction. "I've met him and gotten to know him," Moses quietly admitted. "It was him who came and got me, last February, when Sarah fell at the cabin. He risked his life to get help for her." Rosie stared wide-eyed at him, her mouth open, and Moses wondered if she *had* heard of the Indian's foray into town from Amanda Culpepper. But just as instantly, he knew Amos would not have spoken of it, even to his wife . . . *especially* to his wife, knowing of her close friendship with Rosie.

"As you'll read in the letter, he's . . . ah . . . his name is Gray Eagle and he's a Sioux Indian." A silence, as still as death, filled the room. Samuel remained as he was, a twitching movement in his cheek, the only sign of the tension he was feeling. "His mother was white. She died when he was very young, and he was raised by his father's people." Moses did not know what else to say. He knew everything else would be explained in the letter that lay on the table before Samuel.

The silence was unbearable. Rosie reached over and

patted Samuel's arm, unsure of how to comfort or console him. Samuel rose from his chair. He seemed unsteady and held on to the edge of the table, as if to keep his balance. His face was devoid of expression and ashen gray. He stared at Moses, a long time, almost as if he could not remember who he was. Then he picked up Sarah's letter, slowly walked to the stove, and pitched it in.

"Oh, no, Samuel!" Rosie exclaimed, raising her hands to her face. Then he turned and left the room, shuffling his feet like an old man, his shoulders drooped, and arms hanging limply at his sides. Moses had seen many men die before, but that was the closest he'd come to it in a long time. Rosie knew, too, that the unexpected blow Samuel had received had killed something inside of him, as surely as if he'd been gunned down.

"Thank you for coming," Rosie whispered, after a lengthy silence. "I'll see you out." Moses stood, wanting to say something to comfort them, but words failed him. He took his hat and went out, sorely aware of the door shutting behind him.

Five days later, as he sat at his desk at the jail, Moses realized he had not seen Samuel or Rosie anywhere in town, since that morning. Their house looked dark and foreboding when he had ridden by, the curtains drawn as though to shut out the world, or to shut out further grief. He wanted to go back to check on Samuel, to say something that might help. But what was there to say? He lay awake at night, reliving each moment, going over in his mind what he had said. He wondered if anything might have eased the pain Samuel Justus had felt. He thought of the way Samuel had burned Sarah's letter without so much as glancing at it first. Thought, too, of the words of love inside—words she had written—that might have eased her father's pain, given time.

He also felt the whole resulting demeanor of Samuel Justus, a portent of things to come. He could feel it in his bones, stronger everyday. It was like a sickness that ate away at a person. You couldn't see it, but you knew it was there.

Moses glanced over at Amos as he worked on reports at a side table. "I haven't seen Samuel or Rosie in town, lately, have you?" He had told Amos of Samuel's reaction to the news that Sarah had left with Gray Eagle. But Amos had only shaken his head sadly, then, not saying a word.

"Nope, haven't seen them," he replied now. "I don't want to say anything disparaging about Samuel, Moses, but at his age he should be getting some sense when it comes to his hatred toward Indians. He's let it override everything in his life, even his love for his daughter. A man has to grow. Has to realize that times change and not all things stay the same." He looked steadily at Moses before going on.

"I like that boy, Gray Eagle. He seemed like a real decent fellow. Sarah could have done a lot worse." Moses glanced at him, a look on his face that Amos recognized from years past. He chose his next words carefully. "A man shouldn't be judged by the color of his skin, or who his people are. Took *me* a long time to learn that," he said apologetically, "too long." He got up and went to stand by the window, watching the activity outside. "I was a fool," Amos stated. "I was young . . . young and in love. That's my excuse. Took me a long time to understand that." He paused, shaking his head, then continued, "It had to do with growing up, seeing the way of different folks as I rode across the country. But most of all, it had to do with seeing things from a different perspective." Moses sat there, listening, feeling a long, never-forgotten wound being eased by the words Amos spoke.

"I learned a lot when I was shot up back in '38 or '39. I don't remember which year anymore. An old priest, Padre Ocampo, cared for me—tending my wounds—at a little mission just over the border. As he worked, he spoke of things I'd never heard of before: of Jesus' love for us, and how He died for all men. *All* men," he repeated. "I laid there, almost two months, listening to his words, feeling the serenity in that little mission."

Amos stopped speaking and Moses watched him: an old man reminiscing about his life, remembering the changes that had occurred, unbidden. "I turned my life over to the Lord," Amos continued, as though he was still in awe of that one act. "Told Him I couldn't go on as I was. Told Him I needed Him to help me. To change me." He sniffled, his back still turned toward Moses. "I gave Him my life that day. Never used my guns again. Felt 'new,' like a babe, just born. Felt clean and free of the hate I had carried so long . . . for you."

He paused, taking a deep breath, and then continued, "Made up my mind that when I left that mission, I would do whatever it took to get myself pardoned." A dog barked outside and ran along beside a buckboard, the sounds of it invading the silence of the room. "I vowed to set things right. Not only with Amanda, but also with you. I hope I've done just that." He turned toward Moses. "Samuel Justus hasn't dealt with his hatred. Probably won't, 'less his eyes get opened. I don't know *what* it'll take to reach him. He's got a good wife, that adores him, and a daughter whose only crime seems to be loving an Indian. He's a lucky man—very blessed—as we both know. I don't know *what* it'll take to open his eyes . . . or his heart." He poured a cup of coffee and then sat down across the desk from Moses.

"Your words explained a lot to me," Moses offered. "I'm not much good with words, Amos. Never have been. But I want you to know I'm glad we've become friends. I appreciate your friendship . . . more than you know."

They drank their coffee in silence then, each lost in his own thoughts, until finally, Moses spoke again. "I believe I'll go over and see Samuel, try to talk to him. I know what was in Sarah's letter. Maybe I can 'reach his heart,' as you said, by telling him what she wrote . . . what she feels for him."

"Would you mind if I come along?" Amos asked. "If he won't listen to you, maybe he'll listen to me . . . to my story. What do you think?"

"I'd like your company," Moses said. And he reached out his hand to Amos, who took it within his own, healing, once and for all, a wound that had spanned nearly their entire lives.

CHAPTER FIFTY-THREE

Rosie opened the door, a tired, overwrought look upon her face. Both Amos and Moses were startled by her appearance. Her hair hung down against her shoulders, and her eyes were dark with shadows. A sadness seemed to prevail, not only around her, but from within her. She stood there, looking small and defenseless, as though a mere wind could blow her over and destroy her.

"Rosie?" Moses spoke. "Are you all right?"

She looked at him, trying to find the words to answer, as tears began to run down her pale and already tear-streaked cheeks. "He's in there," she whispered, her voice cracking. She looked so forlorn that Moses wanted to put his arms around her and comfort her. She looked down at the floor, wiping her tears with her apron, as they stepped inside. Moses wondered—for just one moment—if he could find Gray Eagle and Sarah and bring them back. If somehow, they could mend the devastating pain, their leaving had obviously cost Rosie and Samuel.

Rosie ushered them into the parlor. The curtains were closed, and no lamps burned. It took a few seconds for their eyes to adjust. Then they saw Samuel, slumped in an overstuffed chair, a bottle of whiskey clutched in his hand. Empty bottles were scattered about the floor around his feet. Rosie lit the oil lamp, on the table, by the chair. Both men noticed how her hands shook and felt deeply saddened by what she had had to endure.

Samuel groaned, then jerked awake. The bottle he was holding fell onto the lovely braided rug and Rosie scurried to pick it up, her sorrow more than evident.

"Git outta here," Samuel yelled, unaware that they had visitors. "Ya' wan' me to shell ya' to the Injuns?" His voice pierced the air with slurred and devastatingly cruel words. "Git me a drink," he ordered. "Where's my bottle?"

Rosie looked at Moses, her eyes wide with fright, like a mistreated child. "You have company," she said, standing back from her husband, who grabbed at the bottle she held.

He paid no attention to her, so Moses spoke, hoping to direct his attention away from further drinking, "Samuel, it's me, Moses. We need to talk."

Samuel looked up at him, his head lolling back against the chair, a confused look on his face as he tried to focus. "Who's it?"

"It's Moses Gentry . . . and Amos Culpepper. We need to talk to you," Moses said, his voice quiet and calm.

"You talksh enough," Samuel replied, his tone harsh, "destroyed my life!" He began to cry then, sobs that caused his whole body to heave and shake.

Rosie hurried to him, tears running down her cheeks. "Samuel, honey, it'll be all right," she said, reaching to touch his face. To everyone's horror, he lashed out at her with his fist, hitting her on the cheek, and she fell backwards against the wall.

Amos moved quickly, to support her, speaking words of comfort. She cried loudly, as he walked her to the kitchen, her cheek an angry red where Samuel's fist had hit her. "Rosie," he said, "listen. Samuel's upset and drunk. He's not aware of his actions."

She quit crying and blew her nose on a handkerchief from her apron pocket. "He won't eat," she whimpered. "Drinks and cries, and sleeps in his chair. I come down at night to try to talk to him, and he's asleep, but tears are still on his cheeks." She looked at Amos, a frightened look upon her face. "How long can he keep crying?" She cried then, her body trembling, so sorely grieved was she with concern for her husband.

"Rosie," Amos said, "I want you to go next door to see Amanda. I want you to stay there until I come for you. Will you do that?"

Rosie looked around him and into the parlor. "Yes," she replied meekly. "I don't want to be ... here."

"I'll come get you after we've talked to him and sobered him up. Don't you worry. Stay with Amanda ... talk to her. All right?"

"Yes," Rosie replied sadly, touching the reddened area on her cheek.

When she was safely out the door, Amos returned to the parlor where Moses was trying to talk some sense into Samuel. "You'll never make me 'cept them bastard savages," Samuel yelled. "Hate them stinkin' bashtards! Outta kill 'em ... ev'ry lash one of 'em!" Moses tried to talk to him about Sarah's letter, about the words she had written from her heart. Still Samuel raged on, not listening, lost in a hatred that bordered, it seemed, on insanity. "Outta shoot 'em all," Samuel wailed, his words interspersed with curses.

Moses wanted to throttle the man, or at best, to dunk his head in a tub of water until he gasped for air, and sobered sufficiently to listen. He tried, one more time, to reach the drunken man he had respected up until now. "Gray Eagle is half white," he said. "I don't know if that makes him the man he is, but he's a good man, Samuel. A decent sort who treats Sarah with love and respect."

Samuel glared at him, his eyes blazing. "Respec'! You think a stinkin' bashtard savage knows respec'?" Moses felt his face grow hot, as anger built within him. He tried to reason with Samuel, but he cut him off. "Bashtards, thas what they are! The whole lot of 'em are no good!" Samuel yelled, saliva drooling from his lips as he spoke.

Moses gripped the chair he had brought in from the kitchen, his knuckles white, afraid he would hit the man, if he continued to defile Indians any further. Finally, he could take no more: no more coarse gestures, no more vicious remarks, no more curses or hate toward people who weren't responsible for the color of their skin, or who their parents were. Anger blazing in his eyes, Moses grabbed Samuel by the front of his shirt, lifting him onto his feet, surprising the drunken man to the point of speechlessness.

"Look, you may have good reason to hate Indians. I don't know what they are, but you've driven your daughter away by your hatred, and slugged your wife who always worshiped the ground you walk on! You think Indians are rotten and evil? I'll tell you who's evil, *you* are! You and *every* person that judges a man by the color of his skin, or because his parents were . . . different!"

"Moses," Amos interjected, from the back of the room, "take it easy."

Samuel stood, swaying, his face showing shocked surprise at the angry man before him.

"You think Indians are savages . . ." Moses' voice rose. He felt raw with anger.

"Moses . . ." Amos pleaded again.

"No!" Moses yelled. "This fool has everything a man could want! A beautiful daughter and a devoted wife, and he's *blind*! Blind to how blessed he is!" Samuel stared at Moses, a look of fear in his eyes. "Indians have reverence for the land and animals and every flower that grows! They have more understanding than *you'll ever have*!"

Moses let go of Samuel's shirt, and the drunken man fell back into his chair. Silence prevailed. Then Samuel spoke, "How come you're so knowledgeable of Injuns?"

"Because my . . ."

"Moses . . ." Amos said, looking at the man he'd known since childhood. The man he had wronged so deeply—long ago—by words similar to those of Samuel Justus'. "You don't have to do this," he said. But he knew Moses was too angry to listen.

"Because my *mother* was an Indian!" Moses replied. "And she had more love in her heart, than any white person I've ever known!" The silence that followed was deafening.

For more years than he cared to remember, Moses had carried his secret, silenced by the hand circumstance had dealt him: a white father and an Indian mother. He was a "half-breed," someone looked down upon by whites and Indians, alike. Someone who didn't "fit" in society, who didn't "belong."

Moses had never been accepted by his drunken white father, a man who cursed him and beat his mother, calling her squaw, and laughing at her attempts to please him. She had been pretty when he won her in a card game. Singing Raven was her name. Moses still remembered her sweet voice, hearing it now within his heart, as when he grew from a mere infant to a dark-haired, dark-eyed little boy. Only in his light skin had he shown any resemblance to his father.

His dark features, and his thinking, were from his mother. She taught him many things that helped him find his place in the world. Taught him to read and write and, above all, to believe, not only in the God of his white father, but the Great Spirit of his mother's people, Wakantanka. She taught him to give thanks for each and every blessing he was given, and to always try to do his best.

The day he became a man, though not yet twenty, was the day his father beat his mother for the last time. From that day forward, he had seen to it that no one hurt the woman who had given him life. He stood tall, from that day on, though unsure of himself. Unsure of where he belonged. He felt confused and angry inside, because of the treatment he received from people who laughed and made cruel remarks.

The worst remarks came from an older boy, whom he admired, and often emulated, trying desperately to be *as* accepted. He copied the boy's walk and mannerisms: the way he talked, the way he acted. Especially, around the prettiest girl he had ever seen: a red-haired girl with a smile that stole his breath away when she looked in his direction. The girl, Sarah Mathews, had the prettiest green eyes. They seemed to dance with joy and hope. She was the other boy's intended, Moses had been told. But when she stopped to talk to him, or smiled at him, Moses felt handsome and strong, brave and wise. She never looked at him like the other kids did, who knew he wasn't like them. He prayed she never would.

The day of the barn dance, when he was seventeen, she had asked him to dance, the older boy having not yet arrived. He had nearly stumbled over his own feet, in response, unable to speak. She took his hand and led him to the dance floor amid couples who whirled and spun, laughing, their faces filled with great joy. He remembered, still, how she guided his hand to her small waist and taught him the steps. He was seventeen and had never been to a dance. Never held a girl in his arms. Never held the one "special" girl he had liked for so many years!

As the music played, they whirled amongst the other couples, Moses being very careful not to step on her dainty white shoes. The music soared, as did his heart, and he felt hers beating against him. Or imagined he did, so filled was he, with the magic of the moment.

"I love you," he blurted out in an unbridled burst of exuberance.

"And I, you," she whispered, softly and sweetly, reaching up to kiss his cheek.

A brutally harsh shove sent him sprawling. "Get away from her, half-breed. She's *my* girl. Don't want no filthy Injun touching her, you hear?" Moses looked up at the boy he had so long admired. "You keep away from my girl, Gentry, you understand? She belongs to *me*, Amos Culpepper, and don't you *ever* forget it!"

All the faces stared at him. The music had stopped; the only sound was the cruel words, and the pounding of his heart! Sarah Mathews stared at the floor, tears tracing their way down her soft, pale cheeks. Moses felt anger, shame, and humiliation course through him. The words tore at him, like words his father often spewed at him before he passed out from drinking. He got up, wanting to tear the throat out of the boy he had so admired. He wanted to kill him, if truth be known! But he saw the women's looks of pity, the men's mocking smiles, and vowed never to show his face in Coyote Ridge again.

The next day, after he packed his meager belongings and kissed his mother goodbye, he turned—looking long and hard at the home he was leaving—hoping to make an indelible imprint of it, upon his heart, knowing he would never return. Sadly, he mounted his horse and rode away, a grief so deep within him, he felt it fill his very soul.

As he cleared the hill, only five or six miles away from town, he heard the thunder of horse's hooves; heard someone shouting and wheeled his horse around, in amazement.

When she reached his side, Sarah Mathews spoke the sweetest words. Words he would never forget, as long as he lived. "I'm going with you, my love." she had said, her auburn hair shining in the golden sun, her smile mending the years of pain that had engulfed him. He reached out, clasping her hand, and they turned their horses and rode away. Together.

CHAPTER FIFTY-FOUR

Moses jerked from his memories, as Amos spoke, saying he was going to put on a pot of coffee. His hand rested a moment on Moses' shoulder as he walked past him. He could only imagine what revealing the secret he had kept, so many years, had cost Moses. Amos walked to the stove, thinking back in time, feeling renewed shame for the pain he had caused so long ago.

Moses looked at Samuel, who sat placidly in his chair. His eyes were closed, his breathing raspy, a grim look upon his face. "Samuel, Amos went to make us some coffee. Why don't we go sit in the kitchen?"

Samuel opened his eyes, looking at him with disgust. "So you're an Injun?"

"Part Indian," Moses replied, tired of the whole conversation.

"Whi'sh part?" Samuel asked, laughing coarsely. "No wonder my preddy girl ran off with a Injun." He hiccupped and drool ran down his chin. Moses clenched his fists, anger running through his veins. It took all his strength to turn away from the insults. "Go ahead, grab me ag'in, Injun," Samuel dared Moses, laughing a cruel laugh that tore through Moses, ripping at him until he felt raw.

Moses turned from Samuel, going into the other room, his face flushed with anger. He glanced at Amos, then opened the back door and quickly walked outside, pacing back and forth across the yard, hoping to squelch the anger that blazed inside him.

Amos heard Samuel get up from the overstuffed chair and curse. Then he heard the sound of a drawer being opened. Samuel began to mutter to himself in harsh and angry tones. "Looking for another bottle," Amos decided, shaking his head, saddened by the turn of events.

The coffee finished boiling. After it settled, Amos poured two cups, one for himself and one for Samuel. Moses entered then, once more in control of his emotions.

"Coffee's done," Amos told him, nodding at the empty cup on the table. "Got a cup out for you."

"Thanks," Moses replied, "but I think I'll try to talk to him one more time. He's really a decent man. This has just been too big a blow to him, that's all."

"That, and too much booze," Amos added, turning to go into the parlor, a cup of steaming coffee in each hand.

Moses walked into the room, behind Amos, and glanced toward Samuel, a gasp coming from his lips! In his hand, Samuel held a small, very old Muff gun, and it was pointed directly at him! Amos yelled a warning, but it was too late! A loud explosion filled the room, and Moses was knocked backwards! He hit the floor, grabbing his chest, a pained expression upon his face!

Amos dropped the cups of coffee he was holding, at the same time Samuel dropped the gun. "Shit!" Amos exclaimed, rushing to Moses' side. Moses lay still, his eyes wide open, looking up into Amos' face.

Behind them, Samuel was weeping and repeating over and over, "What have I done? Oh, God! What have I done?" He held his face in his hands, devastated by the outcome of his many years of hatred.

"Moses? Where are ya' hit? Can you hear me? I'll go get Doc," Amos said as he looked at Moses, trying to judge the extent of his injuries. He saw no blood, just the surprised look upon his friend's face.

"Amos?" Moses questioned, rubbing his chest directly over his heart. Samuel Justus continued to cry in the background. "Feels like a sledge hammer hit me in the chest."

Amos saw where Moses' coat had a hole in it. But, to his surprise, no blood stained it. He reached down, opening the coat, and saw the sheriff's badge inside, a deep dent directly in the middle of it. "Well, I'll be!" he exclaimed, moving the badge, and finding no wound beneath it.

Moses watched him, a pensive look on his face. "How bad is it?" he asked, at last.

"Too late," Amos answered, a huge grin beginning to form across his face.

Moses was shocked to see the look on Amos Culpepper's face and felt his ire rise. "You think it's funny I'm shot?" he growled, starting to rise up on one elbow, thoroughly perturbed and confused by Amos, who was laughing aloud now.

Then Amos spoke, erasing the look on the sheriff's face, "You aren't mortally wounded, Gentry, you lucky devil. The only thing 'mortally wounded' is your sheriff's badge!"

"What?" Moses questioned, his eyes wide with astonishment.

"The bullet hit your badge. You'll have a bruise, from the impact, but you're darned lucky . . . the luckiest fellow *I've* ever known," Amos stated, laughing.

Moses felt his chest and the deep dent in his badge. "Well, I'll be!" he exclaimed, a smile crossing his features.

Samuel quit sobbing, shocked to hear the two men laughing. "What? What is it?"

"Mortally wounded," Amos replied. "You'll spend the rest of your days, Samuel Justus, awaiting the hangman's noose!" Samuel's face went considerably more pale, and to their surprise, they realized he was now "sober as a judge"!

"I didn't mean to do it," he whispered. "I'm not a drinking

man . . ." He stopped talking then, as Amos helped Moses to his feet. "I . . . I don't understand." Samuel's hands trembled and his face grew ashen. "What . . . how can he get up? Where is he shot?" Samuel asked, seeing no blood on Moses' coat and the ever-persistent smiles on the lawmen's faces.

"There's no blood, Samuel, 'cause you shot him in the badge!" Amos retorted. "Put a dent in it, as deep as all git out!"

Samuel's mouth dropped open in astonishment, then relief, as the truth sunk in. He got up and walked slowly across the room, coming face to face with Moses. The two men stood there, looking deep into each other's eyes, and then Samuel reached out, hesitantly, offering his hand to Moses. "I'm sorry, Moses. I'm so darned sorry," he stated, as tears once more began to trickle down his cheeks. "I could've killed you . . . could've ruined *everything* . . ." The weight of his actions and intention overwhelmed him.

Moses looked hard at him, then reached out slowly, to clasp the old man's shaking hand. "If you weren't Sarah's father," he replied, "you'd be dead right now." He let his words sink in before continuing, "But since you are, and I'm still alive, I'll just say this . . . it's time to set aside your hatred, Samuel. I don't know why you're so all-fired full of hate for Indians, but you've got a daughter that loves you and a wife that . . ."

At the mention of Rosie, Samuel suddenly exclaimed, "Oh, God! Tell me I didn't hit Rosie? I didn't, did I?"

"You sure did," Moses and Amos both replied at the same time.

"Oh, God!" Samuel groaned.

"You'll need more than God to get back in her good graces, I'm afraid," Amos replied solemnly.

"Never was a drinkin' man," Samuel stated softly, his voice filled with shame and remorse as he walked past Moses to the door. "Rosie?" he called.

"She's over with Amanda," Amos answered. "Wanted no part of you, so I sent her over there."

"Oh, God," Samuel replied, walking weakly back toward the large chair in the corner where he slumped down, holding his head in his hands.

Moses walked around, rubbing his chest, stunned by how close he had come to dying. "I don't know why you've got so much hate in you for Indians, Samuel, but today could have ended in tragedy. Not only for me, but for you, too, needless to say," Moses stated flatly.

"Yes, I know that. I . . . I've been a fool. I let my hate for . . ." Samuel glanced at Moses uncertainly, "for Indians color everything in my life." Shaking his head in disbelief, he covered his face with his hands. Then slowly he began to speak, his voice a mere whisper in the stillness of the room. "Back in 1822, at the fort, I was in command when a group of Indians attacked a nearby settlement. I won't go into all the details . . . I can't."

He shook his head as the memories flooded back, once more, from that day. "There was no cause for the attack. We'd all been gettin' along fine, Indians and whites, alike. Then they attacked." As he described that day, so many years before, anguish filled his voice. "Old Preacher Hollingsworth lost his whole family. Seven kids there were. The youngest only three. They cut off her scalp." Tears began to run down his cheeks as he remembered. "Then they cut out her tongue."

He sobbed aloud now, his shoulders shaking and chest heaving. "Just three, you know," he said between sobs. "My Sarah was two then, and everyday I'd come home and see her playing and smiling up at me, and I'd see the Hollingsworth baby all over again, in my head. Just *three* . . . and they cut out her tongue!" Moses and Amos exchanged looks, unable to comfort the weeping man. "She died in her father's arms, never knowing why she'd been so grievously hurt, never understanding the reason for the cruelty done her. Her brothers and sisters were also slaughtered that day."

His voice drifted off, his mind seeing the horrifying scene once again. "Her mother survived the attack . . . went crazy with grief. The preacher stood at her grave, said a prayer over his littlest girl, then put a gun to his head and pulled the trigger before any of us could stop him. We buried him beside her. Beside *all* his children!"

Samuel looked up at Moses and Amos, a look of intense sadness upon his face. "Nobody knows why the Injuns . . ." he glanced quickly at Moses, "why they had attacked so viciously. The preacher used to ride out to their encampment, considered them friends. Took the word of God to them . . . the heathens!" He bristled with rage. "No one ever knew what set them off that day . . . and I've hated Indians ever since!"

Moses walked over to Samuel, placing his hand on the older man's shoulder. "For what it's worth, Samuel, we're not all heathens."

Samuel looked up at Moses, his cheeks wet and eyes red from crying. He looked at him, a long while, before speaking. "I . . . I was wrong, Moses. I let my hatred nearly destroy everything I've ever held dear. And let it drive me to almost kill you—a man I've always . . . respected. A man who had the guts to tell me he's part Indian. I'm . . . I'm so sorry, Moses. I hope you'll forgive me."

Moses studied the man's face, noting the sincerity in his voice. "You're forgiven," he replied. "I only hope you find it in your heart to forgive Sarah and give Gray Eagle a chance. He's a good man, a decent man, and they love each other. He can't help it, *either*, that he's part Indian and part white."

Amos picked up the cups he had dropped, hoping Rosie would be able to get the coffee stain out of her rug. Then he breathed a silent prayer, for his *two* half-breed friends, and Samuel Justus.

CHAPTER FIFTY-FIVE

Far away to the west, as the sun set that night, a happy couple made camp. The woman no longer felt uncertainty in the decision she had made to go with her companion, to marry him, and live amongst his people. She watched as he lit their campfire, an excitement running through her, at the mere sight of him. All her life she had longed for the kind of adventure she had read about in her mother's books. Now her own adventure had begun, and there was no turning back.

She thought of her father. By now he would know she was gone, but would have read her letter and, hopefully, would have accepted her leaving. Would understand her decision to go with the man who was now her husband.

She thought, too, of the sheriff. Her best friend. The only other man she would ever have considered as a possible husband, if things had been different. She smiled as she thought of the many ways he had irritated her when she first met him. Then, of the camaraderie that had grown between them as they struggled to save Melinda Rose's baby. She sighed as she remembered the kiss they had shared that night on the steps of Melinda Rose's house.

In her mind's eye, she saw the look on his face as he had told her of his Sarah, and of the devastation he felt when she died. Then she had stood face to face with the same Mexican bandit and was certain she, too, was about to die. But, Old

John had thrown his Bowie knife, and she was alive, though he lay dead. She shivered at the memory.

"Darlin'"—Moses always called her that. And funny as it seemed, she knew how much she would miss hearing it. She grinned as she remembered the black eyes he had given her— by accident—as she nursed him back to health after the cougar attack. Yes, if she hadn't fallen for the dark-haired fellow she was with, she would, seriously, have hoped things would have been different between herself and the sheriff. But he was still wed to the memory of his deceased wife, and she loved another.

Sarah smiled at Gray Eagle and then looked out over the land as it rolled endlessly on. A slight haze hung over it in the distance, like the finest silk. "Well, Mother," she began, her voice a mere whisper. "I've made a decision that will change my life forever. I do so welcome the adventure that lies ahead, yet it seems, somehow, like the choice was never all my own. So many things seem to have led to this day. Even your death, and the move to Hastings, that followed."

She paused, thinking back. "And later, Old John's teachings, so many of them Indian in origin. I never did fit in with the other girls, you know. Always was an outcast, of sorts. I guess now we'll see if I'm courageous enough to succeed in following my heart." She laughed softly, before continuing. "If I am, I guess that will make me a courageous outcast!"

She smiled at the thought and then turned, walking contentedly to Gray Eagle's side. From that moment on, Sarah vowed to no longer focus on the past, but to confront the challenge of the future that beckoned.

THE END